HISTORICAL

Your romantic escape to the past.

Miss Isobel And The Prince

Catherine Tinley

Marriage Charade With The Heir

Carol Arens

MILLS & BOON

MISS ISOBEL AND THE PRINCE
© 2024 by Catherine Tinley
Philippine Copyright 2024
Australian Copyright 2024
New Zealand Copyright 2024
First Published 2024
First Australian Paperback Edition 2024
ISBN 978 1 038 91055 4

MARRIAGE CHARADE WITH THE HEIR
© 2024 by Carol Arens
Philippine Copyright 2024
Australian Copyright 2024
New Zealand Copyright 2024
First Published 2024
First Australian Paperback Edition 2024
ISBN 978 1 038 91055 4

Published by
Harlequin Mills & Boon
An imprint of Harlequin Enterprises (Australia) Pty Limited (ABN 47 001 180 918), a subsidiary of HarperCollins Publishers Australia Pty Limited
(ABN 36 009 913 517)
Level 19, 201 Elizabeth Street
SYDNEY NSW 2000 AUSTRALIA

Printed and bound in Australia by McPherson's Printing Group

Miss Isobel And The Prince

Catherine Tinley

MILLS & BOON

Catherine Tinley has loved reading and writing since childhood and has a particular fondness for love, romance and happy endings. She lives in Ireland with her husband, children, dog and kitten and can be reached at catherinetinley.com, as well as through Facebook and on Twitter @catherinetinley.

Visit the Author Profile page at millsandboon.com.au.

Author Note

Welcome to the second book in my Triplet Orphans series—this time featuring the feisty Miss Isobel and the Queen's distant cousin, Prince Claudio.

Prince Claudio—lately arrived in England—is determined to enjoy life, having gained freedom from the restrictions of his father's court. For Claudio, marriage is out of the question for many years yet.

Izzy, meantime, has decided to find a sensible man to marry, as this season will be her one and only chance to escape from her fate as a schoolteacher or governess. The question marks over her origins mean a titled husband is not an option, so she will have to choose from among the Misters of the ton. But should the chance arise, might she try for one glorious kiss from a prince?

Look out for the third book in the series, coming soon. Of the three sisters, Miss Anna is the sensible one, the dependable one, the responsible one. Yet one man is going to make her forget all reason and common sense—and perhaps help her finally uncover the mystery of her parents' past.

DEDICATION

For my husband, Andrew,
with love

Prologue

Scotland,
1796

It was time to leave. Again.

Maria knew it but had been refusing to think about it. Tomorrow she and her three darlings must uproot themselves from this, their home. The only home her daughters had ever known. A place they had felt safe. Until now.

Briefly, she wondered if she should tell milady the truth, then dismissed the notion. It was a story too fantastical to be believed, too risky to be told. Especially now.

Instead, they would leave their haven, their sanctuary, departing before the guests began to arrive. As she had done many times before, she bemoaned the twist of fate that had seen milady—now simply her dear friend Margaret—seek company for the first time in years. Without letting Maria know—and why should she, when she was mistress of the house?—she had invited a group of former friends to visit. Renton Ashbourne. Thaxby. Kelgrove. All had accepted, and all were even now on their way. Milady Margaret had expected Maria to be pleased, that much was clear, and had looked decidedly crestfallen at Maria's response.

'But, Maria, you have been encouraging me to move

on, to accept that my dear husband is gone, to focus on my son, and the future. This is a momentous decision for me—to engage again with the people we knew in London.' She frowned. 'I have had little contact with the *ton* since his death, as you know.' She lifted her chin. 'And now I am ready to try again. I could not face going there.' A visible shudder ran through her. 'But inviting them here, for a quiet house party, that I can do—at least, I *think* I can.'

'Of course you can! For you are so strong. We both are!'

'I have learned from you, Maria. Each time I felt my life was worthless I would see you, also widowed, also young, but with no home, no family. Your determination to see your girls safe and well has been my inspiration!'

Safe and well.

A shiver of fear ran down her spine. Those who loved her, those who hated her, those who were indifferent to her… all would be here for Margaret's party, but she would not.

Margaret had been predictably horrified on hearing that Maria and her girls were leaving.

'But why? And where will you go?'

'I am not sure. Somewhere quiet, out of the way. It is better so. Besides, I have relied on your good heart and hospitality for long enough. Five years and more! You are healed enough now from the loss of your husband to start to engage in society again. You no longer need me.'

'But I do! I need your friendship! Are we not friends, Maria?'

At this, Maria had clasped her hand. 'Of course we are! And I promise to write to you. It is just…' She swallowed. 'Margaret, you have never pried into my circumstances. I will always be grateful for everything you have done for me—'

'Oh, stuff and nonsense! What was I supposed to do—

send you outside to give birth in the stable? And you were so shocked to have *three* babies, not one.' She gave a rueful smile. 'My son was a sturdy toddler by then, but I knew enough to help you in those early weeks, along with Nurse.' Her eyes grew distant. 'And then, by the time you were well and managing, you and I were fast friends.' She eyed Maria intently. 'I must confess to a certain curiosity, though. You seemed...frightened. Of someone or something.'

Maria nodded. 'I could not tell you. I still cannot. But know this—I did nothing wrong. Nothing! Those who wished me harm did so for their own reasons.'

Margaret spread her hands. 'I do not doubt it. And I do not mean to pry. But I ask you to reconsider. Stay with me—with us. This has been your home for five long years. Your girls and my son are best friends—as we are. Stay.'

'I wish I could.' There was a catch in Maria's voice. 'But I must think of my safety. And my daughters' safety.'

Margaret gasped. 'Someone would threaten your children?'

'I know not. But I cannot take that chance.'

Margaret was thoughtful, frowning. 'My house guests. You fear one of them?'

Maria eyed her steadily.

'I am so sorry, Maria! Who? Which one?'

But Maria shook her head. 'I have no proof. Of *anything*. So I dare not accuse. I must simply survive in safety and keep my daughters safe. So please, tell no one about me, if you can. And if you must, you may mention me as a friend—the widowed Mrs Lennox and her three children. No one needs to know they are triplets, and no one needs to know my first name.'

'Very well, but I cannot understand it!'

In the end Maria prevailed, as she had to. Tears were

shed on both parts, then Maria, sorrowfully, packed up their modest belongings. Clothing. The books and music sheets gifted to them at Christmastide, and for their fifth birthday earlier this year. Maria's respectable savings—for dear Margaret had insisted on paying her these past years, as her companion, and for helping with young Xander's education. Opening her strongbox, Maria counted the coin within, feeling reassured there would be enough to keep them for many months, until she found a suitable situation.

Other treasures were there, too. Earrings from her grandmother. His last letter to her. And the other thing. The treasure. Carefully she unfolded the velvet cloth, blinking as the jewels within caught the light. So beautiful! So distinctive!

So dangerous, for the piece would be easily recognised by anyone who knew about it. Even now. Wrapping it up again, her brow furrowed, she set it to one side, along with the letter. The earrings, though, those she would take with her. A legacy for her daughters, and a reminder that once, she had had a grandmother who loved her.

Chapter One

Grantham, England,
March 1, 1812

Being born a prince held certain advantages.

Prince Claudio Friedrich Ferdinand of Andernach stretched, yawned, and left his bed. The day was already well advanced, the serving maid who had warmed his bed last night long gone, and Claudio's head was remarkably clear, given the amount of fine wine he had consumed the night before. Having landed in England only two weeks ago, it was remarkable how quickly his title had opened so many doors. Already he had been invited to drink, to dine, and to carouse with a number of new friends, and now this—a brief trip north to see a horse race in the vicinity of Grantham.

The Angel Inn was, his friends had assured him, suitable for people of their class, even though it was also used by commoners. He had seen little of it, admittedly, for after the race yesterday the gentlemen had simply retired to the nearest village hostelry—there to drink, and speak of nonsense, and dally with a couple of saucy serving maids. The maids had been gratifyingly flirtatious, one going so far as to call him *handsome*, but it was only after Eldon had called him *Prince* that the pretty one with the dark eyes had focused her attention on him. It had been well after midnight when he had slipped her up to his chamber in the Angel, and he now only vaguely remembered her fixation on his princely status.

An hour later, having washed, dressed, and partaken of a light breakfast in his chamber, he made his way downstairs to seek his new friends. Sure enough, there they were, in the taproom, already imbibing. *Lord, these English know how to sport!* It was all such a contrast from the decorum and duty that had plagued him at home. A welcome contrast.

'Prince!' Hawkins raised a hand in greeting. 'How is your head this fine day?'

Grinning, Claudio slid onto the long bench beside him. 'Perfectly clear, I assure you! And you should call me Andernach, you know.'

'Well, I would if I could say it!' A look of concentration appeared on Hawkins's ruddy visage. 'Handernack! There!'

Claudio shuddered. 'Actually, *Prince* will suffice. Now, how does a man get some ale around here?'

'Thank the Lord, we are finally in Grantham!' Izzy gazed eagerly out of the window of the coach. 'What is the name of the inn, Anna?'

'The Angel, I think.' Her sister's gaze remained focused on the streets and buildings of the Lincolnshire town.

'Yes, definitely the Angel.' Rose, Izzy's other sister, nodded. 'The coachman said we could stop here for an hour or two for dinner.'

Izzy's frustration rose. 'Can we not stay here tonight? Why must we press on so much each day?'

Anna's tone was even. 'You know our journey has been planned in detail, and at a much easier pace than people usually travel. We must reach Stamford tonight, for a bedchamber is reserved for us there.' She sighed. 'We are all tired of travelling, Izzy. It has felt like a month since we left Scotland. But we are nearly there. Tomorrow night we sleep in Hitchin, and the day after, we shall finally reach London!'

'There it is!' Rose pointed to a grey stone building, the sign featuring two demi-angels holding a crown. Izzy had a brief impression of an arched entrance before the coach swung into the innyard.

There was a brief silence as they busied themselves with bonnets and reticules. Their matching red cloaks had kept the cold at bay today, thankfully. The farther south they went, the milder the weather. Already the frosts of Scotland and northern England were giving way to warmer temperatures, and in the hedgerows, Izzy had spotted nodding daffodils, replacing the delicate snowdrops and shy crocuses still on display farther north.

We are leaving winter behind, and spring this year holds endless possibilities.

Excitement rose again in Izzy's breast. Until just a couple of weeks ago she and her sisters had lived quietly in a small school for young ladies, which had not suited Izzy one bit. Finally, adventure was upon her, and she intended to relish every moment.

They were handed down from the carriage by the coachman, making their way across the yard and inside the inn. A man dressed in the familiar dun clothing of an innkeeper approached them, his gaze flicking over them in assessment even as he greeted them.

'Good day, good day. And er…good day.'

There it was, the realisation they were identical triplets. Having seen it all her life, Izzy took little notice of the flicker of confusion mixed with surprise. It was as familiar to her as breathing.

'How may I serve you today?' the landlord continued.

He did not say *ladies*, Izzy noted. Their drab dresses, simple red cloaks, and plain straw bonnets had led many inn staff to conclude they were of the servant class—a misapprehension which they had had to frequently correct on their long journey south.

As usual, Anna took charge. Being the eldest of the three, she saw it as her due.

She was born only twenty minutes before me, thought Izzy sourly, then chided herself inwardly. She was not actually cross with Anna—just tired, and a little ill-tempered, and ready for her dinner.

'Good day.' Anna's tone was clipped, and she did not incline her head. 'We require a private parlour, if you please, and dinner. And our coachman will need assistance with the horses.'

The innkeeper's eyes widened briefly. 'Of course, miss! Right away!'

That is more like it!

It was always interesting to note the change in demeanour when people realised they were not in fact servants but young ladies—their educated tones being the usual indication, along with the fact they were travelling by private carriage. Izzy had not been raised to think she was a person of consequence—quite the reverse in fact—but the girls needed the acknowledgement of their status as protection. Three young ladies travelling alone might be subject to all kinds of unwanted attention otherwise. Attentions that they simply were not equipped to deal with.

Izzy looked around her. The place was spotlessly clean and comfortably furnished. A painted notice informed her that the inn had had many royal visitors in its six-hundred-year history, including King John as long ago as 1213 and, more recently, both Charles I and Oliver Cromwell—though not, Izzy surmised, at the same time. To her right she could hear a hubbub through a closed door—the taproom, presumably.

The innkeeper was consulting his ledger and frowning. 'My apologies, ladies. We are busy today, and so I need to find a suitable room for you to dine in. I do have one private parlour that is currently not in use, but it has been reserved by a party of young gentlemen.' He closed the book. 'If you will give me a moment, I shall consult with them. Please, be seated.'

Taking her seat, Izzy became aware of a new noise from the taproom: male voices raised in song.

Lord, they are drunk in the afternoon!

Already she was learning more of the world. Never could she have imagined a life so different from the quietude of Belvedere School. As she listened the chorus ended, a single, clear baritone beginning a solo performance. The innkeeper opened the door, and briefly, the song came to her more clearly.

Why...he is singing in German!

Having an ear for languages, at school Izzy had eagerly devoured Latin and Greek, Spanish and Italian, and then German, making the most of the good fortune that one of the Belvedere teachers had spent ten years near Hanover, tutoring an English family there. Izzy had no difficulty understanding the words the man was singing, a simple drinking song. Something about his voice, though, was disturbing her, causing a feeling almost of pins and needles in her body.

How odd!

After a few moments the singing ceased, and a little later the innkeeper reappeared. Perhaps the singing group were the ones who had reserved the parlour.

'Good news, ladies. You have full use of the parlour for dinner, for the gentlemen do not intend to dine until much later. I do hope that is acceptable, Miss…?'

'I am Miss Lennox. My sisters, Miss Isobel Lennox, and Miss Rose Lennox.'

He bowed. 'Follow me.'

'Thank you.' Anna was every inch the refined young lady as she followed the landlord down a long corridor, her sisters at her heels. Despite their simple clothing, the Lennox sisters were not to be trifled with!

Ten minutes later they were alone, having ordered dinner and used the outside privy before returning to their snug parlour. After divesting themselves of boots, bonnets, and cloaks, Anna and Rose sank into comfortable settees with matching expressions signalling relief. Izzy could not understand it. Pacing about the room, she felt consumed by restlessness.

'How can you sit, when we have been sitting all day?'

Rose groaned. 'Because this settee, unlike the coach, does not bounce or rattle. I declare, my bones are aching!'

'Come, walk with me about the room,' she urged them. 'It is small I know, but at least your legs will get some movement!'

They resisted, and so she continued by herself, walking around the large table a dozen times until she was quite dizzy. It was always this way. Her sisters full of languor while she bubbled with vivacity. Still, at least Anna and Rose had agreed to go to London in the first place. Lord, it had been a close-run thing, though!

Her mind returned to that day a few short weeks ago

when their guardian Mr Marnoch—a lawyer who had been dear Mama's employer before she died—had summoned them to his office. It being the day after their twenty-first birthday, he had informed them that he knew almost nothing of their family background. Mama had come to Elgin with five-year-old triplets, had clerked for him, and had asked him to accept their guardianship during her last long illness, five years later. Mama had died before their eleventh birthday, and so they had spent a full ten years in Belvedere School. Never once in that time had they left the vicinity of Elgin.

In her mind's eye Izzy could recall every detail of the school, the town, and Mr Marnoch's comfortable mansion, where he had bade them visit him occasionally. He was warm and kind and, Izzy reflected, had adapted remarkably well to having three small girls foisted on him. In his office that day, he had offered them the opportunity to visit his widowed sister in London, there to discover what they could about Mama's background and family. He had set each of them a quest, and Izzy's was particularly intriguing.

Your quest is to discover what you can about your father. Your mother rarely spoke about Mr Lennox and informed me she was a widow when she first arrived in the town. Her eyes were hazel while yours are blue, so he may have had blue eyes. Your mama had a London Season, but I am uncertain if that is how they met.

'I am to discover the name of our father? But how?' Izzy had exclaimed on reading the paper. 'How am I to do this?'

Mr Marnoch had shrugged. 'Honestly, I have no idea.

I have written down all I know on the matter. The rest is up to you.'

And so her practical sister Anna and her timid sister Rose, inspired by their own quests, had both agreed to go, and Izzy could not have been more delighted. Going to London, where she might see the sights and dance at a ball and meet people who were *not* from a five-mile radius of Elgin? She could think of nothing more exciting. If only it were not taking so dashed long to get there!

Claudio was happy. Vaguely aware that his happiness was largely due to a haze of ale-induced cloudiness, he was happy nevertheless. In his entire life he had never set out to drink all day with the specific aim of achieving drunkenness, as these English gentlemen did. Never would he have thought to find himself merrily drunk in some random inn in the middle of England, with a bunch of gentlemen he had met only recently, but who seemed to him to be the best of fellows. Yes, travelling to England had been an act of genius on his part—although his father would most certainly not approve of his actions so far. Still, Papa was far away and would never know.

Indeed, it had been Papa's suggestion that he consider making a life in England, given the ongoing machinations aimed at annexing and merging the small German-speaking principalities into larger blocs. Since the fall of the Holy Roman Empire and the work of Napoleon's confederation, the momentum was all in one direction, and it did not bode well for small sovereign states like the one ruled by his father. Claudio's eldest brother would eventually inherit *something*, but it was not currently clear what.

In the meantime, Claudio and his brothers were left adrift, uncertain of their future. Claudio's English was excellent despite never having travelled to this country, and so Papa had urged him to travel here, find an English wife, and settle down. Queen Charlotte—a distant cousin—had introduced him at court on his second night in London, and instantly a group of gentlemen had surrounded him, all keen to befriend the new prince in town.

Some, like Garvald, Ashbourne, and Phillips, had seemed sensible and sober, and remained aloof, if friendly. Claudio however had found himself drawn to Mr Eldon and Mr Hawkins, who had none of the reserve and stiffness he had just escaped from at home. All his life he had played at protocol, adhering to the strictures of his father's court. He had no intention of replacing one set of sensible associates with another. Hawkins and Eldon were fascinatingly different and represented a life as unlike his old existence as Claudio could imagine.

Yes, coming to England must be one of the best decisions he had ever made. Here he could fall down drunk or carouse with comely maids without a disapproving glance from any direction. For the first time in his life, he was enjoying the benefits of princedom, rather than its restrictions.

Rising to his feet he swayed lightly, noting that the room was moving in an alarming matter. Momentarily tempted to sit back down again, he resisted, the need to relieve himself being undeniable. With great focus he put one foot carefully in front of another, determined not to fall down in front of his new friends. Having successfully crossed the taproom, though his head was spinning, he made for the corridor that led to the privies.

Izzy had had enough. Anna steadfastly refused to walk about the room with her, while Rose looked to have actually nodded off on the settee. 'Who will come to the privy with me?'

Rose, naturally, made no answer, while Anna raised a quizzical brow. 'But we went when we first arrived!'

'And? I need to go again.'

'No doubt dinner will be here shortly.'

'Even more reason why I should go now, before it arrives!'

Anna shook her head. 'You should wait, Izzy.'

It was too much. Izzy's chest burned with annoyance.

Anna is not my parent, nor my guardian, nor my teacher!

'Then, I shall go by myself!'

Anna frowned. 'Very well. But take care.'

Gesturing a vague response to Anna's concerned expression—for surely if she thought there was any real danger she would leave her comfortable settee—Izzy left the parlour and began making her way down the dimly-lit corridor.

Enjoying a brief sense of freedom, she took everything in: the painted walls, low ceilings, the scent of roasting meat rising tantalisingly from the kitchens. The corridor was empty, the only sound the shuffle of Izzy's slippers on the flagstone floor, and a distant murmur from the taproom. In this part now the hallway bent to the right, a window illuminating the scene. Ahead of her a door opened, and a man emerged.

Instantly Izzy caught her breath. She was alone, and this man was an unknown threat. Her gaze swept over him, noting that he was young, not more than two or three years older than she, perhaps. Fair hair, a handsome face, strong figure. He wore the clothing of a gentleman, and Izzy's fear subsided a little. Surely he would behave with honour? Thinking quickly, she decided to simply pass him without speaking. The ladies' retiring room was just past the one set out for the men, and she would be safe there.

Lifting her chin a little, she walked on.

Claudio's head had cleared a little. After making use of the privy he had washed his face and hands using clear cold water from the innyard well.

Perhaps I shall drink a little more slowly when I return, he mused.

After drying his face and hands on a clean soft towel provided by a servant, he left the yard—only to catch his breath. There, walking towards him, was the most divine creature he had ever beheld. Corn-gold hair, deep blue eyes, and a perfect complexion…his gaze drifted downwards. She was perfectly proportioned, her form discernible despite the drab brown gown she wore. A serving maid, he realised, taking in her clothing. Instantly, recalling his success last night, he decided to address her.

'Hail, golden Aphrodite!' He bowed theatrically, but she walked on towards him, avoiding his gaze, without acknowledging his words.

'What?' He sighed dramatically. 'You do not return my greeting?'

Now her gaze flicked towards him—a mix of uncertainty, nervousness, and—was that humour in her eyes? He slapped a hand to his chest. 'You wound me, o fair one.' He frowned. 'At least you could say *good day*.'

She was almost upon him. Boldly he met her gaze. 'Good day,' he addressed her pointedly.

Rose-pink lips pursed in disapproval. 'Good day, sir. Now, will you let me pass?'

He was, to be fair, standing directly in her path, and the corridor was narrow. 'First, a kiss!'

Chapter Two

The golden maiden caught her breath. 'No!'

Claudio was conscious of disappointment. Still, never having kissed an unwilling maid, he was not prepared to do so now. Inspiration came to him. 'Not even if I inform you that I am a prince?'

Now he had her attention. She laughed, scepticism clear in the wry twist of her delectable mouth. 'If you are a prince, sir, then I am the Queen of Sheba!'

He blinked. 'But I *am* a prince!' This was not going as expected. Not at all.

'There is but one prince in England, sir. The Prince Regent. I have seen his likeness many times, and I assure you, you are not he!'

'Well, no. I am not *the* prince—not the Prince Regent, anyway. But I am *a* prince.'

'In your own imagination, perhaps,' she countered, eyes ablaze. 'I do know of princes from storybooks when I was a child, and never did they behave like you.'

'Behave?' His mind seemed slow, befuddled. 'How do princes behave, then?'

She considered this, her head tilted to one side. Amid his confusion, he could not fail to notice again how kissable were her lips: perfect rosebuds that he ached to touch with his own.

She held up her hands, as if to mark off her points on her fingers. 'First, princes should be handsome.' She assessed him directly. 'I concede that you are not ugly.'

Not ugly? His eyes widened at her effrontery.

'But princes are also expected to be *honourable*, sir.'

Now his mind was in sharp focus. Drawing himself up, he gave her one of his father's best disdainful looks. 'How dare you suggest I am anything other than honourable!'

She nodded thoughtfully. 'An arrogant air is a feature of princes, I'll grant you. You should cultivate it. But as to the question of your honour, what else must I think when I encounter someone who, while in a state of severe intoxication, accosts a lone maid in the middle of the afternoon and threatens to kiss her? Now, step aside, sir, or must I scream for help?'

Dumbfounded, he gave way a little. Enough to allow her to pass, but only if she brushed against him briefly.

With a muffled sound of exasperation she did so, and his entire body—despite the ale—thrilled at the sensation of her shoulder sliding across his chest, from right to left.

If only...

He watched as she made for the privy, then made his way back to the taproom in something of a daze. What on earth had just occurred? Never had he been spoken to in such a manner, by serving maid or noble.

And I did not threaten to kiss her.

He had simply *asked* for a kiss, as any man might. And if a maiden said *no*, an honourable man like himself would not force the matter. The accusation rankled, as had her defiant air.

Perhaps the English were not so fond of princes as he had believed.

* * *

Izzy remained in the privy and yard for quite ten minutes, in a high state of agitation. Her sheltered life in Belvedere School had not prepared her for such a situation, and she had to admit to being fairly disturbed by it all. Pacing up and down the innyard, she tried to make sense of it all. The Reverend Buchan, in his sermons at the Holy Trinity Chapel in Elgin, had frequently warned his parishioners of the evils of gin and whisky, although he allowed wine was a civilised drink.

'Take ye not the evil soup,' he had exhorted them, 'for surely it is the devil's buttermilk and leads to all manner of vice and sin.'

The man she had met today must surely have been drinking gin, she concluded, for dear Mr Marnoch regularly had a dram of whisky in the evenings and never behaved inappropriately.

Yes, that must be it.

So what was her own excuse? She had imbibed nothing stronger than tea this day, and yet her mind was filled with visions of kissing the handsome young drunkard she had just encountered.

Reflecting on their exchange, she realised that any fear had vanished very early on. Somehow she had sensed she was in no danger of physical harm from him. Now her mind was filled with his image—his strong handsome face, piercing grey eyes, thick blond hair. And when she had brushed past him…she shuddered, recalling the delicious thrill of her shoulder and upper arm brushing across his firm chest.

Men are shaped so differently from us.

Naturally she had known that, but today she had learned how…how *interesting* the differences were.

Pushing away such shocking thoughts, she concentrated

again on his forwardness. How dare he ask for a kiss from her! No one had ever done so, and it was galling to recall his lazy smile, his confidence that she would oblige him. Still, she thought with satisfaction, at least she had put him in his place.

Despite being unused to the ways of the world, she was not foolish enough to believe his Banbury tale about being a prince. Had she been a gambling person—which of course she was not, having been raised to abhor such vices—she would be willing to stake her new gloves on his having used the *prince* ruse on some other unsuspecting female—and with success. too, given his clear consternation at her rejection of his nonsensical claim.

No, he was no prince—that much was certain. Recalling their brief exchange she wondered now if there had been a tinge of a foreign accent in his speech—although given the ever so slight slurring of his words, it was impossible to tell. The expensive cut and finish of his fine waistcoat and buckskin breeches indicated he was wealthy. A merchant, perhaps.

Satisfied with her own reasoning, she returned to her sisters in a fine state of outrage. When they questioned her, she gave no details, saying only that she had encountered a young man who had behaved in a boorish, arrogant way, but she had come to no harm. Seemingly satisfied, they bade her eat her dinner before it got cold, and an hour later they were on their way again.

The rest of the evening was strangely flat. While Claudio's new friends continued to drink, and jest, and sing, he hugged his cup, only sipping from it now and again. The more sober he got, the more annoyed with himself he became. Why had he just stood there like an idiot and allowed a serving wench to question his honour? He, Prince Claudio Friedrich Ferdinand, third son of the ruling prince of Andernach!

And why had the girl reacted so cuttingly to his overtures? There was no harm in his trying, surely? So why had she been so cold towards him, so judgemental?

Might his Aphrodite be already promised to another? He nodded sagely into his cup. That would explain it. If her affections had already been won—in his mind, he pictured a brawny groom or farmer—then, he would allow her to deny the brief spark of interest he had surely seen in her eye.

But no.

Even if she was enamoured of some coarse servant or labourer—quite unfitting to match her delicate beauty—still she had had no need to turn a light encounter into an assassination of his character. Why, she had acted as though *she* were the princess and he a commoner who had dared to proposition her!

Even worse had been their second encounter. He had chanced to pass the main doorway just as she was leaving, following some other girls out the door to the stableyard. Her drab gown had been covered by one of those red cloaks all young women seemed to wear here, her golden curls peeping out from beneath a simple straw bonnet. It was only when she had turned her head that he had known for certain it was her, his breath catching again at the perfection of her features.

Stupefied, he had simply stood stock-still, staring at her, but when she had fleetingly met his gaze she had looked straight through him, almost as if their previous encounter had never taken place. Taken aback, he had felt his jaw slacken, before tightening it up again grimly. Surely she could have given him a hint of a nod or even a disdainful glare? Instead, her cold emptiness had left him feeling as though she thought him worthless. Worthless…almost like a third son in a tiny principality.

And so his entire evening was spoiled. Spoiled because he had allowed an unknown servant girl to pierce his skin, to interfere with the haze of good-natured carousing he had been enjoying.

When the landlord called them through to their parlour for dinner, he ate his fill and afterwards refused to return to the taproom. Ignoring his friends' raillery, he made for his bed, there to dream fitful dreams where Papa frowned in his direction.

London,
March 17

Lady Ashbourne, Mr Marnoch's sister, proved to be every bit as warm and engaging as her brother. Welcoming the Lennox sisters into her elegant London mansion with great warmth and excitement, she declared them to be pretty behaved, and respectful and seemed to be delighted to be sponsoring them. She was curious as to how to tell them apart, and they had explained they tended to wear specific colours or trim their clothing with such colours—Anna with blue, Izzy with greens and yellows, and Rose with pink.

They each had been given a bedchamber of their own as well as a serving maid. Having shared a chamber with her sisters for her whole life, Izzy was loving having a pretty room of her own. The ladies' maid, however, was taking quite some getting used to. Izzy, Anna, and Rose had always done each other's buttons and hair at school, and it felt distinctly odd to be sitting at a dressing table having her hair pinned by a skilled London abigail. Still, it was all part of the adventure, she supposed.

Today Mary, Izzy's maid, was taking much longer than usual, for today was special. Today they were to leave Lady Ashbourne's house for the first time since their arrival.

Their hostess had been surprised, then delighted, to discover they were identical triplets and had hit upon the notion of revealing this in a dramatic way, when she presented the girls at court. Which meant that for the past two weeks they had all been cooped up together in the Ashbourne townhouse in Grafton Street.

Despite Izzy's usual restlessness, she had quite enjoyed the experience. Lord Ashbourne—Lady Ashbourne's nephew and the current viscount—was often at home, and together they all enjoyed elegant dinners and interesting discourse. But even better was the daytime activity, for they were constantly busy with dressmakers, mantua-makers, and milliners, as well as music and dancing classes. Every day brought new adventures, and after a lifetime of schoolbooks and dreariness, Izzy could not have been happier.

Lady Ashbourne was determined to ensure they were as ready as they could be to make their début at St James's Palace. Mr Marnoch, bless him, had sent money for them to be kitted out appropriately for London society, and Izzy was delighting in the new gowns, nightgowns, pelisses, hats, and shoes that had been made for her and her sisters in just a fortnight.

'That's you done, Miss Isobel.' Mary nodded in satisfaction at her handiwork, and Izzy had to admit the girl was highly skilled at dressing hair. 'I shall place your tiara once you are gowned,' she added, touching the diadem reverently. Izzy's eyes went to it for the hundredth time that day.

Lady Ashbourne had loaned each of them a diamond tiara just for today, and Izzy swallowed at the responsibility.

What if I break it, or lose it? It must be worth a fortune!

But no. Izzy squared her shoulders, determined that nothing bad would happen, for today they would make their curtsy before the queen herself.

Rising, Izzy turned to face the gown. She had of course tried it on already, numerous times, in fact, for a team of dressmakers had been visiting on a daily basis to ensure the Lennox sisters' court gowns were ready in time. Clad only in her shift and stockings, and with her hair now dressed and pinned, Isobel felt a certain solemnity about donning the gown. First, the hoop—for the queen abhorred the current fashion for straight, Grecian-inspired gowns. No, all débutantes being presented to Her Majesty must wear a hoop, and a four-foot train, and feather headdresses with lappets. The tiaras were Lady Ashbourne's own addition.

Next, Mary assisted her to put on the petticoat—a soft cotton half-slip tied at the waist. After that were the stays, which Mary pulled as tight as she could, until Izzy protested that she could not breathe. Following this ordeal Mary tied a padded roll around Izzy's waist—to lift and display the skirts properly, she explained.

Lord! thought Izzy. *I wonder how my mama and her friends managed every day, if this is what they had to endure!*

Sadly, Lady Ashbourne had informed them that the surname Lennox was unknown in the *ton*, and so Izzy's quest to identify their father had fallen at the very first hurdle. They had decided instead to focus on Rose's mission, to discover who Mama's family might have been. It had been something of a relief to Izzy to let go of her quest, for somehow it had never seemed quite real to her. Surely the *fu-*

ture was more important than the past—and for Izzy, the immediate future looked like the most exciting thing that had ever happened to her.

After the hip roll, Mary added the stomacher, a flat piece of stiffened fabric dotted with beads and sparkling thread which she pinned directly to the stays. Finally they were getting to the outer layers which would actually be seen.

The gown petticoat was next, and Mary deftly arranged it over the hoop, moving and arranging it until she was satisfied. At last, Izzy donned the gown itself, and Mary secured it with multiple pins, before deftly stitching it to the edges of the stomacher in three places.

I have literally been sewn into this gown!

The notion was strange, but Izzy was fascinated to be trying the fashions of twenty or thirty years ago—probably the one time in her life she would have the opportunity to do so. The dress was of silk brocade, all in white with silver thread and thousands of tiny stones that made it sparkle and glimmer. It must have taken an entire team of seamstresses the entire fortnight to create three such delightful gowns *à la Française* for Izzy and her sisters.

With Mary's help she put on matching shoes, then the maid carefully placed the tiara and headdress on her head. Eyeing her critically, Mary circled all around her before declaring herself satisfied. In the distance, Izzy heard a clock chime. Why, the whole process had taken more than two hours, and she was supposed to be downstairs by now!

'I wonder how my sisters are faring,' she mused, a frown creasing her forehead. 'Dressing for court took much longer than I anticipated!'

'Never worry, miss, you are ready to go now,' Mary declared—just as the door opened to admit the housekeeper.

'Ah, good! You are ready, Miss Isobel. The others are

waiting downstairs, and the carriage is being brought around, for it is time to go!'

Swallowing against a sudden flutter of nervousness, Izzy thanked Mary, then made her way slowly and carefully down the wide staircase, fearful she might trip or that the tall feathers in her headdress might fall. Thankfully they seemed to be secure, and she was able to walk at a reasonably normal pace through the hallway to where her sisters waited, decked out in matching gowns. Only the tiaras were different.

'Oh, my dears!' Lady Ashbourne seemed momentarily overcome. 'You shall outshine them all, I declare!'

Lord Ashbourne, looking handsome in his formal dress, appeared from his library to bow to them all and tell them they looked beautiful. With a gesture he indicated they should precede him out to the Ashbourne coach.

Beautiful! No one had ever said such a thing to Izzy before, and she could not help but be gratified by it. As the coach made its way across Piccadilly and down the hill towards St James's Palace, she reflected upon this. While she had occasionally seen flashes of what might have been admiration in the gaze of young labourers and tradesmen in Elgin, she naturally could have no dealings with such young men.

Having been raised a lady in an exclusive school for the daughters of gentlemen, she knew herself to be too high for such men. Yet the trepidation in her stomach reminded her that attending court had never been an expectation either. With no known parentage, she and her sisters were too high for tradesmen, not high enough for court. Yet why should she not make her curtsy before the queen? Lady Ashbourne was sponsoring them, and their company manners were good.

So why do I feel like an impostor?

Gazing hungrily out of the carriage window, she tried to take everything in: the bustling busyness of Piccadilly, the tall, elegant buildings in St James's Street. Many of the gentlemen's clubs were located there, including White's, Brooks's, and Boodle's, they had been told. Certainly Lord Ashbourne seemed to spend much of his time in his club, and Izzy eyed the neoclassical façade of White's with interest as they passed it. What on earth did gentlemen do in there all day and night? Abruptly, the carriage drew to a halt, and they all looked instinctively to Lady Ashbourne.

'No, we have not yet arrived, my dears,' she chuckled. 'Instead we have joined the queue of carriages for today's presentations at the palace. We must be patient.'

And patient they were, sitting for more than half an hour as the carriage moved slowly, slowly forwards—through the gates and gradually around the courtyard. It was a tight squeeze within, for Izzy and Anna were seated either side of Lady Ashbourne, while her nephew and Rose had the rear-facing seats. Izzy's mind drifted once again to Lord Ashbourne's describing them as beautiful, and her realisation it was the first time she had ever been described so.

Indeed, the closest she had ever previously come to receiving a compliment from a gentleman had been that drunken merchant's clumsy attempt to beguile her at the inn in Grantham. While she could read nothing more than politeness in Lord Ashbourne's words earlier, the merchant had, she reflected, seemed to sincerely admire her—even if such admiration had been fleeting and expressed in a highly inappropriate manner. *Fair one*, he had called her and likened her to golden Aphrodite, no less. Aphrodite, the goddess of love and beauty, the golden epithet a familiar one from Izzy's studies of Homer's epics.

Golden…rather a trite reference to my hair colour, she thought sourly. He might have done better!

She shook her head slightly, catching the direction of her thoughts.

In the two weeks and more since the encounter at Grantham, on multiple occasions she had had to sternly remind herself not to think of him. She was becoming fairly good at *not* thinking of him—in the daytime, at least. And despite strong urgings, she had so far resisted drawing him in her sketchbook, even though she itched to do so.

Izzy loved to draw and paint and had something of a talent for it. She often gave gifts of sketches and miniatures at Christmastide or on her sisters' birthday.

I should do something for Lady Ashbourne, who has been so good to us.

And perhaps she could send a sketch of Lady Ashbourne to her brother in Elgin. Mr Marnoch had always encouraged her art. Yes, there was an entire list in her head of drawings she should work on. And yet the drawing she truly wanted to make—the one image she could never fully shake from her mind—was of a tall, handsome merchant, with fair hair and piercing grey eyes.

'Here we are, girls!' Lady Ashbourne's brisk tone alerted Izzy to the fact they had finally arrived. 'Veils on!' Their hostess was determined to reveal the fact they were identical only at the last possible moment, and so one of the dressmakers had suggested face veils for use in the palace antechamber. Izzy thrilled at the theatricality of it all, and her heart warmed to Lady Ashbourne who, it seemed, also had a taste for adventure.

Fixing her own veil over the bridge of her nose, Izzy attached it using the ear-loops, allowing it to fall below her chin. Carefully, she then descended from the carriage, trying not to knock the tall feathers in her headdress. Looking about with curiosity while she waited for the others to emerge, she saw that the palace was of brick, with tall windows and what seemed like dozens of chimneys. While the king and queen no longer lived here all of the time—seemingly preferring Kew Palace and Buckingham House—the court of St James's was still the primary location for levees and ceremonies—including the presentation of débutantes.

'Ready?' Lady Ashbourne asked. They all stepped towards the double entrance doors to the building, when Izzy's attention was caught by some sort of disturbance behind her. Another carriage had pulled up—the last one in the queue, it seemed—and a middle-aged lady was currently scolding a younger lady who was, like the Lennox sisters, wearing a court gown and feather headdress. Another débutante!

About to feel quite sorry for the girl, Izzy abruptly changed her mind when the débutante replied to her mother's scolding in the strongest of terms and using language Izzy had only ever heard in Elgin's market. Her jaw dropped.

Well! Then she chuckled. *Perhaps, after all, I am not an impostor here!*

Chapter Three

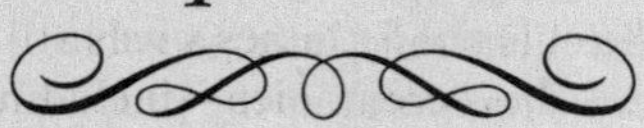

Claudio stood rigidly upright, behind and to the right of Queen Charlotte and her ladies, who had the good fortune to be seated on the dais.

Lord, how many more?

The procession of débutantes had been continuing since noon, until it was all a blur of feathers and curtsies and proud mamas.

All his life he had endured occasions like this. He knew the protocol, knew what was expected of him. Yet here in England, following a number of weeks of a life without any protocol or ceremony whatsoever, he found himself inwardly fighting the necessity to stand still, although thankfully he knew his face was a picture of princely impassivity. Ennui such as he had never known threatened to overcome him. None of the young ladies had even had the grace to faint or swoon, which at least might have been briefly diverting.

Why, even now he might be in an alehouse, or at a cockfight, or playing faro with Hawkins and Eldon. His friends were not here today—indeed they had expressed their disgust at the very possibility—but had promised to meet him later, just as soon as he could get away.

Discreetly, he nodded to a servant who had just made

his way subtly up the Council Chamber—the large hall being used today as the queen's drawing room for the presentations. 'How many more?' he asked quietly, knowing the man had come from the antechamber.

'Three families, Your Highness.'

'Very good.'

Just three more! His relief was palpable. There was to be dancing and refreshments after the presentation, but Claudio had no intention of staying for long. No, once these final few high-born virgins had made their curtsies, he would make his escape. Not long now.

Just three families now stood in the high-ceilinged antechamber. As a red-haired maiden and her mama were taken through the ominous double doors into the queen's chamber, Izzy's attention turned once again to the foul-mouthed girl and her scolding mother. Never had she come across anyone quite like them, and her response was part fascination, part horror.

'For goodness' sake, pinch your cheeks, Charity!' the mother was currently demanding. 'You are as pale as paper. And I have told you before, quit slouching!'

Although pouting mutinously, Charity did as she was bade, at the same time taking the opportunity to send a cross glance in her mother's direction. 'I cannot believe I am to be presented last, Mama. It is not *fair*!'

'Indeed, I must agree with you there. Hold—wait one moment!'

Enthralled, Izzy watched as the girl's mother made her way to the door to address the major-domo. Since this personage looked terrifyingly important, Izzy had to admire the woman's audacity. While the palace maids fussed about, straightening her and her sisters' trains and headdresses,

Izzy's attention remained on what was now best described as an altercation. Voices were raised, the lady seemingly alternating between pleading and demanding. Through it all, the major-domo remained unmoved. As the general noise in the vicinity decreased briefly, Izzy, straining, was able to hear some of the man's words.

'As I have told you repeatedly, Mrs Chorley,' he declared evenly, 'débutantes are presented in order of arrival, and Lady Ashbourne arrived before you did.'

This statement, Izzy saw, had also attracted Lady Ashbourne's attention. Her gaze followed Mrs Chorley as, conceding defeat, she made her way back to her daughter. Abruptly, as if suddenly making a decision, Lady Ashbourne moved purposefully towards the major-domo.

Now what?

Frustratingly, Izzy could not hear what passed between them, but a moment later Lady Ashbourne returned, her eyes sparkling with glee.

'Well!' she declared in a low tone, 'I must say I have outdone myself! By dint of a recent fortuitous conversation with the major-domo, I have managed to ensure you will be the very last to be announced. Indeed it was, in the end, a fairly easy task,' she assured them, 'for normally no one wishes to be last, when the crowd may be restless, the queen bored, and the débutantes miserable with anxiety.'

'But—you prefer for us to be announced last?' Anna sounded puzzled, but Izzy knew exactly why Lady Ashbourne had done it.

She is clever, our sponsor!

'Indeed, I do. You will make an impact, girls, I know it. First or last, never the anonymous middle!' She eyed them all. 'Miserable with anxiety? Ha! Not my girls!' she declared, clear pride in her voice. 'Why, you are as serene as a bevy of swans!'

Serene was not perhaps the best word to describe how Izzy was feeling. Dressed in outlandish costumes from yesteryear, they were about to meet the queen, and judging by the anxiety displayed by many of the other young ladies and their sponsors, they had to behave impeccably. Abruptly Izzy was glad that Lady Ashbourne had made them rehearse their walk and curtsy at home. They had walked up and down her ballroom numerous times in the past few days—feathers on their heads and heavy curtains tied about their waists. Now they must perform it for real. Lord Ashbourne—who had been determined not to spend too long in the Council Chamber—now slipped inside, leaving only the ladies, the palace maids, and the major-domo.

Miss Chorley and her mother were called forward, and the major-domo admitted them. Even through her veil Izzy could discern the stiffness of Miss Chorley's shoulders. The girl was clearly nervous and despite her uncharitable behaviour, Izzy was able to feel a little sorry for her. Suddenly she grinned as she put two and two together. The girl's parents had thought it a good idea to christen their child Charity Chorley, and Izzy thought the absurdity of it entirely fitting.

Finally! At the back of the long hall, the double doors opened once again, and Claudio reawakened his attention. The last girl was about to enter, and soon he would be released from this prison of protocol. Apparently this was the third set of presentations this year, with another to follow next week.

Lord, how do they stand it?

The major-domo's voice rang out. 'Your Majesty, Your

Highness, my lords, ladies, and gentlemen. The final débutantes of the day. Lady Ashbourne presents the wards of her brother, Mr Marnoch. Miss Lennox, Miss Isobel Lennox, Miss Rosabella Lennox!'

Three of them? Well, this was unusual, indeed. Generally sisters were launched one at a time, the younger ones waiting until the older ones were married. Sure enough, instead of a single débutante, three slim figures were now advancing serenely up the central aisle towards the dais. They walked in perfect step—a clever ruse, and one which drew the eye. Their white gowns glimmered and sparkled as they moved, and Claudio noticed that the sound level in the room had changed. First, an increase, as people commented on the audacity of launching three débutantes at once, then a silence, spreading from the back of the hall and running in a wave towards him. They were approaching steadily, and now he could make out the features of the girl leading the way, the eldest, he assumed. Guinea-gold curls, a perfect face—abruptly, he knew that the maiden before him had eyes blue as cornflowers, and that he had once compared her to golden Aphrodite. Briefly, his gaze flicked to Aphrodite's sisters, and his hand tightened on the hilt of the ceremonial sword by his side. His jaw loosened in shock. Three of them! And identical in every feature!

His mind could not take it in. Bemused, his gaze flicked from left to right, as if to check that what he was seeing was real.

They had reached the dais. The two following flanked the eldest, then at some unseen signal they curtsied in unison, all the while keeping their eyes fixed on the queen.

'Lady Ashbourne!' said Her Majesty, the shock in her tone evident.

'Yes, Your Majesty?'

'Where have you been hiding these delectable creatures? I declare I have never seen anything so pretty! Triplets, I declare!' She fluttered an elegant hand. 'La, and I thought only puppies were born in threes!'

Her ladies tittered, but Claudio remained in a state of such shock that he was struggling to know what to think. Not one but *three* golden Aphrodites, all identical.

But which is mine?

Desperately he searched their faces, but their attention was currently given fully to the queen.

Her Majesty rose to speak, and the girls and their sponsor swiftly moved aside. The eldest briefly glanced in his direction, but there were no signs of recognition on her beautiful visage.

Not her, then.

'My friends, I declare we have found our diamond of the Season. And not just one—but three of them!' With a gesture, the Queen indicated the sisters should face the crowd. 'Take your bow, my dears, and then come and sit by me!'

Now Claudio was faced with the sight of the three of them from the rear, again making that curtsy in perfect time with each other. Another realisation dawned. Aphrodite was no serving maid but rather a young lady of consequence, travelling to London to make her début.

What a fool I am! It is no wonder she was so disdainful of me!

Relief warred with mortification within him. Her disdain now had an explanation, and he was an idiot for not having realised she was gently born, and not therefore to be trifled with. But her clothing had been so drab…and of course he had not yet learned to decipher any subtleties of English speech that might have indicated her class.

Also, he belatedly realised, the girl who had afterwards

at the inn behaved towards him as though she had never seen him before was one of Aphrodite's sisters. Who had genuinely never seen him before. His brain felt as though it might ignite in flames as realisation after realisation dawned on him.

The queen's ladies had given up their chairs to Lady Ashbourne and her three débutantes, and as the hubbub in court resumed, Queen Charlotte began quizzing the girls' sponsor about them.

Yes, they were orphans.

No, Lady Ashbourne's brother had no information on their mother's or father's family… *None*—this said with a meaningful nod.

Their dowries were…respectable.

Yes, they had been gently educated and were the *sweetest* girls.

Fascinated, Claudio continued to shamelessly eavesdrop.

'Tell me your names again! And which of you was born first?' the queen demanded.

'I am Annabelle, the eldest.'

Not my Aphrodite.

'By twenty minutes!' the next one clarified, a hint of humour in her voice. 'I am Isobel.'

Is it you?

'And I am Rosabella. I was born a half hour after Isobel.'

Or you perhaps?

'Three babies in one confinement! Your poor, poor mother!' Her Majesty turned to Lady Ashbourne. 'Tell me more, my friend.'

'Well, they were each apparently known as *Bella* or collectively *the Belles* at school,' offered Lady Ashbourne. 'Until I learn which is which, it is how I refer to them.'

'Belle, Bel, and Bella,' repeated the queen. 'Yes, I see. Entirely apt.'

Belles, then, not Aphrodites. Claudio shrugged inwardly. *Belles. Beauties. Yes, just as apt.*

Turning slightly, the queen beckoned him to approach via a raised eyebrow.

Now is the moment. Holding his breath, he stepped forward.

'Claudio, may I introduce Lady Ashbourne, Miss Lennox, Miss Isobel Lennox, and Miss Rosabella Lennox?' Rising, they curtsied to his bow, and he kept his eye on the two younger ones. Miss Rosabella's expression was relaxed and open, while Miss Isobel—

Her eyes were wide, her jaw sagging, and as he watched she threw him a look of utter shock.

Aha! I have you, my Aphrodite!

'It is an honour to meet you,' he murmured, allowing a hint of irony to come through in his tone. Miss Isobel Lennox would know they had met before, and in unusual circumstances.

'Lady Ashbourne, Belles,' the queen continued smoothly, 'this is Prince Claudio Friedrich Ferdinand of Andernach, a distant cousin of mine. He is considering making his home in England. Is that not so, my dear?'

Lord, do not give them expectations of me!

Despite his father's instructions to find an English bride, Claudio knew his priorities for now did not include marriage. His priorities were wine, gambling, sport, bedsport, and more wine. And not always in that order.

'Nothing is as yet decided,' he replied, his tone as neutral as he could manage, and the queen laughed.

'Ah, but I always have my way in the end, Claudio. You know it!' Turning back to Lady Ashbourne and the Belles, she declared, 'Now, you diamonds must all go and mix with the assembly, for how are you to get husbands sitting here with two old ladies?'

'Not *old*, Your Majesty, surely?' returned Lady Ashbourne, a decided twinkle in her eye.

This earned a short laugh. 'Yet not young either, my friend!' The queen patted Lady Ashbourne's hand briefly. 'We bear our trials well, you and I.'

'We do.'

A warm look passed between them, and Claudio realised Lady Ashbourne was likely one of the true friends Queen Charlotte had told him about—a small group of *ton* ladies whom she felt she could trust. Something about the bond between the two women caused a momentary uneasiness within Claudio's gut, something to do with his own friends here. While he was enjoying kicking up larks with them, he could not truly call them friends. Not yet, leastwise. And yet, they were his friends in the usual sense of the word. He sought them out, spent most of his time with them, enjoyed their company.

His gaze searched the room, even though he knew neither Mr Hawkins nor Mr Eldon was there. Recalling his earlier determination to leave as soon as he could, he knew now that he had no intention of leaving. The Belles—the Aphrodites, the triplets, the Misses Lennox, the diamonds—were currently surrounded by admirers and well-wishers, but he knew the first dance was about to be called. He stepped towards the group.

This time, he thought grimly, *she will accept that I am a prince!*

Shock continued to reverberate through Isobel, affecting her ability to think clearly or to focus on the people currently surrounding her and her sisters. Her mind was racing, darting from one realisation to another.

It is him! He is *an actual prince! He is here—just yards from me!*

Her heart was pounding, her pulse fluttering wildly. At the same time, her stomach was sick with mortification and apprehension.

How I spoke to him! Will he wish for revenge on me? On all of us, because of my foolishness?

In the outside world, she was half responding to the group of people who had surrounded them, introducing themselves and making all of the usual comments about just how alike the girls were. *Yes*, she affirmed wearily. *We are identical.*

Vaguely she was aware that to her left some musicians were tuning their instruments, and she remembered Lady Ashbourne saying there would be dancing. Abruptly the crowd around them gave way a little. 'Your Highness,' they bowed, allowing the Prince to approach.

Oh, Lord! Now it comes!

'Good day, good day,' he murmured urbanely, eyeing Izzy and Anna. Those grey eyes, framed by lashes and brows a shade or two darker than his hair, were just as piercing as she had recalled. To their right Rose was busy in conversation with Lord Ashbourne and a dark-haired girl, and the group had clearly not noticed the arrival of the prince in their midst. After looking intently in their direction for a moment, the prince shook his head slightly, turning back to search the faces of Anna and Isobel. Desperately, and knowing exactly whom he was seeking, Isobel tried to keep all emotion out of her expression.

To no avail, for after a pause he bowed to her. 'Might I have this dance?'

Izzy, panicking, gestured towards Anna. 'My sister is the eldest, Your Highness, and by rights—'

'But you were all born on the same day, were you not?'

She nodded helplessly, and he held out his hand. 'Come, Miss Isobel. Dance with me.'

Her eyes widened.

He knows my name!

People usually took months if not years to tell them apart—particularly without the clues of coloured embroidery. Somehow she found herself walking with him towards the dancing area, her hand held in his. She could feel his warmth through her thin glove, and now the kaleidoscope of emotion within her gained a new colour: something golden, and bright, and sparkling. Something unwanted, and frightening, and wonderful.

He knows me!

They had reached the dance floor. Mimicking the other ladies, Izzy wound the long train of her gown twice around her left arm, then took a breath.

I am ready. Now, what will he say to me?

The musicians had not yet begun, and so the hum of conversation was continuing. To Izzy's relief a gentleman addressed the prince, and while he was busy replying, Izzy stole a glance at her dance partner. Yes, he was just as handsome as she remembered—and being sober improved his looks immeasurably, she thought dryly. Yet, even foxed, he had caused her heart to pound in the same way it was pounding now.

His conversation was ending, and instantly she looked about her as though she had been doing so the whole time. Rose, she noted, was in the next set being partnered by Lord Ashbourne, while Anna's hand had been claimed by a tall gentleman who was handsome in a rather forbidding sort of way. The entire situation was beyond belief.

We are in the queen's drawing room, dancing with titled gentlemen, and the queen has singled us out for favour, it seems!

Yet she could not enjoy their collective success, for standing before her was a man she had thought was a merchant, a man who had told her of his princely status and she had laughed.

I laughed at a prince.

Mortification rose within her again but, thankfully, the musicians had finally struck up the first dance.

I shall get through this, then escape.

It was the only strategy she could think of.

Curtsying to his bow as the dance began, she lifted her chin.

I can do this!

He fired the first arrows almost immediately. 'We have met before, Miss Isobel.'

Now, this was an easy feint to counter, for the triplets had all their lives made the most of being identical. Pausing as the dance took them apart for a few steps, she affected puzzlement when they came back together. 'I do not think so, Your Highness. I am certain I would recall—'

He chuckled. 'That will not do, Your Majesty, for I know it was you.'

She tossed her head. 'I am sure I do not know what you mean, Your Highness.' His words registered fully. 'Why did you call me *Your Majesty*?'

'Am I not addressing the Queen of Sheba?'

She flushed as his words hit home.

Oh, if only I had not been quite so scathing that day.

Laughing lightly, she frowned as if confused. 'The Queen of Sheba? What on earth are you talking about?'

When next the dance brought them together, his expression had changed. Now he looked grim, angry.

Oh, dear.

'You may deny it all you wish, but we both recall what happened that day. You were determined to deny that I might possibly be a prince, and you questioned my honour.'

Faced with such a direct accusation, Izzy felt rage rise within her. Ignoring the voice of caution in her mind—a voice that she associated with Anna's calm good sense—abruptly she abandoned all pretence. 'Well, think of it from my perspective. How likely was it that I would meet an actual prince in a random inn in—in *Grantham*, for heaven's sake!'

'You should have accepted my word,' he returned stiffly.

'Aye, and kissed you on your say-so, no doubt!' she returned scornfully and had the satisfaction of seeing a faint flush across his cheekbones.

'I—I did not know of your station when I said that.'

'So it is your habit to proposition maidens of a lower station, then? Always ensuring they know of your royal status? Have you had much success, *Your Highness*?' Her tone dripped with venom, and she felt his hand tighten on hers.

'I shall not deign to answer such a question.' His tone was low, but she knew she had riled him.

Oh, such dignity!

'So the answer is *yes*, then. And so, my *honourable* prince, are you ready to apologise to me for speaking to me in such a manner?'

'*I* apologise to *you*? You are the one who questioned my honour, without evidence or just cause!'

'Evidence? Just cause? You tried to kiss me, a defenceless female, alone in a hallway!'

Now anger flashed clearly in those grey eyes.

Have I gone too far?

'I did not!' he retorted. 'I asked for a kiss and accepted your refusal!'

'I—' To be fair, this was true. Momentarily speechless, yet still the anger within her flared higher at the sight of his self-satisfied expression.

'So are you planning to apologise for your wrongful accusation of dishonour?' he pressed, sure of his advantage.

No! The answer came instinctively. He might not have forced a kiss upon her, but he had made her feel decidedly uncomfortable, and even now it was clear he was not prepared to back down from his pillar of righteousness even a little.

The dance took them apart again—this time for him to turn every other lady in their set, and by the time he returned she was stonily determined. 'I suggest, Your Highness, that we endeavour to put this...*incident* behind us. We are clearly not destined to be friends, but London is surely large enough that we might avoid one another.'

'Agreed.' His tone was clipped, his expression disdainful. In silence they completed the dance, then went their separate ways.

Rose approached her as she left the dance floor, and alarm crossed her face as she read whatever expression Izzy was currently wearing.

'What happened?'

'Insufferable man!' Izzy could barely contain her anger.

'Who? Who is insufferable?' Rose glanced about, a perplexed expression on her face.

'That prince person! He thinks a great deal of himself, that one.'

He dared to ask me *for an apology!*

'As does the Viscount Ashbourne!' Rose retorted. 'He dared to try and advise me, as though I were a junior girl at Belvedere!'

Anna joined them, wearing a slight frown. 'Izzy! Rose! What has got you both in such high dudgeon?'

Briefly, Izzy gave her to understand that Prince Claudio was superior and conceited and thought very highly of himself, while Rose made her opinions of Viscount Ashbourne clear.

As ever, Anna remained calm. 'Izzy, he *is* actually a prince, you know. He may think as highly of himself as he wishes!' While she added some soothing words to Rose, Izzy's attention went inwardly.

He is *actually a prince.*

Well, yes, but did he need to be so lofty and condescending? Vaguely, she was aware that her outrage was tinged with both guilt and mortification, both of which were serving only to reinforce her current anger.

Rose glanced her way, bringing Izzy's attention back to her sisters. 'Still,' Rose declared cheerfully, 'we are here at the palace and dancing in court dresses. Who would have thought it possible just two months ago?'

Izzy snorted. 'Well, I should much rather be back at school, sewing, than suffering such arrogance!' Even as the words were spoken, she knew they were a lie. Coming to London was the best thing that had ever happened to her—despite the arrogance of a certain gentleman—er, prince. 'And Anna,' she continued hotly, 'you are wrong. Just because he happens to be a prince does not mean he can treat others with disdain!'

'Izzy!' Anna breathed in warning, making Izzy stiffen in horror.

Sure enough, the prince had joined them. Bowing, he smiled politely, his face a mask of impassivity. There was no doubt he had heard Izzy's words. She felt herself shrink in mortification.

'Having already danced with Miss Isobel,' he declared urbanely, tilting his head unerringly towards Izzy, 'I should now like to dance with each of her sisters.' He looked from Rose to Anna and back again. 'Which of you is Miss Lennox the eldest?'

Anna identified herself and walked away in step with him, her hand on his arm, while Izzy died a little inside. *Lord!* An instant later two other gentlemen came to claim Rose and Izzy for la Boulangere. Automatically Izzy accepted and was relieved when her partner—a fairly handsome gentleman who introduced himself as Mr Fitch—took her to a set at the bottom of the room, far away from the prince, who had clearly won their latest bout.

As the first couple linked their way around the circle Izzy stood impassively, pretending to watch, but in reality her mind was on Anna's current dance partner. Not by so much as a quiver had he revealed he had heard her insults, and his very composure demonstrated his royal quality. It was *she* who was lacking, she who had been rude, she who had let herself down—and in doing so she had let down her sisters, and Lady Ashbourne, and even Mr Marnoch and the Belvedere teachers, though they were far away in Scotland.

Mr Fitch tried to speak to her and, conscious of the need to redeem herself, she was more than polite to him. As the dance continued, she positively encouraged the man to converse with her.

See? she asked an invisible judge. *I am a lady of quality. I am not always rude or uncivil.*

Yet at a deeper level she was conscious of something that felt suspiciously like shame.

Claudio played his part in la Boulangere, his mind awhirl. The lady beside him was exquisite—the Belles, in his opinion and no doubt in many others, were the most beautiful maidens in the room. Moreover, Miss Anna was demure, polite, and pleasant. They enjoyed easy conversation about his journey to England, and he even told her of his father's pleasant memories of the country from his own visit more than twenty years ago.

Like Miss Rosabella, the youngest of the sisters, Miss Anna was the embodiment of an ideal. So why was Claudio's attention so caught by the middle sister? Why, when he could be enjoying a pleasant dance with a lady who was *exactly* as beautiful as Miss Isobel, was his mind still repeating and repeating the sound of her voice as she described him as arrogant, spoke of him treating people with disdain?

Is it true?

Instantly, he rejected the notion. Being mindful of one's position in life was not arrogance, it was simply a recognition of reality.

I was born a prince.

He could no more change that fact than he could his height or his eye colour. Thus reassured, he completed the dance, made his farewells to the queen, and departed from court without a backwards glance.

Chapter Four

Gradually, Claudio became aware that he was awake. Opening his eyes, he focused on a beam of bright sunshine streaming through a tiny gap in his curtains. Instinctively he glanced towards the clock on the mantel and gave a wry smile. Waking at midday was becoming quite a habit with him, and one that would have been abhorred back home. But then, many things were different here.

Since the clock had been striking four when he sought his bed, his late awakening was hardly to be wondered at. After the court presentations yesterday he had gone directly to White's, there to meet Eldon, Hawkins, and a group of merry young men. While Hawkins and Eldon were a little older, they behaved just as young men ought and indeed at times led the merriment. Together they had drunk copious glasses of wine, played cards, and talked of everything and nothing, before gradually drifting away to seek their rest.

Sitting on the edge of the bed Claudio yawned and stretched, absent-mindedly scratching his bare chest as he recalled yesterday's presentation at court—and in particular the realisation that his golden Aphrodite was part of the *ton*. He had thought to never see her again and had built around the Grantham memories a scaffold of impossible things. Yes, the reality of her was far removed from his romantical notions, for she was pert and judgemental, and her waspish words had stung. Having falsely accused him of being dishonourable—an accusation that still rankled—she had gone on to accuse him of treating people badly. Something tight within his chest burned at the memory.

Dishonour.

Such an accusation went deep, for he had been raised to value honour above everything.

He shook his head, laughing softly at his own foolishness. All those times in his imagination where he had managed to persuade her for a kiss in that Grantham hallway now seemed absurd, for it seemed she heartily disliked him—a lowering notion. He was not accustomed to being disliked. He was, after all, a prince.

Ugh! Annoyingly, his thoughts had already gone to Miss Isobel, and he had only been awake for a few minutes! But he had much to think about. Miss Isobel and her sisters had been the talk of the club last night, with those who had been present at court regaling the others with tales of the impact they had made.

That entire conversation had left Claudio feeling strangely uncomfortable. When they were speaking of the triplets' beauty, he had felt a mix of pride and...*possessiveness*, almost. As if by meeting Miss Isobel in Grantham, it had given him some sort of prior claim on her.

How odd!

It meant, too, when there had been deprecating comments made about their dowries—no better than *respectable*, apparently—he had felt the strangest urge to come to their defence. Surely a person was worth more than their wealth? Naturally money mattered, but did it perhaps matter too much to some of his new friends?

He shrugged, then used the chamber pot before crossing the room to wash before calling for his valet and fully opening the curtains. He himself had an adequate settlement from his father. If he did decide to live in England, it would undoubtedly be clever of him to marry an heiress, but he was in the fortunate position of not needing to do so.

Should I stay in England, I will need a townhouse.

Today he and his friends were to begin the Season tradition of house calls, and from what the others had said most of the *ton* lived within a three-mile radius of St James's Palace. Inwardly he admitted to a growing curiosity about the *ton*, their houses and traditions, their way of life.

This place, these people, might become my home.

Buckingham House, his current residence, was well-known amongst the *ton* as it was Queen Charlotte's favourite residence. Although the Queen herself always travelled by carriage, the distance between here and St James's was no more than a ten-minute walk, and living here suited Claudio very well. It would not do as a permanent home, however. Having grown up in his father's *Schloss*, he had a strange hankering for a different sort of residence, a different way of life. Something proportionate to a man, not a prince. Yes, a townhouse seemed appealing after a lifetime of castles and palaces. *If* he stayed.

His attention was drawn to movement in the gardens below. A gardener was conversing with a middle-aged kitchen maid amid box hedges and daffodils. The woman had a trug on her arm filled with vegetables and was clearly on her way back to the scullery door. As he watched, his mind still elsewhere, the maid happened to glance to where he stood in the first-floor window. Instantly her jaw dropped, a look of shock crossing her face.

What?

A moment later he remembered. English prudishness

meant they were uncomfortable with nakedness, unlike his own countrymen. In his father's principality, the doctors had recommended sun therapy and enjoyment of nature as health-giving. People swam in the lakes and rivers in the summertime, and there were not the same puritanical attitudes as he had been informed were common here. Sighing, he stepped away from the window, and was already donning his shirt when the valet arrived.

As he dressed, his mind returned to last night's conversations about the Belles—which, it seemed, was to be society's name for the Lennox triplets. The most difficult moments for him had been the scathing comments made by some about the girls' parentage. Apparently the sisters had been raised as ladies and were accepted as such, yet no one could say who their parents had been. This seemed to be a matter of some importance to the *ton*, though Claudio was uncertain why this was the case. Of course one's lineage was important, but outside of royalty or matters of inheritance, surely it should not matter that the Belles did not know the names and backgrounds of their parents? The girls were making no claims on anyone, and were surely entitled to be part of the Season without their names being bandied about so critically.

Although Miss Isobel had royally irritated him and had chosen to dislike him—why, he could not fathom—he was man enough to separate that from the inappropriate tittle-tattle being flung about. What had been her other wounding words? Oh, yes. She had accused him of *treating others with disdain.* Since this was something he had not nor would ever do, he was trying to dismiss her tantrum as being motivated by momentary anger. So why did the memory still sting so?

He had come to London for the chance to be himself.

Not Prince Three of Four in his family. His brothers were all that was admirable, but at court, the four sons of the ruling prince had been seen as something of a set. All well-behaved. All respectful of their father and of their positions within the principality. All lacking in individuality, in passion, in distinctiveness. Here, he could be Claudio.

If only he knew who Claudio was.

Miss Isobel certainly believed she knew. Her judgements were based upon the briefest of acquaintance, and it bothered him that she had formed such a damning impression of him. Yes, he had spoken to her in Grantham in a way that had not been appropriate for her station. But he had done her no harm.

I am not a bad person.

Acknowledging briefly the uncomfortable feelings now swirling within him, with determination he pushed them away, diverting his attention elsewhere. The treatment of three sisters who were almost strangers to him was none of his concern, and the opinions of one of them certainly had no relevance to him. His energy would be better spent considering his activities for the coming week.

While there would be visits to the *ton* at-home where he might be in the company of débutantes, there were also plans for fencing and boxing sessions at the hands of London's finest teachers, a card party in Hawkins's bachelor apartments, a trip to see a horse race at Hampstead later in the week, and of course, endless nights of wine and ale.

Life is good.

Striding out of Buckingham House, Claudio's step was light and his heart lighter.

Izzy was in alt.

This is why I came to London!

Yes, she had a quest to try and discover the identity of her father, but since they did not even know who Mama was, and the surname Lennox was unknown, she had no realistic starting point to begin. Sensibly, she thought, she had decided to shelve the matter for now. And besides, it was the *ton* who likely had the information she and her sisters needed. And so mingling with the *ton*, getting to know everyone, was the best way to advance her cause.

Satisfied with her own logic, she turned her attention back to the present. This afternoon Lady Ashbourne was hosting callers, and callers had come in droves. The large drawing room of Ashbourne House was full to bursting with gentlemen of the *ton*, many of whom had brought or sent flowers for the Belles. Many ladies had come too, and the place was thronged.

Growing up in a school was all very well, but for years Izzy had craved company and excitement and a place where one had a wide circle of acquaintances. The Belles would be here until the summer, and Izzy intended to make the most of every moment.

Scanning around the room, it thrilled her to think these were all people she would get to know but did not know yet. And they were all so stylish! With a silent prayer of gratitude for her guardian's generosity, Izzy smoothed her hands over her pretty muslin gown. She tended to wear greens and yellows, and this gown had tiny printed flowers and leaves all over the fabric, the hem trimmed with not one but two ruffles.

Such extravagance!

The court gown yesterday had been astonishing, but to Izzy's eye, today's dress was both prettier and more flattering.

As the afternoon progressed Izzy lost count of all the

people she conversed with. Having desired new company for years, she was eager to become acquainted with as many people as possible. Mr Fitch, who had danced with her at court yesterday was there, as was a Mr Kirby, and both of them offered her flattery and flimflam, which she managed to take without rolling her eyes. Both seemed solid, sensible gentlemen, and while Mr Fitch was rather better-looking, Mr Kirby had kind eyes.

The flattery was novel, though not unwelcome—even if she did not quite believe their outrageous compliments. These past couple of days had given her the impression that she and her sisters were considered good-looking, and such attention was new to her. Briefly her mind flicked to a certain gentleman likening her to Aphrodite, but she pushed the thought away. He had not come, and she was not particularly surprised. Her words last night had been harsh, she knew, and spoken in anger...but she could do nothing about that now.

Excusing herself, she left Mr Fitch and went to greet Miss Chorley and her mother, who had just arrived. They were, she thought, a perfect example of what her teachers had called *vulgar*, and Izzy was gleefully interested in them. She knew herself to be something of a rebel, but never would she behave in a way that was vulgar. To meet people who were so unaware or uncaring of their demeanour was fascinating to her.

'I told you the gentlemen would all be here, Charity. Look, the Earl of Garvald!' Mrs Chorley was muttering to her daughter as Isobel approached.

'Welcome, welcome!' declared Lady Ashbourne, bustling across to them before Isobel could get there. 'Mrs Chorley, it is lovely to see you again. And your pretty daughter! I trust you are well?'

'I am well, thank you. And are you well, Lady Ashbourne?'

Lady Ashbourne confirmed it, and Mrs Chorley continued in a rush, 'I wanted to thank you again for kindly allowing my dear Charity to precede your *delightful* charges yesterday!'

The word *delightful*, Izzy noted wryly, was uttered as if through gritted teeth.

Stepping forward, she exchanged greetings with the pair, then offered to take them to the other part of the room, where there was a vacant settee. 'Just there, can you see?' she said, pointing. 'Next to the Earl of Garvald.'

'Indeed!' Mrs Chorley's gaze swivelled instantly to the Earl. 'How fortuitous! I mean, that there should be *any* settee free, for you have no shortage of visitors!'

'Indeed we are very fortunate,' Izzy replied noncommittally, leading them to the settee and seating herself alongside the pair.

To her no great surprise she was promptly ignored by the Chorleys, whose attention was fully given to conversing with the taciturn earl, whose good looks, Izzy thought, were almost spoiled by his closedness. He answered every Chorley query with equanimity, politeness, and brevity, and Izzy felt an unexpected giggle bubble within her.

Why, this is as good as watching a play!

Not that she had ever seen a play—not in real life, leastways. The scenes she and the other Belvedere girls had played out occasionally at school did not count.

Perhaps I can visit the theatre, here in London.

Oh, it was such an adventure to be here! A pang went through her at the realisation that her visit would inevitably end, but she pushed it away.

After a few moments Garvald bowed and left them, and

the Chorleys, seemingly undeterred, began finally to engage in conversation with her, their gaze flitting around the room all the while. They were clearly in search of a better option—which might have been a deflating thought to anyone more sensitive than Izzy. But she cared nothing for what such people thought of her. In that regard she was armoured against hurt. Unlike—

'Sit up, Charity!' Mrs Chorley's tone was almost a hiss. 'He has arrived!'

Startled, Izzy froze as she put together what was happening. She had no need to turn her head to see who had just entered the drawing room. Keeping her eyes fixed on her companions, she noticed that the hum of conversation in the room quieted for a moment then increased, as though time had briefly stood still and was now rushing to catch up with itself.

The cynic within her curled a lip at the sycophancy of the *ton*, despite the woman in her being foolishly desperate to look at him. Thankfully she had enough strength of character to resist, maintaining her attention on Miss Chorley. Unfortunately the latter was gazing hungrily towards the door—or, more accurately, the person who had just entered.

'Scotland,' she murmured, drawing both Chorleys back to her. 'You asked where my sisters and I grew up,' she reminded them, amused by the identical blank looks they were giving her. 'In Elgin, actually. It is near Inverness.'

'How sad for you!' Mrs Chorley's tone dripped with false sympathy. 'So far away from everyone and everything of importance. We live in London, naturally, and my husband has also purchased a *darling* little country estate for us to take refuge in during the hotter months. No more than forty acres, you understand, but it is in the heart of Kent. It cost a pretty penny, I assure you!'

She went on to add the exact amount paid by Mr Chorley, and an uncomfortable feeling settled in Izzy's chest on hearing Mrs Chorley's words. One did not speak so plainly of such things! It was simply not…polite.

Distaste, she realised. *I feel distaste.*

Then, a moment later, the understanding that somehow, between Mama and Mr Marnoch and the Belvedere teachers, she genuinely did have a sense of what was appropriate behaviour and what was not. Vulgarity was indeed real and embodied in Mrs Chorley and her daughter.

How strange!

She caught her breath. Without conscious thought, as her attention had been briefly diverted by Mrs Chorley, her head had slowly turned, and now the prince was in her line of vision. Instantly her stomach seemed to flip, her mouth went dry, and her heart began thudding loudly. Abruptly, it dawned on Izzy that she had been hoping for his arrival—or awaiting it, at least.

It must be because he vexes me so much.

Hungrily she took everything in at a glance. His fair hair and strong profile. His broad shoulders, trim figure, and strong legs perfectly displayed by the current fashion for tight coats and breeches. Lord, it was unfair that any man should be so handsome…particularly when his good looks were matched by his arrogance!

This day is not for him, she reminded herself. *It is for me and Anna and Rose to finally experience being out in society. I refuse to let him spoil everything.*

With some effort she dragged her gaze away from him lest he catch her looking, instead focusing on his companions. Both gentlemen were older; perhaps in their early thirties, so around ten years older than the prince. One was portly, with a round red face, while the other was tall and gaunt. They had clearly arrived together. She frowned. Why on earth would a young man such as the prince seek the company of men who were so much older? Perhaps he was more sober than she had imagined. Strangely this elevated her impression of him, suggesting a gravitas she had previously thought lacking. Did she *wish* to think well of him? She shook her head, rejecting the notion. She would do better to not think of him at all. Besides, it was entirely possible that the other two gentlemen had coincidentally arrived at the same time as Prince Claudio.

'Who are those gentlemen with the prince, Mama?'

Instantly her attention swivelled to the Chorley ladies. *Yes, I should also like to know this.*

'The tall one is Mr Eldon, and the other is Mr Hawkins. They are the prince's closest companions, by all accounts. Let us go and speak with them.'

With the briefest of farewells to Izzy they were gone.

It is a good thing, she thought wryly, *that I am not easily put out by such behaviour.*

And yet the prince himself had also managed to stir her to an unexpected degree. Because she was still cross with him, no doubt.

Mr Kirby returned to sit with her and engage in empty conversation. It took very little to reply to him, while at the same time her mind was busy ruminating on her response to the prince. Undoubtedly he had been arrogant in Grantham, and his ruse of trying to get a kiss by telling her he was a prince still enraged her. Surely a man should stand on his own merits and not by any unearned plaudits, such as royal birth? And yet, did she not also expect others to treat her with particular respect simply because she had been raised a lady? Oh, it was all too complicated! One thing was certain, though: the *ton* was determined to fawn over him. Which strengthened her resolve to do exactly the opposite.

Lord! I have done it again!

Having resolved earlier not to even *think* of him, she had in fact been lost in thought for quite a number of minutes. With determination she turned her attention back to Mr Kirby who was still talking. Stifling a sigh—for poor Mr Kirby was dreadfully dull—she focused on his words.

'And so I would be honoured, Miss Isobel, if you and your sisters would join me in my box at Drury Lane.'

Suddenly she was all attention. 'The theatre? I should like that!' She frowned. 'But I do not think we can go without Lady Ashbourne.'

He laughed. 'Well, naturally! I shall of course invite a couple of gentlemen to make up the numbers…' He considered the matter. 'The *right* gentlemen. Not—but perhaps—yes, I must think on this.'

All the while, the prince had been standing near the fireplace, fully within her line of vision. With half an ear on Mr Kirby's deliberations, she could not help but notice that Mrs Chorley and her daughter were still with the prince and his friends, and the five of them seemed to be getting along famously. As she watched, the prince turned his head slightly, and their eyes met. Instantly she stiffened, her breath catching in her throat and her heart skipping a beat. After a long moment during which she was trapped by his gaze, she came to her senses.

Lord! I am caught looking at him!

Turning away, she laughed as though Mr Kirby had said something full of wit and wisdom. 'Oh, Mr Kirby, I am certain you will invite exactly the right people!'

Thankfully her companion seemed not to notice anything amiss, and they continued to converse for another ten minutes, Isobel acting as though Mr Kirby was the most interesting person in the entire world. It was only when he commented how delightful and unusual it was for a young lady to remain in extended conversation that she suddenly realised she was perhaps encouraging him in a way she had not intended. 'You are right, of course, and so you must go now, Mr Kirby. I should not wish anyone to think I was paying you particular attention!'

Much struck, he replied with great animation. 'Indeed, no! I would not for the world compromise your reputation in any way, Miss Isobel.' He rose and bowed over her hand. There was a light in his eye that gave Izzy a momentary discomfort.

Oh, dear! Does he think I have a particular liking for him?

Briefly alone again, Izzy's uncomfortable thought was that she did not wish for...*anyone* to think her unpopular. Rising, she made her way to where Anna and another lady were in conversation with the Earl of Garvald. Lady Mary Someone, she recalled. Deliberately, she kept her back turned to the prince and his friends, and when she next looked he was gone.

After that, the party felt oddly flat. Was she really so focused on one arrogant man that she might allow it to detract from this wonderful day? Sadly, it seemed she was. Still, at least he was gone, and she no longer had to worry about inadvertently meeting his gaze or, worse, having to make polite conversation with him. Yes, it was so much better without him.

Having worked out some of his frustrations in Gentleman Jackson's boxing saloon, Claudio prepared for another night out in London. From now on, his friends assured him, their evenings would be taken up with soirées, musicales, theatre performances, and balls as the Season got properly underway. Claudio also had a responsibility to his cousin the queen, who had requested his attendance at some of her own gatherings. Still, at least for some of the time he and his friends could choose their own diversions.

Tonight, Hawkins was taking them to a discreet club off St James's, a club where, he was assured, the stakes were higher than the usual fare. Undoubtedly there would also be good wine, possibly ale, and perhaps even good French brandy. All of the elements were there for another night of drinking, gambling, and generally being free of the sort of scrutiny and expectations he was subjected to at home.

So why was his mind hankering back to the tea and conversation he had endured earlier in Lady Ashbourne's drawing room? Surely those were exactly the sort of tedious events he had so abhorred back home? And yet… something within him had welcomed the familiar rhythms of social chit-chat. Meeting new people, observing others… He had engaged in relatively interesting conversations with some of the gentlemen: Garvald, Ashbourne, Phillips. All had seemed sober and sensible…and dull as ditch-water in comparison to his own merry friends.

All three Lennox sisters had been present—well, naturally they would be, given that Lady Ashbourne was their sponsor for the Season. While he had initially struggled to identify which was Miss Isobel, he had worked out before long that the one in the pink-trimmed dress and the one in the blue gown were unlikely to be her, as they had both greeted him in an unaffected way. The one in the yellow-and-green print muslin, however… He stifled a grin. She had made such a show of *not* looking at him that it had to be Isobel.

And then there had been that moment when they had locked eyes and the world had seemed to pause for a moment. Deliberately he released his breath, shocked by the realisation that this young lady was beginning to become something of an obsession with him.

Perhaps tonight he should seek a bed-mate, someone to distract his mind and return it to the evenness he had taken for granted. Yes, that was a good plan. Most of the clubs had courtesans working for them or serving maids willing to earn extra coin. Deliberately, he took a guinea from his strongbox, the golden colour exactly like her hair. Kissing it, he slipped it into his watch-pocket rather than his purse. Yes, that would banish the ghosts that haunted him, the intrusive thoughts he did not choose to think. A night on the town, some wine, and a willing bed companion, and he would be like a new man!

'Move over, then!'

Izzy shuffled up to the top of the bed, leaning against the wall and rearranging the pillows behind her. Anna and Rose had come to her chamber for a night-time chat. They were getting used to their individual bedchambers here in London, though it was the first time in their lives they had slept apart. Izzy would never have admitted it, but she missed their company: Anna's wise counsel, Rose's dreaminess, the sound of their breathing as they slept. And so they had developed the habit of coming together each night to exclaim at their new experiences and share their impressions of London. Tonight, Rose was sharing novel information, having discovered that the whole aim of the Season—including being presented to the queen—was so that débutantes could attract husbands.

'And so, we are to hope for vouchers to an assembly

room called Almack's, which is the height of this *marriage mart.*' Rose's opinion on this was evident from her grimace and her scathing tone.

'So the whole thing is one enormous social whirl, designed to fire off their daughters?' Anna sounded as incredulous as Izzy felt.

How sordid!

Instantly, her mind reviewed the behaviour of the gentlemen at court and in Lady Ashbourne's drawing room. Given this shocking new information, their behaviour—even that of Mr Kirby and Mr Fitch—suddenly had new significance.

And as for Miss Chorley and her mama, who marched straight up to...

But no, it was the gentlemen who were the buyers in this unsavoury Marriage Mart.

She shuddered. 'And as for the gentlemen… I suppose they circle about, making judgements on the worthiness of the young ladies?' In her mind's eye she could see the prince, loftily judging every young lady in the room. She also now recalled that the queen had sent them off to dance, asking them how they were to get husbands otherwise. At the time she had thought it an idle jest—the sort of thing unmarried ladies were used to hearing. 'I can just imagine… Ugh! How appalling!'

Anna was, as always, leaning towards the practical and calmly pointed out it would actually make sense for them to marry. And it did. Of course it did. Married ladies had more security and more freedom than spinsters. And it would prevent them from being dispatched back to quiet Elgin at Season's end… The thought was an interesting one and worthy of more consideration when Izzy had time to think.

Hmmm...

Regardless, even if she did decide to marry, Izzy could not but be outraged at the thought of being an item for sale in a marketplace.

If I marry, it will be to a man of my choosing, and I shall choose with care.

This led to another thought—a worrying one.

Can we choose husbands from among the ton?

Mama had been a lady; that much was clear. She had had a Season. But that knowledge was not enough. For many reasons they needed to discover exactly who her family had been, not least because it would not do to accidentally marry someone who turned out to be a relative! Lightly, she mentioned the possibility.

'Let us only flirt with gentlemen who cannot possibly be closely related to Mama or our unknown papa,' she declared lightly, and they all laughed. The very notion of flirting seemed odd. And yet, Mr Kirby might reasonably believe that was what she had been doing this very afternoon.

Is he, then, on the hunt for a wife?

Lord, but life here was so much more complicated than in Elgin!

'But seriously, how are we to do so, when we have no idea of Mama's maiden name?' Anna frowned, then an idea seemed to come to her, for she added, a hint of slyness in her tone, 'I suppose foreign princes must be a safe option, eh, Izzy?'

Izzy's mouth was suddenly dry. 'Not at all' she managed, 'for the prince in question let slip that his own father lived here for a few years, more than twenty years ago.' *Ha!* He had told Anna exactly this during their court dance, so she would know it was true. 'Besides—' she adopted a nonchalant air '—I could never consider aligning myself with anyone so arrogant.'

Thankfully Anna did not labour the point, and the conversation moved on to their quest to find out about their origins. It all went back, Izzy knew, to Mama's decision to leave England and live quietly in Scotland. Had she run away from home and family because of her situation?

Anna had clearly wondered the same. 'To be with child is ruinous for an unmarried lady of the *ton*. Perhaps Mama ran away—'

'Or was rejected by her family—' Izzy interjected.

'Because she was with child.'

'With child…us?' Rose's hand went to her mouth. 'Oh, poor, poor Mama!'

'That may not be what happened,' Anna returned, ever cautious. 'We simply do not know. Our first step must be to discreetly discover who she was.'

'That will then lead us to *him*—our father, I mean. If any of his family are here, we should confront them!' Izzy declared, a sense of righteous anger flooding through her. 'I would know the truth, and soon! Why was she abandoned so? Was it her family's fault? Or does the responsibility lie at our father's doorstep? Perhaps these Stuarts—?' Rose had been informed the surname Lennox was associated with the Stuarts of Scotland.

Anna's tone was scolding. 'Lord, Izzy, quit being so devilish, and take your head out of those Gothic novels. This is not a story in a book.' Izzy made to answer, but Anna talked on. 'This is *real*. And real life is always more…'

'Practical?' offered Rose, with only a hint of wryness. Anna was always practical.

'Yes, more *practical* than a storybook. Our papa died, remember? And Mama always described him as a good man. The truth may be entirely prosaic. She may have simply married someone her family disapproved of. But speculation is useless, so I suggest we quit guessing and instead focus on finding out if anyone in the *ton* remembers Mama.'

They left soon afterwards, and as she blew out the candle, Izzy knew sleep might prove elusive tonight. Her head was full of evil relatives throwing Mama out in the cold, of prospective suitors judging her as though she were a prize ewe, and supercilious princes who would no doubt enjoy every moment of the Marriage Mart. After tossing and turning in her comfortable bed, Izzy finally dozed off, only to dream of a dreary life as Mrs Kirby or Mrs Fitch.

Chapter Five

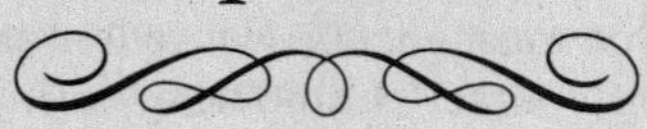

'Sir! Sir!' The voice was relentless, insistent, annoying. Finally though, it pierced his slumbering. 'You have to wake up! It is time to go!'

Groaning, Claudio opened his eyes, wincing as morning light sliced painfully into his skull through his eye sockets. '*Ja, ich stehe auf!* I'm getting up!'

The young woman's face was vaguely familiar. 'Good,' she retorted, 'for I must go to work soon!' Turning away, she finished fastening the buttons on her bodice, and he established that she was fully dressed.

What happened last night?

Turning onto his back, he groaned again as his head throbbed with pain. Closing his eyes, he let memories wash over him. Following his friends through a discreet archway in Mayfair. Gambling in the club in Pickering Court. Flirting with the maid. Her taking him by the hand up some winding stairs. Then—nothing. Nothing at all.

'What happened last night?' he managed, propping himself up on his elbow.

She sniffed. 'You fell asleep. Too much wine.' She raised an eyebrow, adding pertly, 'Your spirit was willing…'

But my flesh was weak. Damnation!

'I thought that quote referred to one's ability to *resist* temptation, not indulge in it!'

She sniffed again. 'Then, wine is surely the solution to the so-called evils of decadence, sir.'

Too much wine.

Shock was now shuddering through him as he realised that for the first time in his adult life he had failed to make the most of a promising situation.

'And now you must go, sir.' Her tone was firm.

'Yes, yes of course!' Lumbering to his feet, he felt woolly-headed and exhausted, while his head was thumping a dull ache with every beat of his heart.

Lord, I am wine-sick!

Never had this happened to him before. Oh, he had seen it in others—occasionally at home, and many times since arriving in England. Hawkins and Eldon were normally incapable of coherent speech before noon, and he had learned not to call on them in the morning, even should he himself feel fresh as a daisy. Which he usually did. Not today, though.

Must have been the cheap wine.

Half an hour later he was back at the palace, his watch-pocket lighter and his head still heavy. It was barely nine o'clock and only servants were about, thank goodness. What he needed was a few hours' more sleep, then he would be right as rain. He stiffened. Was that judgement he was seeing in the eyes of the queen's servants? Stiffening his shoulders, he continued through the lofty hallway with eyes directed straight ahead until he reached the sanctuary of his chamber. There he closed the curtains, summoned his valet, and a little later sank down onto the bed into welcome oblivion.

Izzy was once more in her element. Today they were making social calls, and her mind was dancing with dazzling details of people and places: society families and their beautiful mansions. Tea was *de rigueur*, served in delicate china and with delicious pastries. Lady Jersey had been welcoming and entertaining, the Andertons a little dull, and the Phillipses kind and friendly. Oh, and there had been Lord and Lady Wright, too. It was all a long, long way from Latin lessons in the Belvedere School for young ladies.

And now they were drinking tea yet again—this time in the delightful home of Lady Kelgrove. Izzy stifled a happy grin. The elderly lady had a spark of devilment in her eye that was calling for Izzy to match it. When they arrived she had pushed herself out of her armchair with the aid of a sturdy stick, which was now resting by her chair. Oak, Izzy guessed, with a silver handle.

Lady Kelgrove already had visitors when they entered—a middle-aged couple called Mr and Mrs Thaxby. Sneaking a glance at Mrs Thaxby, Izzy was amused to see a sullen expression on the lady's face. The source of her discontentment was clear: Lady Kelgrove was much more interested in the Lennox sisters than in the Thaxbys.

Human nature is no different here than in Scotland.

Quizzing Lady Ashbourne at length about their presentation—which she had clearly heard about but had not herself attended—Lady Kelgrove wished to know every detail of the queen's conversation about them. At this, the Thaxbys recalled another engagement and took their leave.

They were barely out of the door when Lady Kelgrove gave a self-satisfied chuckle, banging her stick on the floor and declaring wickedly, 'They can take a hint, it seems! Good, for if I was forced to bear their company much longer I might have had a sudden fainting fit or bad turn. Nothing, I assure you, can clear a room more quickly than illness!'

Lady Ashbourne laughed, shaking her head. 'You are a wicked, wicked woman, Lady Kelgrove.'

'Ah, but you know me well, Sarah,' she replied, leaning across to tap Lady Ashbourne's hand with clear affection. 'I am eighty-four,' she informed the triplets. 'And when one is eighty-four, one can say and do almost anything.'

Izzy could not resist. 'Then, I can barely wait to reach eighty-four, for at twenty-one, one can say and do almost nothing at all!'

'Is that so?' Lady Kelgrove's tone was sharp, but Izzy was undaunted.

I have the measure of her, I think.

'I see you have some opinions, Miss Lennox. Which one are you, again?'

'I am Isobel,' Izzy replied evenly. They held each other's gaze for a moment, Izzy understanding she was being thoroughly examined, then Lady Kelgrove cackled with mischievous delight. 'Ha! I predict you will do well, Miss Isobel.'

Turning back to Lady Ashbourne she resumed her questioning, asking about their dowry and family.

'Are there any clues as to their parentage?'

Lady Ashbourne pressed her lips together. 'None. There is no Lennox listed in *Debrett's*.'

'Hmph. Not good. A tradesman or servant, perhaps?'

'Perhaps.'

'It would not be the first time. Nor will it be the last. Still, they are pretty as well as being pretty behaved. They should attract some offers at least.'

Offers.

The Marriage Mart again. Earlier, Lord Ashbourne had told them that with small dowries and the possibility of illegitimacy, Izzy and her sisters might not attract what he referred to as *stellar offers*. Speaking plainly, he had advised that realistically they should look for husbands among the older gentlemen or what he had described as 'those at the fringes of society desirous of a marriage to someone who will appear ladylike'.

Izzy had flinched then and felt her insides clench again now at the notion that in this Marriage Mart, she was less of a prize ewe and more an untried gimmer, a young female with no history of safe lambing behind her, and therefore of less value. And all because of the possibility their birth had been somehow scandalous. That Mama had been unmarried and possibly thrown out by her family.

Not that Izzy wished to marry, anyway. She considered the matter. Leaving school to come to London was the greatest adventure she had ever had, and it had left no space in her mind to think of her future. Perhaps she would marry, one day. Maybe she would fall madly in love, like the heroines in some of the Gothic novels. But no, for she could never be so insipid, swooning and crying over some man. Yet she would like to be a mother someday. Yes, the question bore consideration.

She brought her attention back to Lady Kelgrove. 'Who knows, Sarah?' she was saying. 'They might even outgun the Gunnings!'

The Gunnings? Izzy didn't recall meeting anyone with that name.

Lady Ashbourne then explained that the Gunning sisters had taken the *ton* by storm sixty years before and had both made impressive marriages despite their dubious background.

'Maria Gunning had a tremendous rivalry with Kitty Fisher, as I recall,' Lady Kelgrove said thoughtfully, 'once Kitty became involved with Coventry. They even argued in the park one day. How I should have loved to have witnessed it!'

Involved?

Izzy, realising what Lady Kelgrove must be referring to, felt a sense of shock laced with fascination.

Ladies of the ton *sometimes take lovers. I wonder, if I married Mr Fitch, or Mr Kirby, could I perhaps...?*

'Yes, well, perhaps we should not speak of such matters,' said Lady Ashbourne primly, with a nod to the triplets. 'At least, not in present company.'

'Stuff!' declared Lady Kelgrove bluntly. 'I firmly believe that girls should know of the real world once they make their debuts. I wish I had known more than I did. And I wish I had been more open with my own daughter and granddaughter.' She shrugged. 'But I can do nothing now about might-have-beens. Let me advise you, Sarah. Ensure these girls are well-informed and well-prepared. They have good faces and fine figures, their manners are good, and they have you as sponsor. The Gunnings had no dowries to speak of and had even performed on the stage before their debuts. If anyone asks me, I shall say that your protégées may look as high as they wish for a husband!'

As high as we wish.

Shaking her head against the absurd notion that had just popped into it, Izzy reminded herself that certain men might *look* beautiful, with sculpted features and intense eyes and fine figures, but if, sadly, they were arrogant it mattered not a jot!

They left soon afterwards, and in the carriage Lady Ashbourne warned them that her nephew had the right of it. For all that Lady Kelgrove wished them well, without more details of their parentage she believed they were unlikely to marry well.

If we marry at all! Izzy thought defiantly. And yet…

Somehow a seed had been sown within her. The alternative was what? Returning to rural Scotland to become a spinster teacher or marry a clergyman or farmer who had never gone farther than Inverness or Aberdeen? She shuddered. That would most certainly not do. Having had a taste of *ton* life, she already knew that here was where she wanted to be. And so logic dictated she should give consideration to other possibilities.

Gentlemen like Mr Kirby and Mr Fitch were clearly flirting with the triplets despite being aware of their lack of known background and dowries that were no better than *respectable.* With a ring on her finger Izzy could remain here at the centre of society, avoiding banishment back to Scotland at the end of the Season… Yes, the notion definitely required more thought.

Lady Ashbourne was still explaining why Lady Kelgrove's optimism was, in her opinion, unfounded. 'The Gunning sisters had their Season sixty years ago. What happened then was highly unusual and has never been repeated. I fear my nephew has the right of it when it comes to London society today.'

'So we should not expect offers of marriage from anyone of note?' Anna's voice was low.

Their hostess grimaced. 'I cannot lie. It will be highly unlikely with the possibility of illegitimacy hanging over you. You may look perhaps among the professional classes, but not the *ton.* Or at least, none of the titled gentlemen.'

And certainly not a royal prince.

'Well, that is a good thing,' declared Izzy brightly, 'since we have not come here to search for husbands but to search for information about our parents.'

Which was true, and yet Izzy's brain was currently fired

with speculation. What might be the benefits of a marriage to someone like Fitch or Kirby? Both were gentlemen without a title. Both were clearly part of the *ton*. Both seemed to admire Izzy and her sisters. Could they—could *she* perhaps bring one of them up to scratch? And did she even wish to?

The weeks went on, and Izzy and her sisters became lost in a whirl of excursions and musicales, theatre trips and routs. Izzy loved every minute of it: the fashion, the excitement, the large circle of acquaintances they were building. Naturally, as in any group, there were people she was more drawn to, like the indomitable Lady Kelgrove and the vivacious Lady Jersey. Their own dear Lady Ashbourne was a darling, of course, and some of the other débutantes were warm and genuine, like Lady Mary Renford and Miss Phillips. Both were a little too quiet for Izzy, but Rose had befriended them, and so Izzy counted them in her inner circle of intimates.

Among the gentlemen, Izzy had categorised them into distinct groups, spending quite a bit of her time honing her thoughts and thinking about the categories.

'Miss?' A gentle knock on her bedchamber door alerted her to the fact it was time to dress for tonight's ball at the home of Lady Cowper. This would be their first proper ball, and Izzy could barely wait for the gowns, the dancing, the excitement of it all.

As Mary dressed her hair, adding a pretty silver band at the last, Izzy considered the matter of gentlemen afresh. Firstly, there were the older men, married men, and committed bachelors. These tended to take an avuncular attitude towards all the débutantes and could be relied on for interesting conversation without ogling—always a benefit.

Standing, she stepped into her glittering ballgown, a

delight of white crêpe and satin fringed with gold and featuring a golden satin bodice ornamented with three rows of embroidered leaves. The sleeves were short, full, and edged with the gold satin, while the gown was completed by a short sash of shaded ribbon in a paler gold tied in a fetching bow under the bosom. The maid was adjusting the gown with great reverence and sighed with delight as she finished doing up the buttons. 'You look beautiful, miss!'

'Thank you, Mary.'

Izzy returned to her reverie. Then there were the poets and would-be poets. These were invariably young, romantical, and resoundingly silly. They gave extravagant compliments and pretended to fight for the honour of finding a lady a seat, or procuring a glass of too-sweet ratafia. The poetry they produced was laughably trite, and Izzy often felt that it mattered not to them of which young lady they were currently enamoured, for they listened only for a chance to speak and seemed to be in love with the *idea* of love, rather than with anything to do with the reality of the ladies they were complimenting. Rose and Anna seemed to tolerate them much more readily than Izzy, for she could not help but reflect that if a young lady behaved in such a silly manner, she would receive universal criticism.

Looping her painted fan over her arm, Izzy made her way downstairs, accompanying Lady Ashbourne, Lord Ashbourne, Anna, and Rose out into the carriage. Lord Ashbourne, she thought now, glancing at his handsome face half-revealed by flambeaux, was in a different group to the others. He and Rose were sitting opposite her, and momentarily Izzy had the strangest notion they were *aware* of each other in some way.

Lord, my imagination is running away with me!

To divert her attention from such foolishness, she considered the viscount dispassionately. He, like Garvald and a few of the married men, formed a distinctive group. These men were sensible, intelligent, and—mostly—respectful, although even the cleverest of men tended to underestimate the wit and wisdom of the female sex. However, despite their undoubted good qualities, neither Viscount Ashbourne nor the Earl of Garvald were of particular interest to Izzy, for it had been made clear to the triplets that such unmarried gentlemen—titled, well-respected, and at the heart of the *ton*—could never give serious consideration to marrying a lady whose parentage was unknown.

For the past few weeks they had been making concerted efforts to discover Mama's identity, having decided to investigate all ladies called Maria who had made their debuts around the right time period. Sadly, they had already eliminated most of the options, including Maria Craven who was now Lady Sefton and Maria Berkeley—Lady Kelgrove's granddaughter—who had died of smallpox.

They had arrived. Izzy's heart skipped a little. Receiving an invitation to one of Lady Cowper's events was an achievement in itself. It also meant that tonight, there would be dancing—proper dancing, not like the dances at court, while trying to manhandle a four-foot train over one's arm. Nor would it be like the spontaneous dancing she had enjoyed at some of the less formal soirées, which generally involved no more than four couples taking to the floor at once. No, all night long tonight there would be dozens of couples dancing all at once. *Dozens!*

Having been welcomed by their hostess, Lady Ashbourne and the triplets made their way through the throng—the viscount swiftly taking his leave of them to seek out Garvald and his other friends. Izzy looked around with interest. This was surely the biggest crowd she had ever seen in a house before! The word *house* was of course inadequate in describing the elegant and enormous mansion tucked into the corner of St James's Square. All of the *ton* was here, it seemed. In all directions were people Izzy knew, mixing with elegant people she had yet to meet.

How wonderful!

Her eye fell upon two familiar figures, Mr Hawkins and Mr Eldon. She pressed her lips together. Over the past weeks she had formed a fuller impression of the two gentlemen and their set. In her mind she had dubbed them the pleasure-seekers. They were frequently drunk and liked nothing more than sport, wine, cards, and—in some cases—lechery. Instinctively she checked the group they were standing in, checking helplessly for blond hair and a handsome, sculpted face.

He is not here.

Her heart, a traitor to all rationality, sank in clear disappointment.

Over these past weeks, she and the prince had maintained something of a truce, in that they no longer insulted one another directly—though each time she recalled his arrogance during their early encounters, it still had the power to make her blood feel as though it boiled in her veins. But now she could greet him with an appearance of equanimity, could even make passing conversation. The fact that her senses ignited each time she was in his presence was both unwelcome and extremely puzzling, but she could do nothing about it. Her strange fascination with him continued, despite all common sense.

Their arrival had been noted, and instantly the Belles were surrounded by gentlemen asking for the promise of a dance later. Calmly, Izzy and her sisters allocated some of their dances—but not all of them. Inwardly, Izzy squirmed a little in recognition that, despite his vexing her, she might quite like to dance with His Highness if he were to make an appearance tonight.

Well, he is a good dancer!

Not that she had been able to properly appreciate his skill during their dance at court, being overcome with anger at the time.

I wonder who my sisters are holding spaces for?

Rose, spotting Lady Mary and her family, excused herself, making her way across to her friend. That left just Lady Ashbourne, Izzy, and Anna.

'Now, girls!' said Lady Ashbourne bustling, 'shall we attempt to find a seat, or are you content to wander about for a—Oh! Your Highness!' She sank into a graceful curtsy, and Izzy and Anna followed, Izzy's heart predictably skipping to a new rhythm.

With a conscious effort, she turned, lifting her eyes to meet his.

It is you! something within her declared, a thrill of recognition firing through her.

Quite against her wishes, her mouth went dry, and she could feel her pulse throbbing insistently as she made her curtsy and exchanged pleasantries.

'Miss Lennox, Miss Isobel,' he addressed them, directing his gaze unerringly to the correct sister. *How does he do that?* 'Might I please have the pleasure of dancing with each of you tonight?'

They agreed—well, how could they not?—Izzy's dance with him being fixed for the second one of the evening. Of course, now that he was here and had asked her to dance with him, Izzy's mind was full of righteous indignation. 'It is a sad truth,' she declared once he had joined his friends, 'that politeness does not allow us to decline a dance without good reason.'

'Oh?' Lady Ashbourne raised a knowing eyebrow. 'I quite thought you wished to dance with him.' It was not a question, and yet Izzy, stammering, tried and failed to reply. Mostly because Lady Ashbourne was entirely correct. Lady Ashbourne frowned briefly, then added briskly, 'Let us speak to Lady Kelgrove!'

She swept ahead, leaving Izzy and Anna to follow in her wake. Anna, a hint of a smile at the corners of her mouth, made to speak, but Izzy cut her off.

'Do not, Anna, just do not say it!' While she could not know exactly what her sister had been about to say, she was sure she could guess at the general tenor of it.

The dancing began soon afterwards, and Izzy made sure to sparkle and dazzle her way through the set. Mr Fitch was suitably overcome, and Izzy took his compliments as a balm to her disordered senses. As they left the crowded dancing area when the music ended, he offered to procure for her some ratafia or punch, whichever she should prefer. As he spoke, his left hand was playing with a signet ring on his right, something she recognised as a habit of his. For some reason, it irritated her a little.

'Oh, thank you, Mr Fitch. I should like some—'

'Punch.' It was the prince, two glasses of punch in his hands. 'You always prefer punch, Miss Isobel. As the next dance is mine, I thought to procure your drink in advance. Now, was that not clever of me?'

'It might have been,' she responded sweetly, 'had I wanted punch.'

And there it was—the slightest hint of consternation. She laughed—genuine amusement overcoming her. 'I am jesting, Your Highness. I shall accept the punch.'

Taking it from him, their eyes met, and she was relieved to see similar amusement in his. 'You *almost* convinced me, Miss Isobel.'

'Almost?' Arching a brow, she took a sip from her drink, her eyes never leaving his face.

His gaze dropped to her mouth, then back to her eyes. 'Almost,' he repeated firmly. 'But you have a distaste for ratafia, I think.' His voice lowered and deepened. 'It is too safe for you, too sweet. No, better the thrill of punch for you, Miss Isobel.' His words were rippling through her, stirring feelings she had never felt before. Entranced, she stood there, trapped by his gaze, his nearness, his words. 'Punch is stronger, more potent,' he continued. 'You could never be satisfied with ratafia.'

Yes! she wanted to say. *Yes!*

'Er… I shall take my leave of you, Miss Isobel. Your Highness.'

They both turned to say farewell to Mr Fitch, Izzy having quite forgotten he was there. His interjection reminded Izzy to try and maintain a semblance of normality, and yet something within her continued to thrum in celebration of standing so close to Prince Claudio, of having his full attention. And she had his *full* attention. She was sure of it.

Mr Fitch was barely gone when the musicians struck up for the next dance. Keeping his eyes fixed on hers, the prince raised his glass to her, then emptied it in one swallow. Mesmerised, Izzy took it all in—the strong line of his throat, the lines of his handsome face, the cool challenge in those grey eyes.

'Well?'

Knowing exactly what he wanted, Izzy lifted her chin. *I can do this!*

'Very well.' Taking a breath, she raised her glass, then

tipped it back. As the potent liquid trailed fire down her throat, a recklessness came over her, a desire to *feel* every moment, every sensation, every thrill.

He bowed and held out a hand. 'The waltz is commonplace in my homeland, Miss Isobel. Have you danced it before?'

The waltz!

'No, I have not.' She tutted at herself. 'That is to say, I *have*, but only in dancing lessons.'

He bent his head to murmur in her ear. 'Then, prepare for a singular experience, Miss Isobel.' The way he said her name, with a hint of his accent, seemed to her in that moment a caress, and her entire body now tingled with… *something.* Whatever spell of madness had briefly overtaken her persisted yet.

In something of a daze, she took her place alongside him, forming a set with another couple, Miss Chorley and Mr Kirby. The music began, and Prince Claudio took her hand, turning her under his arm. For an instant, during the turn, she was within an inch of him, his firm body aligned with hers. Then she completed the turn, and they all four formed a circle, stepping forward and back in time. The other gentleman then turned her, and Izzy was astounded to find there was no thrill at all in his doing so. None.

She took a breath. The next hold was the one. His gloved hands came to rest on her shoulders, and she raised her arms to rest on his. This was the first time she had ever touched a man in such a way—or been touched by one. Together they moved, spinning around in time with the music, their eyes locked upon one another and their hands and arms ensuring they were held in each other's embrace.

Embrace?

Yes, for that was exactly what it felt like. Dancing lessons had not relayed to Izzy the full impact of this part of the waltz, for she had felt no discomfort when practising with her sisters or the middle-aged dancing master. They had reached the next couple. Once again, the Prince turned her, once again they completed the circle and the visitor turn, and then it was time for them once again to embrace. This time she was reaching for it, waiting for the delicious moment when she felt the warmth of his hands on her shoulders, sensed his upper arm muscles flex and harden as he led her around to the next place in the set.

Ten times they repeated the pattern, and ten times she felt as though she were in heaven. On the last repetition, he slid his hands down from her shoulders to the bare skin of her upper arms. Izzy had no idea he was going to do it, and when he did so she thought she might die from sheer sensation. Her eyes, still held by his gaze, widened in shocked delight, and he swallowed hard.

'Isobel!' he groaned, so softly she could barely hear him.

Oh, Lord!

What on earth was happening to her? They had returned to the beginning, with Miss Chorley and Mr Kirby. Miss Chorley, Izzy noted absent-mindedly, was currently eyeing the prince coquettishly. Just for an instant, Izzy wished she knew how to flirt with a man, then dismissed the notion.

I can only be Izzy. No one else.

The prince, she observed—with more than a little satisfaction—seemed not to notice Miss Chorley's efforts. He had turned her proficiently and now returned to Izzy for the last turn of the dance. As the music ended he bowed to her—a deep bow, his eyes once again locked with hers. She curtsied gracefully, maintaining his gaze, no words passing between them.

The formal salute completed, Izzy felt at a loss. Unable

to move for the shocking sensations coursing through her, she simply eyed him helplessly, as all around them chattering couples began moving away in search of refreshment.

'So, how did you like the waltz?'

'I-I liked it very much.' Her voice trembled a little. Most unlike her.

Ah, Izzy, quit being such a weakling.

She tossed her head. 'I shall enjoy dancing it again—perhaps with a different partner.' A flicker of something that looked suspiciously like hurt flashed across his expression, and remorse flooded through her. 'I mean—of course I enjoyed dancing with you, Your Highness. I—'

'Enough with *Your Highness*!' he growled, bowing again, this time a curt farewell. 'I wish you well, Miss Isobel.'

Pain arced through her, almost physical in its intensity.

I should not have—

But it was too late. He had rejoined his pleasure-seeking friends. Lifting her chin, Izzy made for Anna.

The next two hours passed in something of a haze. Izzy danced and drank more punch and laughed gaily at the slightest of witticisms from her various dancing partners. After the cotillion, Lady Renton cornered her, asking bluntly, 'Which one are you?'

Momentarily taken aback, Izzy instantly rallied to declare coldly. 'I am Isobel, Lady Renton.'

Though you are not behaving in a very ladylike manner at present.

'Ah, yes.' She waved a hand at Izzy's gown. 'Wrong colour.' Rose must have told Lady Renton's daughter about their preferred colours. With a smile that did not quite reach her eyes, she added silkily, 'Rumour has it the prince is promised to some Prussian princess, you know.'

Already braced for a fight, Isobel did not let any inner shock deter her, although something in her chest twisted in pain.

He is to marry?

'Really?' she smiled. 'I do feel sorry for the poor girl, whoever she is!'

'*Sorry* for her?' Lady Renton's voice was low, her tone sharp. 'When she is to marry a prince?'

Suddenly, Izzy had had enough. Enough of the fawning. Enough of the attention. Apparently all people could see was his title. They seemed not to notice the *man* and all his qualities—good or ill. 'Yes, I am sorry for her, whoever she is. For she is to marry a man-child with no thought for anyone other than himself!' Izzy retorted hotly. 'It is not a fate I would wish on any maiden!'

Pointedly, Lady Renton looked over Izzy's shoulder. 'Your Highness,' she crooned, 'such a delightful evening, is it not?'

Lady Renton must have known he was approaching when she said that!

The woman had timed her barb perfectly, clearly hoping Izzy would say something indiscreet. Which, because of her own dashed hot-headedness, she had. Izzy had fallen neatly into her trap.

Gritting her teeth, Izzy turned. There he was, his gaze fixed on Lady Renton. 'Indeed, yes,' he declared, 'although not all of the company is what I am accustomed to.'

A direct insult. Measure for measure he had met her challenge. Shock stopped Izzy's throat for an instant—but only an instant. 'I *so* agree, Your Highness.' She sighed mournfully as his eyes met hers, too lost to turn back now. 'It is *such* a disappointment to find people are much, much less than their status would suggest.' Her heart was racing, her fists clenched with ire. The truce, such as it was, had ended.

'Like the fools who hang about you with flowers and poetry, I suppose?' His eyes flashed fire.

'Lord, no!' She gave a small laugh. 'They are among the most gentlemanlike of my acquaintance.' She adopted a thoughtful air, belying the rage pulsing through her. 'Indeed, some of them are becoming like friends to me. I do think friendship is a strong basis for any connection, would you not agree?' Her eyes flicked sideways to where Mr Eldon was currently meandering drunkenly through the crowd, apologising each time he clumsily knocked into someone. 'And a true friendship must call to similarity, or affinity, I think.'

His jaw hardened as he glanced briefly towards his friend. 'Much as I would love to continue this delightful conversation, I must go, for I see they are striking up for the next dance. Miss Anderton is waiting!'

He bowed curtly just as, with perfect timing, Mr Fitch came to claim Izzy's hand. Giving the man a smile warm enough to make him blink and stammer, and bidding Lady Renton an insincere farewell, she accompanied him to the dancing area, serene as a swan.

Joining her sisters for supper, Izzy noted Rose seemed uncharacteristically exuberant tonight. She herself was filled with energy—passionate anger thrumming through her.

This place—the dancing—it is all going to our heads, I think.

And she refused to let the thrill of her first proper ball be ruined by a certain royal gentleman—one who had been bestowing glittering smiles on multiple débutantes this evening. Let him carouse himself to death if he chose. And his Prussian princess alongside him. Izzy cared not.

When she and Anna quizzed Rose, though, the youngest triplet gave an unexpected explanation for being in alt herself. Lady Mary Renford had accepted an offer of marriage from Mr Phillips.

Is that why her mother was so odious to me earlier?

Mr Phillips was a perfectly nice gentleman, but Lady Mary's mother had probably hoped for a title for her only daughter. Even as she exclaimed with Anna, abruptly Izzy felt a pang of something that felt suspiciously like panic.

Lady Mary has made her match!

Time was marching on, the Season was well underway, and those from suitable families, like Lady Mary, were able to make matches with the men of their choice.

Not us, though.

Everyone had been most clear. Choices for the Lennox sisters were limited due to their lack of known parentage. Turning away from a strange and unexpected ache in her heart, Izzy focused instead on the prospects that were more rational, more achievable. Mr Kirby. Mr Fitch. Not Mr Phillips—who, to be fair, had made his preference plain a number of weeks ago. Options would likely narrow further over the coming weeks, and Izzy would have to decide very soon whether to marry, and if so, to whom. Something within her shuddered at the very notion, but she suppressed it. Returning to rural Scotland at the end of the Season to become a teacher was unthinkable. She was Miss Isobel Lennox, and she would do what she must.

Chapter Six

Claudio strode to the window and opened the heavy curtains to admit the morning light. The rowan tree outside his chamber was now in full bloom, an abundance of creamy blossoms adorning its branches and creating a soft carpet beneath.

Having woken before ten—uncharacteristically early for his London life—he stood for a moment in the long window, pondering his options. Last night had deeply unsettled him, and he knew exactly why. After Miss Isobel's cutting comment at the end of their dance together, he had done his best. Had danced with half a dozen simpering maidens, eaten a poor supper, and—shockingly—had drunk very little. The appetite for getting thoroughly foxed had left him, as gently and subtly as the blossom petals drifting to the ground. A temporary aberration, no doubt, but Miss Isobel had once again prevented him from doing something he had wished to do.

Not for the first time, last night he had found himself feeling strong irritation at the antics of his own friends. Their teasing about his possible marriage was not new, but it was becoming more of a theme with them. They themselves had not married and seemed determined to make him commit to a similar fate. And he would not.

Last night their teasing had galled him into lying to them by saying he was already promised to a maiden back home. At the time, he had thought only to gain some respite from their relentless appraisals of all the débutantes in London—with the aim, they said, of helping him select his target. Yet the repercussions had been immediate, and he had found himself having to deny the story to multiple people.

'Oh, no!' he had stammered. 'My papa wished for me to marry a certain lady, but nothing is agreed.'

As if that had not been bad enough, he had then been given a very clear understanding of Miss Isobel's opinion of his supposed Prussian princess—a person to be pitied, apparently, since he was a *man-child.* Anger rose within him again as he recalled her scathing tone and her level look towards the extremely bosky Mr Eldon. Such a man, he knew, would not be long tolerated at his father's court, and yet Eldon and his set were Claudio's closest acquaintances here in London.

He closed his eyes, feeling the warmth of the morning sun through the window bathing his body in light. Of course, no sooner had he done so than there she was, in his imagination. She was all golden, her smooth skin glowing with fiery warmth, and he ached to kiss her, to hold her, to—

Hastily, he opened his eyes, stepping away from the window before he mortified himself. Oh, the servants all now knew of his habit of greeting the morning in his skin. He even suspected that some of the maids who happened to be passing through the gardens around noon each day might deliberately tarry there, hoping for a glimpse of the foreign prince who had a tendency to be shockingly naked. Members of the *ton* often walked in the gardens in the afternoons, so he knew to be more circumspect if he rose particularly late in the day. Thankfully, at ten in the morning no one was around—neither aristocrats nor servants—and so he turned back to the room, calling for Jenkins, his valet.

The hours ahead stretched before him with dreary emptiness. His friends he would see later, to discuss nothing but drink and sport and wenches. Yet again. He sighed. Such a life had seemed to him to be so much better than strictures and expectations of his father's court. And now, after only a few short weeks, was he already tiring of it?

Perhaps I shall never be satisfied.

As the clock struck ten, Izzy made her way downstairs to the morning room, a frown on her face and concern lurking within. Something was not right. There was a strange, uneasy air in the house, the servants were acting strangely, and Izzy simply could not figure out what it was about. She had not slept well, her dreams a parade of faceless Prussian princesses, each one more gentle, more refined, more graceful than the last. And now this…whatever it was. Hearing someone behind her on the staircase, she turned.

'Anna!'

'Izzy! What is amiss? My abigail barely spoke to me just now, all the while wearing an air of—of *knowingness* or something.'

'And mine!' She lowered her tone, adding confidentially, 'The maid's mouth was clamped shut the whole time as she helped me dress. I cannot account for it!'

They paused, thinking it through.

Anna spoke slowly. 'It seems as if they know something—'

'But are forbidden from speaking of it.'

Izzy's heart lurched. It had to be something bad, as her maid's demeanour had not suggested a pleasant secret or unexpected treat was on the horizon.

Has Lady Renton complained about my being rude to the prince?

Still murmuring together, they opened the door to the morning room. Inside was Rose, along with Lady Ashbourne, and one look at their faces told Izzy instantly that something was terribly, terribly wrong—something much worse than plain-speaking at a party. Rose was pale, her expression closed and pinched, while Lady Ashbourne's mouth was a grim, narrow line.

Having dismissed the servants, Lady Ashbourne looked to Rose, then turned to Izzy and Anna. 'My brother, your guardian, is unwell,' she began. Izzy froze.

Dear Mr Marnoch, who has been so good to us since Mama's death!

Lady Ashbourne was continuing, 'And so Rose has kindly—'

'No.' Even as Izzy's brain tried to take in the bad news concerning dear Mr Marnoch, Rose interrupted. 'Everyone else may hear that tale,' she stated, her voice low. 'My sisters deserve to know the truth.'

The truth?

What on earth—?

Lady Ashbourne nodded. 'Very well. But you must both swear to repeat this to no one.'

'Of course!'

'Naturally!'

Even as they made their promises, Izzy's mind was racing, desperately attempting to think what might be happening.

Rose swallowed. 'Yesterday, I allowed…a gentleman…to—to kiss me. In a public place. And we were seen.'

Izzy gasped. 'Rose!' A hundred thoughts flew through her mind. Shock at Rose's situation. Disbelief.

Can this really be true?

Dawning horror at the realisation this could be terrible for poor Rose.

Rose nodded grimly. 'If word gets out about this, I am ruined. And unfortunately—' her voice trembled '—you would be ruined along with me, for society judges all three of us as one. I am so sorry. I have failed you. Failed you all. Failed Mama. Failed Mr Marnoch.' She buried her face in her hands, clearly distressed.

Stupidly, all Izzy could think of was Rose's evident happiness at the ball. 'Lord, Rose! Last night I thought you seemed—'

I recognised it because I felt equally happy too, for a time.

A flash of memory came to her. His hands on her shoulders. Their eyes locked together. How wonderful it had been, before all had crashed about her.

A Prussian princess.

Shaking it off, she brought her mind back to her sister and to the true reason for her evident happiness last night. 'So it was not Lady Mary's betrothal, then.'

'Lady Mary is betrothed?' Lady Ashbourne's tone was sharp. 'To whom?'

Izzy's mind, still sluggish from Rose's announcement and with her own waltz memories and quarrel memories tingling through her, made her only stare stupidly at her hostess.

'Never say she has managed to catch Garvald!' Lady Ashbourne declared. 'That is to say, Lady Mary is a sweet girl, but she has not the strength of character for the earl.' She continued, musing thoughtfully. 'Not the prince either, for his passionate nature would terrify her.' She stopped, an arrested expression in her eyes. 'Mr Phillips?'

Rose nodded. 'He spoke with Lord Renton yesterday.'

'I see.' Lady Ashbourne rubbed her chin. 'And I begin to see so much more…'

But Izzy was not listening.

His passionate nature.

She shivered.

How I should love to be kissed by him!

Rose had kissed a man. Or been kissed by him, perhaps. Rose—the quietest, most timid of the sisters. She knew what it was to share a kiss, and yet Izzy, who had long seen herself as the most adventurous, the most passionate, the most headstrong, had not one single adventure to show for all her time in London.

Quit this foolishness! she admonished herself. Rose's situation was a reminder that to be caught kissing a man was a heinous crime for a débutante and not something to be wished for. Lady Mary's footman, it seemed, had witnessed the incident and told Lady Renton.

That woman!

'But my lady, what is to be done?' Anna took Rose's hand.

'Done?' Lady Ashbourne shook her head. 'I have already had this conversation with Rose. She must either marry the gentleman in question, or she must go away.'

'And I have decided to go away. That is why we are pretending that dear Mr Marnoch is ill.' Rose's eyes were suspiciously bright. 'So much deceit! And all because of me!'

Go away? Banished from London?

Izzy's heart stilled at the severity of Rose's punishment. Having decided that she strongly wished to make London her home, Izzy could not in this moment think of a worse fate than to be forcibly banished. With Anna's support, she objected strongly to the plan, but Lady Ashbourne was adamant. She hoped for discretion from Lady Renton, but it could not be assured. Yes, Rose might return at some point in the future perhaps, but for now she needed to leave. Immediately.

Today?

'Oh, Rose! I shall miss you so much!' Izzy hugged her fiercely.

'We have never been apart,' added Anna, wrapping her arms around both sisters. 'How shall we do without you?'

'And I you! Oh, Anna! Izzy!'

Touching her head to Izzy's and Anna's, Rose cried bitterly, and her sisters joined her. All their lives they had been together, even sharing a bedchamber until their arrival in London. Now their bond was to be sundered, and life would never be the same again.

The uneasy feeling within Claudio would not go away. Surprisingly it had been assuaged a little by the fact he had spent more than an hour this morning reading in the Buckingham House library. He had always had a good mind, yet it had astonished him to discover how much enjoyment he had gained earlier from reading a couple of well-crafted essays collected by a man called Dobson.

I have missed using my brain, I think.

Today was four months to the day since he had landed in England. Four months of drinking and gambling, of sports and bedsports, of fencing and boxing. He had been enjoying his body all this time, subjecting it to the effects of wine and ale, exercise and activity—although the desire for bedsport had not returned since his abandoned attempt with the tavern maid that time. *Why?* He shied away from the answer, not wishing to look at it too closely.

Perhaps then, he had not given enough time and attention to the needs of his intellect.

Very well.

Reading—one of his favourite pastimes at home—would return to his days. The book of essays now rested on his nightstand, and he would make time to read more later, before tonight's soirée at Lord and Lady Sefton's.

He glanced at the clock in the long hallway as he passed through. Nine hours until he would make his bow at the Sefton soirée in Arlington Street. He was promised to the queen for dinner, and even with bathing, dressing, and now his plan to read, he estimated he still had five or six hours to kill. His friends would not yet be at the club, and the thought of going directly there, to inhale the odours of stale smoke, spilled wine, and stale bodies from the night before held no attraction. Sighing, and feeling decidedly unsettled, he decided to take a long walk through the Green Park. Perhaps that would assuage the strange restlessness within him.

Rose is gone.

An emotion that felt rather like grief surged through Izzy. She and Anna had left Ashbourne House soon after seeing their sister off in the carriage and were hoping that a brisk walk might distract from the wrenching separation. Even now Rose would be on the outskirts of London on the first stage of the long, long journey back to Scotland. Mr Marnoch was there, and Rose hoped to gain a teaching post in their old school, Belvedere.

Izzy shuddered. Such a fate lay before her, too, should she fail to take this opportunity to make a match.

Poor Rose!

Some young ladies, she knew, dreamed of a love match, but Izzy's options did not now include such luxuries. No, she wanted only a sensible husband with a steady income, who was fixed in the capital. Someone who could be relied upon. Always her mind circled back to two names: Mr Kirby or Mr Fitch. Both were a little dull, to be sure, and she certainly had no desire to kiss them. But then, kisses were not a good measure for a suitable husband. Rose had been near ruined by kisses!

'Izzy,' Anna ventured now, drawing her out of her reverie. 'The gentleman Rose kissed… Have you considered who it might be?' Rose had steadfastly refused to reveal the man's name earlier.

Izzy snorted. 'Who it *might* be, Anna? There can be only one possibility!'

'Viscount Ashbourne?'

Izzy nodded. 'Looking back, it is clear to me that he and Rose share some sort of…' She searched for a suitable word.

'Affinity?' Anna suggested.

'Yes. It is plain to me now. Even last night, in the carriage, I sensed something between them.' She laughed lightly. 'Of course, in my foolishness I did not see what was in front of my face. Not until Rose said someone had kissed her. I do wish she had told us about him. We have never had secrets from one another before.' She sighed.

Affinity.

'We have not the luxury of making eyes at gentlemen who are beyond our reach, Anna.'

Anna slid her hand into Izzy's arm. 'I know. And I never thought to see the day when *you* are the one saying sensible things!'

'These are peculiar times. All manner of strangeness surrounds us.' Like feeling an affinity for someone who had behaved arrogantly towards her. Someone who was as far out of her reach in rank as the stars. Someone who was already promised to another.

And other strange things, now. Like choosing a husband as though he were a new hat. She squirmed uncomfortably at the notion. No, she would be respectful of her future husband. Anything less would be unprincipled. Dishonourable, even.

Even more strangeness. Having a mind that endlessly focused on one person, every day, every night, even though one did not wish it. Did not choose it.

'Oh, my goodness!' Walking towards them was a familiar figure, tall, proud, and handsome—just as though her thoughts had conjured him.

I even recognise the way he walks!

Her heart, naturally, was now pounding, and she even felt a little dizzy.

She swallowed. 'Am I imagining it, Anna, or is that truly the prince before us on the path, strolling through the Green Park alone, like any commoner?'

'It is certainly the prince, Izzy. Now, pray do not—'

'I shall be all politeness, I assure you!' Yet inwardly, Izzy's mind and heart were in chaos. Last night, she had been quite rude towards him, in speaking of pitying his princess. One should not say such things. Unless one was Izzy, who frequently did. She had also snubbed him a little after their dance, earlier in the evening. But why should he care? And why should she not enjoy dancing with different gentlemen?

He had seen them. Izzy knew it from the way his shoulders suddenly stiffened, ever so slightly. His coat today was of blue superfine and… Oh, how it drew attention to the breadth of his shoulders, the colour making his eyes look more blue than grey in the June sunshine. He stopped to make his bow, and as she gave the required curtsy, his handsomeness made Izzy catch her breath briefly. Only her inner determination ensured she managed to play her part in the polite conversation that ensued.

Their health, the weather, and the delights of last night's ball dispensed with, there was a brief pause.

'Are you often about in the mornings, Your Highness?' Anna's tone was polite.

'Actually no, but this morning I rose unexpectedly early.' He grinned. 'I have even managed to read two of the Dobson essays before venturing out.'

'My sister has read that collection. Were we not speaking of it just a few days ago, Izzy?'

Izzy was still trying to control her thumping heart and feeling of joy in her stomach.

Why did he have to smile? I might have coped if he had been dour today.

'We were,' she managed. 'A most interesting volume.'

There was another pause, then he opened his mouth to say something else. With sudden dread, Izzy wondered if he was about to ask after Rose and so jumped in hastily.

'Do you make a habit of strolling in the Green Park, Your Highness?'

'I enjoy walking in natural surroundings as much as any man, Miss Isobel.' His gaze pierced hers, a hint of challenge in those eyes. 'Why do you ask?'

She sniffed. 'I would have thought such activity too… *commonplace* for such a person as a prince.'

His brow furrowed. 'Indeed? Well, it pleases me to inform you that, despite being a prince, I am clearly sadly commonplace.' He turned to Anna. 'Miss Lennox, I shall hope to see you at Lady Sefton's soirée tonight. I shall wish you both good day.'

His bow was stiff, Izzy's curtsy shallow, and then he was gone.

'Insufferable man!' Izzy declared behind closed teeth as they resumed along the path. 'Highness? High-handedness, more like! Did you see how he cut me just now?'

Anna was frowning. 'Enough, Izzy! You were *rude*, as you must realise! And for no good reason! That is not how we were raised to behave, and I am sorry to say it.'

'I—' About to defend herself robustly, Izzy was suddenly overwhelmed with something that felt like regret, laced with a strong dose of shame. 'You are right, Anna. It is just— Being rude to him is all I can do to…'

'To protect yourself?' Anna's voice was low. 'Because you are drawn to him?' At Izzy's gasp, she shook her head. 'I am not bird-witted, you know. While Rose's *tendre* for the viscount is only apparent to me now, I have known all along that you and the prince only behave as you do because you—you *like* one another.'

'I do not think he likes me! And sometimes I do not like *him* at all!' Izzy returned, an image of him laughing with his vacuous, hedonistic friends coming to mind. 'But I cannot be indifferent to him, no matter how I try. And yet I must try, for he is not for me, and if I allow him to take all my attention, it may prevent me from making a sensible match.'

'Then, you will marry?'

Izzy shrugged. 'I wish to remain part of the *ton*, and the only way to do that is to marry. Teachers and governesses are not permitted to dance at balls or sing at musicales. I cannot sit by the side and watch others *live* when I cannot.' She squared her shoulders. 'So yes, I should marry. And there are gentlemen who will consider us, despite our small dowries and our dubious parentage.'

Anna sighed. 'Lady Ashbourne has had a letter from her friend, confirming that Miss Maria Carew is not our mama, for she is alive and well and living in Pembrokeshire.'

'But she was the last possibility! All of the other débutantes called Maria from around the time of Mama's Season are either married or dead. And I have made no headway on my own quest, for how can I discover who our father was if we do not know Mama's maiden name?'

'I know. Lady Ashbourne says we are unlikely now to ever discover the truth. She believes *Maria* may have not even been Mama's true first name.' She shook her head. 'Mama must have been truly frightened, for she went to great lengths to hide her true identity.'

'Secrets. Mama's secrets. Rose's secrets.' Izzy turned to her sister, stopping in the middle of the path. 'I am glad you know of mine—the prince, I mean,' she declared fiercely. 'Let us try not to have secrets from one another from now on, Anna. We never did before.'

They hugged briefly, and when they parted, Izzy noticed that Anna's eyes were bright with unshed tears. 'What is it?'

'Ach, I am as foolish as you and Rose, if you must know! For I, too, have an affinity for someone who is not for me.'

On they walked, sharing secrets and tears, hopes and dreams. Finally they turned towards home. 'You know,' Izzy said slowly, 'I think that the delights of London—wonderful as they are—have distracted me from what is truly important. My quest. My sisters. Family.'

Anna nodded. 'I, too, have been too distracted. And now Rose is gone.'

There was another silence, then Izzy frowned. 'What are we to say to everyone tonight? At the soirée, I mean?'

'About Rose? Lady Ashbourne's tale is a good one—Rose has gone to care for Mr Marnoch, who is ill.'

'It does not sit easy with me to lie.'

'Nor with me. Perhaps we should not go tonight. By tomorrow the worst of the shock may be over for us, and we shall lie with ease!' Her laugh held a great deal of cynicism. 'I told you off for rudeness earlier, but lying to everyone is a much greater sin. And yet we must.'

Lying. Dissembling. Hiding her true feelings. Every hour of every day Izzy had been doing these things. She had even been lying to herself. Well, no more. Having shared her burden with Anna, she knew what she had to do. The prince was not for her, but she should not need to be rude to hold herself at bay. What had happened to Rose was much too serious for her to risk a similar fate.

I shall be polite to him, and distant. I shall protect my heart and allow my logical brain to choose a husband.

The plan was a good one, even if it made her feel a little sick inside. But she was her mama's daughter, and Mama had had worse trials to face.

Chapter Seven

'Out!'

It was the morning after Lady Sefton's soirée—which they had *not* attended—and Izzy was with Anna and Lady Ashbourne in the dining room. The viscount had joined them earlier at the breakfast table, and Izzy had been relieved when he had left. He had been the cause of dear Rose's banishment, and he neither knew nor, it seemed, cared about her sister's fate.

Oh, how she had longed to rail at him, to accuse him and berate him and scream at him. He was a gentleman about town, a *viscount* for goodness' sake, while Rose was an innocent girl just out of a schoolroom in rural Scotland. And yet he had kissed her, and been seen, and now poor Rose was gone. *Ach!* Izzy could barely look at him.

'Out!'

The viscount was standing in the doorway, his face contorted with rage. Both footmen were already fleeing, the viscount stepping into the room to let them pass.

'Leave us, girls,' Lady Ashbourne sounded wearily resigned. 'No,' she waved away their protests, 'I should like to speak to my nephew alone.'

They went, Izzy throwing him a disdainful look on her way out. A half hour later, Lady Ashbourne joined them upstairs in the drawing room, astonishment in her demeanour. 'Well, my dears, he is going after her. He intends to marry her, despite her objections!'

They were all bewildered, and it took some time, but eventually they were persuaded that the viscount had, after all, true regard for Rose and was determined to marry her if she would have him.

'I told him Rose does not wish to marry him.' She laughed, shaking her head. 'I must say I have never seen him so shocked. Still, it will no doubt do him a world of good. He has had things his own way for much too long.'

'So what will happen now?'

'He is following her to Scotland. He is forced to take the old carriage for she is in the new one—and she is almost two days ahead of him. He will likely not catch her until she is already in Elgin. As to whether she will marry him, I know not. That part is between them.'

'It seems,' Izzy remarked thoughtfully, 'as though he may be worthy of Rose, after all. And so I do hope she will have him.'

'We must say nothing of this, girls,' Lady Ashbourne reminded them. 'Our story stands, and my nephew is often away from town. We must hold fast and hope for a good outcome.'

'And in the meantime, we stand together,' said Anna firmly.

'Indeed. Oh, my dears!' Lady Ashbourne reached for her lace-edged handkerchief. 'How lovely it is to think we may become family!'

They embraced then and discussed their plans. Tonight there was to be another ball, and before that they would stay at home. Unusually for Izzy, her feelings on being denied the opportunity for company leaned more towards relief than disappointment. Leaving the others, she made for her chamber and drew out her sketchbook.

It has been a while.

As she found her pencils, she realised how much she had missed her art. In order to be polite and distant with Prince Claudio in public, it was important that she give vent to these unwelcome feelings in private. Taking a breath, she seated herself at the window and began to draw.

The queen was in a querulous mood. Nothing would do. She had apparently not enjoyed her dinner, her gown was decidedly uncomfortable, and she was now regretting accepting tonight's invitation to Lord and Lady Wright's ball. Claudio made sympathetic noises as the carriage rolled through St James's, bracing himself for the evening to come. He sympathised entirely with his cousin's mood, since he himself was feeling decidedly unsettled.

London was not what he had hoped for. No, that was not quite right. He genuinely liked the city and liked England. He was certainly enjoying the freedom of being his own man, away from the strictures and expectations of his father's court. And yet…

'Ach! The truth is, Claudio, that I am finding this Season dreadfully dull.' The queen made a sharp gesture with both hands. 'There has been no scandal, no intrigue, apart from the usual antics of my sons! A few solid matches, but nothing to excite my interest.' She adopted a teasing air. 'Will you not take an English wife, cousin?'

'What?' Matching her tone, he raised an eyebrow. 'Just to alleviate your ennui? I think not!'

'You are an ungrateful pup, and so I shall tell your father when I next write to him!'

Resisting the urge to squirm in his seat, it occurred to

him for the first time that the queen's account of his carousing and drinking his way through England might not present him to his father in the most flattering light. 'Ah, pray do not, for I assure you I am truly grateful to be here, and I thank you for welcoming me.'

Abandoning her teasing tone, she patted his hand. 'And I am glad to have you, for there is no substitute for family.' Cocking her head to one side, she regarded him thoughtfully. 'It has sometimes seemed to me as though you are… discontented. Am I wrong?'

He shrugged, maintaining an air of nonchalance. 'Everyone may be discontented at times, but I have not regretted my decision to come here.'

But I am beginning to question my choice of friends.

'Good! For you cannot abandon me now. Indeed I quite rely on you, you know!'

'You do?' He could not hide his surprise. 'But you are always so poised, so self-reliant…'

'A queen must play a role, Claudio. As must a prince. And yet underneath the mask, we may be as unhappy or as cross or as uncertain as we please.'

A prince. Does she refer to my father? Or to me?

Nodding slowly, he thought for a moment. 'We hide our true selves from the world.'

'But not from certain people. It is important to have people we can be true with—people who truly know us yet remain by our side. For me, as I told you before I have certain of my ladies, my daughters, those few close friends among the *ton*, and—' she patted his hand with affection '—now I have you. Sadly, my sons are largely a disappointment, and my husband is lost to me, his mind gone in a fog of fear and confusion.'

They talked then of the king's madness, of the brief moments of lucidity when Queen Charlotte could see again the man she loved.

My trials are nothing compared to hers.

They had arrived. Feeling decidedly off-balance, Claudio stepped down from the carriage, offering his hand to the queen.

'*Danke*, Claudio.' Their eyes met briefly, then he saw her stand up straighter, mentally applying her mask.

But she is formidable! Just like—

Leaving the thought unfinished, he walked towards the house, the Queen of England on his arm.

'The queen has arrived! Look, she is even now entering the ballroom!' Mrs Chorley's countenance was twisted with excitement. 'And the prince! Charity, for goodness' sake, do not look! And stand up straight, girl!'

Resisting the urge to square her own shoulders, Izzy kept her eyes firmly fixed on the Chorleys. Miss Chorley tonight was glittering with diamonds, an elaborate necklace around her throat and a matching bracelet on her right wrist. Her gown was of white silk, dotted with beads, with the same beads threaded through her glossy brown curls.

Beside her, Izzy felt like an absolute dowd in her pale gold gown—although, she had thought it pretty an hour ago, when checking her reflection in the mirror in her chamber. The gown was unadorned save for some subtle beading on the bodice, sleeves, and hemline, nothing like the elaborate ornamentation on Miss Chorley's gown, which must have cost a fortune. Izzy wore no jewellery and was suddenly convinced she must appear like a pale candle in sunlight next to Miss Chorley.

'Good evening, ladies!' It was Mr Fitch. Conscious that here was one of her most loyal suitors, Izzy gave him a warm smile. As greetings were exchanged, she took a quick glance towards the new arrivals. Naturally they were surrounded, ladies and gentlemen alike coming forward to greet the queen and her cousin.

Let them! I am quite content here and shall pay my respects in good time.

As Mr Fitch drew her aside to request her hand for the supper dance, Izzy remained half-aware of the conversation between Mrs Chorley and her daughter. Miss Chorley seemed to be distressed about something, but her mama was having none of it.

'We have been through this a hundred times, Charity,' she hissed. 'You simply play your part, and we shall have the prince by the end of tonight!'

Have the prince?

What did that mean? Glancing briefly their way, Izzy saw that Miss Chorley looked genuinely anxious, her mother cross. But there was no more time to think, for Mr Kirby had approached, his brow furrowed as he spied Mr Fitch.

'Good evening, Miss Isobel! At least, I assume it is you!' He indicated her golden gown. 'This is one of your colours, is it not? I confess I am not the most quick-witted of men, but I can remember a thing when it is repeated to me often enough.'

Izzy beamed at him. 'Mr Kirby! How delightful to see you! And yes, it is me.' Turning slightly to include her other suitor, she addressed them both. 'You two are among the few gentlemen to unerringly find me and recognise me.'

And they both rely on the colour of my gown. The prince, though, seems to have been able to recognise me from the start...

The two gentlemen were eyeing each other with a degree of hostility, she noted.

'Fitch.' Mr Kirby nodded his head slightly.

'Kirby.' Mr Fitch matched him for coolness. Opening his mouth to address Izzy again, he found himself forestalled by the newcomer.

'Miss Isobel, may I please ask you to save a dance for me?'

'Of course, Mr Kirby. It is always a delight to have you for a partner. And you, of course, Mr Fitch. I know one is not supposed to have favourites, but if such a thing were permitted, you both would be on my list.'

There! Encouragement for both of them, without leaving myself open to accusations of favouring either one.

Mr Fitch gave a sly smile. 'If you are hoping for Miss Isobel's hand for the supper dance, Kirby, you are too late, for she is promised to me!'

Kirby was undeterred. 'Not at all,' he replied serenely. 'I should like to claim the fourth dance tonight, if I may.' He leaned forwards, his tone now confidential. 'For I happen to know it will be a waltz.' At Mr Fitch's sceptical expression, he declared, 'It was a great success at Lady Cowper's ball, and it is nigh on impossible to get a dancing master these days, for everyone is desirous of learning it!'

Mr Fitch was eyeing him sourly. 'Are you sure you wish to risk it, Kirby? After all, one might easily make a fool of oneself if one gets the steps wrong.'

'I have no worries on that score, I assure you. And with such a graceful partner as Miss Isobel—I saw you waltz with the prince that night—I shall be the most fortunate of men!'

Both gentlemen, Izzy realised, were now fairly agitated, and so she set out to smooth ruffled feathers as best she could. By the time she had done so, the Chorleys were long gone, having joined the other sycophants currently surrounding the queen and the prince. Isobel had nothing against the queen, who had been kind and welcoming to her and to her sisters.

But the longer Izzy was about the *ton*, the more she wished that character meant as much as station. As the lowest possible rank tolerated within society—a girl without parents or lineage—she must attract friends and admirers based on her own God-given gifts of intelligence, looks, and character. In addition, she acknowledged wryly, the fact she and her sisters had dear Lady Ashbourne as a sponsor did not hurt…particularly when contrasted with the encroaching Mrs Chorley.

Izzy's gaze drifted to the Rentons, who were currently standing with Anna and Garvald at the long windows. Lady Renton behaved in very similar ways to Mrs Chorley—her ambition for her daughter being no secret—yet was not sneered at, for her birth and title protected her from judgement. As Izzy watched, Mr Phillips, his mother, and his sister approached the party. Lord Renton welcomed them warmly, his lady less so. Lady Mary's engagement to Mr Phillips had not come as a great surprise to people, once they thought about it, for the young gentleman and young lady were clearly partial to one another. The only speculation was around Lady Renton's clear displeasure at this outcome.

The musicians struck up for the first dance, and Izzy realised she had no partner. Having neither the expectation nor the desire for popularity, this did not bother her in the slightest, but as the Earl of Garvald led Anna to the dance floor and both Kirby and Fitch made their farewells, leaving to seek out their promised partners, Izzy found herself standing alone. Despite herself, she could not help but search out a tall, blond, royal gentleman. *There he is!* He had Miss Chorley by the hand, his head bent to listen to something she was saying on their way to the dance floor, and as he straightened, his gaze met Izzy's.

She stiffened but was unable to tear her gaze away. It was not just his looks that compelled her—there were other gentlemen present who were, some might argue, just as handsome—but something more. Something decidedly unwelcome. Briefly, her memory flicked to her sketchbook—drawing after drawing of one man, one face. All day she had tried to capture his likeness, and more. The essence of him.

Power. Strength. Passion. Unhappiness.

The last had surprised her, for he had never before seemed unhappy to her. In public he was assured, smooth—arrogant, even. Yet she had learned over the years to trust her instincts when drawing or painting. And her instincts were telling her something more lurked in the depths of his soul.

Tonight he will dance and laugh with his empty-headed friends and drink as much as he wishes. And it will not be enough.

He was *more* than the others, somehow. The likes of Eldon and Hawkins were both stuck in the shoes of a very young man, caring only for drinking, gambling, and wenching, no doubt. Prince Claudio was perfectly at liberty to enjoy such a life—being an actual young man. But if he had, as she suspected, more depth, then surely it would eventually begin to pall.

The dance had begun, and now he was entirely focused on his partner. With determination Izzy looked away—directly into the eyes of the queen, who was now seated on a raised chair with a commanding view of the room. Never taking her eyes from Izzy, she leaned her head to the right, speaking to her lady. Izzy swallowed.

What on earth—?

A moment later, the lady approached Izzy.

'Her Majesty wishes to speak with you, Miss Lennox.'

Oh, no! Have I offended her?

Racking her brain to try and understand why she was being singled out, Izzy approached the queen with outer calm, curtsying deeply.

'Come, Miss Lennox, sit with me.'

Miraculously a chair appeared, one of the hovering footmen clearly being charged with satisfying Her Majesty's every demand. Izzy sat, folding her hands in her lap and awaiting the queen's pleasure.

'First things first, my dear. Which one are you?'

'I am Isobel, Your Majesty. The middle sister.'

The anonymous middle. Wasn't that how Lady Ashbourne had described it? 'Always first or last', she had said, the day of their presentation.

'Isobel.' She repeated Izzy's name as if committing it to memory. 'I am told you each have preferred colours. Is that correct?'

'It is.' She indicated her gown. 'I tend to wear greens and yellows. Golden yellows, occasionally, like this gown.'

'Noted. How do you like London, Miss Isobel?'

Izzy replied in the positive and conversed with the queen for quite half an hour—just as if it was the most natural thing in the world. After a time, feeling reassured that she was not in any trouble, she relaxed a little, allowing her character to shine through a little more. Before long the queen was asking her opinion of the people and places she had encountered and laughing aloud at some of Izzy's responses. Izzy tried to be kind and couched her witticisms in guarded language, but Her Majesty was both quick-witted and ready to be entertained.

'You are a keen observer, Miss Isobel. I like it!' was her verdict. 'Now, who else must we discuss?' Her eyes drifted around the crowded room. 'Ah, yes, my cousin, Prince Claudio. What do you make of him?'

Izzy stiffened. 'You must know, Your Majesty, that I cannot possibly comment on someone so closely connected to you.'

The queen's jaw hardened. 'Your queen commands you, Miss Isobel Lennox.'

Izzy held her breath for a long moment, then nodded. 'Very well. The prince is not easily categorised. I have spoken of the pleasure-seekers as a group.' Her gaze moved about the room, seeking him out. He had not danced since partnering Miss Chorley and was currently imbibing a long glass of something. 'He is part of their set, yet does not properly belong.' Returning her gaze to the queen, she shrugged. 'I cannot say why. It is just a feeling.' Taking a breath, she decided to share her notion from earlier. 'I think he is...he is *more* than he shows to the world.'

The queen's gaze was unfocused. 'More than... Yes, I believe you are right. I have seen young men become stifled—staying at the hedonistic stage of life when they should be growing beyond it. For now, this is who he chooses to be.'

'But is it not frustrating to you? To see someone limit themselves to—to drinking and sport, when they could be something more? He has every advantage. Birth, position, looks, a good mind. Yet as far as I can make out he spends his days and nights in pursuit of nothing but pleasure.'

The queen chuckled. 'Patience, child.' She patted Izzy's

hand, then catching the prince's eye she beckoned him to join them. Izzy felt tightness rise within her as he approached. *Now what?*

'Ah, Claudio. I do believe the waltz is next. May I commend Miss Isobel Lennox to you as a dance partner?'

Oh, heavens! Even as mortification flooded through her, Izzy noted the tightening of his jaw, the grimness with which he nodded his acceptance.

'Of course!' He was all politeness, but it was clear to her he had no wish to dance with her. 'Miss Isobel, if you would kindly do me the great honour—'

But Izzy was already on her feet, the need to flee pulsing through her. 'Unfortunately I have already promised the waltz to Mr Kirby.'

The queen frowned. 'Well, of course you must not let Mr Kirby down, child.'

'And there he is!' Izzy gestured to her right where, thankfully, she had spotted her suitor, wearing a rather forlorn expression. 'I must not keep him waiting. Your Majesty. Your Highness.' A swift curtsy, and she was gone before the queen should finagle the prince into offering her a different dance.

A wide smile broke across Mr Kirby's pleasant face as she approached. 'Miss Isobel! I had wondered if all was lost when I saw you talking with Her Majesty. A great honour, yet selfishly all I could think of was our waltz.'

He held out a hand, and she took it, conscious that she was being subjected to scrutiny from many people around her. Talking with the queen, she supposed, would be noticed. Particularly being shown such favour for half an hour and more.

And why should she not speak with me, if she wishes?

Lifting her chin, she walked serenely to the dance floor, there to execute the waltz with particular grace.

* * *

Claudio, having hastily approached Miss Anderton for the waltz, could not prevent dissatisfaction from rising like bile within him.

What ails me?

Why should it matter to him what a certain young lady had said? Or what she believed of him? The same questions had been tormenting him since Grantham. Miss Isobel Lennox was a nobody—one of many débutantes, and not even particularly eligible in terms of dowry and parentage. There was no point being cross about it. He was, after all, a prince.

Setting himself out to be charming, he had Miss Anderton blushing and stammering in no time and was forced to stifle a wave of ennui.

Afterwards, his duty briefly done, he took a glass from a footman and downed it with a feeling of defiance. The servant remained nearby, knowing well what was required, and so Claudio set down his empty glass and took another, this time swirling around the golden liquid therein and contemplating it meditatively. His friends were in the corner to his left. He knew their exact location without looking as they were rapidly achieving a state of raucousness that would no doubt have Lord Wright casting them meaningful glances in the next hour or so, indicating it was probably time for them to retire to their club. Having himself drunk very little so far tonight, Claudio knew he would have to make some effort to catch up or be left frowning soberly at his friends' antics.

His gaze searched the room, pausing as he spied the golden hair of one of the Lennox triplets. She turned, and he dropped his gaze.

Not Isobel.

He needed no clues from the colour of their gowns these days. By now he could tell Anna apart from Rose if he looked carefully, but Miss Isobel's visage was instantly recognisable—just as though she was simply their sister, not part of their likeness. On he searched, pausing when he finally located her, bestowing brilliant smiles on the unedifying Mr Kirby.

Still, at least she is here.

Last night he had searched constantly at the soirée, but the Lennox sisters and Lady Ashbourne had not attended, leaving the entire evening dreadfully flat.

Catching the direction of his thoughts, he cursed inwardly. Why should it matter to him whether she was here or not? Setting down his untouched glass, he turned away from Miss Isobel Lennox and made his way across the room to where Mr Phillips was standing with his shy sister. At least Phillips was capable of sensible conversation, and besides, the man had to be congratulated on making a good match with Lady Mary Renton.

Isobel, half-listening to Mr Kirby's enthusiasm, noted the prince's progression across the room towards the Phillipses, and also Mrs Chorley's hawkish stare. She shuddered, uncertain as to why, then turned her attention back to Mr Kirby, who was in alt that he had performed the waltz without mishap.

'Having such a graceful, sure-footed partner is doubtless the reason for my good fortune,' he declared, and Izzy was moved to protest.

'Oh, no! For I have danced with many gentlemen much less agile than yourself, Mr Kirby, I assure you!'

At this he beamed, a generous smile spreading across his homely face.

I could do worse than Kirby for a husband, she mused, *for he is both kind-hearted and amiable.*

They conversed on for another few minutes, then, making her excuses to Mr Kirby, Izzy made for the ladies' retiring room. As she moved silently down the grand hallway, her thoughts on Mr Kirby's amiability, a door opened farther ahead, and Mrs Chorley and her daughter emerged, deep in conversation. They moved ahead of her, perhaps themselves seeking the retiring room, but something about the set of their shoulders, the hissed speech between them, drew Izzy's attention. Without considering the inappropriateness of eavesdropping at a *ton* ball, Izzy skipped silently to catch up, her sharp ears picking up tantalising snatches of conversation.

'But Mama, I cannot! It would not be right!'

'Nonsense! You are simply securing your future, Charity. Do you not think every other maiden would not do the same?'

To this, Charity replied with something unintelligible, to which her mother replied, 'Oh, fiddlesticks! Do not try my patience, my girl! Now, do as you are bid. That library is perfect for our plan, but we must wait a little longer, for all the young men are becoming nicely wine-befuddled.'

Our plan?

Whatever it was, it involved the prince, and Izzy had a strong notion it would not be to his benefit. Stopping, she allowed the Chorleys to enter the retiring room before turning back, making her way unerringly to the room they had recently vacated. Checking left and right, Izzy opened the door and slipped inside. It was indeed a dimly-lit library, with floor-to-ceiling bookcases, a fireplace, and armchairs upholstered in reddish-brown leather.

The room was empty.

Closing the door behind her, Izzy moved forwards, trailing her fingers along a line of books on the nearest shelf, pausing as she recognised a particular title, *Dobson's Essays*. A gleaming side table held a branch of candles and something else: a lady's painted fan.

Standing still for a moment, her brow furrowed in deep thought, Izzy tried to recall whether Mrs Chorley or her daughter had been carrying a fan just now. Abruptly she came to a decision. Scanning the room, she selected a particularly large armchair, the sort with comfortable wings at the top, against which to rest one's head if one fell asleep while reading. It was heavy, but she managed to tug it into a new position—one turned away from both the door and the side table. Quickly she took the book from its shelf—grateful for her good fortune in finding exactly the book she needed—and placed it on the chair, then took one final look about her before departing. With Rose's disgrace fresh in her mind, she had perhaps jumped to a false conclusion, but it did no harm to be prepared, just in case her absurd notion proved to be correct.

Thankfully the hallway was empty when she emerged. Exhaling slowly, she resumed her journey towards the retiring rooms as though nothing had happened.

Claudio spent a good quarter of an hour with Mr Phillips, enjoying a conversation that included multiple topics, not least Mr Phillips's recent betrothal to Lady Mary. The man was beaming with happiness. Indeed he seemed to exude it from every part of him, almost as though there were a glow about him.

Claudio was at once fascinated, uncomfortable, and, truth be told, a little envious. What must it be like to know love and to have one's love reciprocated? He had never thought on such matters before. Beyond fleeting infatuations with unattainable ladies in his youth, he had never felt anything as deep or as all-consuming as that which was clearly currently affecting Mr Phillips.

As always, his mind flicked to Miss Isobel—his image of her, as always, surrounded by golden light. She was a glowing candle, a blinding ray of sunshine, a blazing fire… Could it be?

But no.

It must not be. He would never choose to fall in love with someone so…*difficult*, and challenging, and direct. Someone who could see clearly every one of his flaws and hold them up for inspection in the clear light of her soul. Someone who knew her own worth, and his. He pushed away the uncomfortable thoughts, focusing his attention once again on the newly-betrothed gentleman beside him.

Afterwards, instead of returning to his friends, he stood there, vaguely unsettled. Where should he go next? Viscount Ashbourne was not present, having apparently gone out of town on a matter of business.

Where can I find sensible conversation?

Looking about, he espied the Earl of Garvald, and before he had even thought about it, he found himself making his way across the room.

Supper was called, and Izzy allowed Mr Fitch to accompany her, following their dance together. 'I noticed,' he began carefully, 'that you have been enjoying the queen's favour.'

Izzy shrugged. 'The queen has never before fixed her attention on me and probably will never do so again.'

'It is a singular honour, and one which many here must envy.'

'I had not thought much about it. The queen is, naturally, the Queen, but she is also a person like everyone else.'

His eyebrows shot up. 'How absurd! She cannot be a person like everyone else, for she is always the Queen.'

About to deliver a heated retort, Izzy decided to give the man a chance to redeem himself. 'Whatever can you mean?'

'Just that Her Majesty must be treated with…a certain *reserve*. As a sign of respect. No—' he held up a hand '—I will not hear an opposing view. My own mama reminds me constantly that the royal family are truly appointed by God to rule over us, and as such I cannot see them simply as—as *people*. The very notion offends!'

'I see.'

Respect?

A hundred words were on her tongue—not least the shocking profligacy of the Prince Regent and, by all accounts, his estranged wife. 'And I have no intention of arguing with you, Mr Fitch.'

There was no point in arguing with such a person. Still, the conversation had been enlightening. Mr Fitch was better-looking than Mr Kirby and had probably a quicker mind, but a habit of being dogmatic would not bode well for marital harmony. And his putting a hand up towards Izzy's face to stop her from talking had not been well-received. Not at all. No, if she had to choose between them right now, Mr Kirby would have the upper hand.

As she ate, idly making conversation with Mr Fitch, she tried to imagine her life a year from now, should she marry.

Is this what my future holds? A husband who tells me what to think? Or—she pictured the amiable Mr Kirby—*a husband who acknowledges he is not quick-witted?*

She stifled a sigh. These were the limitations of her choices. She could no more choose a different husband than become Queen of England. Glancing towards the large table at the top of the room, she saw that Her Majesty had been joined by the prince, and they were currently deep in conversation. Unable to resist, she allowed her eyes to linger on Prince Claudio's handsome features, then looked away before she should be seen. The Chorleys, she noted, were seated at the next table to hers and Mr Fitch's. Mrs Chorley was currently attacking a well-filled plate with gusto, while Miss Chorley seemed to have little appetite.

After supper the retiring rooms were busy for a time, but once the dancing was underway again, the ballroom was soon crowded. Those not dancing were ranged around the edges of the dance floor or sitting and standing in groups. The noise level had increased, no doubt down to the increasing effects of the wine, ratafia, and strong punch being offered by Lady Wright's footmen. Having danced a quadrille with Mr Phillips, Izzy thanked him and made her way to the side, where the open windows gave some relief from the heat of the packed room. Most of the ladies were at this point making good use of their fans, and it reminded Izzy to observe the Chorley ladies. There they were—and Mrs Chorley was making for the prince!

Someone passed in front of Izzy, blocking her view, and by the time she moved to a better vantage point, Prince Claudio was in conversation with Miss Chorley, her mama having left them to converse. Miss Chorley, from what Izzy could see, had no fan.

Claudio was fighting the urge to yawn. To do so at a *ton* party would be the height of rudeness. To do so while in conversation with a young lady would be unforgivable. He was not drunk enough to take Miss Chorley's giggled inanities with any forbearance. Indeed he was not drunk at all, which was probably a mistake. If he were, he would probably be able to bear Miss Chorley's clumsy attempts at flirtation a little more easily.

'Do you like to dance, Your Highness?' Her tone was arch, and quickly he reminded himself he had done his duty by her earlier. Indeed—he ran through a list in his head—he had danced once with nearly all of the eligible maidens, as well as a few of the married ladies. Nearly all. Despite the queen's machinations he had yet to dance with Miss Isobel tonight—an omission that was bothering him much more than it should.

'I do. I think an appreciation for music is one of the higher arts.'

'Well, I know nothing of such matters, but I do love to dance!'

He ignored this, having no intention of asking her for a second dance. His own comment, had he directed it to Miss Isobel—or indeed to Ashbourne, Garvald, or Phillips—would likely have resulted in a lively debate as to the place of music and dance in the civilised world, but with Miss Chorley there was no such opportunity, for she was among the most hen-witted persons of his acquaintance.

Yes, Miss Chorley, and Eldon, and Hawkins…all alike in that respect. He frowned. That was not quite correct. Hawkins and Eldon had the benefit of thirty years and more on this earth, and so had gained knowledge that younger persons like himself could not yet possess. However, it seemed to him his friends used their worldly wisdom simply for their own advantage: to bet on a likely fighter, or to contrive an invitation to a race meet. And why should they not?

His thoughts were interrupted by the realisation that he had been standing in glowering silence next to Miss Chorley, and as he focused on her again he saw that she was bringing a hand to her head.

'Oh, dear,' she said weakly, triggering all his gentlemanly instincts.

'Miss Chorley! Are you unwell? May I be of assistance to you?'

'Yes, I… I feel unwell. The heat…'

'Indeed it is extremely warm in here. Can I fetch your mother for you?' He looked around but could not see Mrs Chorley's plump form anywhere.

'No! Please do not!' Her tone was forceful, and he reflected that Miss Chorley might be quite nervous of her mother. The woman was formidable—and *not* in a good way. Before he had the time to consider who might actually be formidable in a good way, Miss Chorley swayed slightly, so he applied a steadying hand to her elbow.

'Thank you,' she murmured, looking up at him.

'How may I assist you, Miss Chorley?'

'My fan… I left it on a table…' Vaguely she gestured toward the door leading to the hallway.

'Then, I shall fetch it for you! In the meantime, shall I find you a chair?'

She laid a restraining hand on his arm. 'No…please do not make a fuss. If you try to find me a chair they will all be looking at me, and my mama will be displeased.' She squared her shoulders. 'I shall fetch the fan myself, but thank you.' She stepped forwards, swaying ever so slightly.

With a muffled expletive, he started after her. What if she collapsed in the hallway?

'Miss Chorley! I shall accompany you.' His sense of responsibility would not allow her to go alone. Something about her behaviour was a little strange, and he wondered if she was overcome by ratafia as much as by the heat of the packed ballroom.

Izzy could not keep her eyes away from the prince, but this time, instead of an idle or intense perusal of his form and features, her senses were on full alert to his conversation with Miss Chorley. As she watched, she saw Miss Chorley put a hand to her head, and a moment later the prince took her elbow.

Is she unwell?

He looked around, as if seeking someone. Miss Chorley's mama, most likely.

Izzy's eyes widened. He would not find her, for Mrs Chorley was currently hiding behind a pillar to Izzy's right—and seemed to be leaning slightly as if peeping around to watch discreetly. Whatever the Chorleys' plan was, they were clearly currently executing it.

Swiftly, Izzy made for the far doors to the hallway. Time was short, for if her suspicions were true, Miss Chorley and the prince would imminently be on their way to the library.

The hallway was empty, apart from Claudio and the apologetic Miss Chorley.

'I cannot thank you enough, Your Highness! Now, where did I leave that fan? Oh, I remember now!' She paused, opening a door to her left. 'It is in here, I believe! They have the most amazing collection of books—just look! Not that I am a great reader, you understand. You must not think me bookish!'

He frowned. Now was not the time for visiting a library in someone else's house—particularly when it was so dimly-lit in contrast to the bright hallway. Just as his awareness began to send a warning, she half collapsed inside the room, grasping the back of a leather sofa for support.

'Oh! Oh, dear! I feel most unwell!'

'Let me assist you, Miss Chorley.' Gently, he guided her round to the other side of the sofa, bidding her sit. She did so, her breathing agitated and her face flushed.

I must find her mother.

But when he made to move away she reached for his hand, preventing him from leaving.

'Oh, please stay with me, Your Highness. I shall be well in just a moment, I promise.'

Reluctantly, he stayed, his discomfort growing. Her hand gripped his tightly, as if he was saving her from some danger by his very presence. But, *Lord*! It would look bad if someone came upon them. And the hallway outside was the main route to the retiring rooms. He glanced towards the door, which was slowly swinging from open to half-open.

The devil take it!

What if someone should see him? Yet he could not leave Miss Chorley, for she was clearly in some distress. His mind was racing, but for now he could see no way out of the dilemma.

His heart sank as he detected a surge in noise as the doors to the ballroom opened, then closed again. Was someone even now making their way down the hallway?

Thankfully the door had closed farther and was now ajar rather than fully open, so hopefully whoever it was would not even notice but continue to make their way to the retiring rooms. Now he could hear voices. He tensed as he recognised the tones of their hostess, Lady Wright, who seemed to be directing someone. 'You see, the room set aside for ladies is just along here.'

'And what is this room, Lady Wright? Such a delightful house!'

Everything happened at once. As the door began to open he snatched his hand from Miss Chorley's vicelike grip, even as he recognised her mama's voice and realised the trap that they had sprung between them. A trap from which there could be no escape.

'Charity! Your Highness! What on earth are you doing in here, all alone?' Mrs Chorley's manufactured outrage was belied by the delight in her eyes.

Almost, he could feel the blood draining from his face. His mind was frozen. Oh, he had heard of such plots, but never would he have thought himself foolish enough to be caught in such a snare.

And I am not even drunk!

His gaze swung to Lady Wright, who was frowning. Oh, she might suspect that he had been deliberately ensnared, but she would be forced to confirm that he had indeed been alone in the library with Miss Chorley.

His gaze flicked back to the mother. As he looked her expression changed, her jaw sagging—this time in genuine shock. A familiar voice from behind him declared sunnily, 'Oh, but they are not alone, Mrs Chorley. For we are all here together!'

He swung around—to meet the innocent gaze of Miss Isobel Lennox.

Chapter Eight

Izzy's heart was pounding so loudly she could swear Lady Wright might hear it all the way across the room. Having barely made it into the library before the prince and Miss Chorley had opened the ballroom doors, she had hidden herself in the armchair, remaining stock-still and barely able to think. Thankfully, Miss Chorley's histrionics had covered up the sound of Izzy's own ragged breathing.

What if I am wrong? What if they walk straight past the door?

But only a few seconds later her worst suspicions had been confirmed. The door had been pushed open and in they came, Miss Chorley saying she was unwell and the prince—very properly—assisting her to sit. Izzy could hear the rustle of Miss Chorley's silk dress, her dramatic, fast breathing.

Lord! She is really going to do this thing!

Doubts suddenly assailed her. What if the prince *wanted* to be alone with Miss Chorley? Was she to remain here, hidden in a large armchair, while he kissed another maiden? Pain knifed through her at the thought, and abruptly she realised since the day she had met him she had considered his request for a kiss to be an unfinished matter between them. One that could only be resolved by—

Voices in the hallway had distracted her from the thought,

and as she became aware of who was approaching, suddenly she knew that Prince Claudio must not be compromised by this cheap trap. No, she had the power to save him, and save him she would! So when she heard Mrs Chorley's faux outrage, she rose from the chair like an angel of justice, declaring, 'Oh, but they are not alone, Mrs Chorley. For we are all here together!'

The effect was instant. Mrs Chorley's jaw was sagging and her visage turning a sickly grey. Lady Wright was eyeing her approvingly. Miss Chorley's mouth was opening and closing silently. And as for the prince—even now he was turning to face her. Anxious that he not given himself away, she continued brightly, 'And here is the collection we were speaking of, see?'

She held out the book, and he took it, saying, 'Dobson? A most excellent collection.' His face was deathly pale, but as his eyes met hers again they softened a little at the corners, making her heart melt and her knees tremble.

Swallowing, she moved away from him, turning her head left and right as if seeking something. 'Miss Chorley, your fan is here!' Walking across to the side table, she picked it up. 'We came in to look for it, but I then got distracted when I saw the very collection of essays His Highness and I talked of recently. I simply had to sit for a moment to look at it.' Handing the fan to Miss Chorley, whose mouth was still opening and closing in the manner of a goldfish, she turned back to the prince.

'And now, if I am not mistaken, Your Highness, I am promised to you for the next dance.' She waited, her breath caught in her throat. Had she managed to pull the thing off?

He bowed, placing the book back on the shelf, while behind him Lady Wright declared, 'Yes, go and dance, Your Highness. I think you could not find a better partner.'

Turning back, he took Izzy's hand, murmuring, 'I quite agree. Ladies.' He bowed formally to all three of them, then led Izzy from the room.

Claudio could barely take in what had just happened. Disaster had been averted, and by the intervention of the one woman who was rapidly becoming an obsession with him. His mind awhirl, he walked beside her down the hallway towards the ballroom, the warmth of her gloved hand on his arm the only anchor in a world that suddenly seemed much more dangerous than it had a half hour ago.

'I must thank you, Miss Isobel.' Turning his head slightly to meet her gaze, he found her expression to be one of amusement, mixed with a strong dose of relief.

'Well, I was not certain I could carry it off, you know. I am glad you were quick-witted enough to follow my nonsense about the essays!'

He grinned. 'Mr Dobson to the rescue! But no, I can give him no credit, for this was all your doing.'

They had reached the doors. Lifting her gloved hand to his mouth, he pressed a kiss there, and as he lifted his gaze to meet her eyes a shudder of desire powered through him—desire that was surely reflected in her eyes?

'Isobel!' he breathed, as their gazes caught and held.

Beside them, the doors began to open. Instantly both donned matching masks of nonchalance, unconcern, and polite distance, nodding politely towards the gentleman who emerged, clearly seeking the retiring rooms.

'Another waltz!' Claudio declared, as the sound of the musicians' opening bars came to them. 'Perfect!'

Leading her straight to the dance floor, he tried to manage the maelstrom of emotions within him. Relief, yes, and outrage at what the Chorleys had tried. But mostly, he found himself thrumming with warmth and gratitude towards her.

'You are formidable, you know,' he told her as they began to move. 'In a good way,' he hastened to add, conscious that she often put the worst possible interpretation of his words. 'Like the queen.'

Glancing towards Her Majesty, he saw that she had been joined by Lady Wright and was listening intently to whatever their hostess was saying.

Lord! My cousin will have the whole story in a moment.

Still, Lady Wright was discreet, and so he had every hope that the incident in the library would not become common knowledge.

As he moved through the waltz in harmony with Miss Isobel, he felt decidedly strange. All of the usual feelings were there—desire and fascination chief among them. For once, though, there was no argument between them. Instead they talked about what had just happened…and *almost* happened. Isobel had, it seemed, heard the Chorleys making plans earlier.

'Then, it was not just serendipity that brought you to the library?'

'Lord, no! I had to run to get there before you both left the ballroom. Through those far doors.' She frowned. 'I could not know with certainty what they were planning. Indeed, it was only when I heard Mrs Chorley's voice in the hallway that I was sure.' She shook her head. 'I still cannot quite take it in!'

'Nor me,' he replied grimly. 'Even now, I might be informing the queen of my unexpected betrothal.' He thought for a moment. 'So it was all play-acting. No wonder I could not find Mrs Chorley when her daughter first told me she was unwell!'

'As to that—' Isobel's eyes were dancing '—she made certain of it by secreting herself behind a pillar!'

'No! Really?'

'Yes—a very *large* pillar, I must say!'

On they danced, talking and laughing together, oblivious to the attention they were drawing. Claudio knew only that his fascination for her had reached new realms, for their present harmony contained an unexpected addition, the connection of something that felt oddly like friendship. Like, yet strangely unlike. For never before had friendship been so intense, so all-consuming, so…magical.

'I cannot believe it!' Anna's face was a picture. It was almost three in the morning, they were in Izzy's bedchamber, and Izzy had just told her sister the full, sorry tale. 'That Miss Chorley would do such a thing!'

Izzy grimaced. 'It was her mother's plan. My impression is that Miss Chorley was a reluctant participant.'

Anna snorted. 'Yes, but she carried it out regardless.' She shook her head slowly. 'This place… The Marriage Mart…'

'It is all rather sordid, is it not? They reward the *appearance* of goodness, not goodness itself.'

'Yes. Rose must go away, while Miss Chorley might have finagled a prince for a husband!' She sent Izzy a piercing look. 'When you danced with him tonight, you seemed to be getting along famously.'

'Yes, we had just returned from the library and were caught up in what had just happened. I would not read anything into it.' Yet inwardly, her mind kept playing again and again certain memories. The kiss upon her hand. The feeling of connection with him as they danced. The way his eyes had softened when he looked at her that time… She shrugged. 'A temporary truce, no doubt. But I—I asked

Lady Ashbourne about his father's visit to England all those years ago.'

'And?'

She shrugged. 'Prince Claudio's father was apparently devoted to his wife. The *ton* always knows,' Lady Ashbourne said, 'for gossip, *on-dit*s and the latest *crim. cons.* are the currency of every *ton* conversation.'

Anna's eyes widened. 'I have certainly seen shocking behaviour from some of the married gentlemen and ladies. I must say I should prefer to marry someone who would not behave in such a manner.' She frowned. 'But I suppose if a man were tricked into marriage, then he might not feel the same respect for his wife.'

'Or vice versa! Remember that Rose might have been forced to marry Ashbourne—although we know the case is different, for she loves him. I am sure of it.'

'What did the Chorleys do after you foiled their dreadful plan?' Anna was frowning. 'I do not recall seeing them in the last hour or so of the ball.'

'They left early.' Izzy grinned. 'Apparently Miss Chorley had a headache!'

'And what of the queen? She spoke to you not once, but twice!'

'Indeed.' Briefly, Izzy summarised her first conversation with Her Majesty. 'She seemed genuinely amused by my observations. I do hope I did not inadvertently offend her.'

'And the second time?' Anna prompted.

'Ah. Lady Wright told her about the library, so she summoned me again. That time our conversation was brief. "I believe I have reason to thank you, Miss Isobel Lennox," she told me. "You have the gratitude of your queen."'

Anna put a hand to her chest. 'My goodness!'

'I know!' She grinned. 'Who would have thought that a

trio of unknown girls from Elgin with small dowries and no known parents could come to the notice of the queen!'

'And do not forget we are her diamonds!' Anna sighed. 'Such a pity Rose is gone. She should be here, hearing this tonight.'

They hugged, and Anna departed for her own bedchamber. Alone in the darkness, Izzy allowed herself to remember other moments. The rush of desire she had felt with him in the hallway. The swell of possessiveness she had felt in the library. Yes, she would marry a London gentleman—Mr Kirby had the upper hand at present—but before that, she had another task to accomplish. Somehow, somewhere—discreetly and safely and avoiding scandal—real (Rose) or contrived (Miss Chorley), she would find a way to kiss the prince.

Lady Kelgrove was in fine form. Having summoned Claudio to sit by her, the elderly lady was now regaling the prince with a mix of anecdotes, biting observations about members of the *ton*, and piercing questions, which she would throw at him at the most unexpected moments. They were ensconced near the fireplace at Lady Kelgrove's elegant mansion, drinking tea and observing the other guests. Lady Kelgrove was today at-home to visitors and was clearly enjoying every moment.

'And of course Mr Phillips managed to catch Lady Mary Renford—an impressive feat, do you not think?' Her black eyes held a clear challenge. Would he say something banal and meaningless, pretending to not understand her implication?

He decided to match her. 'Given her mother's ambition, yes.' Throwing her an equally challenging glance, he added, 'The most impressive feat of the Season, perhaps?'

'Perhaps—or perhaps not. The queen's diamonds are not yet betrothed, and they are discerning enough, I think, to wait.'

Feeling rather as though he were playing chess with a master, he managed to maintain an unchanged expression. 'The Lennox sisters?'

She chuckled. 'Why? Are there yet more diamonds of which I am unaware? Yes, of course I mean the Lennox sisters. They are quite my favourites, you know.'

'They are? And why so?' Perhaps by keeping the attention on Lady Kelgrove he might be able to manage the disquieting flutters currently tormenting his innards.

No, he would not look towards Miss Isobel again. She was currently by the window, enjoying an animated conversation with Kirby or Fitch. He could never remember which gentleman was which, for to him there was no difference between them. Neither were leaders of society, with nothing of note about them—not their opinions, nor their appearance, nor even their fashion sense. They dressed conservatively and—he would wager a pony on it—used the same tailor. What they also had in common was their devotion to Miss Isobel Lennox, a devotion which entirely grated on him.

'They have been fêted for their beauty, and their manners, and their lively minds. But it is more than that. The Lennox girls are not just admired, they are well-liked. They have *countenance*, my dear. And unlike beauty, countenance is not lost with time.' She sighed. 'So few young ladies have that firmness of character when they have their Season. Often they are too ready to obey their elders unquestioningly. Or, worse, to behave in the silliest way possible.'

Her words were resonating within him, more powerfully than he wished. He knew himself to be drawn to Miss Isobel, knew also that it was for more than simply her beauty, for her sisters—almost identical in looks—did not attract him in the same way.

'I had a granddaughter, you know. She died a long time ago.'

He frowned in sympathy. 'I was not aware. I am sorry, Lady Kelgrove.'

She waved this away. 'My Maria had countenance. I often wonder how she would have fared as she matured. But no matter, for we are speaking of the Lennoxes. So alike, and yet so different. Rose, deceptively quiet. Anna, deceptively commonsensical.'

He waited. 'And Miss Isobel?'

The chuckle came again. 'Not deceptive in any way. Headstrong, obstinate, and opinionated. Just as I like her!'

Something like pride began burning within him—which was nonsensical as he was not connected to the Lennoxes in any way. 'Then, you can tell them apart, my lady?'

'As easily as you can,' she retorted. 'Oh, I am aware there are many who claim to believe they are so identical it would be impossible for anyone other than their mother to know the difference. Now, to be fair, I had the benefit of knowing their preferred colours to begin with, but now it seems to me their faces are different enough to make them seem like sisters only, not triplets.' She sent him a searching glance. 'And you share this, too, do you not, Your Highness?'

He shrugged. 'I do. It is strange to me when people appear to genuinely mix them up.' And yet he could not tell Isobel's suitors apart. 'Of course, Miss Rose has been gone for a few weeks now, so there are only the two of them.'

She pressed her lips together. 'I am told Rose may not return this Season. I am most displeased that Lady Ashbourne allowed her to go away. Surely someone else can take care of Lady Ashbourne's brother? Has he no servants, for goodness' sake?'

He had no answer to this, although inwardly he wondered yet again if Isobel was missing her younger sister. It mattered to him, somehow.

'She may opt for Kirby rather than Fitch, I think.'

Now Lady Kelgrove had all his attention. 'Miss Isobel? You think she will *marry* one of those fools?'

She raised a quizzical eyebrow. 'You have reason to think otherwise?' At his dumb silence, she continued. 'I thought not. From what I know of Miss Isobel, she is practical enough to know she needs a husband. And since many of the *ton* are foolish enough to bemoan the lack of information about their parentage, a Fitch or a Kirby is exactly what she needs. What? You disapprove?'

'Why must she marry at all? Or why can she not wait a few years?' His heart was suddenly pounding in a most distracting way, and there was a sick feeling in his stomach.

'Did you not know? Lady Ashbourne's inestimable brother—the one who has become unwell at quite the most inconvenient time—has paid for a single Season for the girls. He is, I understand, a solicitor and, as such, has limited funds. If they are not betrothed by summer, they may have to return to wherever they have been living. Somewhere in rural Scotland, I understand.' This last was said with a scathing tone.

'Then—she—they will not return after the summer?'

'Unlikely, unless at least one of them marries.'

'But—but we are already well into June! The Season is almost done!'

'Indeed. Once July arrives, the *ton* will start making for their country homes for the summer.' Eyeing him closely, she waited.

'I see… I see.' And he did. A little, at least. For the first time, he tried to understand what it might be like to have options restricted by one's level of wealth. Oh, not abject poverty. That, he understood, albeit from a distance. Both at home and here in London, he gave alms and carried out good works, as he had been raised to do. No, this was altogether different. The Lennox triplets had the *appearance* of wealth—gowns and fripperies, the benefits of a good education—but, he reflected now, no jewellery. So enough wealth for one Season, but no more. Instantly a wave of something like fear rippled through him.

She should have all of it. Everything she wants.

'So why must Miss Isobel limit herself to gentlemen such as Kirby and Fitch?'

'Because no titled gentleman has offered for her. Yet.' She eyed him levelly.

He swallowed.

I am not ready for this!

'And if they do not, then she will do what she must, Your Highness.'

What she must.

He could not like it. And if he had been a few years older, perhaps things might have been different. As it was, how could he think of marriage—even with someone as wonderful as Isobel—when he did not yet know who he was?

Chapter Nine

'What a glorious day for it!'

The sun was shining, Greenwich was sparkling, and a cavalcade of carriages was currently dispensing its *tonnish* occupants out into nature.

'Delightful!' was the reply, the same sentiments being echoed among the rapidly increasing group of lords, ladies, and gentlemen spilling out into bright sunshine, cerulean skies, and lush, green grass.

Izzy played her part, meandering through the throng with Anna, parasol resting delicately on one shoulder. Her dress was of buttercup-yellow muslin, with a fine line of ivy leaves embroidered at the hem. Carefully she angled her parasol as she walked, ensuring the blazing sun should not touch her face, for there was nothing worse than to be sunburnt. The gentlemen, she guessed, would be uncomfortable in their jackets and waistcoats, and she could only be grateful for the current fashion for loose muslin gowns for ladies. How her mama would have managed in the stiff brocade gowns of twenty-five years ago she could only imagine.

Today had been appointed as the day for a casual luncheon on the grass, on the hill above Greenwich. Those attending had agreed which foods they would provide, with

Lady Ashbourne's cook contributing five blancmanges, which were even now being unstrapped from the back of the carriage, still in their copper moulds. The food was being gathered in a central location, whence servants would distribute it to each cluster of elegant persons. The Ashbourne servants had also packed cutlery and crockery, along with cloths for them to sit on and ale and orgeat for them to drink. The carriage was the hired one they had been using for weeks now, as both Ashbourne carriages were currently in Scotland.

Rose had written to say she had arrived safely and was to begin teaching at Belvedere on the morrow, but at that point the viscount had clearly not yet arrived.

Will she have him?

Lady Ashbourne was dubious, but Izzy privately thought she would.

I believe she loves him. I only hope he loves her.

She and Anna had spoken briefly of what it might mean for them, should Rose become a viscountess. Surely then, they would be more acceptable to the high sticklers, as sisters-in-law to Lord Ashbourne, rather than orphans with no known family? While they still could not expect similar good fortune—for Rose's marriage, should it happen, would be seen as surprising, and probably assumed to be related to propinquity, since the Lennox ladies had been living in the Ashbourne townhouse all Season. Still, it might reassure Mr Kirby or Mr Fitch about the advisability of offering for Izzy.

To be fair, neither gentleman seemed to need such reassurance, for both—possibly fuelled by dislike of the other—were becoming marked in their attentions towards her, to the extent that she was beginning to avoid them a little. Once a proposal was made, she would have to decide, and she was not quite ready to do so. Stifling a sigh, she continued to greet the various ladies and gentlemen. The notion of being actually married to Mr Kirby—or Mr Fitch—was beginning to feel all too real, and she was developing an understanding that it would take an inordinate amount of courage to make vows of lifetime devotion to either gentleman. Thankfully, neither was to be present today, as Mr Kirby had an unavoidable appointment with his man of business, while Mr Fitch was apparently visiting his elderly mother somewhere south of London.

Her heart skipped, for finally she espied the blond hair and strong shoulders of Prince Claudio. He had his back to her, but she knew every line of his shape. Excitement fought with relief within her, for events always seemed flat when he was not there. Oh, she knew he was to marry his Prussian princess—although the gossips could not agree on just how fixed his betrothal was. It would always have been impossible for a prince to consider a maiden such as herself, but still, she dreamed. Even when he frustrated her. Even when he vexed her.

Hearts are not minds, she told herself. They are permitted to be foolish.

So for now she would allow herself to dream. Would indulge her foolish heart, a little. Soon the time would come when her dreams must be overruled, when she would agree to marry someone—anyone—for safety, for security. For the chance to remain here.

I shall have to be honest, she reminded herself.

Mr Kirby—or Mr Fitch—must know that she did not love him. And from what she could understand of *ton* marriages, this would not be a particular barrier.

Love matches were apparently rare. And she must not yearn for *rare*. She must accept *common*, *normal*, *ordi-*

nary. Once again, she sighed inwardly, bringing her attention back to the present.

This was real. Being here now, with the sun shining, her dreams intact, and Prince Claudio in her eyeline. Her heart lifted.

Claudio looked around surreptitiously, knowing he could not settle until he had established where she was. Thankfully, his friends—who had just been commencing their card games when he had left the club last night—would not be here today. No doubt they would sleep for many more hours yet. Good, for that gave him the opportunity to be himself without their ribbing, which was constant.

It seemed he could not speak to a young lady without being teased about courting her, although that had decreased a little since his fiction about a Prussian princess, which was now, he hoped, suitably vague enough to avoid speculation about her identity. Nor could he speak to a sober-minded gentleman or an older lady without his own set accusing him of being staid and dull. And yet, he enjoyed their company, too, when in the mood.

Why can I not be more than one person? he wondered as he and the queen made the rounds, glad to stretch their legs after the journey out from London. *Why can I not be the drunken gambler on occasion, while still remaining my father's son, with an interest in all sorts of people and activities?*

No answer came to him, and so he pushed the conundrum to the back of his mind. The day was bright, Eldon and Hawkins were snoring in their beds, and Miss Isobel was here. He could wish for nothing more.

Isobel remained in a sunny mood. She had managed to spoil the Chorleys' abhorrent scheme, Lord Ashbourne was on his way to Scotland to offer for Rose, and she was determined to steal a kiss from Prince Claudio before accepting her fate as Mrs Kirby or Mrs Fitch. Having—for now at least—given up fighting her mysterious *tendre* for the prince, it was astounding how it had spread through her, as if sunlight had penetrated every part of her. It seemed concentrated behind her breastbone, with a fierce glow that made everything in her life seem better.

As the servants laid out the cloths, she kept a subtle eye on the prince, willing him to approach. He had greeted them briefly in the initial melée, but she hoped he would return for a more meaningful conversation. *Yes!* Finally, he was heading in their direction.

Her heart skipped.

Soon I shall speak to him, and our eyes will meet again, and perhaps I will feel again what I felt in the hallway, when he said my name...

The sun was shining and life was good, and she was determined to avoid thinking of future storms. Today was today, and she would simply enjoy every moment.

The queen wished to sit with her ladies, and so Claudio had decided to make one more circuit of the gathered assembly, wondering if he might secure an invitation to join Miss Isobel and her family. Most of those present would probably welcome his company, not because of who he was, but because of *what* he was. Today, he wanted Miss Isobel and her companions to welcome him because he was *Claudio*, not because he was a prince. The notion was unsettling, challenging him to look more deeply into it, but for now he shoved it away.

In all directions cloths were being laid out, with elegant people of all ages and sizes arranging themselves on the ground. Lady Ashbourne and the two Misses Lennox were to his left, standing beneath the generous canopy of an oak tree as their servants made everything ready, but as he approached he saw that a gentleman had just joined them. His heart sank, for really he could not bear another half hour of hearing Mr Fitch—or had it been Kirby?—extolling the virtues of his horse.

He had, of course, already greeted them all, during that first frenzied ten minutes—Miss Isobel's dazzling smile seeming to be momentarily brighter than the sun. Aphrodite! he had thought again, recalling her effect on him the very first time he had laid eyes on her golden beauty.

Indeed he had greeted everyone bar the Chorleys, whom he had avoided—not precisely cutting them, but making it clear he was not inclined to welcome their company. Both mother and daughter were present today, and as he approached Lady Ashbourne and her party, he saw with horror that his path would take him directly towards Miss Chorley and her mother. Since their attempt to trap him into marriage in Lady Wright's library, he had had nothing but disdain for the pair of them but was well-bred enough not to give them the cut simply because they deserved it. Besides, a gentleman should never deliberately insult a lady. Briefly, his mind flicked to some of his previous encounters with Miss Isobel, generating a flash of shame.

What should I do?

He had only a moment to decide, for already he was near them.

'Your Highness.' The Chorley ladies curtsied, and he made his bow.

'Good day, ladies.' No enquiry after their health. No comment about the weather or the occasion. His words delivered in a hard tone. He moved on, satisfied, making for

Lady Ashbourne's area. To his great relief, the gentleman with them was neither Fitch nor Kirby, but—

'Garvald! Good to see you.' Pumping the man's hand with genuine pleasure, he realised that men like the earl, and Ashbourne, and Phillips—sober, sensible gentlemen—were becoming just as much his favourites as his drinking set.

Perhaps I should make the effort to get to know them better.

He made his greetings to everyone, then graciously accepted Lady Ashbourne's invitation to join them for luncheon—an invitation which seemed genuine. *Ah, yes,* he thought as he seated himself beside Miss Isobel, being careful not to sit on her skirts. *This is where I wished to be.*

Izzy was in alt.

This is heaven!

A beautiful summer's day, the joy of eating delicious food out of doors, and the best company. If only Rose had been here, it would have been perfect.

'May I offer you some of the beef, Miss Isobel?' Prince Claudio asked, his grey eyes meeting hers and sending a shiver of delight through her. Garvald was deep in conversation with Anna, and Lady Ashbourne was directing the servants at length about what further food to bring from the central area, where masses of shared food awaited. No one was paying any attention to Izzy and her prince.

'Yes, please.' She held out her plate, allowing her eyes to meet his and linger there. Instantly, breathing became difficult—or unimportant, perhaps. The only reality was his eyes on hers, his face so close… She swallowed, adding, 'Just a little, if you please.'

Watching as he served her, she studied the lines of his

face, the way his hair fell across his brow, his expression as he concentrated on the food…

Oh!

He looked up unexpectedly, and she gave him a sunny smile. He blinked, causing a wave of remorse to ache through her.

He is not used to pleasantness from me.

But things were different now. Following the incident with the Chorleys, there was now harmony between them. Dangerous harmony.

Dangerous?

Her heart quickened at her mind's use of such a powerful word.

Yes, dangerous.

To her peace of mind. And to her heart. For the first time she allowed herself to look forward to the day when she would be Mrs Whomever and he would marry his Prussian princess. Pain lanced through her, hot and fierce and searing. She gasped.

Concern flitted across his features. 'Isobel—Miss Isobel? You are unwell? May I be of assistance?'

'I am well, I assure you.' She took a breath. 'Indeed, I am *very* well at this moment.' Her look was intent.

He seemed to take her meaning. 'As am I.' His voice was low. 'Once you have eaten your fill, perhaps we could walk a short way together? These surroundings are idyllic.'

She nodded. 'I should like that.' *Like* it? She would love it above all things.

Sure enough, once a good half hour had passed, Garvald rose, helping Anna to her feet. The prince, a warm glint in his eye, performed the same service for Izzy, and their hands remained clasped just a moment too long.

Lady Ashbourne, a thoughtful expression on her kind

face, declined to go with them, stating she intended to find Lady Wright and Lady Jersey, if someone would help her to rise. And so the gentlemen offered her a strong hand each, and she made a breathless comment about enjoying the attentions of not one but two handsome young gentlemen. The two handsome young gentlemen exchanged a wry glance and assured her they were happy to be of service.

After seeing Lady Ashbourne off, the four of them—Izzy and Claudio, Anna and Garvald—strolled towards the tree-lined patch at the side of the hill. Just two ladies and two gentlemen, with the sun shining and nature sharing an abundance of delightful sights and aromas. No additional chaperones were needed, for who could object to a group of young people walking together in broad daylight?

Entering the blessed shade of the woods, Izzy resolved to fix the memory within her. The sound of birdsong. Sunlight shafting through gaps in the canopy, dappling the undergrowth here and there as if to say *Look here—foxgloves! Or here—wild garlic!* Some late bluebells were even dotted here and there, nestling amid the ferns with tenacious beauty. The scent of the garlic soon gave way to honeysuckle and hawthorn as they made their way through the woodland. Deliberately, Izzy noticed it, too.

But most of her attention was given to the man by her side. His height and strength. The way he moved. The way his arm felt beneath her gloved hand.

Anna and the Earl of Garvald were behind them, and frankly, Izzy wished them both at Jericho. If only they would vanish, she could perhaps contrive to get the kiss she craved. A kiss from a prince—just like in the old stories…

By unspoken agreement, Izzy and Prince Claudio maintained a brisk pace, allowing the others to fall behind a little. Still, Izzy felt watched. If she were to kiss the prince, she wanted no possibility of them being seen. Trapping him into an unwanted marriage was an abhorrent notion. It still made her shudder to think how appallingly the Chorleys had behaved. And as for poor Rose, she had undoubtedly kissed Ashbourne because she loved him, not because she wished to compromise him. Indeed, Rose had left London rather than force the viscount to offer for her. No, Izzy's wish was simple: one secret kiss from the prince before resigning herself to a life with Mr Kirby. Or the other one.

And Prince Claudio wanted to kiss her. She knew it with absolute certainty. From the way he looked at her. From her awareness of this thing—whatever it was—that thrummed between them.

Frustratingly, she could still hear Anna and her beau behind them and knew that the privacy she craved was not within her power to achieve. Still, the opportunity might not be entirely wasted. Here was the chance for private speech at least.

'Your Highness, I—'

'Please do not call me that.'

She eyed him quizzically. 'Then, what should I call you?'

He sighed. 'I should like you to call me Claudio…but that would cause a scandal, would it not?'

She nodded, her eyes dancing. 'Then, I shall call you Claudio when we are alone—and only then.'

Abruptly the air between them changed. 'Say it again!' Claudio's eyes were ablaze.

'Claudio.' She could barely breathe.

His gaze had dropped to her lips, and strangely, she could feel something there, almost as though he were touching her.

'Again!' he demanded.

'Claudio.' Her heart was pounding, her knees decidedly shaky, and her innards had melted in a most unexpected manner.

He groaned. 'To hear my own name on your lips… I have used your name a few times in error. Forgive me. But may I?'

She nodded. 'Isobel. Or Izzy, which is what my sisters call me.'

'Izzy.' He tried it, then shook his head. 'No. It has your fire, but Isobel is better. More romantical.'

'You think me romantical?'

'Most certainly. Romantical. And passionate. You live in your body in a way that many people do not, I think.'

The look that accompanied his words sent flames licking through her.

What is happening to me?

She swallowed, but for the moment words eluded her.

'You were saying…?' he prompted.

'Oh, yes. I was recalling the first time we met, and how much has changed since then.'

He frowned. 'My behaviour was not what it should have been. I apologise.'

'For what?'

'For causing you discomfort. I should not wish you any vexation or distress—no, not for an instant.'

His eyes blazed with intensity, and her heart melted.

He thinks me romantical, and yet I have never heard anything so romantical as the words he has just uttered.

Determined to try and conceal his effect on her—for it was both disconcerting and fascinating—she laughed lightly. 'I am no delicate flower, I assure you.'

He frowned. 'You are, and you are not. I see your beauty and your determination. I sense the strength within you. So maybe not a flower, then. Perhaps you are a tree in blossom.' He smiled. 'We have a special tree at home—*der Dorflinde*. You remind me of the *Dorflinde*, Isobel.'

'The village linden tree,' she translated.

He raised an eyebrow. 'You speak German?'

She confirmed it, adding—in his language, 'I have heard of linden trees, but I do not believe I have ever seen one.'

'But you speak German perfectly!' He shook his head. 'Honestly, I never expected to find—' He took a breath, continuing in a much more superficial tone, 'Lindens are not common here, I understand. Where I come from they are important. Strong, beautiful, and with the sweetest-scented blossom. Traditionally, courts were held under the protection of their branches.'

*What had he been going to say just now?*To find *what*?

Knowing she could not quiz him, she asked simply, 'Courts?'

'Yes, courts as in justice. But also courts as in courting.' He leaned closer, and her breath caught in her throat. 'There is even an old love poem called "Under der Linden".'

'Do you know it?'

Throwing him a challenge with her eyes, she hoped he would accept, as in this moment she wanted nothing more than to hear a love poem on his lips.

'"*Under der Linden*,"' he began, his voice deep and resonant, '"*an der Heide…*"'

She translated in her mind.

Under the linden, on the heather,
Where we two rested.
There you might find—beautiful together—
Pressed flowers and grass,
Beside the woods in the valley.

His voice tailed off, and her entire body was consumed with longing. In this moment she wished for nothing more than to find a secret place under a tree and lie there with him in the sunshine. Vaguely she knew she needed more than just his kiss but did not know exactly what. All she was certain of was that kissing him was *necessary.*

His mind seemed to have gone in a similar direction. 'That first day, I asked you for a kiss and you said no.'

'I did.' The entire world seemed to pause, as her attention remained riveted on him.

'And if I asked now?'

She swallowed. Now that he had said it, caution threatened to overwhelm her.

Remember what happened to Rose. Remember what the Chorleys tried.

'A kiss,' she began, 'may be thought to be more than a kiss.'

His brow was furrowed. 'I would not wish for anyone to misinterpret…'

Disappointment speared through her. He could not have made it plainer that he was offering nothing more than a kiss.

But that is all I am asking for, is it not?

She was all confusion.

She tried again. 'I mean to say, if someone saw a maiden kissing a gentleman, they might misinterpret what they were seeing.'

His brow cleared. 'Ah! I understand you. What the Chorleys tried was reprehensible, and I do not believe for an instant that you would ever attempt such a thing.'

'Indeed not!' she declared hotly. 'However, in this instance I was also referring to the need to protect the lady's reputation. She, too, might be compromised and forced into a marriage she did not desire.' Briefly her mind flicked to a couple of gentlemen she found abhorrent.

His eyes widened briefly. 'I see… I see.'

What? What does he see?

This conversation was not going as she expected. 'And so,' she continued with determination, 'a maiden should only kiss a gentleman if she wishes to, *and* if she can be certain they will not be observed. And since débutantes are never alone in company, I suspect it would be nigh on impossible.'

'But not hopeless!' He sent her a sideways glance, and a delicious shiver ran through her. 'There was some talk of a masquerade at Vauxhall…'

She gasped. 'I am shocked you would even suggest such a thing. Young ladies, I am informed, must never set foot in Vauxhall, which I am told is a place for all manner of vices.' She frowned. 'Not that I know *precisely* what they might be. But I am certain my sisters and I would never be permitted to visit such a place.'

'You must remember that I, too, am new to London. I did not intend to offend. Very well. No Vauxhall.' Placing his other hand over hers, he squeezed it gently. 'Then, I shall take this as a test of ingenuity. For, Miss Isobel Lennox, my wish to kiss you is unabated.'

Unable to speak, she simply nodded. Fire was blazing through her—a fire that needed his lips on hers.

'And your opinions? If they are unchanged, I shall endeavour not to speak more of this. But I believe—I hope—that perhaps you *do* now wish to kiss me?'

She took a breath. 'I do.' *There!* She had said it aloud, and to her it sounded like a vow.

Their eyes caught and held, depriving her of the power

of speech. Mutely, she nodded, and his eyes kindled again with desire. 'Isobel!'

Voices from behind reminded them both that this was neither the place nor the time. Grinding her teeth together, Isobel walked on, her entire body thrumming with frustration.

Chapter Ten

'And so, if I can find an opportunity, I am determined to kiss him. And nothing you can say can deter me from this, Anna!'

It was the morning after the trip to Greenwich. Izzy and Anna were ambling southwards through the Green Park, and Izzy's mind, body, and heart remained focused on Claudio.

'I shall not even try!' was Anna's response. 'I know you too well, Izzy.' She sighed. 'But be careful. Remember what happened to Rose.'

'All may yet be well with Rose. Ashbourne intends to offer for her, as you know.'

'That is true, and she may accept him. But Rose went away because she did not wish to *force* him to offer for her. I would not wish for you to face the same fate.'

Izzy shuddered. 'Decidedly not! Which is why I must not kiss him unless I am certain we will not be discovered.' Her eyes danced with glee. 'It will be such an adventure, to kiss a man!'

'Especially to kiss a prince! But tell me, is this simply an adventure to you? Or are you… Do you still feel…?

'I still have a *tendre* for him, if that is what you are asking. Indeed, it seems to be going deeper and deeper into me.' She frowned. 'It is most disconcerting, but it feels as though he is *part* of me. Is that not odd?'

'Izzy, I hate to be the one to say this to you, but the chances of a prince marrying a lady with a small dowry and no known parents—'

'It is impossible. I know it! But I have quite given up hope that we shall ever discover the truth about our parents. Without knowing who Mama was, my quest to discover the identity of our papa cannot even begin.' She shrugged. 'I am entirely resigned to being an unsuitable bride for anyone of consequence. Which is why all I want from the prince is a kiss. Just one kiss, and then I shall tie myself to Mr Kirby or Mr Fitch and be perfectly content with my life.'

Anna looked dubious at this, and so Izzy pressed on along the flower-bedecked path, changing the subject. 'I do hope we hear from Rose soon. Not knowing is killing me!'

Thankfully, her sister allowed the conversation to be diverted, and as they continued through the park towards the Buckingham House gardens, Izzy was conscious that she was steering them towards the mansion where Claudio even now was resting. Claudio. Not Prince Claudio. Just… Claudio.

They would not see him, she knew. Despite that one morning when they had met him in the park, Izzy knew that gentlemen invariably stayed out late and rose even later. But to know that her feet were even now taking her closer to where he was? That was enough.

Claudio woke, turned over in his comfortable bed, and stretched. Once again, he had returned home early. Once again, he was awake at a time more suited to his life back in his father's principality, rather than the late hours held by the *ton*. Rejecting the uncomfortable notion that this meant he did not belong here, he rose, making straight for the window.

Isobel. For the hundredth time he went over in his mind the events of yesterday. His name on her lips. The way she had looked at him.

She wants to kiss me!

The thought made him feel like a colossus, a god, a king. He, who had enjoyed kisses and more from many a woman, had never before felt so…so *überwältigt*!

No English word would do, but he tried them out. *Overwhelmed. Dazzled. Astonished. Overpowered. Defeated.* She was everything, and he was overcome by her. Aphrodite? Yes, and more. Never had he known anything like the frustrated desire which was these days his constant companion.

And alongside his body's frustrations, Isobel had also left his mind in turmoil. Last night while out with his friends he had been too distracted to be fully part of their usual pattern of cards and wine, inane raillery giving way to ribald buffoonery as the night progressed. He had left, discontented and distracted. Because of the war raging within him. A battle between euphoric confidence and crippling doubt.

Despite wanting to kiss him, Isobel had made it crystal clear that she would not want to be trapped into marriage with him. A lady might be 'forced into a marriage she did not desire', she had said. Yet Lady Kelgrove had told him Isobel and her sisters needed to marry.

It made no sense unless, somehow, Isobel had seen through his princely regalia. Seen the unworthiness beneath. Seen that he was a fraud. Born to royalty, yet never having earned his position. Drinking, gambling, sporting… She had depth, and energy, and *purpose*, somehow. Yes, he knew she was a lady, limited by her sex and her class just as much as he, yet she seemed *whole*. Sure of who she was.

She would kiss him but not marry him. So…

A motion below in the gardens caught his eye. Two women had just appeared, turning a corner to enter into the pretty wildness below his window. In an instant he took in the details—embroidered muslin gowns, parasols—ladies! He looked closer, noting slim figures, identical golden locks…it could only be Isobel and her sister. Transfixed, he stood frozen, trying to discern their features. No. They were as yet too far away. The gowns! The maiden on the left wore a muslin printed with tiny blue flowers. The other? His heart leapt. Yellow flowers—the motif in her signature hue.

Isobel!

Had he conjured her up through his intense thoughts and feelings?

It all had taken only a few seconds. Now, with dawning horror, he realised he had been observed. As one, the sisters' hands flew to their mouths in shock.

Instantly, he dived back, leaning against the wall beside the window, his breathing shallow and his heart pounding. He was naked, and Isobel had *seen* him. His body, belatedly reacting, had begun to respond in a predictable manner, but his mind was spinning. *She is here!* What should he do?

Reluctantly, he acknowledged that by the time he had dressed and ventured outdoors she would be long gone. And besides, he had to hope that he had not been recognised. They had been far enough away that he had been unable to divine their features, so hopefully they had not divined his. Yes, surely they could not know it was him? His mind was awhirl. Golden Aphrodite in golden sunshine.

And it is me she wants to kiss.

* * *

Still idly chatting, Izzy and Anna entered the pretty gardens around Buckingham House. Members of the *ton* were always welcome there, the queen being relaxed about such matters, and the gardens were one of Izzy's favourite walks. The fact that *he* was there, sleeping somewhere nearby, simply provided an added thrill.

'I cannot believe the Season will end soon,' Anna was saying, 'for it seems like only yesterday that we arrived!'

'I know what you mean, and yet it also seems as though we have been here for an age,' Izzy offered thoughtfully. 'So much has happened—'

She froze, the thought lost, for movement at one of the first-floor windows had caught her eye. There, right in front of them, completely naked, was a man. Young, strong, and well-proportioned, he stood there as if greeting the day and seemed unaware of their presence. Even as her eyes widened and her hand flew to her mouth in shock, Izzy had recognised him. It was Prince Claudio, she was certain of it. Fair hair, the right height and build, and more…she *knew* him. Between her artist's eye and her smitten heart, she knew it could be no other.

'Oh, my goodness!' Anna sounded as shocked as Izzy felt. As they watched, Claudio abruptly moved away from the window, perhaps realising he could be seen. 'That man was naked!'

'He was.' Izzy could not help but giggle a little. 'The first naked man I have ever seen in the flesh.'

And entirely fitting it should be him.

'Why, have you seen other naked men?'

Izzy snorted. 'Of course! Now, do not look at me like that. My study of art has led me to peruse the great masters of painting and sculpture. You also must have also seen reproductions of Michelangelo's *David.* And what of all those classical paintings?'

'The paintings,' Anna replied primly, 'usually have a fig leaf or drape of fabric to hide the, er…'

Izzy chuckled. 'No fig leaf today, that is for certain.' She adopted a thoughtful tone. 'And I am not sure a fig leaf would be adequate to the task. It was much larger than the ones I have seen on classical statues. The shape of it was most interesting, do you not think? The way it—'

Anna clapped her hands to her ears, half laughing. 'Stop! No, it was *not* interesting, Izzy! Indeed as gently born maidens we must never let it be known that we have seen such a thing!'

'Ah, that is a shame, for really it was fascinating to see how it nestled there, amid—'

'No more!' Anna turned. 'I want to go back home now. If one of the queen's hedonistic sons wishes to parade around naked, then that, I suppose, is his privilege. But I do not have to look at his—at *him*, I mean!'

Izzy took this in good humour, inwardly relieved for Claudio's sake that Anna had not recognised him. 'Oh, very well. But you must admit that what we saw was a fine specimen of manhood.'

'Do you mean the man? Or his—?' She shook her head, laughing outright. 'Now you have me joining you in this madness, Izzy. Lord, who would have thought moving to London would expose us to such an education!'

'But we must always be ready to learn, Anna. Lady Kelgrove has the right of it, you know.'

'Why? What is her view?'

'She often says that young ladies should be taught about such matters—the marital bed, childbirth, topics that no one will speak about to us. We have brains for thinking, too, and are not such fragile creatures that we would swoon from hearing the truth!'

'But how can you know you would not swoon, when you do not know the truth?' retorted Anna, with inescapable logic.

'If Rose marries the viscount, we could ask her! For she would surely tell us.'

'You know,' said Anna slowly, 'that is not the worst idea you have ever had, Izzy!'

On they went, jesting and teasing one another, while inwardly Izzy saved every detail of the memory and allowed her pulse and thudding heart to gradually return to normal. Claudio in all his glory had had a profound effect on her and would not be forgotten.

An hour later, having washed, dressed, and broken his fast, Claudio strode down the ornate hallway in Buckingham House to the queen's quarters, determination in every nerve and sinew. The queen was a female relative. Surely she could advise him? Having been admitted to her suite, he was disappointed to find her surrounded by her ladies, and with at least three servants standing mutely to the side in case they should be needed. After a frustrating half hour he finally suggested a walk in the gardens, and to his relief she agreed.

Her retinue accompanied them, of course, but he was able to walk with her a little ahead of the others. If he kept his voice low, then he should be able to speak freely. The problem was he now was unsure of what to say. The queen, seemingly oblivious to his dilemma, prattled on about the weather, the gardens, her dog, while pausing frequently to deadhead roses and geraniums as she passed.

'I was speaking to Lady Kelgrove yesterday. She adores the Lennox girls,' declared Her Majesty in a casual manner.

'She does?' Strangely, for a man of four-and-twenty, abruptly Claudio felt like a boy caught stealing sweetmeats from the kitchen.

She sent him a sideways glance. 'Out with it, Claudio! You might as well tell me. Is it Miss Isobel?' She frowned. 'Or the Chorley creature?'

'I…' Feeling as though he should not admit this, he sought refuge in generalities. 'I cannot say. But…you are a woman.'

'I am.' A gleam of humour lit her eye.

Persisting despite deep discomfort, he managed to continue. 'I seek counsel from you. Wisdom, if you are content to share it. About how the minds of women work.'

'Ah, the eternal question from men. But you intrigue me! What is your specific question?'

He squared his shoulders. 'How should a man respond to a woman—say, a young lady—who indicated she would welcome a kiss but would not welcome marriage?'

The queen chuckled. 'Not Miss Chorley, then! Very well. A man should *admire* such a lady even more than he already does. Let me ask a question of you, Claudio. Have you ever wished to—er—kiss a girl and *not* wished to marry her?'

Dozens of times.

'Well, yes. But—'

'But nothing. Women are not so different to men, after all.'

'But young ladies, *débutantes*…?'

'What? Did you think they would all take one look at your princely title and swoon at your feet?' She harrumphed at the notion. 'A true lady is not blinded by such things as titles or parentage. A true prince ought to be the same.'

Her words pierced him like arrows. So it was possible

for ladies—like gentlemen—to want kisses only, with no hope for marriage? Well, naturally, he knew that there were many such women—widows, willing servants. Had he not enjoyed bed sport with many of them? But the Marriage Mart was such an important enterprise for young ladies of the *ton*, it was strange to acknowledge that a débutante such as Miss Isobel might not wish to marry him.

'Did you think,' the queen continued, briskly pulling dead flowers from a rosebush, 'that because Miss Chorley tried to entrap you, Miss Isobel Lennox would do the same?' She sent him a keen glance. 'No, she has too much strength of character for such a trick. And furthermore, she is too open, too *honest*. One knows exactly who she is after just a few minutes in her company. My advice? Kiss the girl, and enjoy it. But do not *think* of compromising her, or you shall have me to answer to!'

'I should not dream of it!' he retorted. 'Not that I would not *wish* to, but I myself am not ready for marriage, and so...'

'You are nearer to readiness than you realise' was her response, 'but I am glad to hear you are more honourable than my own sons, who have struggled to give me a legitimate grandchild between them, despite their tomcatting.'

He did not take the bait, instead diverting the conversation to her social engagements. 'I know you do not often host large events, but I had heard that young ladies are not permitted to attend Vauxhall, so I wondered if perhaps—'

'Ha! You seek my assistance in creating opportunities! Very well, I shall plan a light masquerade—a *bal masqué*—but no more than kisses, mind! And you shall assist me. But do not get found out!'

He agreed with alacrity, expressing his gratitude in forthright terms.

She patted his hand. 'It will do you good, you know.'

'What will?'

'Having to woo her properly.'

'But I have no intention of wooing any lady! I am too young for marriage.'

If I could have only one kiss from Isobel, then I would be satisfied.

'You may believe so, but that does not make it true. Now, about this masquerade ball, let us plan it together.' She chuckled. 'I shall be a demanding queen and require all the ladies to wear white, even the older ones. Or wear a rosebud, perhaps…' Ruthlessly, she pulled a wilted flower from its stem, discarding it. 'Let me think… The gardens, naturally. A civilised version of Vauxhall…*not* a ridotto, of course. Everyone must behave with propriety… Half masks, white for the ladies, black for the gentlemen…'

'Excuse me, miss. My lady has need of you.'

Izzy looked at the maid blankly. Having positioned herself so that her small easel was facing away from the door, thankfully any servant entering her chamber would not be able to see the shocking image that Izzy had been sketching for the past two hours. Ostensibly a study of da Vinci's *Vitruvian Man*, in reality her inspiration was the glorious sight she had seen earlier.

'Hmmm?'

'In the drawing room, miss.' She paused. 'There are letters lately arrived. Something from the palace. And letters from Scotland.'

Now Izzy was attending. 'From Scotland?' She rose, closing her sketchbook. 'I shall come at once! Thank you, Mary.'

Hurrying to the drawing room, her mind was racing.

The information in those letters was important not just for Rose but for all three of them—Lady Ashbourne, too.

'What news?' she asked breathlessly, entering the drawing room, at the same time taking in the expression of delight on Lady Ashbourne's kind face. Anna was there, too, and currently engaged in reading a letter. Further missives—unopened—sat on the low table beside Lady Ashbourne.

'They are to marry! Which I must say I *knew* just as soon as I saw my nephew's determination on the day he decided to follow her. Travelling all the way to Scotland. And in the old coach, too! No, it was more than duty or a sense of honour. He loves her, and I knew it in here!' She tapped her generous bosom. 'Anna, show her!'

Anna handed her the letter, a tremulous smile on her face. 'Oh, Izzy, it is true! He says they are to marry in Elgin—and look at the date! They are already married by now!'

My dearest aunt...

Izzy read the letter, her eyes flying over the viscount's words.

Delighted...
My affections are returned...
Truly happy...

'How wonderful! A love match!' Izzy picked up the other letters. 'This one is for us, Anna. From Rose!'

The final letter, from Mr Marnoch, was addressed to Lady Ashbourne, and so Izzy handed it to her.

Rose was just as delighted as the viscount, it seemed, and her sisters were left in no doubt about her feelings for her now-husband. All three ladies expressed their joy, read each of the letters multiple times, and even—it had to be admitted—shed a few happy tears.

Having called for tea to settle her exalted nerves, Lady Ashbourne shared another missive with them. On top of the wonderful news of the recent nuptials, they were also invited to a masquerade ball at Buckingham House.

'The queen's ball is likely to be the event of the Season,' she declared. 'I suspect Her Majesty has waited until now in order to ensure it is the last major event before Season's end.'

Season's end. Must I accept a proposal that night?

The thought was lowering. Refusing to allow such a shadow to discourage her on a day of such happy news, Izzy responded brightly. 'It says all ladies must wear white. Our court gowns will be perfect! I still love the beading, the way it catches the light. I had begun remaking mine, but perhaps we should ask the dressmaker to adjust—?'

'Oh, no!' Lady Ashbourne looked horrified. 'You cannot attend a ball in a made-over dress!' She grew thoughtful. 'And something else. I am minded to keep the news of James and Rose's wedding to ourselves for now, my dears.'

'But why?' Izzy wanted to shout from the rooftops about her sister's joy. 'Is it—I mean, since we do not know about our parentage, will this marriage harm the Ashbourne reputation?'

'Lord, no! A good marriage is the making of all of you, my dears. My nephew has shown that he values Rose's *character* above her *name*—or lack of it—and so, if we handle this correctly, we may silence those who would criticise you… But the handling is important. Yes, I think it best if we allow James and Rose to make their own announcement once back in London. And besides,' she chuckled, 'will it not be delightful to hold such a wonderful secret to ourselves for a little while?'

'I suppose,' replied Izzy doubtfully. They had to trust Lady Ashbourne's superior knowledge of the *ton*. Still, at least Rose was happy. That was the most significant part of all of this.

Chapter Eleven

In truth there was something delicious about holding such a secret, Izzy had to admit, as she dressed for the Queen's Masquerade Ball, ten days later. Rose was happy, and being sister-in-law to a viscount might serve to counter some of the criticism levelled at Izzy and Anna for their unknown parentage.

True to Lady Ashbourne's request, Izzy had not breathed a word about Rose and the viscount to anyone. It had been difficult at times to resist the temptation, particularly when people like Lady Renford and Mrs Thaxby continued to adopt a sneering tone towards her. The Chorleys, thankfully, continued to give her a wide berth—unlike the prince, who was decidedly showing her some marked attention.

In one sense their conversations were perfectly innocuous—they discussed books, and philosophy, and politics, as well as history, and even a little gossip. She found him to have a well-formed mind, quite at odds with his hedonistic friends, who could discuss nothing but sport and fashion. But there was more: deeper conversations where they allowed each other to see something of their true selves. He told her of his upbringing, and she shared with him something of her life in Elgin.

I know him now.

It had become a habit for him to sit with her, dance with her, or walk with her at whatever events they both attended, and he also had slipped into a pattern of asking her plans for the next day—she knowing that, unless promised elsewhere, he would endeavour to attend the same events.

'Oh, miss, you look beautiful,' Mary cooed, fastening the final tiny buttons on Izzy's white satin gown. It had been fashioned from the masses of fabric from her court gown, Izzy having taken the scissors to it herself, sewing it into the more modern straight silhouette. Lady Ashbourne had had to be persuaded, deploring made-over gowns as a sign of poverty. However, given the queen's decree that all ladies irrespective of age must wear white to her ball, she had reluctantly conceded that the glittering, beaded fabric could not be bettered. Also, she had mused, it did no harm to remind society of the Belles' success at their presentation.

With this in mind she had once again loaned Anna and Izzy the same diamond tiaras as they had worn at court, this time without the feather and lappet headdress. The effect, Izzy acknowledged, was delightful. Raising a gloved hand, she touched the glittering tiara reverently.

'Thank you. Now I just need my fan. Lady Ashbourne said earlier that she has our masks.'

Having accepted the fan from Mary, she glided downstairs, feeling decidedly princess-like. Anna arrived a few moments later, followed by Lady Ashbourne and her maid, a cluster of masques clutched in her ladyship's hand.

'Girls, you look delightful!' Smoothing her own gown, she added, 'It has been an age since I wore white, but I must say I like it! We matrons are not normally afforded the opportunity. Now, take one of these each, and try them.'

Izzy took a half mask, allowing Lady Ashbourne's personal maid to tie the strings behind her head, then rearranging her coiffure to cover them. The masks were of white satin to match their gowns and were lavishly decorated with embroidery, beads, and feathers. No sooner had Izzy donned the mask than she felt *different.* Yes, anyone who saw them together must realise they were looking at two of the Lennox girls, but there was a certain freedom provided by assumed anonymity that sent the excitement of *possibility* thrumming in Izzy's veins.

I feel daring!

Which of course was exactly why young ladies were not normally permitted to attend masked balls at Vauxhall. The combination of anonymity and dark alleyways had led to many a young lady being compromised. A shiver ran down Izzy's spine at the very notion. No, she had no intention of being compromised or even ravished—whatever that involved. But tonight she had every intention of kissing a prince.

Following the others out to the carriage, Izzy was unsurprised to see clear skies and a glorious sunset. Tonight would be perfect. She just knew it.

Claudio stepped through the glazed doors and onto the western terrace, drawn by the golden rays of the setting sun. The stage was set. All around, the queen's servants were making the final arrangements for tonight's masked ball—tables, chairs, floral displays... Soon the flambeaux would be lit, and over the next hour darkness would fall, slowly, gently, cloaking them in invisibility. His black half mask dangled from his hand, the metal beading reflecting the evening glow.

Making one final tour, he declared himself content. Organising the ball with the queen and her staff had been strangely satisfying—a reminder of the duties he had chafed at in his father's court.

I missed this—being purposeful.

If tonight's ball was a success, then he could justly claim some responsibility. The notion pleased him.

'Your Highness.' A breathless page was hurrying towards him. 'The queen desires your presence. The first guests are arriving.'

'Very well.' Securing his mask, he made his way back inside to the large reception room where the queen would receive her guests and where they would be served with food and drink. The musicians were already outside on the terrace, the dancing area a cleared square of ground below. On three sides there were walkways which, as soon as darkness fell, would no doubt be used by intrepid couples seeking the cover of darkness. With a little luck and ingenuity, he was determined to be among them, Isobel by his side. And then…

'Claudio!' Arrayed in white and gold, the queen allowed him to kiss her hand. 'I am so glad you asked me to do this. I declare I have not been so entertained in an age!' As she spoke, the doors opened, the major-domo announcing the first guests, and Claudio prepared himself to greet them one and all. It being a masquerade, none gave their true names, but instead used pseudonyms such as Madame Incognita and Lord Inconnu. When two golden-haired beauties accompanied by an older matron finally arrived, his attention was transfixed.

'I am Lady Hera,' declared the matron, 'and these are my charges, Athene and Aphrodite.' She indicated with a hand which was which. Athene made a polite curtsy, while Aphrodite… Hunger flashed in Aphrodite's blue eyes as she glanced at him, before she adopted a more acceptable expression. *Lord!*

'Ah,' said the queen. 'No doubt Artemis is off on a hunt, is she not?'

'Indeed, Your Majesty,' replied Lady Ashbourne. 'But we do believe she will return before long.'

As the queen and her friend spoke further of Rose, Athene-Anna joining in, Claudio stepped off the dais, extending a hand. 'Fair Aphrodite! Will you dance with me?'

She dipped her head. 'I shall, Lord—' She tilted her head questioningly.

'Tonight, I believe I must be Ares, God of War and Aphrodite's one true love.'

Taking his hand, she curtsied gracefully. 'Ares,' she breathed. 'Ares the valiant.'

Lady Ashbourne and her charges were the last guests to arrive, and so together Ares and Aphrodite walked across the room, lost in a sea of masked revellers. The air was feverish, the company enjoying, it seemed, the freedom of privacy in a crowd. Outside the last rays of the setting sun sent warmth across dancers and musicians alike. A quadrille was already underway, and so Claudio stood with his Aphrodite to await the next dance, talking softly and savouring the moment. Tonight, if she remained willing, he would find a way.

Izzy closed her eyes briefly, savouring the warmth of the setting sun on her face, the warmth of his strong arm sensed through her glove and his jacket. Like all of the gentlemen, he wore black, with white knee breeches, a snowy cravat, and a waistcoat of white and gold. Mr Brummel had long held that gentlemen should wear only black coats in the evening, and tonight Izzy could only agree with him.

Claudio looked dangerous, other-worldly, enticing… To her he had never looked better—apart from the fact she could only see the bottom half of his face. Still, this held unexpected benefits, for her gaze was constantly drawn to his lips. How had she never noticed before how perfect they were? Their colour, their shape—the lower lip full and beautifully carved, the contrast between the strong angles of his jaw and the soft curves of his lips causing the most delicious flutterings within her.

Turning his head, he looked at her, his eyes glittering behind his mask. Leaning towards her, he murmured in her ear, 'If you keep looking at me like that, then I shall kiss you right here in front of everyone!'

She caught her breath. 'No, you must not!'

He laughed. 'Of course I shall not! Not here, leastways. After dark.' The promise in his voice sent a shiver through her.

They danced la Boulangere together—a perfectly civil undertaking—and yet Izzy had never been more conscious of him. His warmth beside her, the hunger in his gaze each time he looked at her… Honestly, the anticipation of his kiss was the most delicious sensation she had ever experienced. And since the reality might turn out to be something of a let-down, she could not imagine sharing spittle with another person to be in any way pleasing—then *this* was the moment of peak enjoyment. This was the moment she must remember forever.

At the end of the dance he saluted her, his lips pressed to her satin glove. 'Until later, my Aphrodite,' he murmured softly, and her lips curved in response.

'I look forward to it!' she declared boldly, locking her gaze with his. With satisfaction, she heard him catch his breath, but before he had time to say more she spun away.

Nearby a lone figure stood scanning all of the dancers, his left hand playing with a signet ring on his right. She shuddered, walking in the opposite direction.

Tonight I can avoid my dull suitors was her gleeful thought as she dived into the crowd.

Two hours later supper was served inside, and Izzy made a show of putting a few things on her plate, though in reality she was too agitated for food. Her pulse was tumultuous, her attention fragmented, and she—like many others—was constantly scanning the crowd to try to figure out who was whom. Except in her case, she was looking for a specific man: blond hair, tall, strong form, wearing a waistcoat of white and gold. She had seen him a few times after their dance, dancing, sipping wine, or conversing with a gentleman or lady.

But tonight he is mine!

Fierceness rose within her as she imagined claiming him in front of everyone, wrapping herself around him and feeling his arms tighten about her. Yes, she would claim him tonight—just not in public. Smiling, she turned to respond to the plump matron beside her, agreeing that the queen had outdone herself with such a marvellous event.

Aphrodite and Athene were everywhere—and nowhere. Yet they had not, Claudio noticed, stood together. Not even once. This was highly unusual, for the Belles often gravitated towards each other at events. Chuckling inwardly at Isobel's ingenuity, he realised that most people could have no clue which of the slim, white-clad maidens held the surname Lennox. Fair hair, tiara, identical masks and gowns, yet never together at once, revealing who they were. If any of the guests had been trying to keep track of them, it would have been almost impossible, since no one could say at any time which of them they were seeing, or even whether they were looking at one of the triplets.

Yet he knew. The tiaras were different. And she even *walked* differently to her sister, her movements always purposeful, always fired by the restless curiosity within her. Vitality. Spirit. *Lebenskraft.* Truly, he had never known anyone like her.

There she is!

His heart leapt as he spotted her, seated at a supper table and making conversation with a plump lady next to her. Keeping her in view he seated himself at a nearby table, noting that outside it was now fully dark. After supper he would make his move.

'Excuse me.' Rising, Izzy left the supper table, making her way to the ladies' retiring room as it was likely to be quiet just now. In fact it was entirely empty apart from the serving maids stationed there to assist with toilette or sewing repairs, all the ladies currently engaged in enjoying the delicious supper provided by the queen. Emerging afterwards, she felt her heart leap as she saw a familiar figure walking towards her. Prince Claudio!

'Hail, golden Aphrodite!' His voice was soft as he invoked their first meeting, back in a hallway in Grantham.

This time she allowed her eyes to smile. 'Hail, Lord Ares.' She had reached him, and he stood stock-still in the centre of the deserted hall. 'Now will you let me pass?'

He remembered, too. 'First, a kiss!'

She caught her breath. 'Here? Now?' Someone might come upon them at any moment. Reluctantly, she shook her head. 'Too dangerous.'

'I agree. I shall meet you at the statue of Hermes in a few minutes. Do you know where that is?'

She nodded. She knew every corner of the royal garden. The statue of Hermes was at the very end of a shady path, perfect for a dangerous encounter.

'Very well—but only a kiss, mind!'

He chuckled. 'As I mentioned previously, your manner often reminds me of the queen. Strong women, both of you. I like that.' Stepping back, he motioned for her to pass, and this time she deliberately brushed against him as she did so, enjoying the shocking feeling of his warm body against hers.

He had not moved, and she refused to look back, simply relishing the picture she had in her mind's eye of him frozen there in the hallway.

I did that to him.

The sense of power was heady, intoxicating.

Without pausing she walked straight through the supper room to the terrace beyond, looking neither left nor right. Straight through the dancing area she glided, feeling as though she were truly Aphrodite, with the power to turn men's heads and leave them longing for her. Well, it seemed to be true of one man, at least. And he a prince!

Calmly, elegantly, she moved gracefully down the dimly-lit path, the velvety darkness enveloping her in a warm cloak. On either side, small flambeaux lighted the way, the gaps between them enveloped in inky darkness. Reaching the statue, she stepped off the path into the shade of the hedge, concealing herself there lest someone else appear unexpectedly. Now all she had to do was wait.

She lifted her eyes to the heavens. A thousand stars twinkled approvingly towards her—a diadem of stars, a cascade, a shower of silver light. As her eyes adjusted to the darkness, she saw that there were not a thousand stars. Ten thousand, a hundred thousand, a *million* stars—and all of them combining to provide exactly the right amount of light, strong enough to see him, gentle enough to protect them from prying eyes.

Her breath caught, for her ear had detected the sound of someone approaching. She watched him approach, every step confirming the familiarity of his shape, his gait. He passed a flambeau and she briefly saw his face, that jawline she had sketched so many times. Might she, tonight, touch his face, learn it as best she could through gloved fingers?

He had arrived. As he turned his head left and right she stepped forwards, feeling as though this one step was the most daring action she had ever taken.

Their eyes met, his glittering in the dimness of the night, and she shook with the power of his gaze.

What is this thing between us?

No words were exchanged between them. Instead he walked to her, took her hand, and kissed it. As if reading her mind he placed her hand on his cheek, and she thrilled to feel the warmth of his skin through the fine fabric of her glove. His own right hand continued upwards, his knuckle caressing her chin, her jaw, her cheek. Now he was trailing his fingertips over her face to her ear, and she gasped as a sudden sensation ran through her. Skin on skin. With his hands on her face and her hand touching his, she hardly knew what sensation to listen to most closely. Of its own volition her other hand came up, and finally she traced his beloved jaw, his cheekbones, every moment a miracle of discovery.

Now his thumb was tracing her lower lip, and she gasped as the movement brought her insides to life in a novel, unexpected, and entirely delightful manner. Leaning closer, he nuzzled her face with his, and she responded, enjoying the sensation: the warmth of his breath, the silkiness of his skin interrupted by rough stubble in places. *My, how thrilling!* Never had she experienced anything like it. She knew only that she wanted his lips on hers, wanted it more than she had ever wanted anything in her life.

Being Izzy, she did not hesitate but boldly moved her face to align her lips with his. A surprised groan sounded in his throat, making Izzy's knees somehow soften. Afraid she might swoon—not something she was prepared to accept—she slid her hands to his shoulders as she had during their waltz, even as he slanted his head a little, moving his lips on hers. She gasped, and suddenly she was in his arms, her body pressed to his and his arms encircling her so tightly she could feel the buttons on his waistcoat. And either he had something unexpected in his breeches, or his manhood was significantly larger than when she had seen him naked at the window. A delicious hardness was pressing into her nether regions, and even as his lips moved on hers, his hips swivelled a little, making her gasp again. This time he was ready, and his tongue darted into her parted lips, connecting with hers and adding to the maelstrom of sensation pulsing through her.

Lost, she kissed him with all the passion that was in her. She would devour him, and he her, and together they would die of bliss. Desperately, she pulled at her gloves, managing to wrench one off, and now her hand could enjoy even more: fistfuls of his hair, the smooth skin of his neck, his strong back and shoulders… It was for this that she had been born. This man. This kiss.

His hands were roving now, releasing her a little to sweep across her breasts, cupping, squeezing. Boldly he swept a hand inside her bodice, exposing a nipple to the cool night air. Shocked, she could only close her eyes as he rubbed his thumb over it, backwards and forwards until she thought she might die from pleasure. But she knew nothing, for a moment later he replaced his thumb with his mouth, at the same time hitching up her skirts to caress her bottom with his bare hands. Entirely undone, all she could do now was cling to him and try to remain upright.

Now he was upright again, and her legs felt cool air all around, and his hands on her bottom were pressing her to him, closer, closer as they kissed again, feverishly, fervently.

Once more he groaned, taking his hips away and releasing her skirts, leaving her bereft. In vain did she thrust her own hips forwards, but he was evasive.

'Hush,' he murmured. 'Hush, my Aphrodite. We cannot.' His arms were around her again, and their chests were connecting, but his hands were no longer enticing and inciting her to madness. Now they moved up and down her back in soothing strokes, his lips on her cheek, her jaw, her lips—featherlight kisses that ached with tenderness.

Tears started in Izzy's eyes. She, who *never* cried! It was all so much, so beautiful. Truly, this moment was for her life-changing, and her heart knew it.

'Ah, hush now, *Liebling*,' he said, kissing her tears. '*Alles ist gut*.'

All is well. Is it, though?

A fleeting thought, lost almost before it had appeared.

'I should not have—this was supposed to be only a kiss.' He shook his head. 'At least I stopped before… I apologise, Isobel.'

'No!' She put a finger on his lips. 'Do not apologise, Claudio, for that was truly wonderful.'

She felt him smile. 'Do you know—' he kissed her fingers '—that this night is for you? Only for you?'

Confused, she could not answer.

'The stars, the darkness, the ball itself. You are the goddess at the centre of it all. There is magic in you, for you have bewitched me.'

His kisses slowed, then stopped. They simply stood there, wrapped in one another's arms. Izzy had never in her life known such happiness.

'We should go back.' She voiced what they both knew. 'If we stay too long we might be missed.'

'And of course you would not want that.' Was it her imagination, or was there a hint of hardness in his voice? Trying to read him was impossible, for there was not enough light for such subtleties.

'No. And the ball is not only for us—for me. There are over a hundred people there who believe it is for them as much as anyone.'

'But it was I who asked the queen for a masquerade… for you, Isobel.'

She swallowed, lifting her face to his. 'Truly?'

'And now I must kiss you again, for how can I resist when you look at me so?'

He was as good as his word, and once more Izzy lost herself in him, now poignantly aware that this was ending, and that she would never know anything like it again. Ever.

Eventually they had to stop, and Izzy steadied herself before going back to the ball, Claudio waiting a few minutes before himself returning. He had replaced her glove, kissing her hand front and back before he did so. She could still feel the imprint of his lips in her left palm, and closed her fingers protectively, as if to keep it there for all time.

Making for the refreshments area, she took a glass of punch, made brief conversation with a couple of masked ladies, then went with them back to the dance floor. As she went through the performance—dancing, talking, going home in the carriage—she was aware that she was no longer truly present, for her soul remained in that other world, the world of his lips, his arms, his words. The world of the stars and the velvety darkness and the enchantment. Soon enough, she knew, reality would intrude, but until then she would hold onto the magic for as long as she could.

Chapter Twelve

'Well? Did you get your kiss?' The queen's gaze pierced Claudio uncomfortably, and he stammered an answer in the affirmative. Her servants were nearby but hopefully would not understand their conversation in German.

'Hmph!' she declared inelegantly. 'Well, I must say it was worth it for me, regardless. My ball was an undoubted hit!'

This was safer ground. 'Indeed, it was! Everyone seemed to enjoy it prodigiously.'

'I am surprised you noticed, Claudio, for you seemed to have eyes only for Miss Lennox. Do not think I did not perceive it!' She patted his hand. 'I approve, by the way. A most suitable choice, for I care not that her parents are unconfirmed. She is clearly a well-brought-up young lady…and with enough fire in her to manage you, Claudio!' She chuckled at her own wit. 'Miss Isobel's character shows her breeding, and your fascination with her shows that you see it, too.'

'But I have not made any choice! As I have said before, I am too young to even consider—'

'You are four-and-twenty, Claudio,' she said firmly. 'Most ladies are married with little ones at that age. And if more gentlemen were sensible enough to find a good woman and settle into marital harmony at four-and-twenty, then the *ton* should be a happier group!' She sighed. 'My own dear husband was but two-and-twenty when we wed, and I have observed that marriages where the couple are both young to start with do remarkably well. You grow together, you see.'

He frowned in puzzlement. 'Then, you do not believe there is a requirement for the man to be…' he sought the right words '…fully formed?'

She snorted. 'Absolutely not! The requirements are simply two things: affinity and constancy—or passion and purpose, if you prefer. Knowing oneself fully and understanding the other person—those take a lifetime.'

Loath to argue, he simply let it go, but her words sat uncomfortably with him, for in truth they strengthened an uncertainty now raging within him. Was he truly too young to wed? What if he married, then regretted it?

Instantly denial blazed within him. He could not imagine regretting marrying Isobel. She was…she was everything. But he himself was a part-formed thing, unsure of himself, who he was, where his future lay. What if the hedonistic side of him came to dominate?

Eldon—despite his predilection for bed sport—had never married, nor had Hawkins, whom Claudio had never seen truly sober. He shuddered.

Is that my future?

Abruptly, he felt a wave of fierceness run through him.

I am glad they are bachelors!

Men such as Hawkins and Eldon could never make a wife happy. Indeed, the wives of such men could only ever be miserable.

So why do I count such men among my friends?

Questions raged within him, doubt and uncertainty clouding his mind. The queen's words had given him much to think about.

Of one thing he was certain, though. Never had he experienced anything like the desire and tenderness he had felt last night. His mind, heart, and soul were full of Isobel. He had not lied when he said he felt bewitched by her. No other maiden earned anything more than a fleeting look from him now. He could acknowledge that some of them were attractive—beautiful, even—without feeling an ounce of attraction for himself.

His overwhelming feeling today, though—as well as elation—was shame. Having promised the queen he would do no more than kiss Isobel, he had nearly ravished her, right there in the gardens. Worse, he had made the same promise to himself and had broken it within moments of being close to her, protected by a cloak of darkness. What sort of man was he, to succumb so readily to lust when Isobel deserved every respect? Yes, she was beautiful, and maddeningly desirable, but he had three years on her, and experience. He should have been better at controlling himself. One thing was certain: it could not happen again. Not because he did not wish it to, but because he had very little confidence in his ability to stop next time.

To everyone's surprise and delight, James and Rose—now Viscount and Viscountess Ashbourne—arrived in the late morning, sparking great celebration in Ashbourne House. They looked entirely happy, and Izzy noted a little enviously how their eyes followed one another at all times.

What must it be like to marry someone you love and who loves you in return?

Having achieved her aim of kissing the prince last night, and it being better than her wildest imaginings, Izzy understood now that he had spoiled her. No man could ever compare to him. His looks, his lively mind, his warm heart, and now, his fiery kisses that had left her in an eternal state of longing. She would never be his bride, never sit by his side with his ring on her finger, letting the world know that they belonged to one another.

On the occasion of her marriage, Rose had received from their guardian a pair of earrings that had belonged to Mama, as well as a letter from her. They read it together, shedding a tear at their mother's beautiful words, and bemoaning again the lack of information about her origins or the identity of their father. Izzy, having believed she had become accustomed to being an orphan of dubious parentage, momentarily railed against the cruelty of her circumstance.

Had I been the daughter of a known, respectable couple, might the prince have considered me?

But no, such daydreams were useless. Her fate was as it was, and she must not dream of the impossible.

'We shall visit Lady Kelgrove first,' the viscount declared. 'Rose and I have discussed it, and we believe it makes sense. She is highly influential, and we all have a fondness for her. If we can achieve her approval for marrying in Scotland, then it will make it easier for the rest of the *ton* to follow.' He took Rose's hand. 'Not that I should care about any disapproval, for marrying Rose has been the best decision I have ever made.'

The happy pair left for Lady Kelgrove's townhouse a couple of hours later, and Izzy, Anna, and Lady Ashbourne—who had now officially become the Dowager Viscountess despite, she said, believing she was far too young for such a title—made ready for the evening, being promised at a soirée at Lord and Lady Renton's. However, before dinner had been served, they received an unexpected but urgent message bidding them all come to Lady Kelgrove's mansion immediately.

'Oh, dear! I do hope nothing has befallen her, for I do

have a great affection for Lady Kelgrove!' Lady Ashbourne looked troubled and fiddled with her reticule the whole way through Mayfair, but when they were ushered into the drawing room by a rather bewildered looking footman, Lady Kelgrove was there to greet them. Worryingly, she did look rather pale and was clutching a handkerchief in her crabbed hand.

Has she been crying?

Rose and James were there, too, and Rose had definitely been crying. The butler stood by the fireplace, wringing his hands. Never had Izzy seen a butler in a state of agitation, but there was no other way to describe it, and butlers were *never* agitated.

Cutting across Lady Ashbourne's distressed greeting, Lady Kelgrove bade them sit. 'Which of you is Annabelle, and which Isobel? Wait.' She held up an imperious hand, looking from one to the other. 'You are Anna. And you are Isobel. I should not have needed to ask, for I know you well.' She closed her eyes briefly. 'Naturally, I know you both.'

Inwardly Izzy's mind was racing.

What on earth is happening?

'It seems,' began Lady Kelgrove, steadying herself, 'that the earrings currently being worn by the new Lady Ashbourne belonged to your mother, Maria.'

All of the hairs at the back of Izzy's neck were suddenly standing to attention, and she could not breathe.

'I recognised them instantly,' Lady Kelgrove continued, 'for they were a gift from me to my granddaughter, Maria.'

Maria Berkeley?

Could it possibly be—? But how?

'A granddaughter,' Lady Kelgrove continued, the slightest hint of a quiver in her voice, 'whom I was informed had died of smallpox at eighteen years of age. Brooks—' she waved a hand towards the elderly butler '—has informed me in the last hour that Maria's supposed death was a lie concocted by my husband after Maria ran away.' She smiled tremulously. 'I am your great-grandmother, my dears.'

Much embracing followed, and copious tears. Lady Ashbourne declared herself delighted and reflected, giggling, that those who had sneered at the triplets would get quite a shock in discovering the girls were of the Kelgrove line. They stayed for dinner, abandoning all engagements for the evening, and agreed that while the news of Rose's marriage was to be shared, for now they would keep their discovery about Maria Berkeley to themselves.

Lord, the ton does love a secret! thought Izzy, her mind still reeling from today's news.

Still, it was fitting that Rose and James announce their own good news. As Lady Ashbourne pointed out, the sight of them would put paid to any suggestion there had been something havey-cavey about the nuptials.

'For,' she said, 'the two of you are smelling of April and May, and this is clearly a love match!' She preened a little. 'And I can say with perfect truth that I knew you were to be married, and it was better done in Scotland where you grew up, Rose.'

'And *was* there something havey-cavey about it?' asked Lady Kelgrove sharply.

Lord Ashbourne held his hands open a little. 'I was seen kissing Rose by Lady Renton's footman, which is why she went away to her guardian and her old school.'

'And you did not offer her marriage?' Lady Kelgrove's brow was furrowed, her shoulders stiff. Indeed every inch of her signalled displeasure.

'I did not get the chance! She was gone before I even knew we had been seen. I followed her immediately—that is to say, two days later, once I was made aware of the situation—and was greatly relieved when she agreed to be my wife.' The look he threw Rose made Izzy's insides melt with joy for the two of them.

He adores her!

'Hmph. You should have offered for her the moment you put her reputation at risk. And *you*—' she pointed a stabbing finger at Rose '—should not have run away.' A wistful expression appeared in her eyes. 'And nor should my Maria.' Her expression changed. 'I must warn you, girls, that I find myself hungry for information about my darling granddaughter. Tell me again, how did you come to have your colours—the blue, the green and yellow, the pink?'

Anna explained that the midwife had tied coloured ribbons around their wrists as each of them was born, and that Mama had kept the colours initially so she would always know which was which, then because each of them liked having their own colour.'

'She even had songs for each of us,' added Rose. 'Mine was ring-a-ring o' roses.'

Lady Kelgrove looked to Izzy. 'Greensleeves,' she said with a shrug.

Her face crumpled. 'I used to sing Greensleeves to her when she was young.' She swallowed hard, then looked at Anna.

'Ah, Mama created a song for me—perhaps she could not think of a suitable nursery rhyme. I mean, *Little Boy Blue* would not have been welcome!'

'Indeed not! So what is your song? Can you remember it?'

Anna glanced mischievously at her sisters. 'Well? Shall we?'

Izzy rose instantly, remembering every word, every

action. They stood together, grinning, then Anna started her song.

'The Lady Blue she points her shoe,' they chanted in a singsong tone, each pointing her right foot as though beginning a dance, simultaneously dipping in a sweeping curtsy, just as though they were wearing huge panniers.

'You find the line to find the kine,' They swept their right arms out as though following an imaginary line. Izzy could almost see the herd of cows she had always pictured in her mind.

'The key is three and three times three.' For this they weaved around each other, the three of them changing place three times each.

'The treasure fine is yours and mine,' and they finished by forming a circle, clapping hands together and against each other's palms.

Laughing, they returned to their chairs, acknowledging the smiles and applause of their small audience.

'Thank you, my dears.' Lady Kelgrove again made use of her handkerchief. 'I can honestly picture Maria's enjoyment as she created this for you. A silly little ditty, but it has her sense of mischief.' She sighed, 'I only wish she had come to me.'

'Do you think,' Anna offered, 'that she ran away because of our father? We were in February the following year—'

'And we came two months early,' Izzy added.

'So she was not with child when she ran away. She disappeared almost a year before you were born. Where could she have been, for a full year? Ah, Maria, Maria. What was so dreadful you could not trust me with it?'

There was a pause.

Izzy swallowed against a sudden lump in her throat. 'I

must ask...do you know who our father might be?' Perhaps, after all, she would find the answer to her own quest.

'I have my suspicions, but let us speak of it at another time. The important matter now is that we have found one another. That is to be celebrated!' She thought for a moment, then slammed her stick on the floor. 'I have it! I shall host a ball for you here, my dears,' she declared briskly. 'A ball at which I shall announce your identity. It will give me great satisfaction to shock the likes of the Thaxbys, Lady Renford, and others. It will have to be next week, for everyone will leave London soon for the summer. Ha! The queen may believe her ball to be the last significant event of the Season, but mine will outshine them all!'

Lady Ashbourne instilled a note of caution. 'You do realise, my lady, that announcing this will add to speculation that Maria might never have wed. Running away, her own father cutting her off...'

Lady Kelgrove snorted inelegantly. 'I do indeed realise it, but I care not. These girls are not to blame for any errors made by their parents, and my patronage added to yours—plus, of course, Rose's recent marriage—will ensure they will suffer no longer for the previous vagueness regarding their parentage.'

She repeated this theme numerous times during dinner, adding that she should have realised the triplets were Maria's daughters, for she had taken to them instantly. 'And you, Miss Isobel!' she declared, making Izzy start and eye her rather warily. Since the events of last night at the Queen's Masquerade Ball, she was half expecting someone to suddenly declare she and Claudio had been seen—as had happened to Rose and James. Lady Kelgrove, however, was on an entirely different tack.

'I was speaking of you recently to Prince Claudio. I described you as headstrong, obstinate, and opinionated. Just as I like you!' She nodded approvingly. 'I see now that you get those gifts from me. Use them well!'

'I am not sure everyone would see such qualities as gifts.'

She was speaking to Claudio of me? Lord, I should love to know what else was said.

But the conversation moved on, and her curiosity remained unsatisfied.

There she is!

Lady Ashbourne had just entered the Renton drawing room, followed by the Misses Lennox. Claudio's eyes widened.

Three of them!

Miss Rose had returned, then. He was glad, for Izzy's sake. The viscount was also with them, and Claudio was reminded that something in him had wanted to make a friend of the viscount. Yes, and Garvald, too. Instead, here he was, standing listening to empty-headed nonsense from Hawkins and Eldon. His eyes roved hungrily over Isobel.

What a beauty she is!

It struck him now that he had absolutely no notion what to say to her tonight. How to *be* when he was around her. What had taken place between them had been so profound, so affecting, that it would be practically impossible to behave with any sort of normality. And yet, he must. They both must. To give any hint of what had occurred would lead to the most vulgar of speculation, and Isobel must not be exposed to any such distress.

Pretending to laugh at something Hawkins had said, Claudio glanced towards the Ashbourne–Lennox party again. Isobel was talking with one of her sisters in an animated way, and his heart turned over just at the sight of her.

A flash of delicious memory came to him: the liberties he had taken with his hands and his mouth. The memories, though, were laced with something that felt suspiciously like shame. Yes, she had been willing—he thrilled each time he recalled the passion within her. But that did not excuse what he had done.

Here she was in a society drawing room, dressed in the pale colours of a débutante—a lady to be respected, admired, treated as an innocent. And she *was* innocent, of that he had no doubt. Yet he had behaved as though she were an experienced tavern wench or a Cyprian. He felt like a despoiler, someone without honour.

If Papa knew what I had done...

And so, when it was finally time to greet them all, he found himself to be tongue-tied, taciturn, reserved. Inside, all was turmoil. She was close enough to touch, yet he could barely look at her. Self-loathing, a familiar enemy, reared its head within him. Isobel was a goddess, and he the mortal who had dared to touch her. He would never be the same again.

Making his excuses as soon as he was able, he encouraged his friends to leave earlier than planned, then spent the rest of the night in a disreputable tavern drinking enough to fall down. Enough to forget.

Izzy watched him go, feeling confused, bereft, bewildered. While of course he could not have alluded in public to what had taken place between them—no, not so much as by a look or a glance—still, she had hoped for something more than *this*. He had been withdrawn almost to the point of rudeness. Even Lady Ashbourne had commented on it, wondering aloud if something ailed him. Izzy knew better.

It is me. I am his ailment, she thought fancifully, imagining herself taking a sweeping bow to the entire assembly, before announcing *Good evening, everyone! I am Prince Claudio's ailment.*

He was clearly regretting his actions in the garden, which in turn was now making Izzy question hers. What had seemed so wonderful—the passion and tenderness she believed she had sensed between them—now seemed overlaid with the taint of corruption. Anger surged through her. These past weeks she thought she had found a friend, yet his actions tonight had shown her clearly that she had been mistaken. He was evidently no friend to her.

All through the evening she worried over it, railing between fury and pain even as Lord Ashbourne made the announcement about his marriage, and the crowd thronged about him and Rose, wishing them happy.

Claudio should have been here to be part of this.

Catching the thought she frowned, questioning her assumptions. He had shown a preference for her company in recent weeks, it was true, yet tonight he had treated her as though she were a near stranger. Was it possible he had befriended her only to persuade her to commit indiscretions at the queen's ball?

Surely not.

Normally Izzy counted herself a good judge of character, but with him all logic was overset, and perhaps she could no longer trust her instincts. What did she know of princes or lords? Having always had an impulsive streak, had it on this occasion veered towards recklessness?

And had he, his object achieved, moved on to try to captivate another? His set was known for wenching, as well as for drinking, gambling, and sport. Were they now on their way to visit courtesans? And would Claudio do to some unknown woman what he had done to her?

Her mind reeling and her stomach sick, she managed to smile and please her way through the evening, vaguely remembering afterwards that someone had mentioned Mr Kirby was to return to London on the morrow.

Lord! Fitch, too, would be back. Having avoided him at the masquerade, she had been relieved to hear of his latest trip to the country to visit his mother. He seemed to visit his dear mama a lot, which was no doubt a good thing. But now he was returning. With only a week left of the Season, either or both of her suitors might well propose marriage, and her mind was in the clouds. She could not think about it now. Her head was beginning to ache, and it was all too painful.

Thankfully Mary was waiting at home to help her undress, remove her uncomfortable hairpins, and offer her a tincture. 'It is this heavy weather, miss. My head has been pounding all day. If we could only get a thunderstorm, then all would be well again!'

Izzy, naturally, did not contradict the girl, but once the maid had gone, she blew out the last candle and cried herself to sleep.

Chapter Thirteen

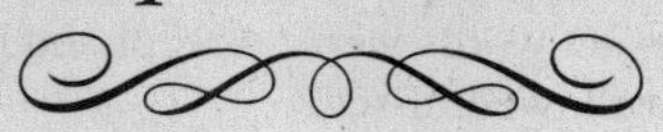

'What day is it, Jenkins?'

'Monday, Your Highness.' The valet's voice was neutral, with no hint of criticism. It mattered not, for the self-critical voice within Claudio—the one held at bay by wine, ale, and beer—was beginning to reassert itself.

You are a disgrace, it said. Foul. Worthless. Drunken sot. Despoiler of gentle maidens.

Monday? The soirée at the Rentons had been on Wednesday.

Have I really been drunk for four days and nights?

'My engagements?'

Jenkins listed today's invitations while Claudio hoisted himself carefully into a sitting position, the room spinning slightly as he did so. Last night he had made it back to Buckingham House before midnight—hardly surprising that he had faded, since he had been drinking since breakfast. Tentatively, Claudio looked towards the window. The midday sun was bright but not as painful as Claudio had feared.

'And tonight, you are promised to Lady Kelgrove's ball. Shall I cancel everything for today again, Your Highness?'

'Lady Kelgrove is hosting a ball? I do not recall...'

'The invitation arrived only yesterday, Your Highness.'

'And I accepted it?' Madness, for the Lennox sisters

were certain to be there, given the mutual fondness between them and Lady Kelgrove. Dimly, he recalled meeting Ashbourne in one of the clubs and congratulating him on his recent marriage to Miss Rose.

Lucky bastard.

The valet stood his ground. 'Er…yes, Your Highness. In fact your exact words were "Accept and be damned!"'

Claudio swallowed. 'I see.'

Might as well go.

He would have to see her sometime. Why not tonight?

'Breakfast, Your Highness? Or ale?'

Claudio shuddered. 'Ale? No. I have had enough ale to last me a lifetime.' The very thought made him feel sick. 'A bath, and then some beef, eggs, and rolls, please. And tea. Yes, tea.'

Jenkins bowed. 'Very well, Your Highness. Er… Her Majesty has requested your presence today, if it pleases you?'

The sick feeling in Claudio's stomach intensified. 'Yes, of course.'

An hour later, hair still damp from his bath, Prince Claudio sauntered into the queen's apartments. After the usual greetings he took the seat she offered and accepted refreshments. She eyed him closely, and he managed to maintain equanimity. At moments like this she strongly reminded him of his father.

'How do you like your tea, Claudio?' Her tone was deceptively mild.

'Oh, as it comes,' was his reply, his air of unconcern probably not fooling her for an instant. He had seen his red-rimmed eyes in the mirror and knew his dissipation was visible to anyone who knew where to look for it.

'What are your plans for today?'

As he listed his chosen engagements, she tilted her head to listen carefully.

'And then,' he continued, 'this evening I am promised to Lady Kelgrove's ball.'

She snorted. 'Well, I must say I am glad to hear it! She may have announced it only very recently, but all of the *ton* holds Lady Kelgrove in great respect. It would not do to miss it.'

'No, indeed,' he answered mildly, and she flashed him an irritated glance.

'No doubt she will give prominence to the Lennox girls, for she continually reminds us all that they are her favourites.' She sniffed. 'Before she knew them, they were *my* diamonds first, of course!' Taking a sip of tea, she continued, with a nonchalant air, 'Of course, the youngest Lennox girl's marriage to Ashbourne has changed all their fortunes.'

Now she had his attention. 'How so?' His expression was neutral, but there was a tightness in his shoulders that had not been there a moment earlier.

She shrugged. 'They will be seen now as more marriageable. Although the Season is almost done, so the time is short. Some may still sneer at their lack of parents, but I would not be surprised if Garvald came up to scratch and offered for one of them.'

'Garvald? The *Earl* of Garvald?'

'The very same. A man of taste, and wit, and intelligence. The girls themselves of course may not realise this and settle for a plain mister.' She shrugged. 'Ah, well. With the Season at an end, those who remain unbetrothed must choose from the options available to them, I suppose.'

'But Garvald is not seeking to marry, is he?'

'I rather suspect he is very close to it.' She raised an eyebrow. 'You sound surprised.'

He frowned. 'How old is Garvald? Do you know?'

She considered the matter. 'Let me think... Three—no, four-and-twenty. And he is among the most liked of gentlemen, far more so than the dissipated wastrels at the edge of the *ton*. I am sure you have noted it.'

Just four-and-twenty?

He swallowed, making a noncommittal answer, but she was undeterred.

'Many young men face a crossroads, Claudio.' Her gaze became unfocused. 'One path is brightly lit and enticing, with promises of drink, sport, and a lifetime of irresponsibility. The other has neither glitter nor glamour but holds depth, warmth, and enduring satisfaction.' Her words were disturbing him greatly, and his mind was awhirl.

'Despite my husband's madness, I have never regretted my choice, and together we have lived a relatively quiet life—so much so that the king has earned the soubriquet Farmer George.' She shook her head slowly. 'A quiet life, but a happy one...despite everything.'

He left soon afterwards, her message having been received loud and clear. Garvald, a sensible, sober man of just four-and-twenty, was more admired than the likes of Hawkins and Eldon, whom she had described as—what was it?—'dissipated wastrels'. The memory of her words pierced him.

I chose wrongly. I chose badly. And now it is too late.

'No, can you lift it a little higher, please?'

Izzy stifled a sigh. Mary, her usual maid, was sick, and so another of the housemaids was dressing her hair. *Poor Mary!* Strange to think that in the months since she had arrived in London, she and Mary had come to an understanding about the way she liked her hair done, among many other preferences.

I am a lady of the ton *now, apparently.*

'Is that all right, miss?' The maid sounded anxious, and Izzy stifled a sigh.

'It will do just fine. Thank you.'

It had been almost a week since the masquerade. Five days since she had even laid eyes on him. He had attended none of the *ton* gatherings since leaving the Renton soirée so abruptly. A throwaway comment from one of the other gentlemen had given her to understand that the prince and his cronies—she refused to call them his *friends*, even in her mind—were not out of town but rather had been drinking in clubs and taverns for the past few days. And to think she had judged Claudio to be a man of sense, of reason, of sensibility and feeling! Clearly, he was nothing better than a tavern drunkard, despite his princely title. And looks. And manner.

Her mind went back to their very first encounter, in a hallway in Grantham. Yes, her first impression of him must have been correct. He was a wastrel, a seducer, a man who would not hesitate to use his royal title for his own sordid purposes. Her more recent error of judgement had been monumental, and now she was being punished for it. When she thought of the liberties she had allowed him in the queen's garden, she burned with mortification. Clearly, once he had achieved his sordid aim, he had vanished, leaving her wretched.

The sense of hurt and betrayal was not becoming any easier to bear. The pain within her was like a living thing, scalding and piercing as it twisted and writhed. Worse, her foolish heart still retained an affection for him that was as unwelcome as it was idiotic. Not seeing him was agony. Yet seeing him in the Rentons' drawing room and realising he was ignoring her—that had been a thousand times worse.

Will he be there tonight?

The thought had plagued her these past days, each time she entered a drawing room or a ballroom. Each time, the answer had been *no.* Yet that did not stop her imprudent heart from hoping. Even though she *knew* he was not the person she had imagined him to be. Even though he had rejected her in the plainest possible way.

Her head ached, and her heart did, too. And it was not getting any easier. In fact, it seemed to be getting worse, for tonight her very bones were aching, and it hurt to move her eyes. And the new maid had tied her half stays too tight, making it difficult to breathe. Yet still she smiled and pleased, greeting Lady Kelgrove with genuine warmth, and enjoying the elderly lady's air of repressed excitement. Tonight, she would claim the Lennox sisters as her own long-lost great-granddaughters, and she was clearly relishing the prospect.

'Tonight we shall shake them up, girls. Just wait and see!' Lifting her quizzing glass, she studied the triplets from head to toe. 'Delightful! You are a credit to your mother, my dears.' Discomfort rippled through Izzy at the words. Would Lady Kelgrove still say that if she knew what Izzy had been doing in the dark with the prince?

'Now,' Lady Kelgrove continued, 'go and enjoy yourselves. I shall make the announcement at supper.'

Izzy tried. She really did. She made her curtsy to the queen and made empty conversation with a dozen or more ladies and gentlemen. Mr Fitch was there and informed her with an air of sadness that his mama had advised him he was too young for marriage.

'I have taken her advice to heart, Miss Isobel. I, er, do hope no young lady will suffer hurt by the withdrawal of my attentions.'

Relief flooded through her. 'Indeed not, Mr Fitch, though it shows you in a very good light to think of such a thing. And I do think it is important for you to listen to your mama.' They parted amicably, and with relief on both sides, and Izzy continued to circulate amid the large crowd.

Thankfully Rose's marriage had caught the attention of the *ton*, and Izzy lost count of the number of people coming to congratulate again the new Lady Ashbourne, who was now appropriately decked out in a gown of deep rose-pink, a shade that would never have been permitted for an unmarried lady. It was her first event dressed in such a way, and she had been in alt earlier when the first of her new clothes had arrived.

Despite Rose's evident happiness and success, to Izzy all seemed flat, and empty, and meaningless. And the warm weather was not helping. One moment she was shivering, and the next suffocating with the heat. Even dancing was difficult, for her legs felt as though they were made of lead. It hurt to move. Everything and everyone was irritating her, and she wished only to return to the haven of her bedchamber at home.

An excited babble reached her ears, and she turned to see what had caused such consternation, her eyes meeting the gaze of Prince Claudio, who had just arrived. Late, but he had arrived. Instantly she looked away, trying to ignore the sudden thunderous tattoo of her heart.

Be calm, she told herself.

He had to reappear eventually. It still did not change who he was or what he had done.

'Yes, of course!' Mr Kirby had come to claim her for the next dance and willingly she went, flashing him a bright smile. Subtly, as she moved through the figures of the dance, she tracked the prince's progress around the edges of the dancing floor, the people he spoke to, helplessly observing the way his coat of grey superfine enhanced his cool colouring… He was spending quite some time with Garvald, she noted. Not his usual company. But then, his own friends were not here, so he probably had no choice but to converse with some of the more sober, thoughtful gentlemen. He would no doubt leave before long, the ball being rather too staid for his liking, she thought, briefly wondering if he would be here for Lady Kelgrove's announcement. He probably would not care.

He does not care.

'…if I might speak with you later. In private.' Her attention snapped back to Mr Kirby. Red-faced and earnest, there was no doubting his meaning or his intentions. Unlike with Mr Fitch, there was no controlling mother in the background to rescue her this time.

Lord! Here was a new riddle. Before Rose's wedding and Lady Kelgrove's revelations, Izzy had been in danger of being banished back to Scotland next week, her one Season done. That was no longer the case, Rose having assured both her and Anna that they could live with the Ashbournes for as long as they wished. Lady Kelgrove, too, had invited Izzy to come live with her, stating that Izzy was one of the few people she could tolerate.

'Aye, and your husband too, once you are wed,' she had added, and it had taken all of Izzy's self-control not to emit a sceptical snort. Now that she *need* not marry, she was not sure she would ever *wish* to. And, despite her plans of just a couple of weeks ago, she now knew she could never, ever marry Mr Kirby. Or Mr Fitch.

I must tell Mr Kirby.

A ripple of guilt ran through her. The man could reasonably argue that she had encouraged him for, to be fair, she had. He was awaiting her response, and now the dance had brought them together again.

'I will speak with you, Mr Kirby. But I must warn you that my situation…has changed recently.'

He looked crestfallen. 'I see.' They parted again, and when they returned he had squared his shoulders. 'Very well. On the terrace, perhaps, after this dance?'

'Ten minutes after.' She needed to go to the retiring room, for her head was throbbing with pain, and she felt decidedly strange. For the first time she began to wonder if she was in fact ill, rather than just heartsore. Her mind flicked to poor Mary, laid low with what Cook suspected was influenza. Yes, that could be it. She stifled a sigh.

Wonderful. Just wonderful.

Claudio laughed at something Garvald said. The man had a dry wit that was both entertaining and admirable, and Claudio was now regretting not making a friend of him from the beginning. The Season was nearly done, and he was only now discovering the true value in the people around him. The queen's revelation that he and Garvald were similar in age had astounded him.

A man of taste, and wit, and intelligence, eh? I could have been described so, perhaps. Had I made different choices.

Here, then, was another way to be. Personable rather than raucous. Unafraid to show one's intelligence. Garvald was a little shy and had seemed standoffish to Claudio at first.

I was distracted by gilt, when all the while gold was before me.

Gold. He had been subtly observing Isobel since his arrival. What to do? She crossed the ballroom, and Claudio watched her go, realising she was making for the retiring room. Remembering their previous encounters in various hallways, there was an inevitability to it, perhaps. A symmetry that might help him. Lord knows he needed all the help he could get.

As he made his bow to Garvald and moved subtly towards the corridor, giving her time to complete her ablutions, his mind went over their previous encounters. The inn in Grantham. The library at the Wrights' ball, when first she had behaved as though she might like him, a little. The hallway in Buckingham House, where they had arranged their garden assignation. And now this. Claudio had no idea what he would say to her, only that he needed to speak to her where others could not easily hear them.

Damnation!

Two footmen stood in the hallway at either side of the ballroom door, two more farther down near the retiring rooms. Of course the wealthy Lady Kelgrove would have many more footmen than any household would consider reasonable. Taken aback, he had not yet recovered when she emerged from the room set aside for ladies, walking towards him with a frown and drooping shoulders. He waited, holding his breath for the moment she would recognise him.

There!

Pausing for the briefest of instants, she then continued towards him at a faster pace, chin raised, and an expression of determination on her beautiful face.

She went to pass him, and he took her hand.

'Unhand me, sir!'

She is angry. Livid, indeed.

In a cajoling tone, he attempted to reach her with humour. 'Now, now, Miss Isobel. You know that my title is *Your*

Highness, not *sir*.' Retaining her hand, he gave a sweeping bow—a royal bow.

She was unmoved. 'Titles should be earned, not given. You are no prince. Indeed, I am not sure you are even a gentleman.'

His jaw dropped. 'If this is because I left the Renton soirée early, I—'

She held up an imperious hand. 'You may do as you please. I care not.'

Conscious of listening ears all about, he dropped his tone. 'I assure you, Miss Isobel, that despite what you may believe, I am a gentleman. And yes, a prince, too! Now, please allow me to apol—'

Her lip curled. 'Let me pass, for I am promised to speak with someone.'

He frowned but could not make sense of this. Letting it go for now, he focused instead on her superior tone, still trying to connect with her. Surely, somewhere inside, was the Isobel he had laughed with? The Isobel who had become his friend? She looked flushed and was clearly agitated. Giving her a humorous look, and ignoring the growing feeling of dread within, he teased her. 'And you, I suppose, are the Queen of Sheba?'

She dipped her head. 'I may be.' Throwing him a scornful look—a look that seemed to sear into him like a brand—she added, 'In comparison to persons of no honour, I suppose I must be higher in true rank.'

Anger flared within him, and he dropped her hand. No honour?

How dare she?

'No honour? I have been a man of honour my whole life. My father, my friends, all could vouch for—'

She cut him off again. 'I know nothing of your father, but I can tell you this. You have no friends, Claudio. Do you think that the likes of Hawkins or Eldon would bother with you if you were not a royal? They are cronies, hangers-on, leeches. They care nothing for you. They are nothing but sycophants who would be gone in an instant if you were not a prince.'

As she spoke, he felt the colour drain from his face. Each word was a knife wound, stabbing him with hurt, leaving white-hot rage in its wake.

How dare she say such things to me?

'Well, at least,' he shot back, 'I *have* a father. Yes, and I had a mother, too. I should hate to go through life with no name, no history, no parentage.'

Too far.

He saw it in the stricken look in her eye, heard it in the gasp she uttered. 'No! Izzy, I am sorry. I should not have said it. Please—'

She was ice-cold. As though he were not even speaking, she turned, gliding serenely away from him. For the rest of his days he would remember the sight: her back, her golden hair, the way she moved…away from him.

Have I lost her?

Izzy entered the ballroom in a daze. Claudio's words were worse than hurtful, worse than cutting. He had attacked her very soul, or so it seemed to her. To hear such sentiments from anyone would have been devastating, but the fact such condemnation had come from the very man she—

She refused to finish the thought, conscious that she needed to survive the evening for just a little longer. A waltz was underway, and her mind tried to take her back to another waltz, another night. But she would not think of it, of what she had lost, for it was clear now that he had never been hers in any way.

Mr Kirby was standing by the terrace doors on the far side of the room.

Oh, Lord! she had quite forgotten her assignation to speak with him. Catching her eye, he gave her a meaningful look, and she nodded. As he stepped onto the terrace, she began crossing the room, avoiding the eye of anyone who might delay or detain her. After the waltz, she knew, supper would be called.

I shall speak with Mr Kirby, allow dear Lady Kelgrove to make her announcement, then go home.

Duty. Honour. *La politesse.* These were morals drummed into her by all of the important people in her life. The Ashbournes. Lady Kelgrove. Her sisters. Mr Marnoch. The Belvedere teachers. Mama.

She would not even have to feign illness to escape, for she genuinely felt dreadful. Her head was now thumping as though tiny creatures with a thousand hammers were labouring inside. Her legs were decidedly weak; she could not have danced now even if she wanted to. And she had begun to shiver as though she were outside in the winter snow, rather than in a sweltering ballroom at midsummer.

Concentrating on every step, she managed to reach the terrace. As her eyes adjusted to the gloom, she saw Mr Kirby was there, waiting for her, and as she approached her heart was sore at the sadness she saw in his kind eyes. Other people were there, too, she vaguely noticed, but in this moment she had one task, and one task only. To disappoint this man—a good, kind gentleman—who had done nothing wrong except believe her when she had encouraged him.

'Mr Kirby.' She gave him her hand, and he kissed the back of it. Moved by regret and compassion, she allowed him to keep it. He would not misinterpret her action now, she knew.

'You said you had something to say to me, Miss Isobel.'

'I did. I do. I must apologise, Mr Kirby, but my circumstances have changed. I thought I might marry you, if you asked me. Or Mr Fitch. But my sister's marriage means now that…' She now searched for the right words.

'That you may look higher for a husband. I understand.' His voice was tight.

Pushing away the image of Claudio in his full princely regalia, as she had seen him during the presentation of débutantes, she shook her head.

'No! Well, yes, but not because of position or title.'

He thought about this for a second, then nodded slowly. 'Your heart is engaged. I had wondered about it.'

She gave him a sad look. 'Hearts may do what they will. Marriages are for more than the passing wants of the heart. Companionship, friendship, children… I think we could have shared these things.'

'I know we could.' His tone was low.

'But that is not my reason.' She squeezed his hand. 'The truth is that I no longer need to choose a husband this Season. My sister and her husband have invited me to live with them.'

'I am glad for you.' He swallowed, managing a smile. 'And I hope we can continue to be friends.'

'Of course!' Without thinking too much about it, she pressed her lips to his cheek for a fleeting instant.

Now his smile was genuine. 'I thank you for your honesty, Miss Isobel. I—' His eyes widened in confusion, then dawning horror, as he looked at something over her shoulder. Turning, she gasped as she saw the prince bearing down upon them, his face contorted in rage.

* * *

Conscious of the footmen's fascination, Claudio coughed, adjusted his cuffs, then returned to the ballroom—just in time to see Isobel disappear through the doors leading to the terrace. Pushing his way through the crowd, he made his way across the room in double-quick time, murmuring vagueness at those who tried to detain him with meaningless utterings.

I must put this right!

With the focus of an arrow, he made for the terrace, driven by regret and something that felt suspiciously like fear.

I cannot lose her. I must not lose her.

Stepping through the doors he paused for a moment, letting his vision adapt to the dim light. To his left, a group of matrons were fanning themselves and seemed deep in conversation. To his right—

He froze. Isobel was there, her pale gown and golden hair dappled with moonlight. She looked ethereal, other-worldly. And standing with her was Kirby, and he was holding her hand and speaking to her in an earnest manner.

No!

Terror raced through him. Everything fell into place.

Lady Kelgrove telling him a few weeks ago, 'From what I know of Miss Isobel, she is practical enough to know she needs a husband.'

The queen's words yesterday, that the Misses Lennox might not realise their fortunes had improved with Miss Rose's marriage and might 'settle for a plain mister'.

Isobel's cutting words earlier had contrasted people with titles who did not live up to them, like himself, and those whose honour was apparent from their deeds. So even if she knew she might attain a titled husband, she might yet choose Kirby. For his character.

He went cold as he now recalled Isobel's other words a few moments ago: 'I am promised to speak with someone.'

This, then, was an assignation, so that Kirby could make his proposal.

If she accepts him, I have lost her forever.

Even as all these thoughts were flashing through his mind like so many lightning strikes, he was striding across the terrace. As he did so, Isobel leaned forward and kissed Kirby on the cheek, driving rage, pain, and loss through Claudio.

I am too late.

And he had no one to blame but himself.

My stupidity. My tardiness. My failure.

At the last moment Kirby saw him, his eyes growing round as saucers. Now Isobel was turning, trying to see what had startled her suitor. She opened her mouth to speak—and Claudio stopped it with his own mouth, firmly planted onto hers. There was no plan there, no thought, just a howling chasm of loss and pain and need within him. Kirby might have won her, but Claudio would kiss her one last time. After this, his life was pointless, anyway.

Her mouth was hot, her lips sweet as honey. But she was frozen, unresponsive.

Isobel!

Izzy froze in shock. Claudio was kissing her, and she was drowning. His arms held her firmly, his chest pressed against hers, and his mouth was moving, begging her to respond.

She could not. Instead, influenza chose its moment to strike. Blackness overcame her, and her body sagged in a deep faint. As the dark waters overcame her, her last thought was that at least he had kissed her again, even though this time he was motivated by anger.

Remember! she told herself. Remember!

An age later—a year, perhaps, or maybe a day—she heard voices. Ladies' voices.

'He just marched across the terrace and kissed her! I saw it with my own eyes!'

'Shocking!'

'Which one is it?'

'Miss Isobel, I understand. Certainly Mr Kirby called her Isobel, before he went to get assistance.'

The blackness came again, interrupted by an acrid smell, making her cough and awaken. Opening her eyes, she saw three matrons and a serving maid who was waving hartshorn under her nose. The acrid smell stung, bringing hot tears to her eyes. Above them—far, far above—the stars. Memory returned in an instant.

I am on the terrace. Prince Claudio...!

'Now, now, my dear,' one of the ladies soothed, patting her arm. 'You have just had an ordeal. These gentlemen think they may do as they wish!' She tutted, shaking her head. 'Still, you have won a prince for yourself. That ought to cheer you up.'

This made no sense. Struggling, Izzy got up into a sitting position, realising someone had placed her on the stone bench on Lady Kelgrove's terrace. Looking left and right she realised Prince Claudio was nowhere to be seen. Behind the ladies, wringing his hands and looking distressed, was Mr Kirby. She met his eyes, attempting a tremulous smile, and he exhaled in relief. Inside, the gong sounded.

'Supper time!' declared one of the ladies. 'I expect you may wish to go home, Miss… Isobel, is it?'

She nodded abstractedly. 'Yes. Isobel.' They exchanged

knowing glances, which Izzy could not understand. 'And no,' she continued, 'I must see Lady Kelgrove at supper before I can leave.'

'May I bring you something to eat, Miss Isobel?' asked Kirby.

'No, but thank you.' His compassion and care were important, somehow. The ladies were saying all the right things, but the expression in their eyes was one of glee, rather than kindness. *Why?*

'Stay with her,' one of the ladies instructed the maid, who nodded. 'We shall go in. We do not wish to miss out on our supper! Miss Isobel, once you are feeling a little better, you may come inside. It is a little cooler out here, so it will be more comfortable for you.'

Izzy managed a nod, her brain sluggish and her body strangely numb. Kirby and the maid stayed with her, while she breathed and sat and thought of nothing. It took great determination, for her mind was all chaos, but she managed.

After what felt like an age, she took a deep breath, then lifted her eyes to Kirby. 'I should like to go in now.'

'Are you certain?'

She confirmed it and took his arm, remembering to thank the maid. He took her to her sisters, who were seated with Rose's husband and Lady Ashbourne. Supper had ended, and the servants were clearing the tables.

Rose, eyeing her closely, frowned. 'Are you unwell, Izzy?'

She nodded. 'I think I have caught the influenza from Mary. I feel dreadful.'

Instantly both sisters were all concern, offering to take her home instantly. Lady Ashbourne, too, although she gave Izzy a keen glance. 'You wish to stay for Lady Kelgrove's announcement, do you not?'

Izzy nodded. Amid all of the events of the past hour, that was the one thread she was hanging onto. Lady Kelgrove deserved all the drama she desired for her announcement. And the triplets' presence was essential for the heightened drama. Besides, Izzy herself needed this small triumph amid all of the pain and horror of her mind, her body, her heart.

'Very well. But we must leave immediately afterwards.'

Lady Kelgrove was soon ready. Without even glancing in their direction, she had her butler strike the supper gong again, drawing all eyes to her.

'My lords, ladies, and gentlemen,' she began, her voice slow and assured. 'I thank you for attending my ball tonight. As you will know, it has been some years since I hosted such an event, but tonight I have a special announcement to make.' A murmur of interest rippled through the crowd. 'Some of you may remember my granddaughter, Maria Berkeley, who died many years ago. However, I have recently discovered that the manner and timing of her death was not as I had been led to believe, through smallpox when she was eighteen. No.'

Pausing to allow this to sink in, she waited. Once the crowd was again entirely silent, she continued.

'In fact, Maria ran away from home that day. My dear husband decided to put it about that she, too, had fallen victim to the smallpox that was rampaging through the village. But it was not true.'

'She is alive?' Mrs Thaxby looked astounded, and Lady Kelgrove shook her head. 'I have just said she died, but in fact that occurred a number of years later.' Addressing the crowd again, she continued. 'Before she died she made arrangements for her children's care.' Lady Kelgrove smiled. 'Yes, I have great-grandchildren. Three of them, in fact.

Maria arranged for them to be placed in the guardianship of Mr Marnoch in Scotland, a gentleman to whom I owe a debt of gratitude.'

At this, a couple of people seemed to realise what was happening. Lady Mary Renford's jaw dropped, her head swinging towards Rose. Miss Phillips's, too.

'Come and stand beside me, girls.' Lady Kelgrove threw out an arm, and Izzy rose with her sisters, making their way through the tables to the top of the supper room. 'I present to you my great-granddaughters: the new Lady Ashbourne, Miss Lennox, and Miss Isobel Lennox.'

I am now the lowest in ranking among my sisters, Izzy noted absently. *Rose's marriage has put her first. I am happy for her.*

It was just…her mind could not continue, struggling as it was to hold any thread of logic, sequence, or understanding.

Applause rang out, thunderous to Izzy's ears. There was cheering, too, from some quarters and much excited chatter. And then it began—just as at their presentation to the queen at the beginning of the Season, the triplets found themselves surrounded by well-wishers.

There is a symmetry in that, Izzy thought dazedly.

Beginning and end.

To be fair, one or two—Lady Renford, Mrs Thaxby—seemed to congratulate them through gritted teeth, but most of the others seemed genuinely pleased for them. And Lady Kelgrove was in alt, a sight Izzy was glad to see.

Strangely, there was something unusual about how people were looking at her. Or was she imagining it? Tittering behind fans, arch looks… And had that lady really just murmured, 'It seems Prince Claudio has made his choice'? No, her imaginings must be running riot.

But why was Lord Ashbourne looking so grim, listening to quiet words from a middle-aged gentleman with a saddened demeanour?

Surely, this is a happy occasion?

But her mind was gone again, dancing away before she could apply any rigour or logic.

Of Prince Claudio there was no sign.

Perhaps he left after...after...

'I think we can leave now,' declared Lady Ashbourne. 'Isobel, how are you feeling?'

She is referring to my illness. Nothing else.

'Unwell, my lady. Dreadfully unwell.' Nausea had now begun to swirl within her. 'I think I might be sick.'

'Lord, not in Lady Kelgrove's supper room! Quickly, let us go outside. We can leave from the garden.'

'My sisters should stay, though. It would be best for Lady Kelgrove…'

'Yes, of course! Now, go!'

The nausea was manageable, allowing Izzy to make brief farewells on her way to the garden doors. Lady Kelgrove was sympathetic and appreciative of the fact Izzy had waited for her announcement. 'Now, go, child. The Dowager Lady Ashbourne will take care of you, I know.'

They left, and an hour later Izzy was in her bed, shivering with cold and glad to close her eyes. 'I shall be better in the morning, no doubt,' she told Lady Ashbourne, 'for I am *never* sick. I shall defeat this in double-quick time. Just wait and see!'

Chapter Fourteen

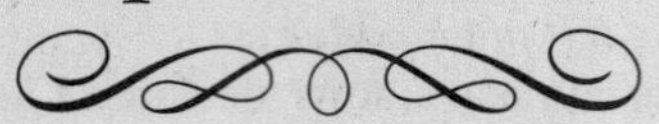

Claudio felt confused. The church clock in front of him had just struck eight. Morning or evening?

Having left the ball directly from the terrace, he had stridden through the districts of Mayfair and St James's for hours, trying to work through the anger, remorse, guilt, and fear pulsing through him. Unable to calm himself through endless walking, he had eventually found a grubby tavern. After only two mugs of ale he had put his head down on the table and slept fitfully for an hour or so. On waking, he had paid his reckoning and stepped outside into bright sunshine.

Looking about, he saw tradesmen and servants bustling about their business.

It is morning, then.

A new day. A fresh start. Yet there was nothing fresh about Claudio's heart. Or his head. Over and over he recalled Isobel's words to him. Her curled lip. Her clear disdain. As a prince, he had never before seen disdain from anyone. And this had been earned. Justified. He felt raw, exposed.

She sees me. And she does not like what she sees.

Isobel was right. Eldon and Hawkins had never been his friends. He had no one.

She had seen him naked, though she might not have realised it at the time. Now he was naked in a new way. His soul had been ruthlessly exposed and found wanting.

Now more memories returned. The pain in her eyes when he had hit out at her with words designed to hurt. He had hurt the woman he loved. Deliberately. Knowingly.

Yes, he himself had been suffering at the time. But he had no excuses. On he walked through the lanes and thoroughfares of London, dodging milk carts and butchers' wagons, street hawkers and jarveys. A hearse almost ran him over, which was strangely fitting. By ten o'clock he had achieved a reasonable state of numbness. By noon, reluctantly, he set his feet towards Buckingham House.

What to do? How could he possibly put this right? He groaned aloud as a new memory drew his attention. Instead of speaking to her, trying to apologise again, he had ended by kissing her in front of the man she was probably betrothed to. And she had not even responded, for she was already lost to him. Never before had he kissed an unwilling woman. He had been so sure of her response, so arrogant...

Self-loathing rose in a wave within him. He was nothing, worse than useless. A failure to his father, to the queen, to himself.

A carriage was waiting just outside the gates. He passed it, not particularly looking, for his mind was most definitely elsewhere, and he had no vitality for noticing. A moment later, he was hailed by someone and he turned to see Lord Ashbourne descending from the carriage, just as a cloud passed over the sun, rendering the day suddenly dull and grey.

Bracing himself for social discourse, Claudio managed what he hoped was a polite smile.

'Your Highness.' Lord Ashbourne's bow was shallow, his face tight.

'Lord Ashbourne.'

Something is not right here.

The hairs were standing to attention at the back of Claudio's neck.

What can he have to say to me?

Better in the morning? How wrong Izzy had been.

In the morning she was worse, much worse, with sickness, fever, and aching bones. Her mind, too, was fevered with no ability to think straight or even form clear thoughts. The doctor was sent for, and he poked and prodded her with hands that were cold, while Izzy wished him a hundred miles away.

'Influenza!' he declared, to no one's great surprise. Rose and Anna were banned from the sick room, for fear they would also succumb, and Lady Ashbourne arranged for a daywatch and nightwatch of maids to tend to Izzy's needs. These were not many, for Izzy simply lay there, tossing and turning feverishly at times, and needing only cool cloths on her forehead when overheated and a hot brick by her feet when she shivered. She could not eat, for even the lightest of soups brought on sickness.

'Tisanes,' the doctor had ordered. 'Tisanes and teas. She must drink.' And so they gave her tisanes. Every half hour, or so it seemed to her. The only time she put her foot to the floor was when she needed the chamber pot, and the maids had to support her—just as though she were a child. That was good, for as a child she held no responsibilities. She had no heart to be broken and no memory to make her feel things she did not wish to feel.

'I have been waiting for you.' Lord Ashbourne's tone was clipped, his face pale. He cast an eye over Claudio's rumpled grey coat from the night before. 'I see you have not yet been home.'

'Yes? Is there something I can do for you?' Even as he spoke, Claudio's mind was working feverishly.

Isobel!

Had she told Ashbourne about his harsh words last night? Or his kiss later? Surely Kirby would not have spoken, for he would not wish any rumour to sully the good name of his affianced bride?

'I shall not waste your time with preamble.' Taking off one of his leather gloves, he slapped it across Claudio's face. 'As Miss Isobel's closest male relative, I challenge you to a duel for her honour.'

All the blood had drained from Claudio's face. 'Her honour?' His mind was befuddled. 'But why?'

Ashbourne's eyes blazed. 'You think it nothing to kiss a maiden in full view and not immediately offer to marry her? Instead you walked away, left the ball entirely.' His scornful tone made his opinion clear. 'No.' Ashbourne held up a hand. 'I care nothing for your excuses. Name your second!'

Who will stand with me?

A series of names flashed through his mind, but there could be only one man—save Ashbourne himself, under other circumstances—whom Claudio would want as his second.

'Garvald,' he declared grimly, and Ashbourne nodded. 'Very well. I shall ask Phillips to call on him. I shall see you at dawn tomorrow.'

Then he was gone, leaving Claudio in a state of shock. Helplessly, he watched Ashbourne's carriage until it was out of sight, his thoughts disordered and his heart sore.

I shall die in the morning, then.

He had no intention of firing at Rose's husband, for to

injure such a man would hurt Isobel. And besides, he was in the wrong. He could not, in good conscience, defend himself, for he had done precisely what Ashbourne had accused him of.

It mattered little if he died, after all. No one would even miss him.

Prince Claudio's suite was the most luxurious in Buckingham House, save those of the king and queen and their many offspring. Both the bedchamber and drawing room were opulent and well-furnished, with paintings hung upon the walls and the best of carpets, curtains, vases, and statuary as embellishment.

But the suite also contained a third chamber, accessible only by using a discreet handle in the drawing-room panelling. This room was small and windowless, but spotlessly clean. Here the prince's clothing was stored, washed, and mended, and here Jenkins slept, ready at all times to respond to the small bell, should His Highness have need of him.

And His Highness did have need of him, Jenkins was certain. Something ailed the young prince, but Jenkins was not privy to the details. All he knew was that when Prince Claudio had arrived two hours ago, he had been in a strange mood. Discarding his clothes from the night before, he had bathed and taken to his bed without so much as a bite to eat. And he had not been in the least bit foxed, Jenkins was certain. No, he knew his charge well enough after all these months serving him to know that he was sober as a judge, and just as inscrutable.

As he went about his duties—washing the prince's linen shirt and cravat, methodically cleaning his coat and knee breeches, polishing his boots and cleaning his dancing shoes—all the while Jenkins's mind was racing.

Something is not right.

Breaking off from his work to straighten and stretch, on impulse Jenkins decided to leave the suite, despite his sense of duty reminding him he should not. Seeking out the queen's personal maid, he quizzed her about the evening before. Had anything unusual taken place at Lady Kelgrove's ball?

'Aye, you could say that. Her Majesty told me the Lennox triplets have been claimed by her ladyship as the daughters of Miss Maria, Lady Kelgrove's granddaughter. Such a to-do! Long-lost family, and the girls all now heiresses to a sizeable fortune!'

Thanking her, Jenkins returned to his post, pondering how this news might account for the prince's strange mood. Rumour among the queen's servants held that he might have had an assignation with a young lady during the masked ball, and one servant had sworn he had seen one of the identical Lennox girls in that part of the garden.

So has he a tendre *for one of Lady Kelgrove's great-granddaughters?*

Yet why should this make Prince Claudio unhappy? For he *was* unhappy, of that Jenkins had no doubt. Unhappy, and unsettled, and with signs of chaos beneath the surface. If he wanted to marry a Miss Lennox, her happy connections should make that an easier task, surely?

Sighing and returning to his tasks, Jenkins continued to ponder over the riddle. Something about Prince Claudio's demeanour was reminding of something or someone else, but he could not figure out who, what, or when. Yet all his instincts were calling upon him to pay attention, and so he would.

* * *

'Come, now, Miss Isobel, and let me change your bed.'

Izzy was vaguely aware that her fever-racked body had soaked the sheets, and that they were really uncomfortable. The problem was that she was unable to move. Helplessly she lifted an arm to the maid, and between her and the housekeeper they managed to lift Izzy into a nearby chair. Her head ached, her throat was agonisingly raw, and she knew she would need to be sick again before long. The maid put a fresh nightgown on her while the housekeeper changed the bed, while Izzy clutched her sick bowl, shivering and sweating all the while.

How can I be both red-hot and freezing-cold at the same time?

Thankfully she was then allowed to lie down again, a willow-bark tisane dutifully swallowed despite the pain.

Sometime later she became aware that her bed was on fire. At least, that was how it felt. The flames were in her, on her, all around her. And why were firm hands holding her ankles?

Something is in my mouth.

Gagging, she opened her eyes, trying to bring her hands up to her mouth, but her wrists, too, were being held. Shocked, she met the eyes of Mrs Coleby.

'Thank the Lord!' the housekeeper declared, letting go of Izzy's right hand and right ankle. 'You can let go, Sally. And Jane, take that spoon out of her mouth. The convulsions have ended.'

Convulsions?

I had convulsions?

Izzy had heard, of course, that one could put a wooden spoon in the mouth of a fitting child, to prevent them from accidentally biting their tongue, having been called upon to assist occasionally when younger girls at school had been unwell with a high fever. It had never happened to her, though. Not until today. And she was now certain that it was the worst advice ever.

After that the doctor came again, and vaguely Izzy knew this was not good. Twice in one day.

Is it still today?

Forcing her eyes open, she managed to see his grim expression, the concerned looks he was exchanging with Lady Ashbourne.

'Her fever is too high,' he muttered. Then there was something about seizures…but Izzy had lost the ability to understand. Letting go, she sank back down into blackness.

'Your Highness.' Then again, more loudly. 'Your Highness!' It was the blasted valet.

Blearily, Claudio opened one eye. 'What the devil do you mean by this, Jenkins?' he muttered. 'Can you not see I am sleeping? Or at least I *was*.'

'I apologise, but the Earl of Garvald is here to see you. He insists on being admitted.'

Claudio sighed. 'Very well. He will have to give me ten minutes. What time is it?'

'Eight in the evening, Your Highness.'

He sat up.

I shall not sleep again in this life.

'I shall wear the blue coat, please.' He thought for a moment. 'And the white and gold waistcoat.'

'Very good, Your Highness. Knee breeches?'

'No. Buckskins, if you please. I do not mean to attend any engagements tonight.'

Twenty minutes later, his valet having taken some time to speak to Garvald and to help him into the requested clothing, Claudio left his bedchamber for the drawing room that was part of the suite allocated to him by the queen.

Garvald was there, pacing, but stopped when Claudio came in. 'Your Highness!'

'Call me Claudio.' He gave a tight smile. 'You are to be my second, after all.'

'It is t-true, then?' The earl ran a hand through his dark hair, clearly agitated. 'I could scarce believe it when Phillips called.'

'What has been agreed?'

'Dawn. Hampstead Heath—a well-known spot. And… er…pistols.'

'That I had surmised. So much cleaner than a swordfight to the death, do you not think?'

Garvald seemed momentarily bereft of speech. 'I—I cannot understand why you are so calm about it.'

Claudio shrugged. 'Shall we meet outside here before dawn? What time?'

They agreed on the arrangements, Garvald offering to bring his carriage and to arrange a doctor. Claudio waved this away. 'If you must.'

'You know,' offered Garvald a little more conversationally, 'when I was at Oxford I ran wild.'

Claudio raised an eyebrow. 'You did? I cannot see you as a wild young man.'

'Oh, but I was.' He grinned. 'Perpetually drunk, wenching, gambling. It was the first time I had ever had any freedom, you see. My poor mother must have been in despair at my antics—at least, those she heard about.' He eyed Claudio closely. 'It does not mean I am a bad person.'

'Of course not.'

He is not me, though.

The earl was a sensible, sober gentleman, who no doubt

enjoyed a drink and a flirtation as much as any man, but he had not Claudio's reputation. He had not done to anyone what Claudio had done to Isobel.

At least my father is not here to share my shame.

'I must write some letters. I shall see you as agreed.'

'Wait.'

Claudio paused.

'It is the role of the seconds to try and see if the duel can be prevented, if an accommodation might be reached.' He took a breath. 'I understand Lord Ashbourne has taken exception at an insult to his wife's sister.'

'Miss Isobel, yes. He says I kissed her in the presence of witnesses and did not afterwards offer for her hand.'

'And is that true?'

'It is.'

Garvald's eyes widened briefly, then grew hard. 'And do you intend to offer for her?'

Claudio shrugged. 'My understanding is that she is betrothed to another. To Mr Kirby, in fact.'

Garvald was frowning. 'Something is not right here. If she is betrothed and the betrothal stands, then her reputation will withstand this. I must speak with Ashbourne.'

'As you wish.' Claudio, not wishing to think of her wedding to Kirby for as much as an instant, brushed this off, and Garvald left soon afterwards.

Standing before the mirror in his bedchamber, Claudio forced himself to look at his own reflection. Shame rose within him like bile, but he squared his shoulders. The very least he could do was to go to his fate with acceptance. He had brought this upon himself through his own dishonourable actions, yet he would do his best to face the consequences like a true prince.

* * *

Lady Ashbourne was there again. Vaguely, Izzy could hear her giving instructions.

'Above all, the doctor has said we must prevent the fever from harming her. When she is feverish you must sponge her down. Yes, and open the window, too!' She lowered her voice a little. 'And if she has more convulsions, you must send for me at once.'

'But, my lady, we were always told to keep the window closed in a sickroom.' The maid's voice was timid.

My bedchamber is now a sickroom.

'Well, I trust Dr Crawford's opinion. You will do as he says.'

'Yes, my lady.'

Claudio sat down to a delicious dinner with the queen, setting out to entertain and charm her, so that she might not realise anything was amiss. She had been at Lady Kelgrove's ball, of course, but seemed not to have heard about his actions on the terrace. Not yet, at least. Instead she had other news for him. Astounding news. The Lennox sisters were the great-granddaughters of Lady Kelgrove herself!

Claudio was astonished and inwardly delighted for them. No more would his beloved Isobel suffer the cruelties of those who whispered in corners about the triplets' lack of parentage. Of course, he himself had been the most cruel, throwing it angrily in Isobel's face. Still, his punishment was on its way, and he was resigned to it.

Afterwards, sitting at his desk, he spent the dark hours of the night writing letters—to his father, his brothers, the queen, and Isobel. It was quite the most difficult thing he had ever had to do. Just how many ways could he find to apologise to them all for his failings and foolish acts?

Glancing at the clock on his mantel, he stood. *It is time.* Gathering up all his failed drafts, he placed them in the grate and set fire to them with a taper. Then, tucking the completed letters into a small folio, he looked around his suite for the last time, before heading out into the darkness.

'Oh, Izzy! Izzy! Please live!'

Vaguely, Izzy realised that Anna and Rose were with her, and that Anna was crying.

But why?

Anna *never* cried.

'Girls, girls!' It was Lady Ashbourne.

The Dowager Lady Ashbourne, Izzy's mind briefly reminded her.

'You should go now. I do not want either of you to catch it as well!'

'Absolutely not!' Rose's tone was firm. 'We know what the doctor said.'

'We lost Mama and could do nothing for her.' Anna spoke quietly, her voice ragged. 'We will stay with Izzy until we know she will be well.'

A deliciously cool cloth was placed on her forehead, and she moaned at the wonderful sensation—a tiny moment of relief amid an agony of pain and discomfort.

'Hush now, Izzy, we are with you.'

Someone squeezed her hand, and somewhere deep in her soul, Izzy felt the love of her sisters.

I am not alone.

Jenkins woke, briefly confused. Why had he left a branch of candles burning? And why was he lying on top of his truckle bed, fully dressed? Then he remembered, and rose swiftly, realising the sound that had awoken him had been that of the prince leaving his suite. Taking the candles, Jenkins emerged into the prince's drawing room, his mind furnishing him with recollections of half-heard exchanges from the day before. Jenkins had tried to eavesdrop unashamedly, but all he had heard were snatches of conversation—something about Ashbourne, and Kirby.

Perhaps they are all going early to a race meet or a cockfight, and I am foolish to be concerned.

The prince had been writing letters when he had dismissed Jenkins and, most unusually, had not asked the valet to remove his boots.

'I may yet go out' had been his explanation, offered with an insouciant air, but it had added to Jenkins's concerns. Why on earth would he want to go out *after* one in the morning? Unless he had meant to leave very early the next day. But if he and his friends were simply going to a cockfight, why would the prince not ask his valet to help with his boots? Ladies might disapprove of such pursuits, but valets had no opinion on such matters. It made no sense.

Glancing towards the desk, he saw that Prince Claudio had made use of the sealing wax, yet no letters were on the desk awaiting Jenkins's collection for sending.

Where are they?

A small fire was lit in the grate, despite the heat of the summer night, and the incongruity struck Jenkins as significant. Drafts, perhaps? Something that might provide some insight into the prince's odd demeanour. Swiftly he bent to the fire, rescuing a small fragment of paper. Only a few words were visible…

…my shame…
…most heartily sorry…
…is for the best…

Not a cockfight, then.

In an instant Jenkins caught the memory that had been dancing around the edge of his mind, and he recoiled in shock and horror.

I must follow him!

Wasting no further time, he moved swiftly through the building, using back stairs and servants' corridors that the prince would not be aware of. Concealing himself in the dark garden, to his satisfaction the prince emerged a few moments later, his face briefly lit by one of the flambeaux at the front door. Drawing up the hood of his dark cloak, he walked stealthily towards the gates, and Jenkins followed.

To Jenkins's surprise, a carriage was waiting outside—a well-appointed carriage at that. Quickening his pace, Jenkins saw a groom open the door to allow the prince to climb inside, heard a male voice greet him. He broke into a run as the groom hopped up behind, reaching the carriage just in time.

'Well, help me up, then!' he said testily to the groom, keeping his voice low.

'And who might you be?'

'I am the prince's valet.'

As he had hoped, no further questions were asked, the groom helping him up to the second perch at the rear of the carriage. Belatedly, Jenkins realised the prince would likely not be best pleased when he realised his valet had followed him.

He might call for me to be dismissed.

Yet Jenkins *knew* he was doing the right thing. As the carriage rolled through the predawn streets of London, he allowed himself to remember that other case, the one from ten years ago. A young footman had drowned in the

Thames—accidentally, they had said. But then, they'd had to say that so the poor man could get a proper burial in holy ground.

Jenkins had always wondered, though. The man's sweetheart had broken with him a few days before, and Jenkins would never forget the young man's strange demeanour on that last day. An unnatural calmness, belying the turmoil that must have been going on inside him.

I am the prince's valet.

Over the years, as part of a team of royal valets, Jenkins had attended to many distinguished guests and visitors, both in Kew Palace and in Buckingham House. Yet never before had he spent so long with a single master, and he had developed an unfortunate attachment to the young prince. Unfortunate, for the Season was almost done, and the *ton* would shortly disperse to their various country estates, leaving Jenkins under the direct orders of Her Majesty's butler. Jenkins foresaw a summer of cleaning silverware and—worse—covering for the valets to the queen's sons.

Jenkins, naturally, was not privy to the prince's intentions, but he guessed the young man would either return to his home on the Rhine, or marry and settle in England. Either way, Jenkins's time serving him was coming to an end, and he discovered he would sincerely miss the young man. Despite his shocking habit of parading around naked with the curtains open, he was a kind and generous master, considering Jenkins's own comfort at times.

Perhaps he simply kept his boots on to avoid having to rouse me at this unearthly hour.

Doubts once again filled Jenkins's head.

Lord! I am a fool, and so he will tell me!

He gasped, and the groom turned to look at him. The first glimmers of dawn were showing, obscured by the early-morning fog that regularly featured at this time of year. The sun would burn it off by midmorning, but for now it was difficult to see more than ten paces away. 'Never say we are making for the Heath!'

'We are.' The groom nodded grimly. 'An affair of honour, I believe. My master—Garvald—is to be second to His Highness.'

It is as I feared, then. 'And his opponent?'

'Ashbourne.'

'Lord Ashbourne? But why?'

The groom shrugged. 'Something to do with a lady.' He chuckled. 'Is it not always so?'

Jenkins's mind was working furiously. Lord Ashbourne had lately married one of the Lennox sisters. Had the prince seduced the young bride? Jenkins could not believe it. From what he knew, Prince Claudio had limited his dalliances to willing tavern maids and the like. No, that could not be it.

He considered the matter. The prince had been acting a little distractedly recently, and Jenkins had already suspected him to be lovesick. One of the other Lennox girls? The one he may have dallied with at the Queen's Masquerade? That had to be part of this.

They had arrived. Through the grey gloom Jenkins saw two other carriages. As the coachman wheeled around to stop between them he realised that one contained Ashbourne and his second, the other a doctor.

Much use the doctor will be, if my master intends to die today!

That could be the only logical conclusion to the words in Prince Claudio's letter.

...my shame...
...most heartily sorry...
...is for the best...

His heart sank. How on earth was he meant to avert such a disaster?

Chapter Fifteen

I am ill. Very ill.

This was the first and only thought Izzy had had since the nightmare had begun. All other thoughts were variations on that theme.

I need the basin—I am going to be sick. I am too hot. Why is it so cold? My head hurts. It is agony to swallow. Why is this night lasting so long?

Despite being exhausted she could only achieve brief snatches of sleep. And every time she opened her aching eyes it was still dark.

Why is it still night?

Anna and Rose were not there. Vaguely, she remembered telling them to go to bed, that she would be well. They had protested, but she was Izzy, and so she insisted with all the determination she was capable of. And they had gone in the end.

'Open the curtains,' she murmured, knowing her voice was weak, but thankfully the maid heard her.

'Now, then, miss, it ain't quite morning yet.'

'Please,' she begged. 'I just want this night to be over.'

'Ah, dear, dear. Very well, but I hope the housekeeper does not slay me for this.' Rising, she crossed the room and opened the heavy drapes. In the candlelight the outside world was black as pitch, but a breath of cool air wafted gently from the world outside. 'Morning will be here soon,' she added in a reassuring tone.

Izzy closed her eyes.

Claudio was numb. He could feel nothing, having retreated into a place deep within himself where there was safety, where reality had no meaning. They descended from their various carriages with identical grim expressions on their faces, completing the usual social greetings just as though they were at a ball and not a duel. Yet the black cloaks they all wore gave the gathering a funereal air, which was entirely appropriate.

Mr Phillips carried a small wooden box containing a pair of pistols, and he and Garvald stepped to one side to examine them, while Ashbourne and Claudio simply stood there. All around them swirled the fog, giving the entire experience a sense of unreality. They were in a clearing in the woods, their world bounded by a cage of tall trees, straight, black, and resolute—massive headstones towering over this place. A place of death.

Surprisingly, dawn was breaking, the greyness lightening every moment. A bird called, then another. They, too, could sense the dawn. As the calls became a chorus Claudio listened, conscious of the beauty of the sound. Never before had he appreciated such a simple thing. Closing his eyes, he immersed himself in the birdsong, just for a few breaths.

Footsteps. He opened his eyes. Garvald and Phillips were ready, Garvald drawing him aside for one last conversation. 'Keep your cloak about you and stand sideways on,' he urged. 'That will make you a harder target for him to hit.'

Claudio did not respond, knowing he intended to ensure that he was as easy a target as he possibly could manage to be.

'Wait—do you intend to delope?' Garvald asked.

Claudio frowned briefly, trying to recall the meaning of the English word. *Ah!* Shooting into the air instead of at his opponent. He nodded.

'Yes. I could not harm or injure her sister's husband.' He handed Garvald the neat folio he had tucked into his cloak. 'Letters for my loved ones, if you please.'

Garvald sighed, taking it and perusing the names on each cover. 'This is a bad business. A very bad business.'

Claudio made no response, and so, shoulders drooping, Garvald walked with Claudio back to the others. After exchanging glances with Phillips, who shook his head, he spoke.

'I ask you both one last time, can you resolve this? Your Highness, can you apologise?'

'Willingly,' replied Claudio promptly. 'Though I do not believe that will satisfy Lord Ashbourne.' He looked his opponent in the eye. 'I apologise sincerely. I never meant to do her harm. But I am, nevertheless, conscious of the fact that is exactly what I have done.'

Ashbourne raised a sceptical eyebrow. 'You are correct. My sister-in-law's reputation cannot be recovered through words. Only deeds.' Rage was apparent in every line of his body, in the harshness in his voice. 'Will you agree to marry her?'

Claudio's heart swelled at the notion.

I should love it above all things.

'Gladly, though I do not believe she would have me. And besides, I understand she is already betrothed to Mr Kirby.'

Ashbourne frowned. 'To Kirby? I think not!' He glanced to the seconds.

'Mr Kirby is out of town,' Garvald replied, 'having departed early yesterday morning, and when I called at the house yesterday I was informed Miss Isobel is unwell, so I was unable to establish the truth of this.'

She is unwell!

Claudio had no doubt that Isobel's heart was sore, not her body.

She has been laid low by my actions. This responsibility I must also bear.

Ashbourne shook his head. 'Yes, she is ill. And no, to my knowledge she is not betrothed. In the absence of her guardian, Kirby should have come to me. Unless…' He frowned. 'It is possible, I suppose, that he is on his way to Mr Marnoch in Scotland.'

Naturally the staid Mr Kirby would wish to do things correctly. And Claudio had no right to come between them, if Kirby was Isobel's choice.

'This is a dreadful muddle,' Ashbourne continued. 'Still, one thing is certain. Each day she continues without a betrothal, and with news of your actions circulating, her reputation suffers more.' His eyes hardened. 'Honour must be satisfied. If she is to marry Kirby, then the responsibility falls to him. But I have no notion of such a betrothal, and so I stand as her closest male relative in London. And no maiden in her right mind would turn down an offer from royalty. I say you dissemble, and delay, and prevaricate, and all the while she suffers.'

There was no point arguing. 'Then, let us do this. Right now!'

Though the final words had been his, Claudio had no regrets. This was how his life was fated to end.

That is it, then. No reprieve.

Slowly Claudio walked with Ashbourne to the centre of the clearing, feeling every step, every breath, every heartbeat.

Just as Garvald was preparing to give the combatants their instructions, a cry rang out from the direction of the carriages.

'Stop! You must not!'

All heads turned as a vaguely familiar figure stepped forward. Recognition dawned.

'Jenkins!' Claudio was astounded. 'What do you mean by this?'

What have I done?

Jenkins was trembling so badly his knees were genuinely knocking. As a servant, he was meant to be unobtrusive, invisible. Never seen or heard unless required by his master.

Well, my master needs me now, whether he knows it or not.

'Your Highness.' He made a deep bow. 'My lords and gentlemen.'

'Who is this person, Claudio?' Garvald sounded exasperated.

'My valet. Speak, Jenkins, and this had better be good!'

'He—I—the queen will be most displeased, Your Highness. If you die, I mean.'

'And what of it?' The prince looked furious. 'Honour, as Lord Ashbourne has already highlighted, must be satisfied.' Dismissing Jenkins with a wave of his hand, the prince turned away. 'Shall we proceed?' They began to walk away, then Lord Ashbourne paused, turning to look at Jenkins, a curious expression on his face.

'Is there more, Jenkins?' he asked in a low voice.

Jenkins nodded. 'Two things. I believe he *intends* to die today. And I believe he is enamoured of the lady.'

Ashbourne's eyes narrowed, then he shrugged. 'Noted.' Then he, too, walked on while Jenkins made his way back to the shadows of the carriages.

'Better than a play!' the groom was muttering, clearly entertained by Jenkins's intervention. Jenkins ignored him.

Claudio was experiencing severe mortification. That a servant would dare do such a thing—follow him to his assignation, then interfere with the actions of his master! Never had Claudio known anything like it. And what was more, he had succeeded in turning this tragedy into something of a comedy. A farce, even. Falling back on his dignity, Claudio schooled his features into impassivity and listened to Garvald's instructions.

'You will each take a pistol from Mr Phillips and stand back to back here. When I give the word you will walk twenty paces at my count, then turn and shoot. Understood?'

Claudio nodded grimly. Randomly selecting one of the pistols, he checked it and weighed it in his hand. It mattered not anyway, for he had no intention of shooting Rose's husband. Isobel's brother-in-law. Ashbourne, on the other hand, was checking his pistol assiduously, ensuring it was primed and ready. Claudio, feeling rather sick, looked away.

Lord James Arthur Henry Drummond, the Viscount Ashbourne, was vexed. Recently married to the wonderful Rose Lennox, he was fiercely protective of his beloved wife and her sisters and had been white-hot with rage when informed of Prince Claudio's insult to Isobel.

How dare he!

Even now, anger surged within him as he pictured the prince accosting Izzy in full public view. Reports had confirmed Isobel had not responded to his kiss, had seemed deeply shocked, and had sunk into a faint. Granted, Izzy had been in the early stages of influenza at the time, but this to James was further proof of the fact Isobel had not wished for the prince's attentions, for who could even *think* of such things while so unwell?

It was also significant, he reflected grimly, that the insult had taken place *before* Lady Kelgrove's announcement that the Lennox sisters were her great-granddaughters. Would Izzy have suffered in the same way if the prince had known of her illustrious parentage? James doubted it. No, the man had clearly believed he could insult Izzy, with no intention of offering marriage, and get away with it.

Checking his pistol, another aspect struck him anew. What of the man's insult to the Ashbourne family, to which Isobel now belonged? His own recent marriage to Rose was common knowledge—indeed he recalled the prince offering congratulations—and yet still Prince Claudio had assaulted Izzy.

Does he care nothing for my family's name and lineage?

Or had the prince believed James to be a *laissez-faire* protector, interested only in Rose? Well, if that had been the case, the man knew differently now. With a fair degree of satisfaction, James recalled how Prince Claudio had blanched when he had slapped him.

Yes, you did not expect me to take an interest in your sordid actions, did you?

The house and line of Ashbourne would be a laughing stock if honour were not satisfied. Ashbourne had no choice but to see this through.

Turning his back on the prince, he awaited Garvald beginning the count.

The next time I see him, I shall shoot him through the heart.

A flash of sanity appeared now in his brain, highlighting the enormity of his intentions just when he needed to be resolute. Never had he killed a man, yet honour demanded it for an outrage such as this.

The count began, and Ashbourne paced slowly in time with Garvald's words, his steps measured, for the closer he ended up to the prince, the easier it would be to hit his target. Oh, he knew the *theory* of what his role required today, and he was no coward, and yet…

'Four…five…six…'

His mind flicked briefly to his beautiful wife, sleeping soundly at home. Thankfully, Izzy's fever had broken a few hours ago, and Rose had climbed into bed a little later, cold and exhausted, murmuring to him of her relief. She had not stirred when he had crept out of their bed an hour ago. He swallowed. The possibility of himself being shot and killed was very real, the knowledge swirling uncomfortably in his gut. Reminding himself that Claudio, and not he, was in the wrong, he hoped the young prince would have honour enough to acknowledge his sin by firing into the air.

For himself, though, he must have no intention of deloping. Honour must be satisfied. Even if, having killed his man, he would have to flee the country. Rose could join him in Paris or Vienna… But such matters were for another time.

'Eleven…twelve…thirteen…'

It was a pity, for he had found himself quite liking the prince before this. Yes, the man had been sporting all around London with the feather-brained, hedonistic duo of Hawkins and Eldon, but James had seen another side to him: charm, and intelligence, and what he had believed to be a sense of honour and dignity. An inconvenient memory now assailed him—of himself kissing Rose in the park, before they were betrothed.

That was different. I loved her, and my intentions were honourable.

He pushed the recollections from his mind, focusing once again on the task at hand.

'Sixteen…seventeen…eighteen…'

As the seconds ticked by and he paced on, Ashbourne's mind was now working furiously. The valet's words were sinking in.

I believe he intends to die today.

From what little he had seen of Prince Claudio's demeanour today, this could well be true. Regret? Guilt? A sense of honour? Perhaps the man was not without merit, then.

I believe he is enamoured of the lady.

If the valet was right about the first, perhaps he was also correct about the second.

So why will he not marry her?

Because of Kirby? Nothing made sense.

Time had run out. Despite the valet's best efforts earlier, the duel had not been prevented. It was time. *Twenty.* Turning, Ashbourne raised his gun, took aim, and fired.

Chapter Sixteen

'Twenty.'

Turning, Claudio pointed his gun into the air and fired, knowing that he was about to feel the fatal shot. In that instant, his thoughts—all disordered just a moment ago—now became clear. In his mind and heart at this moment there was only one person.

Isobel.

At least he had done right by her in this one thing. He had not argued, or evaded, or tried to flee England. He had stayed, accepting his fate. And she did not even know how much he loved her. Not yet, at least. Would Garvald give her the letter he had written? He hoped so.

The sound of a double report rang out, shockingly loud, and the stench of gun smoke filled Claudio's nostrils. When the smoke cleared he was still standing, his heart beating furiously and his stomach sick.

What? Why no pain?

Bewildered, he looked down. His white and gold waistcoat was an easy target, framed by the edges of his dark cloak. Indeed he had selected it for that very reason. Why was there no bloodstain seeping through the fabric? And why could he not feel anything?

'By G-god, Ashbourne, you m-missed!' Garvald's shout held a great deal of relief.

Strangely, Claudio's knees decided to melt away at that moment, and he fell to his knees, the gun sliding from his loose fingers.

Ashbourne missed!

His breathing sounded strange, ragged, and his brain would not work.

'Maybe not!' Phillips was running towards him. 'How do you, Your Highness?' Crouching down, he swept a hand across the prince's chest to check. 'Winged?' He checked Claudio's shoulders and arms, the left then the right.

'No,' Claudio croaked. 'He missed.'

Phillips exhaled loudly. 'Thank the Lord for that!' Rising, he eyed Ashbourne, who was approaching at leisure. 'You never miss! What the hell—?'

'Your pistol pulls to the left, Phillips,' Ashbourne declared mildly, handing the gun to Phillips. 'Besides, shooting a wafer at Manton's is a little different to shooting a man in a duel, do you not think?'

Claudio did not believe a word of it. Rising, he offered a hand. 'I am most heartily sorry for my insult to your sister-in-law.'

Ashbourne took it briefly, his expression grim. 'Honour has been satisfied—for now. But you *will* marry Isobel.' His tone did not allow for dissent. But then, Claudio had no intention of dissenting.

'Agreed.' He grimaced. 'If she will have me.'

'That part is up to you. But you must manage it.' He shrugged. 'You are a prince.'

'And Kirby?'

Ashbourne shrugged. 'Whatever may have been agreed between them, he has not formally sought her hand. In her guardian's absence, I imagine he will come to me.'

Claudio bowed. 'Then, may I formally request your permission to pay my addresses to her?'

'Granted. Once she is well again.'

'Of course.'

Ashbourne rubbed his hands together. 'Now, then. I find myself to be starving. Breakfast, perhaps? At White's?'

They assented and took to the carriages, Claudio still shaken by the fact he was, in fact, still alive and was expected to share breakfast with his opponent. Bewildered, he stole a glance towards the horizon, where a perfect sunrise was mocking recent events, slicing through the fog with hopeful intent.

'I am not dead,' he said aloud, making Garvald chuckle.

'No.' His brow furrowed. 'Though, you should be. Ashbourne rarely misses at Manton's.'

'Then, he deliberately spared me—even though I deserved to die.'

Garvald sent him a piercing look. 'Not many men live beyond the day they are fated to die. What do you intend to do with the opportunity?'

Elation flooded through Claudio. He had been fated to die and yet had lived. He felt renewed, reborn, washed clean of his past. He set his jaw, his voice thick with emotion.

'I intend to *live*, Garvald. To learn, and do, and love. To do more than play.'

'Good man.' Garvald nodded approvingly. 'Playing is still good, though—just…in *moderation*. And with the right company.'

Claudio's eyes narrowed. 'And would you have me? Allow me to be part of your set? Even though I have made so many errors, have wronged Miss Isobel and shamed my family and my name?'

Garvald punched him lightly on the arm. 'I thought you would never ask.'

* * *

Finally.

The next time Izzy opened her eyes there was light at the window. It was morning, and she had survived the night. She felt empty, exhausted. The headache and raw throat had not eased, but just now her bed was *not* on fire, and for that she was grateful. Turning onto her side, she looked towards the window with aching eyes. Outside the world was still wreathed in fog, but each moment brought more light, until finally the sun broke through.

Claudio was stone-cold sober yet had never been more contented. Having spent four hours in White's with Ashbourne, Garvald, and Phillips, eating, conversing, and drinking nothing more interesting than tea, he wondered at how he had ever thought their set to be staid and dull. He had been delighted to discover commonality of thought with the other gentlemen and to learn it was entirely possible to enjoy oneself tremendously while not being drunk.

Raillery there was, and plenty of it, but the humorous slights shared among his new friends were rather more intellectual in nature than the tavern-level insults traded among Eldon and Hawkins's set. Intellectual, yes, but all the more hilarious for it.

Claudio found himself watching and listening, and he realised that here, finally, was a group of men more akin to his character than either the dour courtiers at home or the drunken sots of his previous acquaintance in London. These gentlemen could go from a discussion of Napoleon's latest exploits in Western Russia, to gentle raillery, then on to a discussion of Hume's theory of knowledge without so much as a blink.

The day continued, the clock struck noon, and acquaintances came and went. Hawkins came by briefly, and Claudio rose to speak with him. Having stood for a few moments of empty speech, he informed Hawkins that he had committed to other engagements for the remaining few days in London and also that his summer plans had changed, meaning that he would not now be able to join him and Mr Eldon at Mr Hawkins's country residence as previously arranged.

'Ah, that is a shame! Still, we shall hope to see you in the autumn, yes?'

Claudio confirmed it, reflecting that the autumn was a long way away.

I might be a married man by then, if I can persuade Isobel to have me despite my appalling treatment of her.

Ashbourne's confirmation that Kirby had not formally sought permission for her hand gave him hope, although he knew he would have much to do if he was to court her successfully.

Crossing back to his new friends he retook his seat, then realised with a start they were all looking at him.

'Well?' Ashbourne's brows were raised. 'Have you made an assignation to meet your friends later?'

Claudio shook his head. 'I informed Hawkins that I will not spend the summer with him after all, and that I have other plans for this week.'

'Other plans?' Garvald arched a brow. 'Are you assuming we shall include you?' Hardly waiting for Claudio to react, he instead slapped his arm in an amicable manner. 'Which we are. Am I right, my friends?'

They confirmed it, sending a glow of gratitude surging through Claudio, then outlined the engagements they had agreed to attend. 'Afterwards, we go to the clubs for a few brandies or some late-night wine, but we are not fond of tavern fare, and we have outgrown the need for regular gambling,' declared Ashbourne soberly.

'Although we enjoy a good race meet or card party as much as the next man!' added Phillips, grinning.

'That sounds ideal,' Claudio confirmed, meaning it. 'I look forward to maintaining a more balanced approach to my leisure!' His expression changed. 'But I must ask you to advise me on matters of substance.' He took a breath. 'As you know, I intend to offer for Miss Isobel Lennox.' He gave a wry smile. 'In truth, I adore her, and nothing would make me happier than to win her hand. But as you are also well aware, I have made a complete—what is the phrase you use?—mill…mull?' They nodded at the latter. 'Ah, yes! I have made a *mull* of it, and I think she will not have me.'

'Kissing her without permission in full view of the gossips was not, perhaps, the best strategy,' offered Ashbourne dryly. 'Nevertheless, it happened, and as soon as she is well enough, I intend to inform her of her obligation to marry you.'

Phillips was frowning. 'But—forgive me—can there be any doubt about the matter? If she is not, after all, betrothed to Kirby, then what maiden will turn down a proposal from a prince? She will have you and be the envy of every débutante in London!'

Claudio grimaced.

I am not fit for my title, and Isobel knows it.

'I know how strong-willed Miss Isobel can be,' he offered cautiously. 'Indeed, it is one of the qualities I admire about her. But in this instance I fear it will work against me. I should inform you that she and I had words in the corridor just before the, er…incident on the terrace. I am afraid I said hurtful things to her.'

'And she to you?'

He shrugged. 'That is of no matter. But how am I to overcome the very real anger and antipathy she is likely to hold for me now?'

Ashbourne was frowning. 'So why did you kiss her on the terrace? I can understand that you may have been roused to anger following your argument, but what purpose—' His brow cleared. 'Did you mean to punish her?'

'No!' Claudio closed his eyes briefly, shaking his head. 'Though, I suppose that is what she may believe.' He eyed Ashbourne steadily. 'The truth is that when I went to the terrace Kirby had her by the hand, and I saw her kiss his cheek. After that I—I suppose I wanted one last kiss from her, before she wed him.' He brought a hand to his forehead. 'I was not thinking straight. Indeed, I have not been thinking straight since our argument—and even before.' He tapped his chest. 'All is turmoil within me.' He looked around them all. 'What? What have I said?'

They all bore startled expressions, Garvald now rolling his eyes and Phillips beginning to grin.

'"One last kiss", you said.' Ashbourne looked stern. 'Have you kissed her before?'

Claudio groaned. 'Lord, I should not have said that!' Sighing, he accepted the inevitable. 'Yes. At the Queen's Masquerade.'

'And she was willing?'

He nodded. 'We had an assignation to meet in the garden. She had previously told me that a maiden should only kiss a gentleman if she wishes to *and* if she can be certain they will not be observed.'

'How enterprising.' Ashbourne did not look impressed. 'I begin to understand that the sooner Miss Isobel is safely married, the better!'

Garvald was following a different scent. 'Then, she

wanted to kiss you that time? You have a…a connection, an affinity?'

'I believed so.' Hurt pierced him, dagger sharp. 'But that is gone now. How am I to marry a wife who no doubt detests me?'

They had no answer to this.

'Never mind,' declared Ashbourne. 'You will have a lifetime to convince her. Yes, and you have time now to plan how you might approach the matter. She is ill, and likely to remain so for a couple of weeks. It is influenza, according to the doctor.'

Influenza? 'Then, she is not unwell because of…what happened?' *Because of me.*

'No, of that you are absolved. She caught it from one of the housemaids.' Ashbourne frowned. 'She is quite unwell, actually. The doctor was concerned last evening because her fever was so high.'

Claudio caught his breath. 'That sounds worrying.'

So I might lose her, anyway, to illness. Lord, what is the point of me living if Isobel does not?

Ashbourne nodded. 'My wife refused to rest last night until the fever broke.' He glanced to the clock. 'I suspect she will soon awaken, and I intend to be there when she does.' Rising, he bowed and bade them farewell.

Phillips left soon afterwards, being promised to Lord Renford. His marriage to Lady Mary Renford was fixed for late July, and he and his future father-in-law were building a better acquaintance. A little later Garvald and Claudio departed, Garvald handing the prince his folio of letters when they got outside. Claudio went to take it, but Garvald paused, a curious expression on his face.

'A word of advice, Your Highness?'

'Call me Claudio.'

He nodded. 'Burn all these letters, save one. I know not what you wrote to Miss Isobel, but it might prove useful in your courtship.' His brow furrowed. 'In fact, it might be best if I keep it, for now. With your permission?'

Opening the folio, he extracted the letter addressed to Miss Isobel, then handed the rest over. Taking the folio, Claudio clasped his hand. 'Thank you for being my second. I appreciate it.'

'Any time.' Garvald grinned. 'And no, I do not mean you should engage in any further affairs of honour!'

The next few days passed in a daze of sickness, of aches and pains, sweats and shivers. While Izzy was nowhere near as ill as she had been on that awful night, she was still dreadfully unwell. Sometimes her sisters were there, sometimes Lady Ashbourne. Always a housemaid was with her, tending to her needs. Once she was capable of doing so, she expressed her gratitude to them incessantly, saving all of her grumpiness for Anna and Rose.

Knowing her well, her sisters ignored her petulant complaints, giving her only kindness and patience.

'Look!' Anna declared cheerfully. 'More flowers for you!'

Lady Kelgrove had already sent a large bouquet, which currently adorned one of the polished side tables in Izzy's bedchamber. This bunch was even larger and consisted of perfect red roses and delicate violets entwined with ivy and tied with a simple ribbon. Rose had just brought it and was currently arranging the blooms to her satisfaction.

'How lovely!' Izzy attempted a smile, but the muscles in her face were too tired, so she subsided. 'Who are they from?'

Kirby, perhaps. Not Mr Fitch, for I am out of favour with

him and his mama. But Mr Kirby is kind enough, even in his disappointment, to—

'They are from Prince Claudio!' Rose's tone was bright.

Instantly a slice of pain—different to the physical pains of illness, yet just as potent—stabbed through her. 'Take them away!'

'But, Izzy—'

'No! Take them away!'

Rose sighed. 'Very well. I shall bring them back to the drawing room, where we can at least enjoy them.' A look passed between her and Anna, a look Izzy knew well.

They are humouring me.

Still, in this moment the only battle she had to fight was to get all traces of Prince Claudio from her chamber. Would that she could cleanse her heart and mind so easily.

Having finally plucked up the courage to visit Ashbourne House while the ladies were at-home, Claudio was close to regretting it, for the Dowager—the Viscount Ashbourne's aunt—was clearly vexed with him. Oh, she was all politeness, but there was none of the warmth that had characterised their previous conversations.

Isobel's sisters had sensed it, too, departing after only a short time using the pretext of bringing his flowers up to Miss Isobel. After they had gone he had politely quizzed the elder Lady Ashbourne about Miss Isobel's health, and while she answered readily enough, all the while her eyes flashed with anger.

'Yes, she was dreadfully ill,' she continued. 'Influenza is a terrible, terrible illness, and she has suffered greatly.'

Claudio swallowed. 'But she is recovering, you say? She will be well again?' Lord, how difficult it was to feign polite concern when inwardly his gut was knotted as he awaited news of his beloved.

Lady Ashbourne sniffed. 'I daresay. And no thanks to those who would wish her harm!' She glared at him. 'Including those who would harm her reputation!'

'My lady,' he began, 'I am glad you have referred to this, for I must be honest with you. May I speak plainly?'

She assented, regal as his cousin, the queen, and he spoke. He had no plan, no prepared speech. He simply spoke from the heart, being careful to omit any mention of events on Hampstead Heath. Duels were not for the ears of ladies, for they tended to abhor such things.

At first her ladyship was unreadable, then astonished, then exasperated.

'Oh, for goodness' sake! Never—' she sent him a fierce look '—have I heard such folly! Or at least only rarely. You young men! Why, you are just as bad as… But never mind that.' She sighed. 'And now it is all a muddle, and she will not have you!'

His heart sank. 'I know. And yet, because of my impetuous actions, she must. But I want no unwilling bride.'

Lady Ashbourne knew Isobel. As did he. Her strong will and stubborn character would not be easily persuaded. *She will not have you.*

'And my nephew?' Her ladyship eyed him keenly.

'Lord Ashbourne has insisted I marry her.'

She gave a nod of approval. 'Quite right, too.'

'And it is my dearest wish. But my own stupidity means—'

He broke off as Rose entered, carrying the same bouquet she had left with not long before.

'Izzy will not—Oh! Your Highness, I beg your pardon. I had not realised you were still here.' Her cheeks were flushed with colour as they all realised what she had been about to say.

'And yet, here I am,' he replied dryly. 'Miss Isobel will not have my flowers in her chamber?'

Rose bit her lip.

'I see.' He stood. 'I shall call again tomorrow, with your permission, ladies?'

Rose agreed politely, but with a hint of a furrow in her brow.

The dowager fixed him with a direct stare. 'London begins to empty,' she stated casually, 'but we are fixed here until such time as Isobel is well again.'

'Understood.' Ignoring the concerned glance Rose was throwing at her husband's aunt, he bowed and made for the door. The dowager understood what must happen to mend Miss Isobel's reputation. Hopefully she would persuade the Lennox sisters of the same.

Chapter Seventeen

As Izzy's health improved, her temper did not. As if it was not already hard just to *breathe* without coughing, to swallow without lifting her shoulders in pain, to move her legs and arms without groaning, now her family were all trying to send her mad, she was sure of it. First Lady Ashbourne—the elder Lady Ashbourne; it was impossible to remember that Rose now had that title—then her sisters. One after another they tried to make her speak of the prince, and Kirby, and the thing that had happened on the terrace.

So people know.

Well, it stood to reason. Now that her brain was beginning to function again, she recalled the gleeful interest of the ladies who had witnessed everything, the interested looks she had been receiving in the supper room.

'I had to go away, Izzy.' Rose was eyeing her steadily. 'All the way to Scotland, because my reputation was at risk. And James and I were only seen by a servant! The prince kissed you in full view of some of the greatest tattlers in the *ton*.'

'And?' Izzy glared at her. 'He is the one who has behaved abominably, not I!'

'But can you not see? He must marry you now.'

'Oh, must he?' She fixed her sister with a hard stare.

'And when you were told James had to marry you, you chose to leave rather than force him in such a way.'

'But that was different! I loved James and did not wish him to marry where he did not love.'

Izzy nodded, as a pang went through her. 'Exactly. No one should marry where there is not love.'

I want no cold-hearted prince as husband.

Rose frowned. 'But Mr Kirby? Mr Fitch? The last time we spoke, you were deliberating which of them to accept.'

Izzy gave a short laugh, which turned into a fit of coughing. Afterwards, she lay back on her pillows, exhausted. 'I have no need to marry now, for so long as I can make my home with you, Rose, I need no husband.'

Moved, Rose took her hand, assuring her that of course Izzy could live with them for as long as she wished, but that dear Izzy must consider her reputation.

Snorting at this, Izzy felt another wave of weariness overcome her. Squeezing Rose's hand, she closed her eyes. How weak she was, that even a conversation could exhaust her so!

Phillips was leaving for a visit with the Rentons prior to his wedding, and the gentlemen had gathered in White's for their last meal all together until the autumn.

'You will come back a married man, my friend.' Ashbourne was clearly delighted. 'I am sorry to miss the wedding, but we cannot yet leave town.' Claudio's ears pricked up as they always did at any mention of Isobel, no matter how indirect. 'The doctor is pleased with my sister-in-law's progress and hopes to permit her to travel in a week or so.' He grimaced. 'I fear he may recommend Brighton or one of the other watering holes—all of which will be full to the gills. London-by-the-Sea is not my idea of a restorative summer.' He frowned. 'No, I must try to persuade him that a country retreat would be more efficacious.'

Phillips was eyeing Claudio. 'So do you intend to spend the summer at Kew with the royals?' he asked, making Claudio grimace.

'I suppose so. While I greatly admire the queen, her children are not, perhaps… Still,' he said as he lifted his chin, 'it is the least of my worries.' He frowned, glancing at Ashbourne. 'I hope the doctor will agree to your taking Miss Isobel to your country seat, wherever that is. If it is anywhere near the royal residence, perhaps I may call on you?'

'Naturally, although—Miss Izzy's health permitting—we shall not be there all summer.' He glanced at Garvald, who grinned.

'What Ashbourne means to say is that my mother has invited Lord Ashbourne and his entire family—including his wife and her sisters—to my home in Scotland for a party in August, along with some others.' He inclined his head. 'You are most welcome to join us.'

Claudio shook his head. 'Much as I would relish the opportunity—indeed, I can think of no more delightful opportunity—I must decline.' He spread his hands. 'You have been more than generous to me, but I cannot forget that just a week ago I was on Hampstead Heath believing I was about to die.'

They protested, but he would not be moved. It was too soon, he knew, to trade on their goodwill, and much as he wanted to cement a friendship with them, instinctively he felt it would be wrong to accept the invitation Garvald had just been pressured into offering. Despite the opportunities a country house party would offer, from here forward he must be guided by his conscience. This was his new life, his second life, and he was determined to behave as he ought. Even if it cost him in the short term.

Ten days after Lady Kelgrove's ball, Izzy came downstairs for the first time. For the past few days she had been spending most of her time in a comfortable chair by the window. While her body remained weak, thankfully her mind was now mostly free of the cloudiness which had beset her since falling ill. It was now mid-July, and London was hot, bereft of the *ton*, and dreadfully odorous. Lady Ashbourne insisted on keeping the windows closed, for the stench from the streets was overbearing.

Grateful, Izzy had brought her sketchbook to the drawing room, having first ensured all her foolish drawings of a certain unprincely prince had been pulled from it. On the verge of destroying them, something had held her back, and so she had contented herself with secreting them in a drawer.

They shall serve as a reminder of my foolishness, she had told herself.

Currently, she was sketching dear Lady Ashbourne who, when not sermonising about reputation and marriage, was still a darling. Drawing was Izzy's relief, for while engaged with pencils and charcoal, she had no thought for anything outside the present. And so she was quite astonished when Lady Ashbourne suddenly rose, declaring,

'Visitors! How wonderful!'

Izzy lifted her head to see the door open and two gentlemen entering. Instantly her heart began to thump wildly with anger. While she had no argument with Garvald, the last time she had seen his companion he had been disgracing her in public. Nor had she forgotten his hurtful words in the hallway.

At least I have a father. And a mother, too!

'Your Highness!' Rising, Lady Ashbourne held out two hands to him. He took them, bowing and greeting her with every appearance of warmth. The maids had told her he had been a frequent visitor to the dowager during Izzy's illness, and she had no doubt been the subject of many conversations.

'Miss Isobel.' His brow was creased as he studied her face, and fleetingly she wondered if she looked terrible. 'I am glad to see you so much better. I was concerned about you.'

My, he is clever!

His expression held just the right amount of warmth and worry to be credible, and yet she knew better.

'Good day,' she offered, inclining her head in a greeting that was not quite an insult. 'And Garvald!' Allowing a natural smile to break through, she greeted the earl with perhaps more warmth than was strictly necessary, just in case Prince Claudio had missed the point.

They sat, tea was ordered, and Lady Ashbourne and the earl covered up any suggestion of an awkward silence with chatter. Yes, Rose and Anna were shopping. The doctor had agreed the Scottish air would be just the thing for Miss Isobel, and they were looking forward to visiting Garvald's home. How was his dear mother?

Unusually for her, Izzy was at a loss. Enormous feelings were running through her—of hurt, and loss, and grief. But most of all she felt anger. She turned towards it. Yes, anger was safe. Picking up her sketchbook, she began slashing lines on the page—the fireplace, Lady Ashbourne's chair, an impression of side tables and paintings and the ornate clock on the mantel.

He was seated near her, and the entire right side of Izzy's

body was tingling with awareness. Then he spoke and oh! her foolish heart thudded with joy. 'I remember you told me you enjoy drawing, Miss Isobel. May I see?'

Meeting his eyes, she was attempted to deny him, to throw up her head and flounce from the room, but something held her back—perhaps a vestige of *la politesse*, perhaps the realisation that she was suddenly as weak as she had been five days ago and could not trust her legs to carry her. Wordlessly she handed him the sketchbook, watching his face as he flicked through the book, viewing her work. And all the while she was hating herself for hoping for a compliment from him.

She was not disappointed. 'But these are astounding! Look, Garvald, this study of a vase. And this—one of your serving maids, I presume?'

'Yes, that is Mary who then gave Miss Isobel the influenza! But our Izzy is mightily talented, is she not?'

Garvald agreed, and together the gentlemen perused the book, pausing over her studies of Rose and Anna.

'Astonishing! The differences between you are small, yet I think this one is of Miss Lennox, and not your youngest sister?'

Izzy nodded. 'Yes, that is Anna.' Even though she was out of charity with the prince, she could not help but be pleased at both gentlemen's response to her work.

Prince Claudio turned to the next page. 'Your presentation!' His eyes roved over the scene, where Izzy had attempted to capture both the elegance of the room and the sense of a huge crowd within it. 'That you remember these details so well, yet surely you cannot have returned there recently?'

'Oh,' Izzy said as she waved this away. 'My drawings are out of sequence in the book. I usually open the book at a random page and just start drawing. That was one of the first sketches I made when we came here.' Clamping her mouth shut, she regretfully realised that had been much too long a speech when she was trying to show him by word and deed that she despised him.

They continued to go through her book page by page, praising each drawing, and in doing so showing insight into her work. Proportions, lines, expressions... The details they noticed showed perception into exactly what she had been trying to achieve with each piece. Despite herself, she could not help but feel a little gratified.

Dropping her gaze to the book, she watched Claudio's smooth hands as he turned another page.

I could draw those hands...

Both gentlemen gasped at the same time, and Izzy froze in horror. There in all his naked glory, was the prince at the window. Yes, it was clearly him, and yes, he was naked.

Her eyes flew to Claudio, who met her regard, something like stupefaction in his expression. Seemingly unable to speak, he simply gazed at her. Similarly voiceless, her hand flew to her face, while with the other she wrenched the book from his grasp.

'Let me see that!' Lady Ashbourne, sharp as ever, had realised something was amiss. Taking the book, she shrieked, 'Lord save us!'

Snapping it closed, she eyed Izzy and Claudio grimly. 'Well, that puts an end to it. I shall leave you both alone now, and when I come back into this room, you had better be betrothed. Do you understand me?'

Never had Izzy seen Lady Ashbourne so angry.

'But, Lady Ashbourne, this is not—'

The lady put up a hand to silence her. 'I do not wish to hear one more word from you, miss! Come, Garvald!'

Lord Garvald bowed. 'Gladly.' His eyes were dancing with amusement.

Oh, Lord! Could this moment get any worse?

Apparently it could. No sooner had the door closed behind them than Claudio dropped to one knee before her, taking her hands in his.

'Isobel! I—'

'No!' Wrenching her hands away, Izzy took two steps back, gripping the back of a gilded chair. 'I do not wish to hear what you have to say!'

He rose, looking pale but determined. 'Nevertheless, you will hear it. Isobel—Izzy—I know I have made a mill of it—'

'Mull.'

'Excuse me?'

'A mull of it. You have made a *mull* of it.'

He swallowed. 'I have. I have behaved abominably, thinking only of my own heedless pleasure, when all along another life was calling to me. I have been a drunkard, a gambler, and a fool.'

With some difficulty she maintained a neutral expression, but inwardly his words were having a powerful effect on her. She had expected either a determination to marry her despite his best instincts, or a flowery display of false sentiment. What she had not anticipated was brutal, self-critical honesty.

Or is he simply telling me what he believes I wish to hear?

'And the worst thing is that I hurt you. I lashed out with cruel words that I did not even mean. For that night, you held up a mirror to me, showing me myself in all my meanness and baseness. Those men whom I called friends were indeed sycophants, and part of me knew that, but I confess

I liked their attentions.' He shrugged. 'It is no excuse, but as one prince among four at home, I was never myself, I think. Coming here to England was a chance to discover who I truly am.'

'Who are you, then? For it seemed to me you have been showing me your true character all along. The man who chooses Eldon the Lech and Hawkins the Sot for friends.' He winced. 'The man who cared nothing for my reputation or my feelings, only his own anger.'

His head bowed. 'I accept all that you say of me. And it is true that when I kissed you on the terrace, I was not conscious of what it might do to your reputation. But I was not angry with you.'

The second part she ignored for now. 'Lady Kelgrove had not yet made her announcement that my mother was her granddaughter. But for that, my reputation would have been quite ruined. You did not care. And your words to me were very plain. You said you would hate to go through life with no name, or history, or parentage. And you were right in a sense. It has been difficult for us all our lives, but particularly since coming to London. But that is not what you intended. You meant it as an insult.'

'I was angry. I should not have said it.'

She folded her arms. 'It cannot be unsaid.'

'But we must marry. You know it as well as I do.'

'That is not true!' she declared hotly, uncaring that her voice was raised.

We cannot be trapped into marriage like this.

'The gossips will soon move on to a new target.'

'Lady Ashbourne, however, will not. And she, like my cousin, the queen, is formidable. As are you,' he added softly.

'No!' She almost shouted it, so great was her distress. Here, in front of her, was the man she loved more than life itself, talking of marriage, but she must not give in. She must be strong. Her mind flashed back to the library at the Wright house, when Miss Chorley had tried to entrap him. 'I am no Miss Chorley!'

His eyes widened. 'Is that what you think? For I can tell you right now that—'

The door opened, and Garvald marched in. 'From my position outside the door, it seems to me that this conversation is not proceeding as it should.' He handed her a letter. 'On the morning of his death, the prince wrote this to you. And then he did not die.' Turning on his heel he departed, leaving Izzy staring down at the letter in numb shock.

'Death? What does Garvald mean?' Her own recent experience was all she could think of. 'Were you unwell also?' Her brow furrowed. 'Did I, perhaps, infect you with influenza when you kissed me? If so, it is no more than you deserve!'

The prince said nothing, his handsome face rigid as granite.

Her mind was made up. Turning the letter over, she broke the seal and opened it.

My darling Isobel,
If you are reading this then I am gone—killed in a duel by a good man defending your honour.

I have wronged you, and I know my fault, so I shall delope.

Too late I see my errors, but at least I see them. I have wasted the opportunity I was given. Wasted it on wine and cards and people I thought were my friends but who, as you eloquently pointed out, were in fact only hangers-on. Instead of carousing in taverns, I should have been forging friendships with the honourable young gentlemen of the ton—men like Garvald and Ashbourne and Phillips.

And I should have told you what my heart has known for a long time.

I love you, Isobel. You are my match, my twin, my perfect missing piece. No one but you would dare to tell me such truths as you did that night. You bring clarity, and light, and challenge to my life. You see the man, not the prince, and for that I am eternally grateful.

If you have chosen Kirby for your husband, then he is the luckiest man on God's earth, and I wish you happy.

Please know that I am calm as I go to my fate. I am ready to die. For all the wrongs I have done you. For the foolish choices I have made. For the small chance I had of gaining your affections—a chance I wasted as I have wasted my life. But to die—this will be the one truly noble act of my life, and I am ready.

Forever yours
Claudio

His signature was unadorned. No titles, no flourishes. Not *Prince Claudio*. Just *Claudio*. Stunned, she could barely take it in. A duel? To the *death*?

Lifting her head she met his eyes, and instantly he knelt again, keeping his eyes on hers.

'Isobel,' he said, and his voice seemed to reverberate through her very soul. 'You are my life, my light, and my love. I know myself to be a fool, and I know I do not deserve you. But will you marry me?'

Sinking to her knees before him, she reached for him with both hands. 'You idiot! You might have *died*!' she declared fiercely. 'That would have been the greatest foolishness of all!'

His arms slid around her as they moved towards each other. 'How so?' he muttered, his gaze dropping to her mouth.

'Because I need you to *live*!' Then her lips were on his, the letter fluttering to the floor beside them as they surrendered to one another in the most wonderful kiss of their lives.

'Then, you will marry me?'

It was a long time later—Izzy had no idea how long—but they had moved to sit together on the settee, and were now ready to talk again. Their kisses had been frenzied, then gentle, and Izzy had felt tears prick her eyes at how beautiful everything was. The letter—which Izzy knew she would treasure all her life—was safely folded and tucked away in her reticule, the sketchbook safely closed.

She smiled at his words. 'I shall, and gladly! I love you. But I did not know, you see, that you loved me. I would never do what Charity Chorley did—or at least she tried.'

He shook his head. 'Of course you would not. You have honour. A quality I am determined to nurture in myself, having perhaps slid from the high standards I was raised to believe in.' He chuckled. 'But tell me, did her parents really name her Charity Chorley? It is like something from a masquerade!'

There was a discreet tapping on the door, then Lady Ashbourne entered cautiously, followed by Garvald.

'It has been quiet in here for quite a few minutes, so we dared to hope that perhaps you have—Oh, I can see that you have! Well, thank the Lord for that!'

Smiles and congratulations followed, and Izzy was shocked to realise that her whole conversation with the prince—including all the delicious kisses—had taken only a quarter of an hour. 'Garvald insisted on intervening, you know!' continued Lady Ashbourne, dabbing at the corner of her eye with a lace-trimmed handkerchief. She patted the earl's arm. 'I know not what you said, Garvald, but it appears to have done the trick! Oh, and here are your sisters! Come in, come in, girls, for Izzy has news for you!'

Epilogue

Prince Claudio Friedrich Ferdinand, third son of the Prince of Andernach, married Miss Isobel Lennox in a quiet ceremony in St George's, Hanover Square, a week after Isobel had read his letter. Given the bridegroom's royal status, there was no difficulty in procuring a special licence.

The newly wedded couple spent two weeks in Shropshire before travelling to Scotland to visit her sisters as part of a large party of guests at the main seat of the Earl of Garvald. The following spring they journeyed to Andernach-on-the-Rhine, where Claudio's brothers and father gave Princess Isobel the warmest of welcomes. During their stay they were able to share the good news that Izzy was in the family way, with the baby expected in the summertime.

With the blessing of both families they made their home with Lady Kelgrove—an arrangement which suited everyone, for Lady Kelgrove was delighted to share her life with family, and the young couple had all the privacy and independence they needed in her substantial London mansion as well as in her country estate.

Prince Claudio became universally respected as a man of sense, and taste, and honour, and was known to be firm friends with Ashbourne, Garvald, and Phillips—as fine a group of young men as could ever be recalled among the *ton*.

Izzy, while deliriously happy with her prince, pursued her love of art with a great deal of fervour and commitment, and if she made drawings unsuitable for sharing with guests, she always made sure to carefully keep them in separate sketchbooks.

* * * * *

Marriage Charade With The Heir

Carol Arens

MILLS & BOON

Carol Arens delights in tossing fictional characters into hot water, watching them steam and then giving them a happily-ever-after. When she is not writing, she enjoys spending time with her family, beach camping or lounging about a mountain cabin. At home, she enjoys playing with her grandchildren and gardening. During rare spare moments, you will find her snuggled up with a good book. Carol enjoys hearing from readers at carolarens@yahoo.com or on Facebook.

Visit the Author Profile page
at millsandboon.com.au for more titles.

Author Note

You are the best. Without you I would have no one to share my fictional friends with. Thank you so much for choosing to spend some time with Olive and Joseph. I hope you enjoy their story.

Have you ever found yourself in a spot where doing the best thing for someone else is not quite what you really want to do?

It happens to our Olive. "Oh what a tangled web we weave when first we practice to deceive" is her life's motto. Sadly for Olive, one thing leads to another and she finds herself becoming ever more entangled in the web. One good thing, though, is that she's not entangled alone. Her new neighbor, the handsome heir to a viscount, is ensnared as tight as she is.

Together they build a pillar of lies...all with the best of intentions, of course. You must guess that it does not take long for sparks to fly between them.

But what will happen when the pillar tumbles? Will their love survive having the truth exposed?

As you know, in the world of romance love conquers all. Thank you so much for taking the journey with Olive and Joseph and discovering how they manage it.

DEDICATION

Dedicated to the memory of Joseph De Cuir.
You are always in our hearts.
Love cannot be separated.

Chapter One

Fallen Leaf, North Yorkshire, 1871

'Oh what a tangled web we weave when first we practice to deceive.'

Olive Augustmore recited the motto she held dear while yanking the handle of her trunk and dragging it from its hiding place under a tool cupboard.

The screech it made scraping across the stones of the stable floor caught the attention of Gilroy, a highly curious goat. He uttered a bleat, sending her an inquisitive stare.

Many people would not recognize the stare as inquisitive, but Olive did. Gilroy was the father of most of her goat herd. She had raised him from the time he took his first leap.

'I do not know why you should be so curious, my boy. This is not the first time you have seen me drag out this trunk in the deep, dark dead of night.' She arched a brow at the goat. 'You would not guess it by what I am about to do, but I am an honest person. Scrupulously so. Until recently.'

For some reason, Olive found it comforting to speak to the animals.

Rain pattered on the roof, curse it. Haunting the road was easier in dry weather when moonlight shone bright on the path.

Ordinarily, Olive would not stoop to deception. As she had just explained to Gilroy, she was the very beacon of honesty. But in this case, what could not be helped, could not be helped.

Olive dug deep, then dragged out yards of gauzy fabric hidden at the bottom of the trunk. Sitting back on her heels, she unfolded it, then rose and carried it to one of two horse stalls.

'Don't you dare nibble it, Star,' she said to the horse while she spread the filmy fabric across a wooden rail.

Going back to the trunk, she withdrew the dark, fearsome-looking costume which had taken hours upon hours of sewing in the wee private hours of night to create.

It had turned out quite well, and she did not consider it vain to admire the garment. Honest appraisal of her handiwork was all it was. She might as well be honest in something.

'I make a right proper highwayman, Star, and you a right proper ghoul.' Olive glanced at Gilroy peeking out from his pen slats. 'We are a fearsome pair, you must agree.'

She untied her apron, then unbuttoned her dress to change. She was halfway shed of her petticoats when her sister rushed inside the stable, dripping rain and sobbing her poor heart out.

Olive opened her arms. Eliza rushed in. She wrapped her sister up even though the hug was wet and cold.

'Is Laura well?' Olive asked.

'She clung to me and cried when I left. I think she senses I am her mother. I cannot bear it any longer…truly, sister, I cannot.'

When Eliza's sobs evened to a sniffle, she glanced up,

seeming to be aware for the first time that Olive was standing in her shift.

'Is Father drinking?' her sister asked, her eyes taking on a round, horrified expression. 'Is he set on going to the tavern again?'

'It is what he intends. He is looking for his coat, so we must hurry. He is better at finding it than he used to be. Place Star's costume over her while I get into this.' She snatched the highwayman's trousers from the stable stones and stepped into them. Oh, but they were cold.

When her sister seemed about to dissolve into another bout of tears, she said, 'Hurry, Eliza. I must get into place before Father comes out, or everything will be ruined.'

'I will be, at any rate.'

Yes, Eliza would be, and no other way about it. Bearing a child out of wedlock was a shame which could bring a lass down quicker than anything else.

Urgency was the word of the moment. Olive must take to the road and scare Father away from the pub. If he managed to get there, he was sure to drink even more than he already had and speak of things he needed to keep quiet about. It was his way to blather indiscreetly when he was in his cups.

Such a disaster must be prevented at all costs. As far as Olive was concerned, Eliza was only ruined if the 'crime' was discovered.

Her sister was a kind, tenderhearted woman who had suffered a brief lack of judgement and was paying a heart-wrenching price for it.

'I am so sorry, Olive.' Tears spurted from Eliza's eyes again. 'You should not have to do this. I am the guilty one.'

'Sister, you are hardly the first girl to be led astray by

a sweet-talking snake in the grass, and you are unlikely to be the last.'

'You have never been led astray.'

'I am not as trusting as you are. And to be fair, he was the proverbial wolf in sheep's clothing. He did present himself rather respectably for a low-down cad.'

Laura's sire was a wandering poet and singer. Far more charming than an honest man had any right to be. From what Eliza had wailed against Olive's shoulder that night nearly two years ago, her deflowering had taken a shockingly short time…moments only.

Olive had no experience in the human act, but that did seem rather quick for much pleasure to be involved. She believed Gilroy gave more time and thought to the matter.

What she wondered, but did not say to her sister, is how many other young women the villain had seduced during his brief stay in Fallen Leaf.

As far as she knew, Eliza was the only one to pay the piper for her indiscretion.

But, of course, her niece was the sweetest child, and her existence could not be regretted in the least.

However, the price her sister had paid for the circumstance of her child's birth was wretched. Continuing to pretend that Laura was their neighbours' child instead of her own was tearing Eliza up.

'Thank the Good Lord for Mary and Harlow,' Olive said. 'They are the best people we know.'

The Stricklands had taken in Laura just days after she was born to raise along with their own baby girl, who was born the same week.

No doubt there was a special paradise in store for those good souls one day.

'Chin up, sister. No more tears. Laura is living close by. And our secret is safe. We cannot know the future. One day this situation might turn around.'

She could only pray it would. Although the road this far from the village was not frequently travelled, especially at night, there was a risk of being caught out in her deception.

So far the only person she had frightened was her inebriated father, and that little more than half a dozen times. One good scare tended to keep him home at night for a long time. But when he was drunk enough, he forgot how scared he had been the last time.

Forgot that he could not speak of baby Laura, his adorable grandchild, to anyone else.

Olive hastily shrugged into the rest of the highwayman costume.

Eliza made quick work of draping the horse in ghostly gauze.

'Give us a dreadful snort, Star,' Eliza sniffed while Olive mounted the saddle.

Having been secretly trained to do so, the horse made a fierce noise while rolling her eyes until the whites showed.

'Good girl, Star! You are a smart one.' Eliza fed the horse an apple from the barrel.

'Be quick. I think I hear Father singing like a strangled cat.'

Eliza rushed for the doors. She pushed them open.

Lantern glow shone out ahead of Olive. The path went dark when her sister drew the doors closed again.

Urging Star to a trot, she wondered why it was that when Father saddled his horse for the ride to The Shepherd's Keep, the tavern, not the chapel which shared the name… but to the point, how was it that Father never noticed that

Star was missing? Perhaps because he was well along in his drinking by then and his attention was set on only one thing...drinking even more.

And chatting. Father would talk about anything that crossed his mind when he was drunk and in the company of neighbours.

It was before dawn when Joseph Billings mounted his horse and rode along a rural path toward his father's newest property acquisition in North Yorkshire.

Having spent the night in the village of Fallen Leaf at a quaint tavern with rooms to let, he was able to venture out before daylight. It was the time of day he enjoyed most, when night and morning were nearly balanced.

Joseph could not help but grin while he rode though a pretty valley dotted with cottages and small farms. He smelled smoke, but the light was still too dim to see it rising from chimneys.

While he was doing his father's bidding, seeing to the condition of the new property, he found it a pleasure and not a duty.

It was worth the travel north if only to escape London, where people of rank tended to sleep past sunrise and miss dawn's splendour.

More than that, though, he was glad to be rid of Lady Hortencia Clark's attention. In London, there was not a time he did not feel her avaricious eye cutting him between the shoulder blades.

The woman had an unhealthy obsession with him. Or not him so much as the Claymore fortune. She was determined to have him and all that came with him.

Joseph snorted, resentful that the grasping woman even occupied his mind for a moment.

He would not let her ruin this special hour of the day.

Out here in the country, he could breathe. Life in the city and the social obligations that went along with being Viscount Claymore's only child were not what he was made for. Damned if it didn't feel like a polished boot heel pressing on his soul.

He may have been born into society, but he had never particularly felt like a part of it. Just because he had been raised to respect the rules of proper etiquette did not mean he was going to dance to them…insofar as was possible.

Nothing in London could compare to sitting atop his horse, Dane, while watching the sky turn pink behind the hills. The manor house was said to be located on the hilltop where this road ended.

At first Dane's hoofbeats were the only sound he heard. Then birds began to chirp. One, then two, and within moments the trees growing along the path seemed fully alive.

From what he could tell so far, this might be his father's finest purchase. The land leading to the new property was the prettiest he had ever seen. Even while it was half-hidden in the shadows of near dawn, he sensed the estate would be exquisite.

He had not felt such peace in a place since he was a boy and had spent his summers in Scotland with his father's cousin, as his own father had done as a child.

The estate in Scotland was not a grand one, but humble and comfortable. More of a farm, really, he thought, where he and his cousins were free to run and leap. Father's cousins' home was a place where the most common sound was laughter… games were played and books read around the hearth at night.

Each year when it was time to return to London, he'd felt the loss of family and freedom keenly.

It was not as if he did not love and miss his parents during those summers, but their lives were focused on social commitments, and the travel which was required of their positions. Even when they were at home, it often felt as if they were not. Back then he had imagined society to be a thief, robbing him of his family…always taking them here and there, away from him.

When the day came for him to take the title, he would not travel far and wide. If he had a family, he would put them before any social obligation.

'It isn't that I am not appreciative of what I was born to,' he said to the horse. Only, it felt good to say things to an animal which you could not say to anyone else. When one spoke to a horse, there was no chance of being misunderstood. 'It's a bit like how you would be grateful for having a good stone stable to be in during a storm, plenty of oats and hay to eat rather than not. You'd be grateful, aye?'

He patted Dane's neck. 'But what if the cost of the comfort was being away from the other outdoor horses? You'd be safe but lonely. What if all you could think about was leaping the paddock fence and going to them?'

His parents had always loved him. He well knew it. It was only that with all they had to do for Claymore, they were simply too busy to spend much time with him.

He was grateful that his father had sent him to his cousin's estate where there were aunties, uncles, and cousins aplenty who loved him, too. They never looked at him differently because he was the only heir to a very wealthy title. They were close enough to one to not be impressed. To them he was simply Joseph.

In London he had no cousins, only a few friends. But did those friends even like him? He never really knew if it was him they admired or the Claymore wealth and influence.

'I shall tell you a story from my past.' The horse's ear twitched. 'As an example of my two lives. Once when I was in Scotland, I was sick as anything…fever, cough and the like. My parents were in Paris and could not come to my bedside. My aunties were there, though. I remember how there was always at least one of them sitting beside me, stroking my brow and singing to me.'

Joseph paused, remembering…smiling while he thought of his sweet aunts and how devoted they'd been to spooning broth into his mouth.

'Another time, and this was in London, I was sick again, much like before. This time my parents were in Spain and could not be with me. There was a doctor at my bedside and a nurse. Highly qualified, both of them. But they did not sing or call me their sweet handsome boy.'

Dane snorted and shook his mane.

'You understand then how cut up I was when Father decided it was time to end those childhood visits. Time, he said, to be trained to one day take his place as Viscount Claymore.'

Ach, he'd been crushed for a time, putting that part of his life away. Back in London he had worked hard, studied hard, and yet he still felt he did not fully belong amongst the glittering nobility.

The sense of having two lives never really went away.

'I will tell you another secret, Dane. There is more than a whisper of Scots left in me.'

Riding past several farms, rich and fertile-smelling, he felt the land begin to rise toward the hills. Trees here became thick, branches arched over the path, creating a leafy canopy.

While he rode, savouring the fresh, crisp scents of morning, the sky began to brighten.

He heard a goat bleating, looked that way and noticed a path which led from the narrow road to a cottage. A distance beyond the first cottage, he spotted another.

A woman was singing. He paused to listen. Someone must enjoy daybreak as much as he did. It seemed that the voice came from outside the first cottage, but he did not see anyone.

Seconds later, he heard the faint cry of a baby coming from the second cottage. It reminded him that morning was moving on and, just as the child's mother certainly had things to accomplish, so did he.

Father would be waiting for his report, a detailed narrative about the property's condition. The house, the land, the area surrounding it...his father would be anxious to read every detail.

A short distance past the cottages, there was a bridge. Dane carried him over a wide stream. The water looked cold and sounded as if it rushed rather than gurgled. He swore it sang a song as lovely as the woman's had been.

On the other side of the bridge, the path rose sharply, carrying him to the top of the hill where the manor house was reported to be. If it turned out as he imagined, the view of the property's acreage would be stunning.

Something stirred him about this place. From the moment he'd arrived in Fallen Leaf, he'd felt...well, something...but he knew not what.

The curious sensation had grown while he'd crossed the valley. Now, the further up the hill he rode, the stronger the feeling became. He could not say he'd ever experienced anything like it before, not since those summers in Scotland. There was an abiding sense of well-being here.

Perhaps, having been stuck in London for a year, it was only that he felt stirred by the natural beauty of the land, refreshed by the sounds and scents of nature.

It seemed more than that, though.

The road ended and became a driveway which wound left and slightly up. A grove of trees hid the house from view. All he could see of it were chimneys. Three of them poking over the treetops. The stones would be cold since no one had lived in the house for two years.

At last the full house came into view. It was three stories tall with morning light glinting off a dozen or more windows. A wide porch stood proudly at the front.

Again, a sense of well-being made his heart swell. Odd how a place he had never been to could cause such a reaction. A breeze kicked up, shuffling leaves against one another in a whisper.

He knew they were not whispering 'welcome home,' but it felt as if they were.

How could one feel he had been missing a place he had never been to?

It made no sense.

Sense or not, he was glad to be here.

Once again, Olive sat atop Star under the limbs of a great dripping tree at night.

Truly, she did not feel like a dastardly highwayman riding a ghoul horse.

What she did feel was wet and miserable.

She stared at the curve in the path, wondering how far

out her father was. Straining her ears over tapping rain, she listened for hoofbeats. At their first echo, she would draw her sword, gathering her terrifying persona about her.

It never failed to amaze her that her father, being frightened of the apparition lurking on the road at night, continued to go out. So far he had not made it all the way to the pub but raced for home as soon as he spotted her. A bit of a wail and the brandishing of her foil were enough to give Father the shakes.

As far as Olive was concerned, the deception she played on him was his fault as much as anyone's…if one did not count the drifting scoundrel who had landed them in this predicament in the first place.

Clearly this was completely that wicked man's fault.

What she and her sister needed to do was convince their father to allow Eliza to marry. Only then would they have a chance of putting all this behind them.

To Olive's way of thinking, a married woman had a certain respect in the eyes of the village. If said married lady then adopted a child, no one would remark upon it.

Thinking she heard hoofbeats, Olive rose in the stirrups and unsheathed her sword with great drama, even though Father had yet to come into view. It was important to draw on her character for a moment before letting him loose to do his villainy.

By nature, she was not a spooky marauder, but once she settled into the part, it became alarmingly natural. For a woman who was truth-loving to her core…mostly…the sensation was disturbing.

Whatever sound she thought she heard went away, so she settled back into the saddle to wait, sword resting across her thighs.

It was taking Father longer than usual to come around the bend. Hopefully he had not fallen from his horse. His heart might fail if a hellish brigand helped him back into the saddle.

She and Eliza both loved their father, for all his awful stubbornness and his dependence on the jug. There had been a time before Mama died when he had been a man who laughed and danced…who sang sweet love songs to them all. Mama's death had changed each of them, naturally, but Father most of all. After the grief settled and life began again, he became determined to be in control of everything. He could not control letting go of his beloved wife and so was now fixated on having everything else happen according to his will.

The trouble was, she and Eliza were what he wanted most to control. It was only a shame that he did not direct his stubbornness to turning away from drink.

Still, he was their father, and they loved him. So, with some worry, she strained her ears, listening for hoofbeats on wet earth.

There! *Clop suck clop…*but coming from the wrong direction. While it was not unheard of for travelers to take this path, it was rare. The only two cottages out this way were the Strickland cottage and their own, a situation which had made it easier to keep Laura's existence a secret. As luck would have it, or providence perhaps, Laura's and the Stricklands' babies were similar in appearance. So far, they had been able to make it seem that the two children were actually only one.

Certainly, the older they got, the more difficult it would be. Eliza simply must wed.

*Clip clop, clip clop…*the sound came closer. Who could

it be? There was a mansion on top of the hill where the road ended, but no one had lived there in the last two years.

She backed up into the deeper shadows of the tree. So far, Father was the only victim of her terrorizing, and she would like to keep it that way.

Of all the wicked timing, here came the sound of Father's horse picking her way along in the mud.

Since Olive could not allow her father to go to The Shepherd's Keep, she would have to expose herself to both travelers.

Wouldn't this end in a fine mess?

The riders stopped and spoke quietly to one another for a moment. Neither of the men noticed her lurking in the shadows.

Olive did not recognize the other fellow in the dark, bundled against the rain as he was. She probably knew him, though, since Father did.

Neighbour or not, she must do what she could to prevent her father from speaking of private family matters.

Very well…she took a deep breath then wailed. The sound echoed through the treetops…eerie, sinister. She would have frightened herself if she had not been the very ghoul howling a warning.

She emerged from under the tree, but only a few steps. It would not do to be recognized.

Star reared, snorted and rolled her eyes.

Father immediately turned his horse and dashed for home. The other rider screamed, nearly falling off his horse. The nervous animal raced back toward the village with his rider barely hanging on.

Olive waited a few moments, giving her father the time to get home. Eliza would be waiting in the stable to help him put the horse away. At this point, Father would be too frightened to turn back toward the village.

Please, oh, please let this be the last time she was forced to do this.

The whole matter grated on her. She hated deceiving her father, even if it was for the good of them all.

The worst of the night's affair was that another man had seen the apparition. This was no longer simply a family matter.

Word was bound to spread. News of a spectre terrorizing the road would be the only thing anyone spoke of.

'It was fierce as anything I ever saw. Not even human,' Father declared, sitting close to the hearth in an attempt to chase away a chill which no doubt went to the bone.

'The eyes of a phantom and no mistaking it. Flames is what they were…red and fearsome. Such heat! I must be burned. Do I look burned?' He stared at his arms, turned his hands this way and that. 'Ach, but you would not believe it.'

'You are correct, Father.' Olive handed him a cup of tea, and he curled his fingers around the prettily painted china. It was not likely that he would drink it, but she must encourage him to drink something calming which did not come from his jug. 'I would not believe it. You were drinking and had no business going to the village. When one is not in his right mind, one is bound to imagine all kinds of nonsense.'

'I was in my right mind, daughter. And I was not alone. Just you ask Homer Miles. He wasn't drunk. Only looking for a lost sheep. Got the buzzard scared out of him, he did.'

That was a complication, to be sure.

'Heavens, Father, I am certain as can be there is no phantom highwayman. Shadows are all you saw,' Eliza declared, then sat down in the chair across from him.

'No, my girl. I saw a horse with eyes of fire and hooves that sparked when it reared up. The rider smelled of brimstone.'

'Surely not!' It was entirely inappropriate to feel like grinning…but brimstone? Apparently her performance had been a grand success. She pressed her smile to the rim of her teacup, then sat in the chair beside Eliza's. It was all sorts of wrong to feel proud of her deception and yet…it must be noted that she had put a great deal of effort into her evil persona, even if she only noted it to herself.

'Homer will say it's the truth. From now on, you girls will not go out after dark, not even to go to the stable.'

Olive shot Eliza a glance…a wordless message. Eliza answered with a blink and half a nod.

With any luck, Father was in a mood to be receptive to the idea they had been wishing to present to him.

'If only we had husbands to watch out for us,' Eliza said with a sigh.

'Oh, indeed.' Olive leaned forward in her chair, making sure she had her father's full attention. 'James Foster is a big, strapping lad. A woman would be safe with him as her husband.'

Father set his tea aside with a thump. He nodded, then cocked his head to one side in thought. 'I have long admired the young fellow. A man could do worse than having a baker as his son-in-law.'

A blush rose in Eliza's cheeks. Olive knew it had nothing to do with hot tea or the reflection from the hearth flames. Her sister was more than just a bit taken with James Foster. She was in love with him and had admitted as much to Olive.

Having seen Eliza and James together, how special looks passed between them whenever she and her sister visited the bakery, she believed James returned Eliza's affection.

If Father gave his approval of a marriage between them, it would be an answer to their prayers.

Eliza would have the man she loved.

And perhaps the child she loved as well. Of course, her sister could not marry James without revealing the truth of Laura's birth. It would not be fair to James.

It would take a great deal of courage on her sister's part to do so, because only the best of men would be willing to overlook her fall from grace.

James, she did believe, was such a man, so all might work out well in the end.

Prayerfully, Olive slipped to her knees…mentally, not on the floor. Please, oh please, let it be so. Only then would Olive would be free of the phantom highwayman. Nothing would please her more than being the honest woman she used to be.

'Perhaps, Father…' Olive said, her heart in her throat, her palms as slick as wet leaves. So much depended on what her father's decision would be. If he decided that Eliza should marry James…prayers answered, indeed. If he did not, no amount of pleading would convince him to change his mind. Father was more stubborn than ten men at their worst. 'You ought to speak to James. He would be an excellent addition to our family, and we would no longer have to make our own bread. I suspect other fathers are eager to have him as a son-in-law.'

'I have heard whispers about it,' Eliza added, making a show of shaking her head.

If Olive was this nervous, her sister must feel like a beehive twitched in her veins. Eliza's very future would be determined by what their father decided in the next moment.

'It is indeed time you wed, Olive. Time and past. Your mother was much younger than either of you when she did. So, I will speak to the young man. Make him aware of your interest and my approval if he wishes to court you.'

'Me?' Olive gasped, casting Eliza a horrified glance. 'I do not wish to wed. It is Eliza who wishes to marry James.'

'But you are the eldest and must wed first.'

'That makes no sense.'

'Sense is whatever I say it is, miss.' He stroked his beard between his thumb and finger.

Stunned, Olive leapt to her feet, staring down at her father. Oh, what a horror.

'I should not have to explain it to you, but I do know what is best for you, my daughters. Time is creeping on. You, Olive Rose, are in danger of becoming a spinster. Once you wed, then your sister will be free to do so as well.'

'But I do not love James Foster. Eliza does.'

'Love?' Father spat into hearth. 'We are speaking of marriage.'

'You loved Mama,' Eliza pointed out bravely, for all the good it would do her. Poor thing looked so pale, Olive thought her sister would faint if she tried to stand up.

'Greatly...but to my eventual sorrow.' A shadow passed over his expression. Even six years after their mother's death, Father was not yet over the grief. 'A logical union is what you girls shall have. It is logical for Olive to wed before she grows any older.'

'You make me sound ancient!' She sat back down on her chair…hard. 'I am twenty-four years old. Not even two years older than Eliza, may I point out?'

'My mind is set. You will wed the baker, Olive. Eliza will have the next man I find worthy. Oldest, then youngest. It is the way things will be.'

'But, Father.' Eliza swiped at her cheek. 'I love James. And I believe he loves me.'

'Ah, but this is not the first time you have thought such a thing.' Father's expression was not hard when he said so, but rather soft and concerned. Which did not mean he was going to change his mind about what he had decided. 'You are not at all wise when it comes to love, Eliza.'

With a screech of frustration which was not a bit uncalled for, Eliza leapt from her chair and rushed out of the parlor.

Olive leaned forward, her hands braced on the arms of her chair, her expression hard on her father.

'You are as stubborn as a stone. But so am I. I will not wed the man my sister has her heart set on.'

That said, she stood to follow Eliza out of the parlor.

'I will visit our young man next week and give him my blessing to court you.'

He was not stubborn as a stone, then. Rather, set as a boulder.

Chapter Two

'Come, Dane.'

Joseph led his horse under a large tree. Its limbs nearly swept the ground. What moonlight might reveal would be hidden by brush and branches. This was a good place to watch the road for a dead highwayman.

'Stand courageous while we wait for the ghoul and its fire-eyed horse. Pay no mind when sparks fly from its hooves. Stand your ground in our righteous cause against evil, my good steed.'

Perhaps it was not right to make a jest of the matter. The people of Fallen Leaf were uneasy. It was said the poor fellow who encountered the monster could hardly tell his story for fear. Even so, the tale had spread quickly.

Aye, the poor soul—Homer was his name—had been terrified by something while out looking for his sheep, and another man along with him.

But a creature from the underworld?

It was absurd.

Someone was scaring the people of the village, and Joseph meant to find out who…and why. While the people of Fallen Leaf were not his tenants, they were his neighbours, and he would not stand for them being menaced.

What reason could there be for it? No good one, he would wager.

This was the third night he'd waited under this tree. It was where the witness claimed the horror had happened, so it made sense to watch this part of the isolated road.

The villain might see this as only some sort of jest, but the tavern was suffering from people being too ill at ease to leave their homes.

Ach! The owner of the tavern feared he would soon have to shutter his doors.

'Tonight is our night.' He patted the horse's neck. 'Don't you feel it in your bones?'

What Dane probably felt is that he would rather be in his stall.

It was still early enough in the evening that if he managed to capture the culprit, he would have time to escort him to The Shepherd's Keep, where he would present him to any patrons stout-hearted enough to brave a ride to the tavern. Then he would force the man to explain his mischief.

It was not acceptable that the people in the village should shiver in their beds.

This nonsense would come to an end this very night… as long as the cowardly fiend made an appearance. Each passing moment that he sat here made him feel like he was wasting his time.

All of a sudden the wind kicked up. It howled along the woodland path, twisted branches and made them creak.

'It does certainly set the mood for mischief,' he told Dane.

If one was inclined to fear, this would be the stage to make one quake.

But what was that? His nerves prickled in anticipation.

He leaned down to whisper in Dane's ear. 'I think I hear something.'

Mostly it was wind rushing past his ears. The whistling kept him from hearing the sound which had first caught his attention.

Dane's ears twitched, so Joseph knew he had not imagined the clop of hooves deeper in the woods.

One would not ride through trees, avoiding a proper path, unless one wished to remain hidden, and perhaps was bent on a bit of mayhem.

'I reckon we've finally got him, Dane, but hold here.'

Let the villain be the one to thrash about and announce his presence.

Joseph did not move so much as maneuvered his weight in the saddle.

The terror of Fallen Leaf emerged from the darkened woods, revealed moonbeam by moonbeam. It did not come fully into the open but sat on its underworld mount, keeping to the dappled shadows of the tree on the other side of the path.

The figure sat still as stone, except for his head, which he cocked to the side as if listening for something…for his poor victim, probably.

Aye, but not tonight. Tonight he would be exposed.

As Joseph expected, the rider was mortal. Surely an apparition would sense when its victim was approaching without having to listen.

In a quite benign manner, the rider shifted, bending to pat his horse's neck.

Then he drew a sword from a sheath and rested it across his thighs.

The man was rather slight of build for a highwayman sprung from the underworld.

With the element of fear removed, the fellow did not seem altogether fierce.

One would expect such a dastardly figure to be singed with hellfire. Not look as fashionable as this villain did. To Joseph's way of thinking, whoever had created the costume had done so with great care. Shiny brass buttons winked in a shaft of moonlight. A long red feather fluttered from a hat brim.

Hoofbeats pattered on the path, approaching from the direction Joseph had just come.

All at once the highwayman lifted his sword and charged out from under the tree. The horse gave a fearsome snort and rolled its eyes until the whites showed. The animal did look impressive and quite fierce, rising up and pawing the air.

The approaching rider rounded the curve in the road.

Joseph burst out of hiding, giving a shout. The approaching rider pulled his mount about and dashed back the way he had come.

The highwayman's horse pranced nervously. The rider got him under control, then turned the animal and raced into the woods.

The sound of the second horse's retreat grew fainter while Joseph urged Dane through the trees in pursuit of the highwayman's mount.

'Halt!' he shouted at the fleeing highwayman.

The man did not slow down, but no matter. This night his mischief would cease.

It was evident that the 'apparition' was not accustomed to being chased. The man wobbled in the saddle, his rump bouncing with the horse's fast gait.

It would take only a moment to run the villain to ground and have the truth at last.

'Halt!' he shouted again. Racing madly like this through dense woods was not safe.

An unexpected tree could loom out at one…a low hanging branch could—

Dash it! As if he had conjured the peril himself, it happened.

The highwayman hit a branch, fell off the horse, then grazed his head on a rock.

His horse must have been a loyal animal, because it immediately stopped and spun about, sniffed the fallen man, then turned nervously in a circle. The filmy gauze draped across the horse snagged on the tree branch which had brought down the rider.

Wind caught the fabric, blowing and twisting it in a way which did look ghostly.

The horse finally trotted away.

Leaping off Dane's back, Joseph knelt beside the unconscious rider. With great care, he turned him over.

The red hat fell off, revealing the culprit's face.

What the blazes! A hank of hair fell across his wrist. The lock was the colour of strawberries swirled in honey, then drenched in moonlight. Odd that he should take particular notice of the shade of the lady brigand's hair in this moment, but he couldn't help it as it slid over his palm, the silky strands tickling his skin.

The terror of the night was beautiful with fine features saved from looking aristocratic by an adorable round nose. The mystery deepened.

'Miss!' He jiggled her ever so gently, but she did not stir. 'Wake up, miss.'

Not so much as a fluttered eyelash. A trickle of blood dripped from her temple, down her cheek. Luckily, it was not a great deal of blood, which gave him hope that the injury was not too awful.

It did need tending, though, and right away.

Who was she? He did not recall seeing her in the village.

'I would certainly remember if I did,' he murmured, slipping his arms under her shoulders and lifting her from the dirt.

'Kneel, boy,' he said to Dane.

Luckily, Dane was a well-trained animal, which meant getting a limp woman, as slight as she was, into the saddle was possible.

He steadied the lady, gripping her arm. Then he ordered Dane to stand. Without letting go of her, he lifted himself up behind, clutching her securely to his chest.

With a light touch, he checked the bleeding. So far the swelling was not too bad. He wondered where the nearest physician was. Not in Fallen Leaf. He did know that much.

Even if he knew where to find a doctor, he could not leave the lady alone to summon him.

Dressed as she was, he would not take her to the village to be tended, not until he knew why she was acting the part of a villain. His curiosity demanded it.

There was nothing for it but to take her to the manor house and hope she would rally soon.

What a dashed shame that his first guest to the manor was unconscious and bleeding. This was what he thought while carrying the lady highwayman up the manor steps, then through the entrance hall.

In part, he was to blame, but only to a degree. True, she

had fallen from her horse because he'd pursued her, yet her behaviour was what had caused the pursuit to begin with.

Not that blame mattered in the moment. Only one thing did. Her recovery.

Up another flight of stairs, and then a right turn down a long hallway brought him to his bedchamber. There was no choice but to put her in there since it was the only bedroom habitable, as yet.

It was far from proper to lay a woman upon his bed.

If this had happened in London, he would find himself wed to her as soon as a special licence could be had.

He would have a pretty bride, in that case. On the outside. He had no way of knowing if she was equally pretty on the inside.

She had been terrorizing her neighbours. Not a respectful thing to do any way one looked at it.

Ah, well…until he knew the reason for her behaviour, he would do his best to withhold judgement.

Striding to the water basin, he snatched a clean cloth, dampened it, then brought it to the bed, dragging a chair with him.

He sat down, then lightly dabbed a line from her temple to her chin, wiping away a red smear.

A smattering of dried blood stuck to her curls. He stroked it away.

Light from the bedside lamp reflected on her still form. Interesting how it seemed like she had sunshine in her hair. There was no telling what colour her eyes were. Her eyelashes were thick as a fringe and curled up at the tips.

Even after hitting her head on a rock, her complexion had the same pink hue as the rose he had put in a vase beside the bed this morning.

It must be a good sign that her face did not appear pasty.

And yet he worried. The longer she lay without waking, the worse her situation seemed to be.

There was nothing for it but to sit and listen to the clock tick in the hallway.

He wondered if he should remove some of her clothing so that she could breathe more easily.

With his arms folded across his chest and tipping back in the chair, he wondered if putting her in his bed was inappropriate, then…removing her clothes was completely unacceptable.

Except in dire circumstances.

He watched her chest rise and fall. Which was not proper behaviour either, not by a measured mile, but how else was he to determine if her condition was a dire circumstance?

Her complexion remained rosy. That was encouraging.

Still, it was her breathing that concerned him.

'Damn it.' The curse rolled easily off his lips, but he doubted that she was aware enough to hear it. 'I need to know if your stays ought to be loosened. Even a highwayman ghoul needs to breathe.'

Breath huffed on Olive's face. Masculine breath!

Certainly a woman would not carry the unique sweaty, woodsy scent of a man who had recently been exerting himself.

Heat skimmed her nose, warmed it. She must be in a dream in which she was about to be kissed by someone wonderful. The sort of dream which always left her feeling bereft once she awoke and realized she was not about to be kissed by someone wonderful.

Something cold touched her cheek. Cold and wet.

What on earth?

She tried to open her eyes, to see what was happening. Oddly, her eyelids felt sewn closed. Her head was heavy, and yet at the same time, light with dizziness.

What was the last thing she remembered? Oh dear… someone had spotted her and given chase. Yes! She had been running away, and then…

Then something happened which she did not recall. Whatever it was had resulted in her lying in a bed which was not hers.

But whose was it?

How had she got from racing through the woods to here? Wherever here was.

And why did she smell a rose? Perhaps she was not in a bed, but lying on the forest floor near a wild rosebush.

'Damn it. I need to know if your stays ought to be loosened. Even a highwayman ghoul needs to breathe.'

She had been breathing, but hearing that, she suddenly was not.

Wherever she was, she was clearly not alone. No indeed, there had been a man's breath near her face a moment ago.

A hand touched her middle, lightly pressing the fabric of her highwayman costume.

She tried to bat it away, but her fingers merely twitched at her side.

'No stays,' she murmured but was not certain the words emerged.

The hand lifted from her ribs at once.

'Oh…yes, I probably should have guessed a highwayman would not have them.'

Whoever spoke had a deep, comforting voice. Contrary to common sense, she was not afraid.

Helpless as a soggy butterfly, but not frightened. She ought to be terrified, for all the good it would do lying here as defenceless as said insect.

'Why…' She struggled to speak, to ask why he had chased her. He must be the one who had, after all. The better question was, 'Who…'

No matter how she struggled, she still could not open her eyes.

'Imagine my surprise to find the terrible phantom haunting Fallen Leaf to be a woman. A rather small woman at that.'

'Imagine…' At last she gained control of her tongue and managed to pry open one eye. 'Did you hit me?'

He shook his head, brows arched in astonishment. 'I would never hit a woman.'

Perhaps not, but how was she to know that for certain?

'You were hit, but by a branch. It knocked you off your horse. Then you smacked your head on a rock.'

She had a quick flash of memory…of a branch looming suddenly out at her. She had no recollection of a rock.

'Star!' she exclaimed and tried to sit up. Oh, but it just murdered her head.

'Hold up, there. Don't do yourself more harm.'

'How harmed am I?'

'You are awake and speaking, so I expect you will fully recover.'

She managed to open the other eye. A handsome face came into focus.

'Star is your horse?'

She reminded herself not to nod. 'She is. Did you bring her here? And where is here?'

'She took off into the woods.'

He shrugged, smiled at her. His lips were handsome

with compelling brackets nudging the corners. Her stomach reacted with the oddest shiver. But of course it was due to her woozy head and not a stranger's smile.

'I suppose she went home, then,' Olive said. 'She knows the way.'

'Where do you live? Who should I contact?'

Not Father.

She winced. Truly, she was far too dizzy to have a conversation. What she really ought to do is get up and go home.

Since she could not even sit up, that would be impossible.

With a resigned sigh, she closed her eyes again.

'I'm not certain you should sleep, miss. Not with the way you hit your head.'

'Can't help…it.' She really could not. Everything felt so heavy…so distant all of a sudden.

'Go ahead then. I'll sit right here to make sure you keep breathing.'

At least, that's what she thought she heard.

She believed she said something in reply but may have only thought the words. Hopefully, they reflected gratitude.

Whatever the case, she would believe that's what she would have said.

Although she did not know where she was, or who her guardian was, he had claimed he would watch over her, to make sure she continued breathing.

She was fuzzily grateful for his presence.

Fuzzily grateful?

Had she truly thought that earlier on? Lying in a stranger's bed, in a place she did not recognize?

How much time had passed? She had no way of knowing.

This would not do, not for another instant.

She turned her head to see the handsome stranger sitting in a chair next to the bed, his gaze shifting between a sheet of paper he gripped in his hand, and her chest.

Seeing her awake, he crumpled the paper in his fist and shoved it in his shirt pocket.

'You did not stop breathing.' He gave her a weary-looking smile which crinkled his eyes at the corners.

'You really watched me?'

'For three hours.'

'No one has ever done anything like that for me… Perhaps my mother did when I was a baby. But it is what mothers do. Not what strangers do.'

'Somehow, after spending the night in the same room, it hardly seems as though we are strangers.'

'It might seem so to you, but I slept through it. If we became acquainted, I do not recall the moment. We do not know one another's names. Nor where each other lives, who our families are, or…'

Oh, no! For all she knew, she was sleeping in a married man's bed!

'Or,' he said, bending forward, peering deeply into her eyes…into her very thoughts, 'why you are terrorizing your neighbours.'

Yes, or that.

'I shall begin, then.' He sat back, crossed his arms over his chest, and gave a great yawn. 'My name is Joseph Billings. This is Falcon's Steep. I live here.'

'The manor on the hill?' She lifted to her elbows but a searing pain shot though her skull. 'Ouch.'

Despite the misery, she held the pose.

'You are the viscount?' She tried to sit taller, but light flashes pierced her brain.

'No, I am the viscount's heir.' Joseph Billings made as if he would touch her shoulder to prevent her from rising further but then jerked his hand back. 'Wait a while. There is no rush.'

'There is a great rush. My sister will be worried. How long have I been here?'

'Six hours or so.'

'I must go home.'

He shook his head. A lock of golden-brown hair shifted across his forehead. His gaze on her was intense, penetrating. And when had she ever seen eyes so blue? Although she was not herself in the moment, she could not help but notice their resemblance to the sky.

Good then. She must not be in too wicked a condition if she could appreciate vividly blue eyes.

'You will need to gather your strength first. I shall bring you a bowl of broth. If you can manage to keep it down, we will think about getting you home.'

'Oh, well, I suppose so.' It was the sensible thing to do. She eased back onto the pillow. 'Please thank your cook for getting up in the night to prepare it.'

'Aye, well, about that. I am afraid I have not yet hired any servants.'

'Do you mean to say we are here alone?' She had feared as much. The manor had been awfully quiet.

He nodded, then strode toward the chamber door.

'I am here in your bed, and no one is…there is no one to…'

He turned in the doorway, gave her a half smile. 'I promise your virtue is safe.'

'It was my reputation I was thinking of.' She struggled

to get up. She absolutely must get home. One ruined sister in the family was quite enough.

Oh, dear. She made it to her feet, but the room spun. Blackness tugged the corners of her mind. Her legs went limp. The floor rose to meet her.

Strong arms came under her, lifting her against a firm chest. When she landed it was on the soft mattress, not the floor.

'Do not try that again. It is far too soon for you to get up. I promise to take you home, miss. But not until it is safe.'

'It must be safe to do so before dawn, then. If my father wakes and finds me gone…well, I can tell you that neither of us would wish for that to happen.'

'We shall see how strong you are after the broth.'

'And my sister!' Her voice quavered for an instant. Normally she was not one to dissolve in a fit of weeping, but poor Eliza. 'She will be frantic by now. I imagine she is contemplating searching the woods for me.'

'Very well. After I see that you are able to keep down your meal, I will take you home, even if I must carry you.'

That would not do. To be carried in the strong arms of a stranger…the handsome son of a viscount…no, it would never do.

And yet, she would have been carried by him already. She had not floated from the forest floor to his chamber, had she?

'I am sure it will not be necessary. I will be right as a rainbow once I finish.'

'We shall see.'

'Thank you, my lord…for not leaving me on the ground as you probably think I deserve.'

'We shall discuss what you deserve after you eat.' She

would have been alarmed by what he said except she caught a glimmer of a smile in his expression. 'Please call me Joseph…or Mr Billings, if you must.'

'I am Olive Augustmore. I live in the first cottage we will come to. The one at the bottom of the hill.'

'I know of it. Do you sing in the morning? On the way here my first morning, I heard someone singing…and a baby crying.'

'It was probably me you heard. Singing is how I greet my goats each morning. The crying baby would have been my neighbour's child.'

Perhaps it was the neighbour's child. Or it might have been her niece, although she would hardly admit that to a stranger. She would not admit it to anyone.

Guarding the secret was what had led to her being stranded in Joseph Billings's bed in the first place.

Her stomach fluttered. This time she did not mistake the reason. The viscount's son had a smile that a woman could simply not help but react to.

'I'll fetch your broth.' He gave her a wink…and more flutters. 'Get a few moments' rest, Miss Augustmore. I will not be gone long.'

The very last thing she needed was to feel her heart reacting to a gentleman so above her own class…flapping about like a moth in a beam of moonlight.

Joseph sat on a stool near the stove, waiting for the broth to heat.

'Curse it, then,' he mumbled while drawing the letter from his shirt pocket.

It was from his mother and had been delivered earlier in the day, but he hadn't had time to read it when it first came.

Needing a distraction from watching his highwayman breathe, he had done it then.

Apparently, his parents were coming for a visit. Father was anxious to explore his new property. Thinking about it now, Joseph wished he had not presented such a glowing report of it.

It was not as if he did not wish to see his parents. He did, of course. Only, his mother had written that they were bringing 'Dear Hortencia' with them.

'Dear Hortencia?' Even saying her name made his tongue sting.

The woman was a viper. A pretty one, to be sure. It was why most people, his mother among them, never saw past her smile to the icy soul beneath until it was too late.

Cold as a stone in a stream, it was. Joseph did not wish to share a conversation with her, much less his life.

For years the woman had been after him, and with his mother's full approval.

Appearances meant a great deal to his mother, and Hortencia appeared to be perfect. A lady of good breeding, her father being a marquis…a woman of grace and beauty. Mama believed Hortencia would be a credit to the family's standing in society.

Added to that, his mother and Hortencia's late mother had been friends many years ago. A situation which Hortencia was using to her greatest advantage, he thought. The closer she was to Mama, the easier it would be to get to him.

He had never understood why Hortencia wanted him and only him when she could wed higher. The Claymore wealth, he supposed…and Mama's encouragement.

If only his mother could see what he saw.

He likened Hortencia to a cat who stared up at a bird in a tree while ignoring the mouse who crossed her paws.

He shifted on the stool, feeling tense.

This visit was a trap. He felt it to his bones. Hortencia meant to entangle him in something he could not get out of. Out here, away from society, it might be more easily accomplished.

He stood, looked at the broth and decided it was warm enough.

After placing it on a tray with a slice of bread, he carried it upstairs.

Going up, he strove for a pleasant demeanour. There was no way his pretty guest should have to suffer the dour mood that thinking of Hortencia brought on.

It was evident the lady had troubles enough of her own.

With his hand on the doorknob, he made sure to smile.

He did have another month before his parents came. He meant to appreciate the time. The last thing he wished was to taint the good feeling he had right now for his new home with fear of the future…and of what Hortencia might try to do to it.

Chapter Three

Joseph entered his chamber to find Olive Augustmore sitting at the edge of the bed, her fingers pressing circles on her temples.

It would seem that she'd refused his logical admonition to rest.

Even though, clearly, sitting up was causing her a great deal of pain.

He set the tray he carried on the bedside table.

'Broth and bread,' he announced, then pointed at the pillow.

'Are you always this overbearing?' she asked.

'I am rarely called out on it, but yes, I suppose I am in certain circumstances.'

Although she had ignored his advice to rest, she did seem somewhat improved.

He sat beside the bed, picking up the bowl of fragrant broth. After dipping in the spoon, he brought it to her lips. Swirls of steam curled in front of her nose, drawing attention to its sweetly rounded shape. It gave her face a soft, amenable appearance.

Except that she then pressed her lips thin, casting him an arched brow.

Oh, aye? She was not the only one skilled in the gesture. He sent it back to her, slick and easy.

All at once, her frown vanished, and her lips quirked at the corners. Amusement made her eyes twinkly green.

'Is something funny, Miss Augustmore?'

She pushed the spoon away, her lips now parted in a smile. 'You and I are at an impasse over whether or not I will open my mouth. Aren't we a pair of petulant children? You must admit, it is absurd to be scowling at one another over a spoonful of broth.'

Ah, it was good to know the lady was able to look at adversity with a sense of humour. He liked that about her.

Hopefully her lightened mood indicated that her condition was improving.

'Shall we call a truce?' He grinned because her expression was fetching, engaging in a way one could not help but respond to. 'But you must eat and drink if you wish to have the strength to make it home before dawn.'

'I do not believe a bowl of broth will do that. However, you did go to some trouble for me, so…'

She took the spoon from him, dipped it into the bowl herself, then lifted it to her mouth.

Her fingers trembled. Broth dripped onto the waistcoat of her costume.

With a despondent sigh, she handed him the spoon, then brushed the spill off her clothing.

'It seems that what I wish to do and what I am able to do are at odds.'

He filled the spoon and extended it to her. She touched his hand, helping him to guide the broth to her mouth.

'There is no shame in it. You took a nasty fall, but you will be back to yourself in no time.'

She pressed her fingertips on his knuckles while he scooped the next spoonful, offering it to her.

Ah, good, no more trembling.

Within moments she'd finished the broth and indicated she would like to try the bread.

She managed that on her own. He was not really disappointed that she was no longer required to touch his hand with soft, warm fingertips.

The bread was delicious. Olive recognized it as a loaf that James Foster sold every Monday and Thursday. It had always been one of her favourites.

Between bites she asked, 'What did you intend by chasing me, sir?'

How could she not ask? Although it was no surprise that he had pursued her, she did wish to discuss his motive for doing so.

For all she knew, the man meant to have her charged with a crime, although in her opinion, she had not committed one. Until recently, her mischief had been a family matter. One that involved no one but Olive, Father, and Eliza.

Who was Joseph Billings, really? Just because, for reasons she could not begin to understand, she felt safe with him, did not mean she ought to feel that way.

He might be a liar who had no intention of seeing her safely home…carried in his arms.

The image blossoming in her mind made a sticky lump of the bread going down her throat. Oh glory fire. The fact that he was a mysterious stranger made the image all the more interesting. Bordering on downright fascinating, is what it was.

Enough of that, though.

He would escort her home, and there was nothing gallant to it. He was simply stuck with her unless he did.

Besides, she was the one who had insisted on being home before daylight. He was only doing what she'd demanded of him.

To read anything more into it was not level-headed.

The quirk in his smile was a little too compelling. A prudent lady would not be fooled by it. For all she knew, he was as deceptive as she was. 'What I intended to do was to take you to the tavern, where you would explain why you were scaring people.'

Thank goodness she had been knocked senseless by a rock, then. How would she have explained it to everyone?

'Perhaps you have a good reason for causing fear among your neighbours. If you admit to me what it is, I might keep silent about all this.'

'You must keep silent about it, regardless of my reason. If anyone discovers I spent the night here unchaperoned, our reputations will be ruined.'

'I am aware of it. You need not worry. No one will learn of this. But I am curious. Why are you causing mischief?'

'You may rest assured that I have an excellent reason. I do not haunt the roads for my own amusement, I promise you.'

'Please, enlighten me. Once I understand your reason, perhaps I will no longer pursue you. You do know that the tavern is now suffering a loss of business because of you. I do not wish for the owners to fail.'

'No one does, naturally. The truth is, I never meant for anyone to see me but my father.' Causing fear to her neighbours was the last thing she'd intended.

Small furrows cut his brow while he silently waited for her to elaborate.

'Very well.' She leaned back on the pillow, gingerly so as not to jar her head. 'I will tell you.'

Some of it, but certainly not all.

Even though her only lie would be one of omission, and she told that for the sake of her sister, it did grate on her truth-loving soul to do so.

Choking down the last bite of bread, she began to tell him what she could.

'It all has to do with my father. He drinks, you see, far too much. I dress like this to scare him away from going to the tavern. My sister and I fear he will fall off his horse on his way home and be injured.'

This much was the truth. She did worry about his safety.

'Your method seems extreme. You have all of Fallen Leaf afraid to go out after dark. Perhaps giving your father a stern warning would do. Remind him of the danger.'

'Your bedpost would be more attentive to what I say than my father is. He is as stubborn as anything you ever saw. You cannot imagine what my sister and I must deal with because of it.'

Joseph Billings was an easy man to talk to, even though he had it in his power to reveal her charade to the village.

How odd. She really ought to be less forthcoming about everything. Then again, he was demanding that she be.

He seemed a decent man, and yet he was the one who held all the power here. He knew her secret...well, some of it.

'But surely he would not wish for you to scare everyone half out of their wits?'

'I am sorry for that, truly. I never meant for poor Homer to see me, only my father. It is rare for anyone to be on that path at night. I suppose it is a wonder I did not get caught before now.'

'I am surprised that your father did not tell anyone about what he saw.'

Indeed, it is something that she and Eliza worried about.

'Who would believe him? I suppose he did not wish to be thought a fool.'

With the broth and bread finished, she stood up, grasping the bedpost for balance.

'I am ready to go now.'

He tilted his head, arched both brows. 'Not yet, Miss Augustmore. You still need more time.'

'Ready or not, I must go home.'

But then, perhaps he was right. She was woozy-headed. Without his help, she would not even make it to the doorway.

She lowered herself back to the mattress and sat.

'I am curious about something.' He took the tray which she had set aside and placed it on the bedside table next to the vase. The pink rose looked far too cheerful. Her head hurt too wickedly for it to be of help.

'I am curious about something, too.' It was not quite about the rose, although she did wonder what made an important man like he was put a flower next to his bed.

'Shall we each take a turn slaking our curiosity?'

'I will slake mine first,' she said, since the answer was of the utmost importance.

'Very well, ask me what you wish.'

The smile he gave made her feel…probably not dizzy since she already was that, but as before, fluttery. How curious that the sensation came from her middle and not her head.

'Do you still intend to haul me before my neighbours to admit my crime…which is really no true crime at all but only what a dutiful daughter would do to protect her father?' She did not think he meant to expose her, but she needed to hear him say so.

'I understand why you felt you needed to act the way you did. Your secret is safe with me.'

'Thank you. I am grateful.'

'Now it is time for you to slake my curiosity.'

She could not imagine what more there was to be curious about but… 'You may ask, of course.'

The answer would be as honest as she could make it.

'You mentioned that your father's stubbornness made things difficult for you…and your sister, too.'

'I suppose there is no harm in telling you about it. My father has decided it is past time for me and my sister to wed. He has decreed that I, being the oldest and in great danger of spinsterhood, will wed first. He had also decreed that I will wed the baker, the very one who makes the bread you just served me.'

'And you do not wish to marry him? He seemed a decent fellow to me.'

'He is, of course…but he is in love with my sister, and she with him.'

'That does present rather a problem.' He gave her a long considering glance. 'One thing, Miss Augustmore. As I see it, you are in no danger of becoming a spinster.'

My word, the man was appealing, the way he scrubbed his hand over his grin, as if he wanted her to see it and not see it at the same time.

'Of course I am. Since I will not wed the banker, I will not wed at all. Therefore, I am doomed to spinsterhood.'

What? Why had he burst into a grin which he made no effort to hide? 'I cannot imagine why you think it is funny.'

'It is both funny and not funny, Miss Augustmore.' He leaned forward in his chair, looking as if he had a great secret to share. 'We are birds of a feather, you and I. You see, my mother also wishes to force me into a marriage. However, the lady in question is not at all likeable. I will fight the necessity as hard as you will.'

Joseph stood up. Walked halfway across the room and then held out his arms to her.

'Shall we test how ready you are to make the trip home now?' He flexed long, bold fingers in invitation. 'Come to me.'

'I must be ready, mustn't I? It would not do to add being caught alone together to our troubles.' She snatched up her hat from the end of the bed and tugged it back on her head. 'If Father gets wind of this, it will not go well for either of us.'

She took a step toward him, then another, before her strength gave out.

Joseph was beside her at once, scooping her up in his arms.

'Fathers are funny that way.' He smiled, looking handsome and mischievous all at once. By the looks of it, he was laughing inside.

'This is not a bit funny, you know, Joseph! Viscount or not, you will find yourself wed to me within a week if we are discovered.'

'Son of one. But then, if you and I were married, at least I would not need to worry about the woman my mother has chosen for me.'

'It hardly matters. Wed is wed.'

Going out of the chamber, he paused in the doorway and gave her the oddest look. She could not begin to guess what it meant.

'Is something wrong, Joseph? Is my weight hurting your back?' She doubted that was it since his back was broad and his arms were strong.

'No.' He plucked the feather from her hat, tucking it into the buttonhole of her waistcoat. 'The feather was tickling my nose.'

It was not until they reached the bottom of the stairway that she realized she had called him by his given name, twice. What had come over her to use it so easily and after such a short acquaintance?

'I will walk now,' she said, tugging on the shoulder of his coat. 'You cannot possibly carry me all the way home.'

'It's downhill.'

That said, he did not speak again until they arrived at the arbor where the path met the lane leading to the cottages.

'You must put me down now, sir. Don't you see my sister standing there?' Olive wagged her hand at the shadowed figure wringing her apron halfway between the cottage and the path. 'We should not be seen like this.'

Especially by Eliza, who would think the worst. 'I knew she would not sleep until I was home.'

Spotting them, her sister raced forward.

'Now she will see that she had no reason to worry,' he said. 'Finding you hale and whole.'

And in the arms of a handsome stranger.

'She will see no such thing. She will—'

Breathless, Eliza slapped Joseph's arm, yanking on his sleeve.

'Unhand my sister, you lout!'

'She'll fall if I do.'

'Fall? What have you done to her?'

Joseph loosened his grip, allowing her to slide to her feet, but did not let go of her.

'I am steady enough now, I think. Eliza can help me the rest of the way.'

Her sister slipped an arm about her waist.

'You, sir, are a villain.' Eliza gave Joseph a hard glare. 'You shall answer for what you have done.'

'Good night, Joseph…umm… Mr Billings, I mean.'

This was the worst time for her to make a slip of the tongue. He was not Joseph to her, but a viscount's heir.

'Do not judge him so harshly, Eliza. All the man did was come to my aid when I fell off Star and hit my head,' she explained, making her way toward the cottage one cautious step at a time.

'Heavens, how did that happen? I know you are a better rider than that.'

'Ordinarily. But he was chasing me. It wasn't me, though, was it?'

'Your injury is worse than you are letting on. You are not making a bit of sense.'

'I'm making perfect sense. He was chasing the phantom highwayman.'

'Chasing you.'

'Yes, but the point is, he did not know that.'

When they reached the cottage door, she glanced back over her shoulder.

Joseph was still there, standing under the arbor, watching her go. Her heart went soft. It was not so awful having a future viscount watching to see that she made it safely up the lane.

She lifted her hand and waved.

He waved back.

In the dim, predawn light, she doubted he saw her smile.

'Why are you smiling at that man, Olive?'

'I might like him.'

'Like him how?' Eliza took her by the shoulders, staring hard into her eyes. 'You spent the night with him, and I only pray you did not make my mistake.'

Once inside the cottage, Eliza and Olive went to the kitchen, beginning their day as they normally did with toast and eggs.

Father would not rise for another hour, so she and her sister had a few moments to talk before she would need to dress and then begin the daily chores.

'I did not make your mistake. My time with Joseph Billings was nothing like that.'

'Billings? You cannot mean the viscount?'

'Joseph is his son.'

'It is all the same. He is not one of us.'

'It is the oddest thing, Eliza. I get the impression that he does not wish to be seen as lofty. And he behaved like a complete gentleman.'

'He had his hands on you.'

'Because he feared I could not walk safely on my own, that's all. Like I told you, I fell off my horse when he was chasing me, and I hit my head on a rock. He made me broth and gave me bread.'

'Which he would not have needed to do had he not been pursuing you in the first place!'

'He would not have been pursuing me if I was not terrorizing the village. Someone was bound to come after me at some point.'

Eliza had been about to say something else but seemed to catch her words.

'It is my fault, of course. All you have done is try and protect me. I am sorry, Olive.' Eliza folded her arms on the table, placing her head on her forearms. 'I suppose the truth will all come out now. I cannot imagine he did not drag an admission from you.'

'Naturally, he did. Discovering the truth is the reason he chased me. I told him that I wished to keep Father from going to the tavern and drinking to excess. And also that Father is determined to get me wed to James when you are the one who is in love with him.'

Eliza turned her head. One green eye peeked up at her. 'That is all you told him?'

'It is. But I wonder…no, I think… I have a feeling he would keep our secret even if he knew all of it.'

'It is not wise to have a "feeling" about a man you do not know well.' Eliza lifted her head from her arms and shook it. 'Be very wary of him.'

'Of course. But really, Eliza, Joseph is more of a gentleman than you are giving him credit for being. I would not have made it home without his aid.'

'Oh? He might have brought you home on a horse, not in his arms!'

'I shudder to think how a horse's gait would have jarred my head. The pain would have been awful.'

As it turned out, being carried along in his arms had been gentle. At one point she had even rested her head on his broad shoulder, closed her eyes and breathed in the scent of his coat…of his neck.

It would be a lie to say she did not regret it when he set her on her feet at the lane. She'd felt a silly little lump in her throat when his steadying arms were replaced by Eliza's tense ones.

Her life was so full of lies, she would at least be truthful to herself in this one thing. Despite the situation she had landed herself in, she had been comfortable with Joseph.

It made little sense, but there it was.

'Since he went to such trouble to bring me home, I will take him some of our cheese as a thank-you. Please say you will come along as chaperone.'

'Who was your chaperone last night?'

Olive did not answer because clearly this was an accusation, not a question.

'I promise that nothing untoward happened.'

'You are the one who will pay the cost if it did.'

'You are not the only one who learned that lesson, sister. But come, Eliza. It is time to wake the goats.'

Rising, Olive went out the kitchen door, then walked toward the stable singing, as was her custom.

Once inside the stable, Olive took her gown from its hiding place in the trunk. She put it on while Eliza stowed the costume away, then slid the trunk into its spot under the cupboard.

She ought to be exhausted but actually felt quite recovered. In spite of the risk to her reputation last night had posed, her time with their new neighbour had been interesting.

What a handsome, charming man.

And, by glory fire, she was completely safe from developing an infatuation for him.

A cottage lass and an heir apparent?

It was too far-fetched to give a moment's thought to.

Which did not mean he should not be thanked for taking care of her. She would bring him her small gift of cheese.

It was the neighbourly thing to do. Proper any way one looked at it.

Walking in the woods behind the stable where the stream gurgled cheerfully to the right of him, Joseph went over last night in his mind. It had probably been the most interesting night of his life.

Rising yesterday morning, he would never had guessed how it would turn out. How in apprehending the terror of the village, he had become acquainted with an intriguing woman.

A lovely woman whom he thought he had got to know rather well, for all that they had not spent a great deal of time together. Only hours, but it seemed as if somehow in that time they had become friendly. It was interesting how easy conversation could be when one did not have to weigh each word and decide if society would deem it proper.

Talking to Olive had been natural…an echo of the past, he thought. It took him back to when he was young, when life with his cousins had been unaffected.

Aye, last night, once he knew the lady would recover with no great harm done, had that same quality to it.

A small bird hopped onto a branch to peer at him, first with one eye and then the other. The bird did not care if he was a viscount's heir or a commoner. He had to wonder if Olive Augustmore cared.

Not that it mattered really. It was only that he would prefer it if, when she looked at him, she saw a man and not a future viscount.

They were neighbours, after all.

He would like to fit in at Fallen Leaf. Somehow meld the two parts of who he was. It was not something he could do in London. The social demands of the city would only ever allow the noble side of him to flourish.

But here, yes, he thought it could be done. In time he might make acquaintances of the people who lived here. Hopefully they would come to see him as a man and not simply his father's title.

One good thing about his parents' visit was that he would be able to present his petition to Father to make this estate his home.

Coming out of the woods, he stood at the paddock fence, watching Dane prance in the sunshine.

Aye, this was home and where he meant to make his future. Mama would not be pleased for him to live here and not in London, but she was not the biggest obstacle he faced.

Lady Hortencia Clark was.

Joseph had good reason to dread her visit. He had barely escaped being trapped in a compromising situation with her a few times already.

Here at Falcon's Steep, she might succeed. He could hardly spend every moment of the day with his parents or with the servants his mother was already busy hiring.

Unless he was constantly in company, there was a risk of Hortencia springing out from behind a tree or sneaking into his bedchamber.

Last summer he'd caught her attempting to bribe a footman into claiming he'd witnessed Joseph in the act of compromising her. When the man had refused to do it, she'd berated him. Called him names that Joseph himself had never used.

With his ear to the door, he had then heard Hortencia threaten to spread a lie which would have the footman's employment terminated.

Naturally, when Joseph had stepped into the room to put a stop to her abuse, Hortencia had swiftly put on her mask of sweetness and smiles.

The footman did not dare accuse her of anything, so there was nothing he could do to set the matter to rights.

Nothing but remember, and be wary.

It had done him no good to warn Mama of Hortencia's flawed character. She'd dismissed his concerns as the simple aversion to marriage some bachelors had.

There were a few people, he believed, who saw Hortencia for who she was, but like the footman, they did not dare to speak against a lady of high rank who, with a word, had the power to sink a reputation.

Joseph groaned aloud, slammed his fist on the paddock post. He only gained a splinter for his effort.

'Dash it,' he muttered, then pulled it out with his teeth, spitting it onto the dirt.

Yet it was not really the splinter he cursed. It was that he refused to be bound for life to such a conniving shrew.

Not that he was entirely certain he could avoid it.

Unless…

He'd had an idea last night. An outrageous one. As ideas went, it was one of his worst. There was no way in which it could be successful.

His thoughts were interrupted by the high, happy lilt of women laughing.

Their voices came from the front of the manor. Coming closer, it sounded as if the ladies were taking the path which led to the rear of the house.

Surely there had not been enough time for the maids his mother was hiring to get here.

Looking away from the paddock, he squinted toward the direction of the sound.

Ah, there was a sight to brighten a man's mood. Miss Augustmore and her sister rounded the corner and were approaching the arbor which framed the kitchen steps.

Seeing Olive under a bower of blooming pink roses, watching her smile and chat with her sister, was a cheerful sight.

Cheerful was precisely the balm he needed in that moment.

Olive spotted him first. She and her sister came towards him across the grassy meadow that divided the manor house from the stable and paddock.

Olive carried a basket in the crook of her elbow. It bumped her hip when she walked.

Joseph did not consider himself a fanciful man. That didn't keep him from thinking she looked like walking sunshine, though.

It did not matter that he had spent only a short time with her, and much of that while she was asleep; he found he liked her.

There were certain people he had met in his life who he felt an affinity with straight away. Cousins mostly, and a few friends from school.

The odd thing was, he had never felt that connection to a woman before, unless she was a relative.

Interesting that he felt it now, and for a lady not of his class.

Interesting but not surprising, since given a choice, he

would spend as little time as possible among the class he was born into.

He crossed the meadow in long strides and met the ladies halfway, waving them around a patch of buttercups abuzz with bees.

'It is good to see you again, Miss Augustmore.' He nodded at Olive.

'And you, too, Miss Augustmore.' He nodded at her sister. Eliza, he recalled her name being.

Eliza did not look overly pleased to see him, but at least she was not scowling at him as she had done in the wee hours this morning.

Hard to blame her for it, though. He must have come across as a rake having kept her sister out all night and then bringing her home in his arms.

'Olive explained to me what happened, and I regret that I assumed the worst and glowered at you, sir.'

'Think nothing of it, Miss Augustmore. It was easy to misunderstand the situation.'

'Indeed… Well, I will say this one thing and then not speak of it again. You should not have been chasing my sister. Now I am done with it.'

'Eliza!' Olive shot her sister a reprimanding glance. 'Have you forgotten what we discussed? Did we not agree that it was a fortunate bit of luck Mr Billings caught me out and not someone else? That we can thank our lucky stars he has chosen to keep our secret?'

'I do recall it, of course. And we have brought you cheese from our very own goats to express our gratitude to you, sir.'

Eliza took the basket from Olive and pushed it at him.

'And a mince pie,' Olive added.

In the sunshine, Olive's eyes were a near match to meadow clover. He was so caught up in how pretty they were that he lost track of what the sisters were saying. But it wasn't only her eyes catching him up. It was her lips, too.

With a mental jerk, he reminded himself that it was inappropriate to be thinking of her this way, especially in front of Eliza, who did not trust him anyway.

'Thank you for the cheese and pie,' he said.

What he did not say but felt, was, *Thank you for bringing sweetness to a day which worry over Hortencia turned sour.*

Once again he wondered if he should present the idea to Olive that was niggling his mind. It was preposterous, though, so after another second's thought, he dismissed it. He did not wish for Olive to think him insane.

Too bad, because she did seem to have a gift for acting.

'May I just say…' Hopefully she did not take his compliment in the wrong way, but it was fair to give the lady her due. 'You did make a brilliant highwayman ghoul. I applaud both you and your horse. As a pair, you were truly frightful.'

'Thank you, I suppose. But the truth is, I am relieved it is over. I do not care for being dishonest.'

Eliza crushed a dirt clod under her boot toe, biting her bottom lip.

What a lucky thing he had not told Olive Augustmore what was on his mind, then. Honesty did not play into it.

'How will you keep your father home now?' he asked, because he sensed they were about to leave, and he wished for their company a bit longer.

'Hide the horses, I imagine,' Olive answered. 'It seems more respectful than drugging his tea.'

'Tea?' Eliza exclaimed. 'As if we could get a sip down his throat.'

'We should be on our way.' Olive nodded at her sister. 'We have schemes to invent.'

What would her clever mind come up with next, he wondered? If it was half as inventive as haunting the road, he would be impressed.

'May I help in some way?'

Aye, he would not mind being a part of whatever interesting mischief the ladies devised.

'You could tie him to his chair, but that would be less than subtle,' Olive declared with a quick laugh.

Somehow, and he was not sure how it happened, he found himself staring at her mouth again. This time for far too long. Riveted is what he was, caught by the appeal of humour expressed in her pretty, quirking lips.

She tipped her head, returning his stare in kind. It made his mouth tingle.

Something was happening here, but he was damned if he knew quite what.

It was not something to know, he imagined, but only to feel.

Then she blinked and broke whatever spell had momentarily held them.

Eliza tugged on her sister's sleeve, glancing back and forth between him and Olive with a less than pleased expression. 'We would not wish to involve you in it, sir. We will think of some other way to deal with Father. Come, sister, we will be on our way.'

'Good day, sir,' Olive said, nodding and smiling.

Watching the sisters walk back the way they had come, he clutched the basket of cheese to his middle.

Something was off with him. Hunger, perhaps, since all he'd eaten for breakfast was a slice of bread?

Surely he was mistaken about that long glance between them being a spell.

Olive Augustmore was a friendly neighbour. Nothing more and nothing less.

The good of it was that a social call required an answering one. The Augustmore sisters had paid him a visit, and now he would reciprocate.

Tomorrow he would pay his respects to Mr Augustmore.

If he managed to spend a bit of time with Olive during the visit…aye, well, he would not mind that at all.

Chapter Four

Sitting in front of the hearth that night, Olive had her knitting needles paused, her mind wandering here and there, but mostly up the hill.

What, she wondered, was Joseph Billings doing? Whatever it was, he would be doing it alone. Did he mind being alone? She did not know him well enough to know.

Eliza swept into the room, her knitting bag tucked under her arm.

'Father is in bed for the night.' Her sister plopped down into the chair beside her, heaving a sigh. She drew the knitting needles from her bag and clacked the pointed ends against one another. 'I visited the bakery this afternoon. Father gave James permission to court you.'

'Oh? I imagine poor James was properly stunned. Did he pummel Father with a baguette?'

'A fine waste of bread it would be, for all the good it would do.'

'Will James court you against Father's wishes?'

Eliza drew a skein of yarn from the bag. 'No. He says it would not be the honourable thing to do. I will admit his sense of honour can be trying. Although he did at least say he would not court you either.'

'It seems we are doomed to be old maids, then.'

It was more than that, though. Olive read the thought that crossed her sister's expression. Unless Eliza wed, she would never be able to adopt her child. 'I miss Mama. None of this would be happening if she were still here.'

'I miss her, too.' Every day.

'Wouldn't you think that since Mama wed for love, Father would allow me to do it?'

Yes, she would think so. 'Father was not as wrong-headed when she was alive.'

Their mother had wed beneath her station. Her father had been a vicar and gentry. The story was, their grandfather had been so angry that he had immediately cut her off from the rest of her family.

Olive and Eliza had never met the man. Not that they were terribly sorry for it. Their own family had been happy, and Grandfather's harsh attitude towards the marriage would only have cast a shadow.

If Mama had grieved the loss of her family, it did not show. She'd raised her girls with joy and laughter. She'd been devoted to Father.

Because of their mother's own upbringing, Olive and her sister had always stood out from the other women in the village. Mama had taught them the manners of polite society, and to read and write and talk. Since they spoke with the diction she'd considered proper, Olive and Eliza did not completely fit in with the other villagers. The men tended to pass them over for women who sounded and behaved more like they did. It was nothing so bad as being outcasts, only they were not quite like everyone else, either.

Luckily, James also had some education, so he and Eliza fit well together. If only their father would allow it.

'While I knit this scarf and you knit Father a pair of socks, we must find a way to keep him home,' Olive said.

'I say we feed his shoes to Gilroy.'

Sadly, that was the best idea they managed.

After wasting away the better hours of the night and much of the morning, Olive had not devised a scheme to keep Father at home.

Depriving him of his shoes would not be kind, and so the only other thing she came up with was to warn him of a plague in the village. Travel was forbidden.

Not a viable solution to the problem, but for now her brain was weary with chewing it over.

What she needed was a few moments of carefree fun, and she knew just how to get them.

She hurried down the back steps of the cottage toward the fenced meadow. Even from here, she heard young goats bleating in the warm afternoon sunshine.

Once inside the gate, she ran toward them, singing and laughing at the same time.

The herd was a perfect size. Large enough to earn money off milk, cheese, and soap, and yet small enough to be managed by Olive and her sister.

There were many wonderful creatures in God's beautiful creation. Of all of them, goats were her favourite.

Perhaps because they seemed to view life with humour. At least, that's how she interpreted them. Always leaping, climbing, and nibbling on anything that came close to their muzzles.

Gilroy was the first to spot her. He bleated and came trotting towards her. Four babies followed, not in an orderly line but bounding every which way.

'Hello, Gilroy.' She patted his head. 'Hello, babies.'

She scooped up a kid and twirled about with it. She nuzzled its head with her nose, then set it back on the grass.

The white-and-brown kid dashed away, followed by its mates. One of them got distracted by a bee and gave chase. Another went to its mother for a snack. The one she had twirled around stopped to nibble a flower.

It all looked like great fun. Which was the very reason Olive had come to the meadow.

She dashed after them, lifting her skirt high so she could leap like they did.

Finally winded, she lay down on the grass, arms stretched wide, while she caught her breath and watched a cloud changing shapes in the sky.

Something nibbled her sleeve. Absently she patted a soft little head. A cold nose pressed her cheek. Then brown eyes blinked at her, the pupils humourous-looking rectangles.

Some people thought a goat's eyes were eerie, but to Olive, they were sweet and funny.

'You are the dearest creature alive,' she said in the very second a different face filled her vision.

This one did not have goat's eyes.

No indeed, these eyes stared down at her with lines creasing the corners. This face had a mouth that turned upward in an effort not to laugh.

'Thank you for saying so, Miss Augustmore. But perhaps I have come at an inconvenient time?'

Truly, there could not have been a more inconvenient one. To greet a future viscount while sprawled in the grass with a small but persistent goat clambering over one's bosom would never be a lady's first choice.

'It is perfect timing if you care to frolic with my young friends.'

'Another time perhaps. I came to return your basket.'

His lips twitched. In another second, he was bound to

bend over in a fit of mirth. She knew because it is what she would do in his situation.

Sitting up, she carefully lifted the goat off her. Then she stood, swiping grass from her skirt.

'I assume you've met my father?'

'He seems a pleasant, reasonable chap.'

'Yes, well, it is still early,' she muttered, then regretted the slip. 'I trust you had a pleasant visit?'

'We spoke of your upcoming marriage.' How much longer could Joseph withhold his laughter? Not much, she guessed. 'He informed me that if I had a mind to court you, I would be refused. He did offer up Eliza, though.'

With that, he finally let go of the laugh. The sound gave her insides a pleasant shiver. Or maybe it was the attractive laugh lines bracketing his mouth causing the sensation. Both working together was her guess.

'I told him that, regretfully, I had only come to return your basket.' Joseph grinned at her, his eyes snapping blue with humour. 'Will you walk with me?'

How, she would like to know, was a lady to walk when her knees had suddenly gone soft?

What was wrong with her? She was not developing an infatuation for her neighbour. It would be all sorts of improper.

In her defence, his face would cause any woman's heart to stumble over itself, no matter her social status. It was not her fault that he was so appealing.

'There is a stream close by. Shall we walk beside it?' she asked.

'Yes, I know the one. It runs downhill from my property.'

Glancing back at the cottage, Olive spotted Eliza standing on the back porch, watching them.

Chaperone enough, she decided, in case the propriety even needed to be observed in her own meadow. London rules might require a hovering third presence, but fortunately this was Fallen Leaf, and life was more relaxed.

'I enjoyed the cheese. I assume it was compliments of one of your friends here in the meadow.'

'They do produce the best cheese. The mince pie was from me.'

'I enjoyed it even more.'

Handsome and with a sense of humour…society debutantes must fall at his feet on a regular basis.

'Your father does seem as determined as you said he was. Will you be able to go against his wishes? Refuse to wed the baker?'

'I shall stand firm in my refusal, I assure you.'

As always, the scent of rushing water was refreshing. Given her present company, she felt as if she could walk alongside it for hours.

'As I will stand firm in my refusal to wed the woman my mother has chosen for me.'

Joseph stooped, plucking a blue flower. Coming back up, he offered it to her with a smile. Oh yes indeed, the ladies of London would never be able to resist him.

'Will you allow me the familiarity of calling you by your first name?' he asked.

She thought about it for a full second, not certain it was appropriate. But she had already called him Joseph, and it had felt nearly appropriate.

'We are neighbours, after all,' she decided. 'And allies in the cause of not marrying as our parents decree. So yes, you may call me Olive as long as I may call you Joseph.'

Hopefully she had not overstepped since he was nobility.

She had some idea of who called who what in social situations, but still it was a little confusing. Too late to take it back now, though. And if he was going to call her Olive, then—

'It is agreed, then…we are Olive and Joseph.'

'May I ask you a question, Joseph?'

'Certainly, Olive.'

How pleasant this was, neighbours taking a friendly walk beside the stream, speaking of this and that, and—

'It is just that you know why my father is insisting I wed a man I do not desire. Why does your mother insist on it?'

The question was rather personal, but she really did want to know.

'Mama has been duped. Many people have. From the outside, Lady Hortencia seems a perfect choice. She is a lady of quality who will bring distinction to our title. She has an angelic look about her, speaks and behaves graciously when people are watching. It is not who she truly is. I will not wed her.'

'Surely no one can force you, a viscount's heir?'

Joseph stopped walking, ran his wide hand through his hair while shaking his head. He pointed to a fallen log beside the stream.

'Do you mind if we sit?'

Birdsong, leaves rustling in a breeze overhead…and sitting beside a handsome man…what was there to mind?

And yet Joseph seemed stressed. A companionable sit by the water might be just the thing.

Silently, they watched the stream gliding past. Dapples of sunshine glinted off the surface in a way which was mesmerizing. One could nearly get lost in the moment.

'It isn't true that I cannot be forced,' he said at last. 'A compromising situation would see me wed in a hurry. Men of my position must be wary of it at all times, you see.'

Hmm…would this be one of those situations? They were alone, after all. And not for the first time.

'I have reason to believe you would not compromise a woman, Joseph.'

'Aye, you do,' he answered with a lift of his brows. 'I wouldn't need to do the wicked deed. It would only need to look as if I had.'

He shook his head, and a ray of sunshine caught his hair, making strands of gold sparkle in the brown. Distracted, she nearly got lost in this moment instead. She really did need to keep her attention from foolishly wandering.

Olive clasped her fingers together, focusing her attention on his dilemma. She would be the worst sort of neighbour to act in a way that would add to his worries. Touching his hair would certainly do that.

'So, you fear this woman will catch you in a false but compromising situation and then demand you marry her, is that it?'

'She has tried before.'

'Presently, it does not seem to me that you are in great danger. You are the only one living in the manor.'

He stood up, pacing toward the water's edge and then back again. 'Not for long. I've received a letter informing me that my parents are coming to visit, and they are bringing Hortencia with them.'

He squatted in front of her, apparently to better get her attention. Truly, she could not recall anyone ever having it so completely.

'I wonder if…' he began. 'No, never mind.'

He looked hard at her, seeming to have lost his voice.

One of them needed to say something, so she did. 'You are wondering if luck will smile upon you, and she will not come? Is that it?'

He shook his head, still silent. There was something he wanted to say, though. She could nearly see the thoughts swirling behind his eyes. Not the exact words, naturally. She was not a mind reader, but she recognized the concern pressing upon him.

But who would not be worried, fearing he would be trapped in a marriage he did not wish to be in?

She stood up. Joseph did, too. Continuing to stroll beside the stream might ease his anxiety.

'Oh, she'll come. I am certain trapping me is the reason for the visit.'

'Perhaps if you write to your mother and explain.'

'She would no more listen to me than your father would to you.'

He nodded, almost said something else, but apparently changed his mind again.

'But possibly I will get lucky and she will not come.'

He said the words, but she knew he did not truly believe them.

Olive disliked seeing him so troubled. While the two of them were worlds apart socially, they did share a common problem.

A problem which neither of them had the power to help the other with.

'What if there was a way?' Joseph heard the words come out of his mouth but could not believe he'd gathered the courage to utter them.

'I am not certain I know what you mean.'

'No? Well, I am not certain I do either,' he admitted.

'What are we discussing then?'

'You…'

Curse it. Getting Olive involved in his troubles was wrong. Nor did he wish for her to think him insane.

'You have a gift for playing a part,' he said, deciding he actually was insane.

'You cannot possibly mean it?' Her eyes sharpened on him, and her jaw sagged a bit.

'I have not yet told you what I mean.'

'It is clear that you wish me to reprise my role as terror of the night and scare Lady Hortencia away from Falcon's Steep.'

Olive curled her fingers into fists, which she jammed on her hips. She shook her head forcefully and dislodged a strand of hair from her tidy bun. The curl hugging her neck went a great way towards softening her starchiness.

'I will not do it. I have only just regained my status as an honest woman. I am quite finished telling lies.'

This could not end in his favour. Honesty was the last thing he wanted.

'I was not going to ask you to become a ghoul.'

'No? That is a great relief.'

It was so wrong of him to ask her. She had told him more than once how highly she valued honesty.

Wrong or not…he must.

'Then what is it you were going to ask of me?'

'I was going to ask you to be my wife.'

'Glory fire, Joseph.' She placed her hands on her waist, tilted her shoulders back and gave him a wink. 'Wouldn't I make a fine lady?'

She turned in a circle, making her skirt swirl.

'As elegant as fine lace,' she went on. 'Refined, too. I suppose I will not be able to lift my hand for the size of the ring you will place on my finger.'

That said, she wagged her hand at him, shooting him a playful smile.

'You my friend, are a great jester. I will admit, laughter does go a way to ease the situations we find ourselves in.'

'I've made a mess of it all,' he groaned.

'Not at all. My spirit is quite lifted.'

'Indeed? I was not making a joke.'

'Of course you were. I am a cottager and you…you live in the manor on the hill. I do not believe for a moment that you seriously meant to propose marriage to me.'

She was correct. He had not meant that in the strictest sense.

'What I should have asked is, will you pretend to marry me?'

'What?'

She backed away from him, her expression suddenly blank. But only blank for the space it took to gather a thought, to gasp.

'You, sir, are a…something I shall not say. I retract what I said about you being a gentleman. Only a true cad would make fun of a humble neighbour in this way.'

'I wasn't doing that.'

'Ha! I only just admitted to you that I was happy to no longer be living a lie…how I valued honesty.' Red-faced, she marched back to him, pointed her finger and jabbed it at the centre button of his waistcoat. 'You, Lord of the Hill, may go back to it.'

Seeing her stunned expression and the offence she had

taken to his proposal, he wished he could take it back, present the idea in a more convincing way.

In for a penny, and all that, he might as well press for the pound. She could not think any worse of him than she did in this moment.

Spinning about, she bustled off, her skirt jerking with her angry stride.

He had to run to catch up. 'Wait, Olive.'

'I also retract my permission for you to call me that.'

'Let's discuss this.'

'I would as soon pretend to wed Gilroy as speak one more word to a man who would tempt me to return to being dishonest.'

'Are you tempted?' Perhaps this was a chip in her resolve. 'You did say you would not wed the baker, that you would be a spinster first…and your sister with you.'

'James is the baker. Gilroy is that goat over there. The one pointing his horns at you.'

He saw the animal, but it was, in that moment, settling onto a patch of clover for a nap.

'Olive—'

'Miss Augustmore to you.' She continued on her way without giving him a backwards glance.

He couldn't blame her. Seeing it from her side, it would seem absurd. All he needed was a moment more to convince her of the benefits to them both.

'Will you consider it before you completely dismiss the idea?'

'I have already dismissed it.'

'Don't you see how my proposal is the solution for both of our problems?'

'Oh what a tangled web we weave when first we practice to deceive,' she recited. 'It is my motto.'

'The damned web is exactly what I am trying to avoid.'

'Cursing will not win me to your cause, sir. I would think such language was forbidden to a man of your high rank.'

'I apologize for the outburst. Not the rest of it.' All he needed was the chance to show her the merit of his plan. 'In the name of neighbourliness, will you allow me to explain the benefits?'

'*Neighbourly* is an odd word to use to describe someone you have just belittled as of no importance.'

'It was not my intent. I vow it was not.'

All at once she stopped walking.

'It is clear what you thought. That poor humble Olive—Miss Augustmore, that is—would be oh so grateful to pretend to act the lady for however long you choose to continue with the deception. You should know that I have no desire to be a lady.'

'One week only…and that is not what I meant.'

He might as well turn around and walk back upstream toward home. This had gone all wrong, and there was nothing more he could say. Remaining in her company would only distress them both.

'I wish you good day, Miss Augustmore.'

He was several yards along his way when he felt a tug on the back of his coat.

'Why do think this makes any sense? How would such a deception benefit us both?'

'It is simple enough. If Hortencia believes I am already wed, she will not continue to pursue me. If your father thinks you are already wed, he will allow your sister to marry the baker.'

He nearly lost his train of thought for an instant, distracted by her eyes. The prettiest he had ever seen, even snapping with indignation as they were. No disguising how sweet her lips were, either, despite being pressed into a thin, tight line.

'Very well. While I understand your point, it is a great lie, one which will never work, and I will not be a part of it.'

Giving a sharp nod, she turned and walked downstream.

'Will you at least think about it?' he called.

'No!'

There was nothing to do but make his way upstream toward home.

To the devil with it. He was going to be on his own when it came to avoiding Hortencia Clark. He did not like his odds.

It was dark outside with no moon, only a fierce, stiff wind. Going to the stable, Olive had to lean into the gusts to keep her balance.

She would rather not be saddling Star for a ride to Falcon's Steep, but in spite of the fact that she had told her noble neighbour she would give no thought to his idea, it was all she had done.

One thing was for certain. She was no longer at risk of succumbing to an infatuation for Joseph Billings. Handsome could only take a fellow so far.

A decent sense of morality counted for quite a bit more. Clearly the man lacked that attribute.

To her utter consternation, the idea he'd presented might actually work to both their benefits.

And yet due to its many flaws, it could surely only end in disaster.

She wanted nothing to do with it.

And would not have done if only the possibility of Eliza happily living in the home of the man she loved—while holding the child she adored—had not taken root in her mind.

Taken root and blossomed!

'Glory fire,' she mumbled while riding Star out of the stable. 'I might be as wrong-minded as our neighbour on the hill. Nearly so, anyway.'

It did not take long for Star to trot the distance to the manor.

Hardly a surprise that there were no lamps flickering in the windows, as it was quite late.

No matter. He had left her sleepless, so she did not feel bad about banging on his front door and waking him from whatever sweet slumber he'd managed to indulge in.

It was only a moment before the latch scraped on the other side of the door. Just long enough for Olive's hair to fly about her head, making it impossible to see the man when he opened the door.

'What the bloody blazes! Olive?'

'Who else would it be? Unless you presented some other woman with your pretend proposal and left her sleepless, too.'

She scraped her hands across her face, brushing her hair aside to the right and left so that she could see.

Oh dear, that was a mistake. It would be better to be blinded than to be looking at Joseph Billings's muscular bare chest.

Any true gentleman would have buttoned his shirt to answer a knock on his front door.

He might even have tidied his hair. Who greeted a guest with unkempt locks poking from his head in such a wild-man manner? She would allow for his bare feet since he would not have taken the time to find his shoes while leaving a visitor standing in the dark and teetering in the wind.

The open shirt, though. It did present a problem for her.

If he wished for the dreaded Hortencia not to seduce him, he would have to do better than this.

'Come in before you blow away.' He caught her arm against a gust and tugged her inside.

This visit would be more successful if she was not struggling to ignore how delightfully rumpled he looked.

From a room off the hallway, she spotted a fire blazing. Well, then, it was satisfying to know that he had not been sleeping either.

'It is nearly midnight. What were you thinking, coming out in this weather?'

'That I have questions, and I will not sleep until they are answered.'

'Very well. Go and sit by the fire. I will tend to your horse and be back shortly.'

'Do not bother. I will not remain long.'

He arched a brow at her as if to hint she was mistreating the animal, and then he led her toward the room with the fire and its welcome glow. Her boots tapped the tile. His bare feet padded.

Being a highly bred society horse, perhaps Dane would be troubled by a bit of wind. Joseph was greatly mistaken about Star. She was a hardy farm animal and would not be distressed at all.

Olive nearly wished she had not come. It was probably too bold a thing to do. And yet with his proposal now lodged in her mind, how was she to move forward with her sweet, quiet life until she had the matter settled?

It would be easier to keep a clear head on matters if she was less focused on how the fire reflected in his hair, and how his very capable hand, with its large knuckles and long fingers, brushed it away from his face.

He indicated that she should sit in a chair near the hearth. It was a delicate-looking chair and one of only two pieces of furniture in the parlor. Lord Future Claymore would shatter it if he tried to sit on it.

The other piece of furniture was a couch.

'I do not need to sit. It is late, and I should not be here. I will ask my questions and be on my way.'

'Sit or stand. Either way, you have already ignored propriety by showing up at my door in the middle of the night.'

That was a valid point. She decided to sit.

He took his place on the couch.

'I would not be here were it not for your inappropriate and false proposal of marriage. Make no mistake, sir, although I have questions, I still believe the proposal to be ill-conceived.'

'Desperate, you mean.' He leaned forward, his hands pressing on the knees of his trousers. 'What would you like to ask?'

'Firstly, why do you think anyone will believe you married a woman from the neighbouring cottage? Peers wed equally well born ladies, not commoners.'

'Ordinarily, they would not. You make a valid point. But you made everyone believe you were a highwayman ghoul. I imagine you could act the part of a society lady rather well.'

She *had* learned proper manners from her mother, so maybe...

'You overestimate my ability, sir.' Truly, it was one thing to wail while hiding in the shadows, and quite another to act a part face-to-face with genuine ladies. In addition, one of those ladies was his mother.

'Olive, you have a skill for this sort of thing…acting, I mean. I will teach you what else you need to know. My parents will believe you to be a lady. With luck, Hortencia will, too.'

'You see? You thinking I can do this only proves that you are not thinking logically.'

'Aye, maybe so. But it is my freedom at stake. I might seem unhinged to have thought of it, but given proper consideration, it makes sense.'

In truth, she did not believe him to be unhinged, only possessed of a clever, manipulative mind.

To her shame, it was rather like her own.

'If you agree to live here with me for a short time, I will pay you handsomely.'

Pay? Surely she had not heard him correctly.

'I will leave now.'

She stood, confused at why his offer of payment offended her so badly.

It must be because accepting his money would put her on the same level as one of his staff. Until earlier today, she'd thought there was something special growing between them.

Something that money would diminish. Truly, if she wished for paid employment, it would not be as a false wife.

If only he had not asked her to live a lie, their budding friendship might still be possible.

She half regretted turning to leave. The more thought

she gave to his plan, the more merit it had. There was very little she would not do to ensure Eliza's happiness.

But really! Lie and get paid for it? To her way of thinking, it only compounded the sin.

She had not gone three steps before he strode after her. He reached for her arm as if he would prevent her leaving but then drew his hand back, clenched his fingers.

'Is it the offer of payment which is making you angry?'

'I am not angry, merely incensed.'

'I do not understand.'

She continued toward the door, trying not to let him see how hurt she had been.

He stepped ahead of her and blocked half of the doorway.

Mercy but he was large and impressive, for all that she hated to take note of it in the moment.

Even his fingers pressing the door frame gave her heart a little flip. His toes did the same thing to her. All ten of them peeked out from under the hem of his rumpled trousers.

'Tell me what I have done wrong, Miss Augustmore.'

How was she to explain that this division between them troubled her? Especially when much of it was her own doing. She had been the one to insist he call her Miss Augustmore again.

At the time, it had felt the righteous thing to say…but now? She could not recall ever being so confused.

'When you offered to pay me, it was a reminder of the distance between our stations. And I thought there might be an understanding of friendship between us, I was reminded of who we must be to one another.'

'It is not at all what I intended, Olive. Surely it is only

fair to pay you for your service? Any actress would expect it.'

'But I am not an actress.'

She squeezed past him, caught the scent of his skin. He really should have buttoned up. It was not her fault that she felt a sweet shiver while going past him.

Let it be a warning to you, she told herself. *Acting the part of this man's wife would leave any woman wanting more.*

She had her hand on the front door knob when his voice came softly to her.

'Olive, think for a minute. This would be a way to give you and your sister the freedom to choose who you will spend your life with. It might be worth the risk.'

Softly spoken, his words had the impact of being shouted…because he was correct.

'Even if it were true, and I agreed, I would not accept a penny of your money.'

'Will you do it then, if I withdraw my offer of money… and apologize for offering it? It would mean a great deal to me to be restored to your good graces.'

'You are restored, Joseph…only I cannot say about the other.'

'Will you think about it at least?'

That was the problem. The more pondered, the more inclined she was to think…just maybe.

'I do believe you have not given this enough thought,' she said. 'Caution was called for. What is your plan to get out of the marriage when the acting is over? How do we stop being wed?'

It was a valid point. They could hardly proceed until it was addressed. 'We can hardly be married one day and then the next, not.'

'I do not have an answer for that bit yet.'

'Which only shows that you have not thought this out properly. On the surface the scheme might have a small speck of merit. But the truth is, it cannot believably be accomplished.'

'You may leave that to me.'

'Even if you could, which you cannot, I will fail at playing the part.'

'You were a convincing highwayman.'

'Which I no longer am. No matter how well I might play my part, it will end. I cannot simply exist as your wife one day and then be vanished the next.'

'A problem, yes. One that I believe can be solved.'

'How? I cannot think of a way. I do not see that there is one.'

'It is illusive, that's all.'

'You have until I open this door and mount Star's saddle.'

Dastardly wind! It blew her about, dizzy as a willow. Her insides were dizzy enough as it was.

'May I try something before you leave?'

His grin would do her in one of these days.

'What do you wish to try?'

Not kiss her. And why had she thought that? Just because his hair blew all wild about his face and his feet were bare… Just because… When was the man going to button his shirt?

Even if he tried to kiss her, she would not allow it.

'To rehearse, as much as try. I will act the part of a gentleman, and you will act the part of a lady. Just to discover if you feel you have a knack for the part before you completely reject it.'

Not a kiss, then. Good.

'Very well. But you must instruct me first on my part.'

She knew a lot more than most cottage girls because of her mother, and from what she read in novels, but surely not so much that she could accomplish what Joseph was asking of her.

Rather than playacting, she ought to be halfway home right now.

'We will act a greeting,' he explained. 'Try not to blow away during it.'

Since she was here, she might as well give it a go, just to see what she could do.

'Is this our first meeting, or are we already acquainted?'

'We have met one time already.'

'Do we like each other?'

'Quite well. In fact, we were taken with one another at first sight.' Seen in the dark, eyes should not look so blue. It must be her imagination making them that way…blue and sparkling with mischief. He gave her a slight bow at the waist. 'Lady Olive, what a great pleasure to meet you again.'

He reached for her hand, picked it up, then lifted it to his lips as if he would kiss it.

Although he did not, he might as well have, given the sweet shiver that raced across her fingertips.

'How lovely to see you again, my Lord. I pray you are well.'

She dipped a small, polite curtsy. She had never engaged in this type of greeting before. Such formality was uncommon in Fallen Leaf. She would need to call on what she had read and imagined.

She blinked at him, slowly, flirtatiously, because it

seemed a society thing to do. And also he had said they were attracted to one another at first sight.

'How could I be otherwise in your delightful presence?' He must have had a great deal of practice with saying that.

'Oh, my lord.' She offered a great deep sigh which lifted her bosom. A society lady might do that. 'If we hurry, we can be out of this wind and tucked up as warm as hatchlings in our respective beds. Now, that would be bliss, would it not?'

'Olive...you do have a gift. A debutante making her debut would not appear so accomplished.'

'I do not know exactly what I accomplished, Joseph.'

Glory fire, it was good to say his name again.

'We just proved that you have the ability to act the part of an exquisite lady of society. If you are comfortable with the part, perhaps we can continue with the lessons. It might help you decide if you can do this for us or not.'

'And if I decide not to? Will it change our...' She waved her hand between them, not certain what words were appropriate. 'Budding acquaintance?'

'You must decide as you will, Olive. Whatever your choice, it will not change my admiration of you.'

If it was within her power to unite Eliza and her daughter, Olive must give this false marriage serious thought.

Setting her foot in the stirrup, she felt his hand at her waist, assisting her up. Although she did not need the help, and had been mounting a horse unassisted since she was ten years old, the attention made her feel appreciated. Feminine in a way no man had made her feel before.

For Joseph, treating a lady like this was simply good manners, and she should not take the attention to heart.

He was a nobleman, and she was a cottager. They were acting a part. There was no more to it than that.

And yet, here in the dark with the wind gusting around and between them, with it wailing in the treetops, the world around them seemed to seemed to fade.

When he grinned up at her, the divide between their stations did not seem as wide.

'If the weather improves,' she said, 'meet me tomorrow at the stream where our properties join. I am curious about what other ladylike things you can teach me.'

'I will meet you regardless of the weather.'

She nodded, then turned Star toward the road.

His eyes were still upon her. She knew it as surely as if she had turned around and looked for the proof.

Which did not mean she did not wish for proof.

Drawing Star to a halt, she glanced back over her shoulder.

'Come at noon. I will bring lunch,' she told him.

'I will bring a bottle of wine and a blanket.'

She waved goodbye to him, wondering what it would be like to blow him a kiss…to practice what a loving wife would do.

Something was wrong with her. She had never blown a man a kiss for any reason.

She nudged Star on towards home.

'I think perhaps it might be done.' She patted the horse's neck. 'The thing is, I do not know how it might be undone again afterwards.'

And she was not speaking only of ending the sham marriage. Her heart was far too tender when it came to the future viscount.

She would do well to remember that his station in life and hers were worlds apart.

Still, what harm could there be in indulging in the delightful, tickling warmth she got when thinking of him?

Unlike true love, which endured forever, an infatuation burned bright and in secret for a moment and then was gone.

There could be no harm in pretending.

Chapter Five

Joseph watched a bee crawling on a yellow flower, productively gathering pollen near the blanket he sat on. Sunshine warmed his back.

He rolled his shoulders in pure pleasure while listening to water gurgling in the stream, and to the pleasant tone of Olive's voice as she practiced words.

Not words that were new to her, but she was learning to pronounce them in an even more refined way. Proper diction was crucial if she was to fool his visitors. She did not need much work in this area since, as she had told him, her mother had been gently born.

All at once she stopped speaking, took a sip of wine, then set the goblet aside in the grass.

'This is delicious, Joseph,' she said, giving her lips an appreciative smack. After a sigh of satisfaction, a mask descended over her natural expression. 'But pray, my lord, how long would I be required to engage in this farce? As delightful as it may be.'

If she actually found this exercise delightful, he'd eat that bee. Her true feelings did not show behind her smile, which was a testament to her skill. A born and bred lady would appear to find everything delightful even when she did not. Putting her guests at ease was a lady of privilege's first order of duty.

'One week, that's all.'

'Sir, may I take you at your word? This is an agreement which you vow to honour?'

'Indeed. On my honour, I vow it.'

'Then, yes. I will do it.' She tipped her wineglass at him in salute. 'To our success.'

He tipped his glass back at her, but it took all he had not to leap and shout in triumph. If he were free to express himself, he would pick her up, swing her about.

'To winning our freedom,' he said instead. 'And to our friendship.'

'To our friendship.'

He could not look away from the blush in her cheeks when she sipped the wine. It might be due to the weather, or the drink…but hopefully it was because she was excited about the venture they were undertaking.

Her lips twitched.

'I will hate to see our alliance end, of course.' She cast him a charming smile.

'You really are good at this,' he admitted. 'If we had just met, I would not question that you were not born a lady.'

'I do not think you would believe it,' the genuine Olive said. 'As you see, I am dressed as a commoner. And I smell a little like goats.'

He shook his head. 'More like fresh air…grass and flowers. Natural. Not like some women I know who drench themselves in so much perfume it makes everyone's head ache.'

She laughed. For as much as he appreciated her portrayal as a fine lady, the real Olive was far more interesting to him.

'Tell me your secret, Olive. How do you play a part so well?'

'I've a good bit of it from my mother, as I said. That much is not acting.'

'However you come by it, you are a natural actor.'

'The acting comes from books.'

'You studied acting?'

'I would not call it studied so much as living the adventure. How do you imagine I learned my talent for highway terror? In print, fine ladies are in distress even more often than ghouls haunt the woods. Upon occasion the poor lady is in distress because of a ghoul. I, though, do not expect to be in distress. Rest assured, Joseph, I intend to cause distress.'

Heaven help him if he was not beginning to adore this woman. She was perfection. Lady or lass, he had never enjoyed a woman's company more.

'Oh, I believe that. I nearly pity poor Hortencia.' He did not, but was beginning to wonder if Olive was a match for her.

Not that the women were at all the same. Olive would be acting in an unselfish cause. Hortencia was all about attaining a selfish goal. Matters of right or wrong did not matter to the woman who intended to trap him.

'I need you to tell me more about her, Joseph. As your wife, I should know how to deal with my nemesis.'

It took half an hour to explain all of Hortencia. How selfishness was her guiding light. How she did not care who got hurt in her quest to have what she wanted…his title, the extensive family fortune and lands.

The way Hortencia ferreted out a person's secrets and used them to her advantage.

At that news, Olive frowned.

'I am sorry,' he said, 'but the woman is part hound. Do not worry, though, we are cleverer than she is. She will not discover that our marriage is false. Only…be wary, Olive, she will come across mild and sweet like a newly hatched chick, but you must not trust her.'

'Glory fire,' she muttered when he finished. 'Now tell me about your parents.'

'They are honourable, but still, they will present a challenge. Especially my mother.'

'I have always got along well with mothers.'

Olive looked sad, somewhat melancholy when she said so. Probably because she missed her own mother.

Not wishing to make her feel that he was looking into her thoughts, he gazed at the treetops. Leaves shivered in a breeze which felt soft on his face.

'Tell me more about your mother,' Olive said.

'She is a force in society, and charitable to go with it. But position is important to her. To Mama, family security is gained by allying ourselves with another family of the highest rank we can marry into. Which is why she is set on having me wed Hortencia. In my mother's eyes, she will be a credit to us all.'

'But surely what you wish for your life also matters to her?'

'No more than it matters to your father.'

She reached across the blanket and squeezed his hand. 'We will strive hard for our futures, Joseph.'

He would kiss her in thanks, but he did not wish to scare her off. Aye, and likely scare himself off along with it. Something warned him a kiss of thanks was not all there would be to it.

'My father will be easier. His way of promoting the health of the estate is to add to it. Property is what he has his eye on. My job in the family is to visit his purchases and report on them. In the past, I never minded the travel. It was a relief to get out of London for a time.'

'In the past, you say? Am I to understand that now, you do mind?'

'There is something about Falcon's Steep…' He glanced north as if somehow he could spot the tall chimneys through acres of woods between here and there. 'Of all the properties I have visited, none of them ever felt like home to me. This place does. It grabbed me from the first moment.'

'London does not feel that way for you either?'

'Never did. I think I was born all wrong. I would rather have grown up with your goats than in the city.'

'Do you intend to remain here, then? Once this is all finished?'

'I'll try. I am not sure if it will be possible.' He did his best not to scowl, but damn it! His future was not his own and never had been. 'I was born to obligation, you understand.'

'It seems a tiresome burden. But perhaps once you have discouraged Hortencia, you will find a bride who appeals to you more. Then your future will be bright wherever you live.'

A long shadow crept across the blanket. Joseph jolted in surprise. He was rarely taken off guard.

'May I join the picnic?'

'Oh, do, Eliza. The reason for this meeting concerns you, after all.'

Olive's sister cast a glance between him and Olive.

'I will leave you to discuss this with your sister.' Rising, Joseph nodded politely at them both.

Olive stood up as well, handing him what he had brought.

'Return at the same time tomorrow, Joseph. I still have so much to learn before your family arrives.'

Once again he had the urge to kiss her. Too bad even a brief salute on the cheek would be inappropriate despite the friendship growing between them.

'Good day, ladies.' He bowed, then strode beside the stream toward home.

It had taken Olive all afternoon to explain the situation to her sister, and then until bedtime to convince her to go along with the plan.

Oh, what a night. If convincing Eliza of the wisdom of what she was doing had not been enough of a challenge, Father took it in his mind to go to the tavern.

What a shame it was about the plague, though. However, he would believe the story only until he paid a visit to the village and discovered there was not some wicked illness striking people down.

But that was a problem for later.

Now she was for bed. Having agreed to act as Joseph's wife, she would need her wits rested and alert in order to succeed in the course she had turned her hand to.

Climbing the stairs to her chamber, she had doubts… new doubts.

Although she had spent so much time convincing her sister all would be well, she herself was not as certain as she had been earlier today.

Weariness wore at one's confidence. She had passed the

weary mark while bedding the goats down in the stable, and that had been hours ago.

Entering her bedroom, she fell face first on the mattress.

She and Joseph had settled many things having to do with her being his false wife…how they had met and had fallen instantly and irrevocably in love, which had led to their sudden vows. They did not wish to live in sin, after all. They had even made up a family of rank for her. What a shame it was that they lived all the way down in Cornwall and had never visited London.

Also agreed upon was that she would need to live in the manor house with Joseph. If she did not, Father would not believe she was married.

Was she about to live in sin, or was it pretend sin, she wondered?

She felt bad about leaving all the work of running their small goat farm to her sister. Worse about giving her the full burden of their father's care.

Even though she was doing all this for Eliza, Olive was the one who had chosen this path for the both of them.

She rolled over onto her back, yawned and spread her arms.

Yes, indeed. This was all for Eliza. It had nothing to do with being able to see Joseph Billings every day. To enjoy his smile, to inwardly sigh over the sound of his voice.

She might, in the moment, be indulging in fantasies, but that was not the reason for pretending to be his wife.

Again, this was all for Eliza, who was now quite on the spot. Once it became known that Olive was married, her sister would be free to tell James they could wed.

Which then put her in the position of having to tell him the truth about Laura.

Between them, Olive would rather be in her own challenging shoes than her sister's.

If James rejected Eliza for her indiscretion, this would all be for naught.

No, that was not right. It would be for Joseph.

Joseph, who looked into a woman's eyes so deep and true that she believed she was the dearest person in his world and he wanted her desperately.

She knew this was not the case. It is only how her weary mind wished to see it.

As she drifted off to sleep, her thoughts became jumbled. A bit of this and a bit of that which made no sense. Then an image of Joseph's smile hovering over her lips came to mind. She would take that one to her dreams.

Tomorrow she would worry about what fancy knife and fork were used for what food, about what was the most appropriate word to speak in any given situation.

How to make someone feel welcome in her home when, in truth, they were not.

In the morning she would consider ways to keep Joseph out of the clutches of the evil Hortencia.

Tomorrow.

Now, seconds before sleep dragged her under, she was going to spend time with her pretend husband's lips.

Two days after their second picnic, Joseph invited Olive to the manor. She would need to be familiar with the place if she was to live here for a time and to be believed as its mistress.

'I am lost with all these rooms,' she told him, wandering from one to the next. 'And servants, you say? I will not know the first thing about being in charge of them. I have only ever been in charge of goats and my father.'

'We have a little time before they begin to arrive. But really, Olive, for all that you are not used to servants, I believe you will find them helpful.'

'I suppose I will not mind having someone to do the cooking for me, but you may tell the woman who is to dress me to find something else to do.'

'If I must be dressed by my valet, you must be dressed by your lady's maid.' He could not help but grin at the resistance shooting from her eyes. Green was a good colour for the emotion. 'She depends upon you for her livelihood. It is the way things are done in society.'

'No wonder you want nothing to do with it,' she commented while staring up at hallway's high ceilings. 'How is a person to clean, to dust the cobwebs all the way up there?'

'That is not your chore either, in this house. But come, Olive. Would you like to see your chamber?'

She did not answer but looked up the stairway.

'Is something wrong?' he asked.

'It is only that I have never slept anywhere other than the cottage. I imagine this will be very different.'

'It will not be for long. Only until my parents leave.'

'Not long enough to become spoiled by all the luxury, I suppose.'

'Do not expect luxury in your chamber yet. The furniture I ordered will be here in a few days, along with what is needed for the rest of the house. But there is already a wardrobe with plenty of room for your gowns.'

'I do not own a single gown…work dresses only, and a better one for church. I never even considered the need for fancy clothes. I am sorry, Joseph, no one will believe

I am your wife. Everything I wear smells like cheese and animals.'

'Olive, I never expected you to be responsible for that expense. A seamstress and her team are due this morning to fit you. Before the servants arrive, you will have appropriate clothing to suit our needs.'

'I can only imagine what the help will think of me having a chamber along with a wardrobe full of gowns.' She tapped her fingers at her waist and the toes of her shoes on the floor. 'Yes, I can imagine. They will assume I am a strumpet, a kept woman who sells her virtue for a bit of silk and lace.'

Laughing was not what he ought to be doing just now, but it escaped him nonetheless.

'Your reputation will do just fine,' she said. Her glare might be the prettiest thing he had seen in a long time. 'You are a man.'

'I beg your pardon, my dove. I will present you as my wife when they arrive.'

'Your dove?'

'If I use an endearment, our love will be more believable.'

'It sounds absurd. Dove? I think not.'

'Pet? My dear one? Or perhaps, my sweet.' She shook her head at them all. 'Would you care to pick your own endearment?'

'I ought to. Let me think on it a moment.'

He watched her eyes, wondering what was going on behind them. She might be reviewing the many endearments she had read in her books.

'My treasure...that would be lovely. My kitten...no! My vixen.' She smiled, then winked. 'My vixen. I like that one.'

'Shall we settle on "my love"?'

'I like that one as well, Joseph. And I will call you "my dear".'

All at once her expression dimmed, and she bit her bottom lip.

'What is it, my love?'

'It is only, my dear, that I have no ring on my finger. No vow of any sort. It will be difficult to feel a sense of being wed.'

'Come with me.'

Scooping up her hand, he led her to his study. There was a battered-looking desk which had been left behind by the previous owner. He was using it until the new furniture arrived.

He opened a drawer, drew out a velvet bag and emptied it onto his open palm.

'This ring belonged to my father's mother.'

'Now, that is convenient. But do you bring it wherever you go?'

'I do. I loved my grannie deeply. She gave me the ring during my last summer in Scotland. Keeping it with me makes me feel closer to her.'

'I do not feel right wearing it falsely. I am sure she never intended it to be used for this kind of mischief.'

As always, thinking of his grandmother made him grin. Her smile, her bright laughter, were as fresh in his mind today as they had been years ago.

'Ah, no. Grannie had a fine sense of mischief herself. If you ever hear laughter whispering out of nowhere, it will be her.'

'You have heard such a thing before?'

'I've heard something. I choose to give Grannie the honour.'

'Then she might not mind having a former highwayman ghoul wear her ring for a time?'

'Keep your ear open for a distant giggle and that will be your answer.'

'It is a beautiful ring. I will protect it so that when the time is right, you may give it to your bride—your real one, I mean.'

'I thought you might keep it.'

'Oh no, I would not dare. It is far too precious to be given away. I will give it back to you once we win this game.'

'As you wish, then,' he said.

He circled the ring around her fingertip, thinking he would not mind her having it as a remembrance of him. 'I believe that words of some sort are called for.'

'What sort of words? This is a unique situation.'

He could scarcely imagine one more unique.

'Vows,' he said. 'Suitable to our endeavour.'

With a smile which teased and insinuated that he was addled, she said, 'Very well. You go first.'

He cleared his throat, squared his shoulders. 'I, Joseph Billings, heir apparent to Claymore, do swear by all that is prankish to pretend to be your husband. I will protect you from the wiles of Lady Hortencia Clark to the best of my ability, and be a true and faithful friend to you always.'

He nodded, indicating it was her turn to say something.

'I, Olive Augustmore, loyal sister and friend to goats, do swear by all that is preposterous, to play the part of your loving wife. I will protect you from the wiles of Lady Hortencia Clark to the best of my ability and be a faithful friend to you always.'

He slid the ring on her finger. 'Should we kiss to seal the vows? It would seem appropriate.'

'Nothing about what we are doing is appropriate, Joseph.'

'So then, my love, a small kiss will not hurt.'

'One to practice on, my dear…that might not be amiss.'

If he gave her the kiss he'd been thinking about, it would absolutely be amiss. Friends did not smother one another in a passionate embrace.

Instead, he bent, intending to kiss her cheek.

Ah, but then Olive went up on her toes, touched his chin with one finger, and breathed a kiss on his mouth. He barely felt it, and yet it left him off balance for a second.

'This sort of thing will be expected if we are so madly in love that we eloped,' she said. 'We might as well get used to it.'

Used to what? To kisses that were not genuine…to passion pretended for the sake of their scheme?

Only an idiot would believe it was possible.

While Olive had not considered that she would have nothing fitting to wear…dash it, he had also failed to consider something. What her breath would feel like skimming so close to his mouth, how the briefest graze of her lips would make him imagine so much more.

He may have landed himself in a fine predicament.

There was some connection bubbling between them even if he could not say exactly what. But it sizzled down the back of his neck. Made his fingertips itch so that he had to curl them up into fists.

Just in time, he caught up with his self-control, clung desperately to it.

'To us,' he muttered, lifting her hand, as if he were offering a toast to their success but without flutes of champagne.

'To the success of our endeavour.' She squeezed his fingers.

The ring caught a glimmer of sunshine streaking through an open window. It sparkled.

He was close to certain that was not a ripple of laugher in the curtain when a gust of wind twisted it in the open window.

Five days later, Olive walked toward Falcon's Steep with Eliza.

'It all begins today,' Olive said, seeing three tall chimneys come into view over the treetops.

She carried nothing with her. Whatever she would have brought would have been too humble for a lady of quality to own.

Even the gown she was wearing would not stay here but would be taken home by her sister. She had seen the gown she would change into, and it nearly rivaled the cottage in value.

'We are in this for good or ill now,' Eliza said bravely. 'You cannot come home until it is finished, or Father will know you did not elope.'

'I will be stunned if he believes it in the first place. I am hardly the type to be swept away in a fit of passion.'

'I will weep on his shoulder because you treated us so heartlessly by running away. He might believe it then. But the one thing you must not do is let him see you. You can hardly have eloped and be here at the same time.'

'He is bound to notice all the activity up the hill.'

'We discussed this, Olive. Of course there is activity when the manor is preparing to receive a new mistress. I will tell him before anyone arrives so that when they do, he will not question it.'

'I cannot imagine how you will keep him from getting curious and coming here.'

Truly, this was never going to work. If Father came knocking at the manor door asking for his daughter, no one would believe she was a lady of society. The lie would be instantly exposed.

'I will do it somehow. Perhaps I will be able to convince him that since you are on a grand honeymoon tour, there is no point visiting until you return. But don't worry, Olive. You act your part, and I will act mine.'

'Thank goodness this will only be for a short time.' Otherwise this would fall apart, lie by lie.

Even if Father never set foot outside of the cottage, it might be impossible to accomplish a phony marriage.

Arm in arm, she and her sister mounted the stairs of Falcon's Steep as if they were marching to battle. Which was rather how she felt.

She was not ready to meet any of the people soon to be arriving. However, she had made a vow and would keep it no matter what.

'Of them all, I most fear meeting Hortencia.'

'She will quake before you, Olive. I have no doubt about it.'

The front door opened before she and her sister made the top step.

Joseph smiled at them both. Olive gave her sister a sidelong glance. Eliza did not seem to have gone all breathless over his smile. But then, her sister was in love with James, so that would explain it.

Olive felt breathless, and it bothered her. It was one

thing to feel that way in the moments before falling asleep, quite another now that she was here to assume her role as his infatuated bride.

This, she reminded herself, was all a great act, and squishy feelings had no place here.

'Are you ladies ready?' Joseph asked, glancing between her and Eliza.

'Nearly,' Olive answered. 'When will the servants begin to arrive?'

That was when her role would start. Making them believe she was their mistress was nearly as important as making Joseph's parents and Hortencia believe she was his wife.

'Later in the afternoon.'

'Come to my chamber, Eliza,' Olive said. 'It will take until then to put on all the layers of clothing I will be required to wear. Wait until you see it all. You will never believe the extravagance.'

'I will see you soon, then.' Joseph turned and, whistling, walked down a hallway which she knew led to the garden.

It was a nice sound, his whistling. She could stand here for an hour just listening to it.

'Hurry, Olive. I cannot wait to see your new gowns.'

'Give it a moment and you will be happy it is not you who must wear them every day. It is a great responsibility caring for such fine fabrics.'

'But you will have a laundress to take care of them.'

Eliza rushed up the stairs ahead of her.

'That is beside the point!' She called up after her. 'Each one of them costs more money than a year of selling goat's cheese would earn…no, two years!'

Eliza did not seem to care about that. She continued up, laughing and clapping her hands.

Chapter Six

Days later, Olive stood on the front porch of Falcon's Steep, curling her fingers into her expensive skirt. In an attempt to divert her attention from the arrival of Joseph's family...more, from the dreaded Hortencia...she watched a butterfly flit from one overflowing flower urn to another. There were several urns, a pair of them flanking each step leading to the front door.

The new staff had done an amazing job of preparing the manor for the visit.

Joseph had been pleased with their work and had praised their efforts many times. When the day came to take his place as the next Viscount Claymore, she felt he would be excellent in the role whether he wished for the title or not.

Now he stood next to her, watching the drive. Joseph had not wished to be taken unaware of his family's arrival, so he had assigned the new gardener to trim the hedges where the drive met the road.

A few moments ago, shears in hand, Mr Kathol waved his arm, signaling that he spotted carriages approaching.

And so here they stood, the great deception ready to be played out.

Wind gusted about, billowing Olive's skirt. A chill

whirled up her legs. Dark clouds to the south began to pile upon one another in an ominous way.

Hopefully Eliza would get the goats inside before the thunder began. The animals became agitated by storms.

Joseph took one of her hands and carefully held it in his. 'Do not worry, Olive. You will shine. The servants believe you are my wife, and they are not an easy group to fool.'

'Perhaps they believe I am your wife, but I cannot think they believe I am of the upper class.'

'Perhaps not, but they accept that as my wife, you are entitled to the respect they would give to a highborn lady.'

'What if they say something about it?'

'They will not. It is not their place to do so. Besides, from what I can see, they are particularly taken with you.'

'I wish you had informed your parents of our marriage beforehand. It will come as a great shock to them.'

'It is best this way. Trust me on it. It is better that Hortencia does not have time to plan anything devious in advance.'

'I trust you.'

Too soon, she heard the clop of hooves. Any second she would see carriages rounding the curve of the drive.

Inhaling deep and long, she closed her eyes. She went to a place in her head where Olive Billings lived. She stepped within her fictional self, drew in another breath, and left cottage lass Olive behind…at least, hopefully she did. The strategy had always worked when she was a highwayman.

Blinking her eyes open, she smiled up at her husband.

'Well, my dear,' she said. 'Here we go, for better or for worse.'

'For better. We will prevail. Wait and see.'

He squeezed her hand, then bent to kiss her cheek. From

the corner of her eye, she caught a movement, the carriage curtain being drawn aside and a face peering out.

A streak of lightning cut the clouds, but the thunder was still too far off to hear.

The driver of his parents' carriage stepped down from his perch, lowered the steps, then opened the door. Hortencia would be in that one as well. The second carriage would carry his mother's and Hortencia's personal maids along with his father's valet.

Six more people whom Olive would need to convince that she was his wife. He marveled that her hand was not trembling.

Both their futures depended upon a convincing portrayal.

Glancing at Olive, he saw her smiling. She leaned her head briefly against his shoulder in a gesture of affection and excitement.

Mama was first to step out of the carriage. Her surprise at seeing Olive standing beside him was revealed by a flash of alarm widening her eyes, there and gone in an instant.

His mother also knew how to play a part. Viscountess Claymore was gracious in every situation. Although she could not know the situation she was walking into, she did so with a smile.

Olive went down the stairs before he did, confidence marking each step. He came down behind her, returning his mother's smile.

Seconds later, his father stepped from the carriage. Spotting Olive, he seemed curious, but after an instant, his attention was diverted by the newly manicured grounds.

'Outstanding,' he announced.

Father was easy. It was Hortencia's reaction he dreaded.

The toe of her fashionable travelling boot hit the first rung of the carriage. He set his shoulders. Let the battle begin, then.

As if issuing a warning, a roll of thunder boomed toward the manor.

He clasped Olive's hand, not for show but for mutual encouragement.

'Joseph! We have missed you, dear boy.' His mother rushed to hug him, breaking his hold on Olive's hand.

He understood what was first on everyone's mind. Who was this lady offering them a welcoming smile? And why was it her place to be welcoming them?

Perhaps he was a coward not to inform them immediately of who Olive was. He needed a second more to gather the perfect words before making the formal introduction.

Conveniently, Father filled the second.

'This property is as fine as you told me it was, son!' He clapped Joseph on the shoulder, half his attention on Olive while he added, 'I cannot wait to take a tour of the house and the grounds.'

Next, Hortencia made a move to embrace him. 'Joseph! Oh, how I have missed you.'

'My dear.' Olive subtly changed position, blocking Hortencia's attempts. 'This must be the family friend you mentioned. She is as lovely as you told me she was.'

Hortencia stepped backward, jerking as if the compliment had been a slap in her face.

Well done, Olive, he cheered inside. Clever of her to place herself as his intimate and Hortencia as just a visitor, first thing.

Mama's well-honed smile slipped.

Father's brows rose over a grin. From the beginning, Father had never been Hortencia's biggest admirer.

Hortencia's expression went blank. He didn't want to know what was going on in her head.

'Mama, Father,' he said, intentionally leaving the family friend out of the announcement. Hortencia must be made to understand that she was not, nor would she ever be, a part of his family. 'It is my great pleasure to introduce you to my wife, Olive Billings.'

Father, bless him, found his voice at once.

'My dear girl! Welcome to the family.' He opened his arms. 'May I offer my congratulations?'

Olive stepped into his embrace and returned it.

'I have been so anxious to meet you all.' Olive shifted her attention to the viscountess. 'I would say I have been anxious for a very long time, but your son and I wed too quickly for me to be anxious for long.'

'I...well, what a surprise.' His mother made a valiant effort to gather her social wits but appeared to be stumbling.

Hortencia always had her wits about her.

'My word, Joseph,' she said smoothly. 'What a wonderful surprise.'

Next Hortencia turned a luminous smile on Olive. 'Welcome to the family. I am so pleased to meet you.'

Curse it. The woman was not pleased, nor was she in a position to be welcoming anyone into the family.

Giving every indication of friendliness, Hortencia slipped her arm though Olive's. 'I am certain we shall become great friends. Oh, but you cannot imagine the tears that will be shed in London over the news. Of course, I understand perfectly. In time the ladies of society will as well.'

'There will not be all that many tears,' Joseph pointed out curtly. He was hardly society's bad boy.

'I did not mean to say so, Joseph. But love does result in a hasty marriage…upon occasion.' Hortencia made quite a point of smoothing her skirt where the pleats lay neatly over her middle. 'For some ladies.'

'Hortencia!' Mama exclaimed, her face blanching at the ill-disguised intent of the comment and the gesture.

Olive, though…she pressed her fingers to her slim waist, and laughed in good humour.

His bride turned toward his mother, clasped her hands, then gave them a squeeze.

'Hortencia was merely indulging in a jest, a bit of humour among new friends, isn't that right?' Olive arched a brow at her nemesis.

'Oh, please, do not think I meant any offence, Lady Claymore. Your new daughter-in-law is correct; only a little teasing among us women.'

The explanation might have been passed off as genuine, except that he and Father were among the company, so it was not simply teasing among women.

'Rest assured, Lady Claymore, preventing such a catastrophe is the reason your son and I wed so quickly. I am not with child…not yet.'

Olive said that last with a pointed glance at Hortencia, which his mother would not have seen.

'I fear we have got off to an uncomfortable start, and it is all my fault.' Hortencia wrung her hands, giving every appearance of being distressed.

Very likely she was, only not for any insult she had caused.

Her distress would come from finding him happily married and now beyond her reach.

He could only pray she would accept the situation. He would still need to be wary in case she decided to test his faithfulness to his bride.

No, not in case she did. Rather, *when* she did.

'Come,' Joseph said, waving for everyone to come up the steps and into the house. 'The storm is moving closer.'

He slipped his arm around Olive's shoulders and began the procession inside. In a backward glance at the clouds rushing in, he noticed that Hortencia had slipped her arm about Mama's waist.

The reason for it was clear. She was claiming a spot as the favourite, no matter that she had been displaced as his bride by another.

'Joseph,' Olive whispered, casting him a subtle glance. 'That storm…it isn't coming. It's upon us already and walking into your house.'

Noise in the house increased more than six extra people in residence would account for.

There was really no mystery to it, Olive decided. It had to do with two of them being annoyingly demanding.

Her mother-in-law because she was making sure the staff was living up to the standards she required of them.

And the other, her foe, constantly nagged at the servants, demanding this or that extra service.

She imagined they must be frustrated by the constant attention ladies of quality required. Not that they were likely to let on about it since they did not wish to risk their employment.

Perhaps now that everyone was seated for dinner, things

would settle. Surely the guests were weary from travelling, and with a spoonful of luck, would retire early.

Olive needed a few hours alone to slip out of character and breathe. Being constantly on guard against the war of words Hortencia waged was exhausting.

That woman was a sly one, coming across as sweet and companionable. Syrup was also sweet, yet it made a sticky trap for unwary flies or ants.

Luckily Joseph had warned her to be on her guard. Otherwise she might have been drawn in, stuck as miserably as an insect.

Why, oh, why had the cunning woman made a point of sitting beside her for the meal?

The conversation went on innocently enough until—

'I must apologize for my words earlier. Truly, Olive, I did not mean them as they came across. I would never suggest you were a fallen woman and so forced to wed. I know Joseph well enough to understand he is not easily fooled. Only a clever harlot would be able to trap him that way.'

'You are correct. My husband is ever discerning when it comes to a person's character.' Olive speared a piece of cheese with her fork but did not lift it to her mouth. 'But tell me, do you believe it is only harlots who get caught up in what nature intends to happen when a man and woman… come together, shall we say?'

Lady Claymore must have heard the exchange because her spoon, brimming with turtle soup, hung halfway between her mouth and her bowl.

Glory fire, Olive was too far into the conversation to let it go now.

'A lady would never allow herself to be in a position for

such a thing to happen. A true lady would not even know about "coming together".'

'I see. As a true lady, then, there are matters you do not understand?'

'Naturally not!'

'I must warn you then, in all friendship, that there are men who might take advantage of your ignorance. You might find yourself in trouble without you even seeing it coming. If you do not mind me saying so, your mother did you no favours by keeping you ignorant in the ways of men and women.'

Hortencia blinked. Her mouth opened and closed like that of a fish tossed on a streambank to flop about. It might not be charitable to feel satisfaction at the woman's consternation, but she did nonetheless.

'I know this is a distressing topic for ladies of our station, Hortencia, but it does no one any good to be unaware of certain ways of...well, of biology, shall we say? Do not worry, though. I will explain it all to you, if you wish.'

'You make it sound as if a woman with a dirty secret is a victim. Not the lowest and most immoral of us all.'

Soup dripped from Lady Claymore's spoon...plop, plop, plop, into the bowl.

Olive had done it now. This was not at all appropriate dinner conversation. Not appropriate conversation for a lady to engage in at any time.

Joseph would probably send her home after dinner ended.

What could not be seen but was true nonetheless, was that Olive had steam coming out of her ears. What an outrage it was for someone to call Eliza immoral...pronounce Olive's sweet niece a dirty secret.

Laura might be a secret, but dirty?

Glory fire! She called on what authority she thought the wife of a future viscount might have and pressed on to make her point.

'I understand what you are saying, of course.' And it made Olive want to spit. 'But you speak out of naivety. There are ladies who find themselves in delicate situations and by no choice of their own. Men are stronger than women are, if you understand what I mean. And often women are simply too innocent to know what is befalling them until it is too late. You, my dear, are in danger of that last example. But if you wish for me to advise you on what to watch out for, for the warning signs if you will, I will be happy to do so.'

'This is the most inappropriate conversation I have ever been engaged in.' Hortencia pushed away from the table and stood up. 'I am overwrought by it. I shall retire to my chamber.'

'I meant no offence, truly.' Oh, but yes, she did intend it. It was beyond gratifying to see her foe rise from the table and flee the battlefield. 'Forewarned is forearmed, you must agree.'

Hortencia snapped her fingers at the footman who stood at attention near the wall. 'Have a meal sent up.'

Joseph gave Olive a considering look from under lowered lashes. He would no doubt have heard the conversation. They all would have.

He'd probably decided she was a miserable failure at being his false bride, and who would blame him?

Who would ever consider her an appropriate future viscountess after this? She was certain that Lady Claymore had never engaged in such a conversation.

Joseph could only be thinking he would be better off with no wife at all.

'I suppose Hortencia is weary from travel,' her father-in-law declared lightly. 'We shall miss her.'

One thing Olive was certain of. No one would regret seeing the last of her.

Indeed, what noble family would appreciate having such a bluntly spoken daughter-in-law at their dinner table?

Only half a day into her role as wife and she was an utter failure. She was as far from genteel as a woman could be.

There was but one thing to do. She must leave this fancy home and its refined people before she brought shame on Joseph. More shame, that is.

A rather tricky obstacle stood in her way. What would she wear home? Her own gown was at the cottage, and she could not wear one of the ornate garments hanging in the wardrobe. It would feel like thievery.

She felt the same about the undergarments she wore, but she could hardly abandon them.

Heavens, what a predicament.

She shrugged and twisted out of the elegant dinner gown she had on. It was not an easy task to perform without the aid of the maid who had helped her into it.

When the gown hit the floor, she scooped it up and spread it across the bed.

Shed of the dress, she faced the next obstacle to her escape.

How was she to get out of the house wearing only undergarments? Even if the family was settled for the night, which she did not believe they were, there was the issue of servants travelling the hallways, performing their night-time tasks.

She could not hope to evade them.

And yet, there might be a way… Hmm, with a bit of luck, she might escape the house.

Going to the corner of the room, she yanked three times on the cord which would summon her maid.

Within moments, the woman bustled into the room, saw the gown on the bed and looked surprised.

'My lady?'

Was she supposed to apologize for undressing herself when it was this woman's job to do it? Here was one more failure at acting a lady.

'I shall put the gown away and brush your hair for bed.'

'I would ask a different service of you tonight, Collins. All of sudden I am feeling rather faint.' Fine ladies did feel that way upon occasion, or so she had read. In Olive's opinion, it was a bit of fiction contrived in order to draw attention to oneself. 'I would like a bit of fresh air.'

'Sit down at once, my lady. I will open your window.'

'Garden air, I mean. I need to sit amongst the shrubbery for a time. I have a small problem, though. I do not wish to dress again, but at the same time, I cannot be seen in my shift. Perhaps you know of a private way out of the house?'

Mary nodded, but not without a frown. Going to the wardrobe, the maid took out a lacy robe, then put it on Olive. Next she found a blanket in another trunk, and folded it over her arm.

'The rain only just stopped, my lady. Everything will be will be wet. But if you truly wish it, I will take you down.'

And so, by way of a back staircase which led from the bedchambers to behind the kitchen, Olive was able to get out of the manor unseen.

Convincing Mary to leave her alone in the garden

proved to be more difficult. In the end, given Olive's 'superior' position, the maid had no choice but to go back inside the house.

Once Collins was out of sight, Olive set the blanket on a bench. She shrugged out of the robe, which was far too elegant to take with her, folded it, and placed it on top of the blanket.

Oh, brrr…it might not be raining, but it was chilly. Still, she did not wish to take anything that did not belong to her even if it meant a bone-chilling walk home.

'I'm sorry, Joseph,' she muttered even though he could not possibly hear her from the house. 'I am not qualified to be your wife, even in jest.'

What she was, was a coward. It was not right to leave him struggling to explain to his parents where she had gone.

Worse, she was abandoning him to the wiles of Lady Hortencia.

Worse again, where was she to hide until her sister wed her baker? In the stable, she supposed. There was really no other place.

Rubbing a chill from her bare arms, she glanced back at her chamber window. It had been lovely and comfortable. She would never forget her time there.

'Please forgive my awful behaviour during dinner.' It did not matter that Joseph would never know she apologized. She simply felt the need to do it.

No matter how she tried to act the part, she was not a lady. She was a far better goatherd than a false future viscountess.

'I do not,' said the tall bush she stood beside.

Leaves rustled, and branches spread apart. Joseph peered narrow-eyed at her through the opening.

'Then you will agree that I must be on my way.' It was a relief to know they were of a same mind on the matter… at least, she thought that was what he meant.

The branches snapped back into place. Joseph stepped around the bush, facing her square on the path.

'How can I forgive you for something when there is nothing to forgive?'

Poor man thought she was only asking his pardon over her dinner behaviour. He would feel quite differently when he knew she was backing out on their agreement.

The sooner she made it clear, the better. She would rather not be standing in the cold discussing matters wearing this thin shift which did not even belong to her.

There was not much to the garment. If she was beginning to feel warm, and she was, it had to do with the way Joseph was looking at her.

Had she not just given Hortencia a lecture on the risk to a woman? How a situation might come upon her quite by surprise?

Very well, she would not leave the robe behind after all. It seemed prudent in the moment to put it back on. To tie the ribbons securely at her neck where it might choke her with good sense.

'Of course there is something to forgive. Even at a cottage dinner table, my conversation would have been unacceptable.'

'Which is what made it so entertaining. Olive, it was all I could do to remain in my seat.' He picked up the blanket, tugged it across her shoulders, then bunched it under her chin. 'I came much too close to laughing out loud when Hortencia got up from the table.'

'I nearly made your mother choke on her soup. She must think me the worst daughter-in-law ever.'

'You won over my father, though. He's never been fond of Hortencia. Come, Olive. Let's go back inside. It is too cold to be out here…especially undressed.'

'There is a reason I am out here undressed.'

'To entertain your husband amongst the shrubbery?' He gave her a teasing grin…one that that smacked of shenanigans.

She was struck dumb for an instant by the mental image of the two of them frolicking about the garden.

'When you have a wife, a real one, you may give her that grin. You may not give it to me. I insist you take it back.'

'Tell me, Olive, why are you leaving me, as clearly you are doing? Have I done something to offend you?'

Other than frolicking about the garden with her in his mind, he had not.

'I only assumed after the way I embarrassed your guest you would not wish for me to remain.'

A gust of wind came up, snatched raindrops from the leaves, then deposited them on her face and hair. It blew the clouds away, revealing a bright, fat moon.

Joseph brushed a damp trail from her temple to her chin, giving her a thoughtful look. It was hard not to notice how raindrops also dotted the hair of his forearms.

In all honesty, and honesty being her guiding light, she was not sorry he had, at some point, rolled back his sleeves and left his arms bare to her view. He had nice, muscular arms. She could not be faulted for noticing.

In that instant, she was noticing far too many things about him. Which would not be so awful if it remained merely observation. But no, there was more to it than that. There was reaction.

All around them, moonlight glistened on water drops, sparkling as if brushed in enchantment. And there was the whisper of his slow, deep breathing and her own quick heartbeat in her ears.

She knew quite well she was not warm because of the blanket he bunched under her chin.

Caution was called for here, because she was looking at Joseph in the way Eliza had probably looked at the travelling poet-singer. In the way that Hortencia claimed to know nothing of.

In the way she had no experience with either, but felt by instinct what was happening.

Instinct suggested she open the blanket and draw Joseph close to her bosom, to share heartbeats and…

Experience—Eliza's, not her own—warned her to run from this folly and go home the way she had planned to.

Which is what this conversation was about. It was only her imagination taking it in another direction.

'I must go, Joseph. This all seemed a brilliant scheme in the beginning, but now that I have met your parents and Hortencia, I can only think I will make a muck of it all. You will end up worse off than you would have been without me.'

'I do not think you truly believe that,' he murmured, looking terribly vulnerable all at once.

For as much as she'd thought it best to go home, to avoid the trouble this marriage ruse was bound to cause, at the same time, she felt wicked for letting Joseph down. He was counting upon her. Eliza was counting upon her.

'You were magnificent at dinner, Olive. I have never

seen anyone get the best of Hortencia, and yet you did it quite handily.' Then his lips twitched, and his eyes sparkled…not figuratively, either. She actually saw a glint. 'Admit it, my friend, you enjoyed every second of it.'

'Glory fire, but I did.' Her lips twitched, too. She could only wonder if her eyes were sparkling like his were. It felt as if they were.

'Please stay, Olive. You are only having a bit of stage fright.'

'But you thought I was magnificent?'

Magnificently inappropriate is what Olive thought.

'Oh, aye. Even better than when you were the terror of the road.'

'I suppose you are right about the stage fright. Please forgive me, Joseph. I will not run off again.'

He let go of the blanket he had been holding in place at her throat, then slipped one arm companionably about her shoulder.

'I am grateful, more than you can know.'

'So am I.'

Because of Joseph, Eliza would have her family.

'If you are worried again, please come to me. We will figure things out.' He led her toward the house. 'Now, we should get back before you catch a chill.'

A chill? That would be the last thing she felt with his body heat wrapping her up in delicious waves.

He kissed her hair in a sweet, friendly gesture. He urged her closer to his side. A woman could rely on a husband with shoulders so strong and broad. One day, some lucky woman would.

However, that woman would *not* be Lady Hortencia Clark.

Chapter Seven

The next night, Joseph sat in the parlor after dinner with his father, legs stretched before him, watching the inch of brandy he swirled in his snifter go round and round.

His father smiled and lifted his own glass.

'To a job well done, son. This is the finest property we have purchased so far.'

'I agree. It felt like home here the first time I rode up the drive.'

'Because you were bringing your bride with you, I would think.'

He nodded, grinned, striving to play his role as husband as brilliantly as Olive played his wife.

'I remember when your mother and I were in love.'

'You say that as if you no longer are.' Perhaps he should not have pointed that out, but Joseph had never considered his parents to be in love.

'That is not what I mean, not quite. I am very fond of your mother, naturally. It is only that life happened, and our young passion for one another grew up. Over the years, it became more practical in nature, I suppose one would say. It is an adequate arrangement.'

He was not surprised to hear his father admit this. His

parents seemed much like many other society couples… bound to one another by duty rather than love.

'You are fulfilled with adequate?' Was this even an appropriate conversation for a father and a son to be having? It might be, now that he was married, or at least perceived to be.

'I have my lands. Your mother has society to keep her entertained. Although I suppose her adventures will be curbed somewhat now that you have married. Your mother was certain she would have you wed to Hortencia, and all of society would be gasping with pleasure over it.' Father took the last sip of his drink, long and slow. 'Well done escaping that fate, my boy.'

'This might be an uncomfortable visit for everyone. I suppose I ought to have told you of my marriage before Mama invited Hortencia.'

'If you want to know what I think, Hortencia would have come regardless. The fact that you have taken wedding vows will mean nothing to her.'

Joseph fought back a grin. He and Olive had taken vows, only not the sort his father imagined.

'I fear you are right.'

'Well, I would not over worry it. It does seem that Olive is Hortencia's match. It is good to see you so in love with your wife. I admit, it does bring back sweet memories.'

Olive must be doing a brilliant job indeed if his father saw him as being so much in love.

When the day came for Joseph to wed, it would be for love. He had seen marriages where a spark ignited between a man and wife had lasted over the years.

Father might be content with being fond of his wife, but Joseph would have more…or he would have nothing.

'I have a matter that I would like to discuss with you, Father.' Joseph finished his drink, long and slow, the same way his father had, as a way of giving brief pause to a conversation. 'I would like to make Falcon's Steep my home. I will still explore your new properties, but I wish to settle here.'

'I cannot imagine a better place for you to bring up your children. You never did appreciate London anyway.' Father stood up from his chair, clasped Joseph on the shoulder, and squeezed. 'Please accept the estate as our wedding gift to you and Olive.'

This was both wonderful…and horrible. Feeling a great deal of guilt, he stood to embrace his father. To accept a wedding gift when there had been no wedding made him feel like the worst of sons. And Father had no other.

However, saddling him with Hortencia as a daughter-in-law was unthinkable. She would make all of their lives utterly miserable.

The scowl he felt settling on his face, sinking into his soul, vanished when the women came into the parlor and Olive's smile rested on him.

He and the viscount stood. Olive hurried across the room, hugged his arm, then went up on her toes and kissed his cheek.

This woman sparkled. Her smile looked sincere, he could nearly believe she was truly his bride and so in love with him that she glowed.

'I missed you,' he said. Once the words left his mouth, he had to confess they were true.

What he ought to do was return Olive's kiss, but all of a sudden, he was not certain his motive was only to fool Hortencia.

'We have all missed your company, Joseph,' Hortencia declared, rushing forward to claim his other arm and, therefore, preventing the possibility of a kiss.

For the best, then. Some things were better left undone.

It left him wondering, though. What if he was not only lying to everyone else about who Olive was to him, but to himself, as well?

His pretend bride intrigued him in every way a woman could intrigue a man.

He was far from indifferent to her. Thinking about it now, how much more could he feel for a woman he one day courted than he felt for Olive, here and now?

It did not matter how much. He knew he could never court Olive properly. No more than Olive could accept his courtship.

A viscount's heir and a cottage lass would not be accepted. Not in London and not in Fallen Leaf either.

He shook out of Hortencia's grip on his sleeve, then led Olive to a couch which was barely wide enough for the two of them, even if they squeezed close together.

His intention when he'd ordered the piece was to fit a woman's generous skirt. Now, feeling Olive's thigh pressing against his, the warmth where her elbow rubbed his arm…he was glad it was no bigger.

This piece of furniture was perfect for cuddling, even if it was not genuine cuddling.

Conversation hummed pleasantly along without much challenge from Hortencia.

After about an hour, the viscount said, 'Amelia, let us retire to our chambers. I believe the newlyweds have better ways of occupying their time than speaking to us old folks. Begging your pardon, Hortencia. I did not mean to suggest you are old. Only that Joseph and his bride would appreciate a bit of privacy.'

'Think nothing of it, my dear Lord Claymore.' Flushed, Hortencia stood.

Damn it but the woman was presumptuous. It grated on him that she used the endearment on his father. She was not family.

'As it is,' she went on, 'I am weary from a day in the wilds. My dear Olive, I wonder how you can take living out here with nothing for company but woods and birds…and squirrels, the dirty, chattering little creatures! It must be so dull with no proper company to keep you entertained.'

'It is not so difficult,' Olive answered, giving his hand a squeeze. 'I have Joseph. He is never dull.'

'Yes, I do recall that about him. Good night, my dears.'

Hortencia sent him a smile that was far too intimate to offer a married man, or a single one, for that matter.

With a dramatic swirl of satin and lace, Hortencia swished out of the parlor.

Moments later, Mama hid a yawn behind her hand. She stood and crossed to where he and Olive sat pressed together. She patted his cheek.

'Good night, son.'

She nodded at Olive. Then, linking her arm with Father's, she led him out of the room.

Out of sight but not of hearing, his father said, 'Hortencia is not a good sport, if you ask me, Amelia.'

'No one did, Marshall.'

'I suppose I should not be offended that your mother likes Hortencia better than she does your wife, Joseph.' Olive said.

What could it possibly matter? Olive was not his true wife, nor a true daughter-in-law either.

She was offended for Joseph's sake, that was all.

Oh, very well…it was only fair to admit that was not all there was to her opinion on the matter.

Still, out of loyalty to her son, Joseph's mother should show a preference for his wife.

Especially since Hortencia was so disrespectful of the wife…of her.

There was constant competition between herself and Hortencia. It had begun that first moment on the steps when Olive threw down the gauntlet, so to speak.

Not that the gauntlet would not have been thrown by one of them eventually, and Olive was only glad she had been the one to do it first. For some reason, being first gave her a sense of advantage. A perception was all it was, because in truth, she didn't have the advantage, not in anything.

'I can only hope that seeing me happily wed will open my mother's eyes to who Hortencia is at heart.' With an arm companionably around her shoulders, Joseph led her from the parlor toward the grand staircase which led up to their chambers. He bent his head close to her ear to whisper, 'Now that she has no hope of making a match between me and that woman, perhaps Mama will look at things differently.'

The warmth of his breath made her wish, if only for an instant, that things were different. That this was not just for show.

But no. A performance was all this cottage girl would ever have of a noble gentleman. It would be futile to wish for anything more than what she had in this moment.

Besides, she was happy with what she had. It was true

in life that the present was all one ever had. No living in the past. No living in the future. Only what was offered right then.

They arrived at her chamber door first. His was one door further down the hallway.

She leaned back against the door, looking up into a face that would leave every woman in London sighing, high- or low-born.

'Well, good night,' she said, half sorry the day was over. She had enjoyed most of it.

Joseph braced his hand on the door frame, leaning toward her, his expression intent as if trying to decide whether to kiss her or not.

She got lost in his eyes. Her heart beat every which way of mad.

This, she reminded herself, was not the first time she had anticipated his kiss, and yet it had not happened.

But this time…oh, this time she felt it pulsing between them. There was a dance of sorts going on…a waltz between what was forbidden and what was desired.

Then, just like that, the music ended. 'Sleep sweet, Olive.'

Joseph lifted away from the door frame, nodded and then walked the short distance to his chamber.

At his door, he paused and gave her a considering look. Whatever he meant by it, she could not guess.

Was any of what just happened real? Had he only been acting as if he would kiss her in case someone was looking?

This game she had agreed to play held more risk than she had first thought.

Although the cottage was a distance away, Olive swore she could nearly hear Eliza warning her to be careful.

* * *

It was not wise to meet her sister in the meadow so near the manor. It could hardly be helped, though. Olive could not venture any closer to the cottage and risk meeting Father. Nor could she be away long enough for anyone to question where she had been.

'Everything is going well,' Olive reported, shading her eyes from the sun, which was warm. Also quite bright after the cloudiness of the past couple of days.

'I need more than that, sister. I require details.' Eliza pointed to a large tree which offered an inviting patch of shade. She tugged Gilroy on his lead toward it. 'This poor boy misses you. All the goats do.'

The trees would provide some privacy, but not enough. This would need to be a quick meeting.

Sitting down in the shade, Olive hugged the goat around his shaggy neck. He responded with a special bleat which meant he was happy to see her.

'I am sorry, Gilroy. It will only be for a few more days. How is Father, Eliza? I hope you have not had a difficult time with him.'

'He is doing well and has given James permission to court me. So thank you for that, Olive.' Eliza squeezed her hand. 'It is such a small word, isn't it? But it is all I have… so, thank you.'

'Has Father tried to go to the tavern?'

'You'd hardly believe it, but no. He sends me to the village every day to see if there is a letter from you.'

'I suppose I should have written one and left it for him. That was a bit of a slip-up. But just tell him I will not be gone long enough to write.'

Gilroy lowered to the grass and settled beside her.

This was lovely. She pitied the people of Joseph's circle who were not able to enjoy nature this way. Imagine a genteel lady sitting under a tree with a goat in Hyde Park. Eyebrows would arch so high they would float right off those proper faces.

She smiled at the mental image because, really, it was very funny.

'I want to know about the woman. Is she as awful as your husband claims she is?'

'You know very well Joseph is not really my husband. And yes, she is every bit of it. Pretty, though. She looks like a fair-skinned porcelain doll. And her eyes! You would not believe how blue they are. She is every man's dream and every woman's envy.'

'I do not dream of fair skin. I envy the freckles on your nose. I hope Laura develops them.'

Eliza sat down, looping her arm across Gilroy's back.

'Proper ladies do not have them.'

'Poor them. But tell me what it is like being married to that handsome man?'

'I will not lie. It is fun to play at.'

'My heart gets dizzy at the thought. But imagine, me the sister-in-law of a noble.'

'Imagining it is all you will do. Better you pay attention to your own coming marriage. I imagine James is happy about it.'

Eliza's gaze wandered to the treetops, and seemed to get lost in the shifting leaves.

'Eliza?'

'I have not spoken to him about it yet. Only Father has. I will, of course. It is only...well, I know he loves me as I love him, but I am so frightened to tell him about Laura.'

'You know you must.'

'Of course I do. But it scares me. Whenever I begin to admit the truth to him, I find I cannot.'

'You only have a few more days before I am no longer wed. You will lose your chance.'

'Pray for me then, sister. I have never been so scared to do anything in my life. What if he hates me afterwards? What if he tells someone about my sin?'

'If he does, he is not the man you want to marry, anyway.'

'But I will be ruined, and Laura along with me. No man will want us then.'

'A very good man will. One who loves you. I believe James is that man. You must trust him if you wish for any sort of happiness in your future.'

'This afternoon, then. I will gather my courage and do it.' All at once Eliza straightened. 'Who is that? It's her, isn't it? The porcelain doll.'

Good heavens! It was.

Hortencia had just come over the rise of the hill and was now making her way towards them.

'This is the first time she has been outside. She dislikes nature. So why is she out in it now? Probably up to no good.'

'She has followed you. Stand up, Olive. Pretend you have come to buy cheese.'

'Did you bring some with you?'

'No…you saw me and my goat passing and stopped me to order some…or something of that nature.'

'I am supposed to be new here. How do I know you sell cheese?'

'You saw the goat and hoped I did.' Eliza frowned at

the approaching image of female perfection. 'Perhaps she will not notice Gilroy cannot give milk.'

'She claims to be innocent of male parts and what they do, but even she cannot fail to notice he is a male. Well, we shall carry on as best we can, Mrs…Gilroy.'

The goat looked up at Olive and bleated. 'It is all I can think of in the moment.'

Then Hortencia was upon them, reaching down to pick leaves from her skirt and muttering unladylike oaths.

'Olive, I do not know how you can tolerate it here. Surely you miss London as much as I do.'

'I find the country far more pleasant. But take heart, my dear. Not much longer until you return.'

Eliza, dressed in her work gown, appeared as common as they came. Hortencia acted as if neither her sister nor her goat existed. She looked right through them.

Then her expression shifted from blank to speculating.

So, she did see them, after all. They were simply beneath her regard.

But what, she would be wondering, was the lady of the manor doing speaking with a commoner?

'Hortencia, may I present Mrs Gilroy.'

'Why would you? I am certain I have no interest in making this woman's acquaintance.' In spite of having no interest, Hortencia looked Eliza over with a sharp eye.

'Mrs Gilroy sells the best cheese in the area. I have made a habit of purchasing only from her.'

Hortencia's blue gaze slithered back to Olive. Olive's imagination supplied a hiss because there should have been one.

'It does surprise me, I must say. Why doesn't she come

to the kitchen door and deal with the cook, like any other vendor would do?'

Why indeed?

Olive stepped closer to Hortencia and whispered. Luckily her sister had excellent hearing and would not miss what she said in 'secret'.

'Mrs Gilroy, the poor soul, has had an accident, and she has trouble walking long distances. I promise you, Hortencia, once you taste the cheese she sells, you will not mind that she cannot make it to the back door.'

'Are you certain?' Hortencia did not bother to whisper. 'She does not look lame. This might be a lazy excuse to avoid walking so far.'

'Oh, no, my lady. I suffered a grievous injury when I was knocked flat by a nervous horse.'

'Really, Olive. I do not know why you believe the woman. She looks as hale as you do.'

'The story is true, Hortencia. I have heard it told among the villagers. It was all anyone spoke about for a while because the horse was fleeing a highwayman. The incident did cause a stir.'

'A highwayman?' Hortencia caught the bodice of her gown and twisted a hank of ivory lace. 'Here?'

'Some say it was a ghoul sprung from the underworld, but that does seem rather far-fetched to me,' Olive said.

'I detest this place. Ghouls and highwaymen. It is absurd. Superstitious delusion.'

'Beggin' your lady's indulgence, it is the very truth. Look, I shall show you the wound.' Eliza grabbed her skirt, drawing it up her leg inch by slow inch. 'It is still oozing a bit, though. As long as you do not mind a bit of pus, it is not so bad to look at.'

Hortencia spun about and stomped back up the hillside, not seeming to notice how her skirt snagged on the thistles.

Olive clasped her hand over her mouth, bent at the waist, suppressing hysterical laughter.

She spun away from Eliza and Gilroy, dashing after Hortencia.

Tears damped her eyes with the effort not to laugh because the urge pressed her chest without mercy.

Oh, but nighttime could not come soon enough. It had become custom for her and Joseph to spend a few moments alone before retiring in order to discuss the progress of their scheme. No one would admire Eliza's tale more than he would.

'A word, son.'

His mother's voice caught him as he was about to go to the garden, where the caretaker was at work trimming a rose hedge which had been neglected for two years.

Joseph had hopes of turning the grounds into a showplace one day. Not for hordes of admiring visitors but for himself. And for Olive, if she came to visit him once this was all over.

Only a couple more days. Thinking about that made him…not unhappy exactly, because it had been his and Olive's plan all along…but there was no denying he was going to miss her.

The two of them got along well, even though theirs was an uncommon friendship. Society, both his and hers, said it should not even exist.

'Of course, Mama. Would you like to walk in the rose garden? The weather is perfect this afternoon.'

'It seems private enough. Yes, then, let's go there.'

'Everywhere around here is private, and beautiful,' he pointed out.

'Your father tells me we are giving it to you as a wedding gift.'

'It is very generous of you. Olive and I are grateful.'

'It is so strange, Joseph…you and Olive. It was a shock to discover you had married her. The match is not at all what I had in mind for you.'

'My duty was to wed. You have never failed to point it out. When I met Olive, I knew there was no other woman for me, so I saw no point in waiting.'

'But Hortencia!' His mother shook her head, probably not even seeing the burst of yellow roses she passed by. Mama usually loved yellow roses. 'It was supposed to be Hortencia you married. I am certain you knew that was the plan. She was a perfect match for you.'

'That was your plan, not mine. She was not a perfect match for me, only a boon to the family name.'

'And for the title you will inherit one day. And therefore, for you.'

'One day far in the future, I hope.'

'Very far in the future, but it would have been wise for you to prepare for it now.'

'I am sorry you are disappointed with my choice, Mama. I never got on well with Hortencia. But Olive? I proposed to her the day after we met. She accepted it the day after that.'

This was somewhat true; it was only the nature of the proposal he was not forthcoming about.

'You are a young man in love. Be careful about that, son. Passion is fleeting. Now, duty…that is what is required of a man of your station.'

'Duty to whom? To myself and my wife or to my peers in London?'

'Who is this wife of yours, anyway? I am not familiar with her family.'

'They are not from London. Olive's father is a country baron. Neither he nor his wife has sought a life in society.'

'You must get along with them famously, then, being of like minds.'

Had they been authentic, he probably would have got along with them. A part of him did wish all this was real. What might have happened if Olive's family was titled?

She would not be who she was, that's what.

Which would be a shame. He would not change her for anything. To his mind she was engaging, clever and… perfect.

To chain such a woman to society's rules would be a crime. He could not imagine her being stuffy and stifled.

'The damage is done, I suppose, and we must live with it,' she said, her sigh resigned.

He stopped and stared hard at her, trying to remind himself that she was a product of her time and place. In her eyes, marrying less advantageously would be considered damage.

'I ask you to look at me, Mama.' He paused for a second to be sure he had her full attention. 'Do I look damaged?'

She let out a great huff. 'What you look is in love.'

He'd expected her to say he looked content…or something on that emotional level.

In love, though? He looked in love?

Very well, it was how he meant to look, so why did the statement shake him?

A man could appear to be in love without being in love.

But his father had said much the same thing…that it was good to see him in love with his wife.

At least Olive did not see what they did. She knew this was a sham, understood that the ruse would end in a couple of days.

'Well, my dear, being that things are what they are, we must celebrate your marriage. Share your joy, and ours.'

'Thank you.' He kissed his mother's cheek. He knew giving up Hortencia's family connections could not be easy for her. 'I hope you will become as fond of Olive as I am.'

'There is something about her…she is different than most ladies I associate with. But I can see why you are taken with her.'

All good…except that soon he would need to find a way to be untaken with her.

He had promised Olive he would think of a way out of this mess, but so far, no way had presented itself to him.

'I have spoken to your father, and we have decided to stay longer.'

They'd decided what? No…he must have misheard her.

'Surely you are anxious to get back to your friends in London.'

'Yes, quite. But I've already announced your wedding in the newspapers. We have invited a few friends to join us here. As I said, your marriage must be celebrated. Everyone must know how much we approve of it.'

'Do you approve of it?'

For some reason, he really wanted her to. And yet it might be easier to find a way out of this predicament if she did not.

'Just give me time, son. This has all come as a great surprise to me.' Then she smiled, giving his cheek a happy pinch. 'But as soon as the grandchildren come, no doubt I will be over the moon about it all.'

A wedding announcement…a party…grandchildren. Joseph did not know whether he was flushed or pale. Dash it all if he was not flashing from one to the next with each heartbeat.

'From the look on your face,' she said, 'I can only think the happy day will not be far off.'

How in the great bloody blazes was he to tell Olive of this turn?

To ask her to remain here longer than she'd agreed to and act as the hostess of a house party was too much to ask of her.

Once she heard the news, she would go home. The ruse would finally fail.

He would be vulnerable to Hortencia's attack. It played out before his eyes, making him cringe because he saw himself as a mole snagged in a falcon's claws. The more he struggled, the tighter the claws clutched him.

Chapter Eight

Given that Olive was required to be dressed by her maid in a new gown and her hair arranged just so, she was running a few moments late for tea.

Had she been allowed to dress herself in a comfortable gown, had she not been forced to sit impatiently while her hair was piled on top of her head in frivolous curls, she would have been early.

Rushing down the hallway to the drawing room, she thought fancy dressing was a waste of good time.

Why not spend those moments getting ready for tea, actually enjoying the company of Joseph's family instead?

She paused outside the door to catch her breath, and to listen for an appropriate time to enter. Although she had not learned any particular rule about entering a room, it only seemed right to wait for a pause in the conversation so that she did not interrupt one in progress.

'Apparently it is only you and I for tea today,' she heard Lady Claymore say.

'I do not mind,' Joseph's father answered. 'We spend so little time just the two of us. I miss that. Don't you recall when we were young…'

This was not a moment to walk in upon. From what Joseph had told her, his parents had been close once and then grown apart.

Besides, a frisson of alarm was creeping in her brain. It did not seem that Joseph was in the drawing room. As far as she could tell, Hortencia was not either.

Where, then, was he? Of a bigger concern…where was Hortencia?

For all that Olive was expected to sip tea and nibble on small sandwiches with Joseph's parents, she had made a vow to protect her un-husband from the claws of his enemy.

Tiptoeing back down the hallway, she wondered which way she should go.

She had no idea why Joseph had not attended tea and so could not imagine where to find him.

Since he would be most in danger from Hortencia in secluded places, she would search there first, then work her way towards the less obvious spots.

Coming out of the kitchen door at the back of the house, she wondered if the stable would be the battleground. She took several steps across the meadow between the house and the stable but stopped short when she saw the gardener and the stable boy come out.

Not in the stable then.

Olive closed her eyes, wondering if it was possible to feel another person's presence. She went utterly still while she conjured up Joseph's face in her mind, mentally reaching for him.

No, apparently that was not possible.

However, she did think of a place he might be.

If he'd needed a few moments of solitude, it made sense that he would walk through the woods and then stroll beside the stream.

At least, it is what she would do. Since she had no better idea of where to find him, she dashed the rest of the way across the meadow, then hurried around to the back of the stable, where the woods grew thicker.

It was tough going wearing yards of satin and lace. Oddly, tough going did not prevent a funny image from blossoming in her mind.

This was a time of urgency, not funny images. But still, she saw herself trudging through the woods, thistles snagging in the hem of her fancy gown while she carried a teapot in one hand and a delicate china cup pinched between the fingers of her other hand.

But then, perhaps it was not all that funny. Perhaps the vision symbolized her struggle with being one person and acting the part of another.

What was wrong with her? This was no time for deep introspection. Joseph might be in danger.

Might be. She did not know for certain that he was, only that neither he nor Hortencia was where she expected them to be.

Her hasty dash through the trees was making too much noise. She stopped, listening to the sounds of the woods, just as she did when she was hunting a stray goat.

Close by, she heard a man's voice over the rush of water. It was cursing.

Why would Joseph be cursing?

Peering hard through the trees, she was relieved to see him sitting on a log and very much alone.

Then she saw a flash of ruby-coloured fabric.

Ha! Hortencia should not be wearing red if she expected to successfully hide herself behind a shrub. And the woman considered herself to be cunning.

From where Joseph sat, he could not see his foe. She clearly saw him, though. The wicked woman stared at him with a calculating smile while unbuttoning the bodice of her gown.

'My dear!' Olive called.

She dashed through the high grass, launched herself at Joseph, and toppled both of them off the log.

They hit the ground hard, but she managed to whisper, 'Roll on top of me, Joseph.'

He rolled, giving her a puzzled look…well, not only puzzled, but rather pleased as well.

She curled her fingers in his hair, drawing his face down to her mouth, but turned her lips at the last second to say rather loudly in his ear, 'Ravage me, husband, here by the stream.'

Taking a cue from Hortencia, she slipped three buttons open on the neck of her gown.

'She's here?' His lips brushed her ear.

A swirly little shiver tickled her middle. Her body reacted as if it did not know this was all for show. Her heart did not recognize it either, because it pumped hard against her ribs.

'Peering at us over the log,' she whispered softly. His nod was as imperceptible as her whisper had been. She only knew he had done it because beard stubble scraped her earlobe.

He dipped his mouth to her neck, kissing it tenderly from the hollow of her throat to her jaw.

Glory fire…

'I am a lucky man, my love,' he said, his voice thick and husky. 'No man could ask for a better wife… A more beautiful or passionate lady does not exist.'

Hortencia would hate hearing that!

Completely immersed in her part, Olive did not mind hearing those words, feeling them whisper over her earlobe like curling steam. Nor did she shy from the warmth they gave her in places she supposed might lead an otherwise respectable woman astray.

In the novels, it was called delirious longing. Perhaps the books had the right of it, because here and now, the sensation nearly made her forget Hortencia was even watching… that this was all to convince the woman what a doomed effort it was, trying to seduce Joseph away from his bride.

To press the point, Olive lifted her leg and rubbed the toe of her shoe along Joseph's calf.

Had she read of this seductive movement in a book, or had it sprung from her heart? If it did come from her heart, then this moment was inappropriate. It would mean the line between acting a role and living it was becoming blurred.

She felt cool air when Joseph caught the hem of her skirt and began to lift it.

'Forgive me,' he whispered in her ear.

None of this is real, none of it, she chanted in her mind. *Only an act performed to discourage a villain.*

Olive heard her foe gasp in clear indignation. 'I have never seen anything so disgraceful!'

Joseph rolled off her, the two of them staring up at Hortencia's flushed face.

'Rolling in the grass like a pair of—'

'Newlyweds,' Joseph said, cutting off the rest of the insult she would have flung at them.

He sat up, reaching out his hand to help Olive upright. She could not be certain of the reason for it, but a shudder clamped his fingers tighter on hers.

Anger, she supposed…and shock that he had nearly been caught by Hortencia.

'Further,' he said while standing and drawing her up beside him, 'eavesdroppers have no right to be offended by anything they see or hear.'

'I did try to warn you about what goes on between a man and a woman, dear Hortencia…when they are deeply in love.'

Recalling the moment, that was not quite how Olive had presented the matter. It was more of the risk a woman took when she gave in to forbidden moments.

Until a few moments ago, her only experience had been what had happened to Eliza…and what she'd read in books. Now, though, she rather understood that under certain conditions, a woman's body could speak louder than logic.

If she was especially fond of the man…not in love perhaps, but maybe…oh, never mind. Runaway emotions made everything tricky, that was all.

Even if she did allow herself to fall in love with Joseph, the future viscount could never love her back.

Quick as a minnow, her motto flitted through her mind. This was a fine tangled web, indeed. She had not expected to become entangled in it quite this way.

The day after tomorrow, their charade would be over, she would go home, and hopefully her sister would have eloped to Gretna Green.

'I was merely walking and I came upon you quite by surprise, Joseph,' Hortencia said. 'I do beg your pardon for interrupting.'

At least the sneaky creature had buttoned up her gown.

Olive left her collar sagging open. The point must be

illustrated that between a married couple, certain behaviour was acceptable.

The same behaviour was forbidden to those who were not wed.

What she told the woman without using words was that she and Joseph were a couple in love.

Hortencia was the outsider.

There was nothing more to her gaping collar than a simple message to a nosy busybody.

Olive touched her throat, wondering if her skin looked flushed. It felt hot enough to have blistered. She also wondered if her pretend husband was flustered.

Not likely, him being a viscount who would be tempted by fine ladies as regularly as the seasons turned.

His temptations were none of her concern. Shame on her for wondering.

'Well,' Hortencia declared with a sudden fake smile, 'we are all late for tea.'

'You go ahead,' Joseph said. 'Please let my parents know we will see them at dinner.'

'As you wish, Joseph. I dare say we will miss you.'

If Hortencia had been shocked by what she saw going on between the bride and groom, she seemed suddenly recovered.

As soon as she was out of sight, Joseph fastened Olive's bodice buttons, slowly…one by one. His knuckles skimmed her neck. She wondered what was behind his thoughtful look. If he meant to cool off anything that had just happened in the grass behind the log, he was failing.

The show was over, but her heart had a difficult go of regaining a steady pace.

'Sit with me, Olive.' He drew her to the log. 'There is something we must discuss.'

She sat down beside him, perhaps closer than she ought to have. If he minded, he would move further away.

This conversation was going to be embarrassing since he could only wish to discuss her behaviour. How she might have rescued him from Hortencia in a less scandalous way.

Joseph kept a firm grip on Olive's hand. Once he told her of the guests who were soon to invade Falcon's Steep, she was bound to leap from this log and go home…leave him to his fate. He was not ready for that.

Not that holding on to her made a difference one way or another. He'd never had any intention of keeping his cottage lass forever.

Not that she was his, either. He did not know why he even thought that.

What he did know was that, in this moment, he liked the way her hand felt in his…small yet strong.

These were capable hands, he knew, as comfortable milking a goat as they were wielding a highwayman's sword. He also now knew how her fingers felt twining through a man's hair. Siren's fingers they were, which could draw an unwitting fellow in for a kiss.

Not that he would consider himself all that unwitting, only drawn in.

In the end it did not matter, not now that everything was changing.

'I beg your pardon, Joseph.' When she glanced up, her eyes shimmered, bright and green. 'I acted shamelessly and with Hortencia looking on, too. I am mortified.'

'You were brilliant. No need to feel mortified. It was lucky you happened along just then, or she would have caught me.'

'It was a near thing, wasn't it? I did not just happen along, though. I was looking for you. When you and Hortencia were both missing for tea, I became worried.' She wriggled her fingers out of his. 'I suppose we should join them now.'

'Not yet.' Curse his tongue for turning to a clumsy lump. His brain searched for words. How was he to inform her that Mama had invited guests?

He had vowed to her this visit would last only a week. To ask her to remain in the lie for who knew how long was not acceptable.

It was not what she'd agreed to. Not what she deserved.

'You look troubled,' she said. A sweet-looking frown cut her brow. 'Is there something else we need to discuss?'

'It is the last thing I wish, and yet, yes, there is.' He glanced over at dapples of sunshine riding the surface of the stream. This problem was not going to slide away on the ripples, so he looked back at her. 'Tonight, after everyone has gone to bed, I will take you home.'

'I know I was very forward with you a moment ago. Truly, Joseph, I promise, I have no intention of entrapping you.' She slid along the log, putting distance between them. 'You are safe with me.'

'I know that. And I must admit, a moment ago…it was not all about Hortencia.' He glanced over his shoulder. The grass was bent where they had lain. 'I think we both recognized what was happening…but it is not why we must cease our charade. Something has come up, and I am certain you will not wish to be a part of it.'

He was silent for a moment, working up the words. It seemed to be a failing of his…being at loss when it came to spitting out something important.

'Since you have not revealed what this "something" is, you cannot be certain I will have no part of it.'

'Mama has invited guests from London to celebrate our marriage.'

Olive stood up. Her eyes went wide. Then she blinked.

'That is indeed a complication,' she muttered.

'One for me to deal with. I do not expect you to remain here, too.'

There, said and done.

It might be best for her to go back to her cottage. The scent of crushed grass came to him, a reminder of just how desirable Olive had been a moment ago.

Awareness of her shape and her scent, of the little sound she'd made when he kissed her neck, all that seared him.

For an instant, there had been no Hortencia staring down at them like some voyeur.

There had been only him and his bride, except that she was not really his bride.

One thing was for certain—what had ignited between them was too intense to be indulged in again.

Despite the fact that Olive had lectured Hortencia on the dangers of unwed intimacy, she could not know all that much about it herself.

Teaching her would be the worst sort of repayment for all she had done for him.

'From what I just saw, Joseph…' She wagged her head at him, brows arched and lips pressed thin. No one else he knew of could wear that expression and still look pretty doing it. 'Taking me home to the cottage would be a great mistake. You will not last an hour without me.'

He would argue the point, but she was correct. He could feel his future turning to misery even while sitting here on a mossy log.

Hortencia would catch him and chain him to London, where all his joy in life would shrivel and die.

Olive stared at him, tapping her lips with her fingers. A thousand thoughts appeared to be going on in her mind.

One thing seemed certain—her thoughts could not be moving in his favour.

'What kind of friend do you think I am, Joseph Billings?' She took three strides toward him, bending at the waist to peer into his eyes. 'Not a loyal one, I'd wager. I am insulted.'

'I meant no insult to you, Olive. But this is not turning out as you imagined it would.'

'Ha! Do vows mean nothing to you? I took them, and so did you. Therefore, I am your ally for the duration of our scheme.'

'And I thank you for it. But it is one thing for you to play my wife in front of my parents and Hortencia. How will you manage with all the rest of them?'

'You will teach me what I need to know.'

Nearly nose to nose with her, it was not possible to look anywhere but into her eyes. The urge to kiss her became overwhelming.

'How many of them?' she asked.

'Six, as far as I know.'

'Formidable.' With that she straightened. 'Still, I will not let that woman have you, Joseph.'

'Why?' It was a foolish question. They had made a bargain which she meant to honour. He wondered if it was more than that, though. She was a friend…a loyal ally. Luckily for him, she was also as clever as a fox.

'Very well,' she said. 'I shall reveal something to you. You will be stunned to know it.' She sat beside him again but did not reach for his hand. 'May I trust you to never reveal a word of what I am going to say?'

'Of course.' What was this? Whatever her secret, he would take it to the grave. 'You may count on me, Olive.'

'Alright then. While it is true that the majority of the reason I am not letting you take me home tonight has to do with Hortencia and her wicked threat to you, there is more to it than that, quite a bit more.' She sighed, clearly hesitant to go on. After a deep sigh, she did. 'I am not confident that my sister has wed her James yet, and I cannot go home until she does.'

'Has she not? I would have thought she'd have got him away to Gretna Green as soon as she could.'

'I had hoped she would, but it is rather more complicated than that. You see, there is something she must tell him, and she is afraid to do it.'

'If they love one another, surely they can overcome it? Eliza must speak up.'

'Easy to say, but the fact of it is, it takes all I have to tell you. And all I am asking of you is your silence.'

'You have it. I promise.'

'Eliza bore a baby out of wedlock. She will have to ask James to raise her as his own. She will not marry him unless he agrees to adopt our sweet Laura, too. It is tearing my sister up, wanting her child so badly and not being able to have her.'

'Poor girl. She has every reason to be afraid.'

'You understand, then? If James rejects Eliza...if he speaks of it to anyone, my sister will be ruined.'

'Aye, she will. She will need a great deal of courage to carry through with what she must do.'

'Eliza has a great deal of courage.'

'Like you do.'

'Not like I do. My sister bears a great load. I only help her carry it. I admire her more than anyone I know.'

'Olive, after hearing this, I really must take you home tonight.'

There was danger here that she had not considered.

'But we are not yet finished,' she said. 'You and my sister both need for me to see this scheme to the end.'

'Do you recall when I told you Hortencia is like a bloodhound? How she seeks out other people's secrets and uses them to get what she wants?'

'And you fear she will discover this one? That she will use it to make me give you up so that she can have you?'

'It is precisely what she will do. I might as well surrender to her now.'

'You will not. Nor will I.'

Olive straightened, squared her shoulders. She gave him a smile so confident, so assured, that he felt her courage seep into him.

Perhaps they might pull this off in the end.

'Come, Joseph.' She reached for him. Her hand looked delicate but was as sturdy as the woman's spirit was. 'We are at war, and our next battle is tea.'

'On to victory, then,' he said resolutely, answering the charge.

He wondered if he might be falling a little bit in love with Olive Augustmore...

Chapter Nine

Guests! To celebrate her marriage? What a nightmare.

As he had done for the past three nights, Joseph knocked on her chamber door.

She could not possibly learn all she needed to in a week, but hopefully enough to make the visitors believe she was the lady of the manor.

He entered her chamber looking casual and too appealing with his collar unbuttoned and his shirtsleeves rolled up…and no shoes.

This was how he dressed each time he came. It was why she'd decided that if he could discard his shoes, so could she.

It was quite a freeing sensation.

'Good evening again, Joseph.' She closed the door behind him, thinking she smelled the flowers in the hallway.

'It is indeed good. I like coming here instead of sitting alone in my chamber.'

'Doesn't it seem a little scandalous, though?'

'Scandal is an odd bird. It only exists when someone else judges a situation to be so. Since no one would object to a man visiting his wife's bedroom, there can be no scandal.'

'What odd logic.' But it made sense if one looked at it

in the light if they wished to see it. 'I wonder what you will teach me tonight.'

Something to do with the bag tucked under his arm, she supposed.

He answered with a grimace, tossing the bag onto the bed.

'We covered dancing last night. Lord Helms and Lord Barlow will be taken with you if they have a mind to wind up the music box.'

'All well and good, but I think it is the ladies I must fool more than the gentlemen, and they will not be taken with me.'

'I do not think you need it, but would you like to practice a few dance steps before we begin our next lesson?'

He was correct. She did not need it, but still she lifted the sides of her gown and twirled toward him.

Catching her hand, he positioned them for a waltz. His palm open wide on her back felt warm, possessive.

She had never felt a touch like it. As lessons went, it was quite informative.

Not scandalous, of course, since there was no one present to judge it to be so.

Clearly music was not needed for dancing. Barefoot steps padding on wood, a man's and a woman's mingled breathing, was all the tune required while he glided her here and there…slowing ever so slightly when they passed the bed.

All at once he stopped, cocked his head.

'Is something wrong?' She missed the pressure of his hand when it fell away from her back.

'Probably not. I thought I heard footsteps pause outside your door.'

'Hortencia. I smelled perfume in the hallway when you came in just now.'

'Ah, good then, let her believe us to be so smitten we cannot keep our hands from one another.'

Yes, let her imagine that.

Joseph went to the hearth and squatted to stir the coals.

'What is in the bag? What new ladylike skill will I learn?'

Rising, he went to the bed and sat on it, then indicated she should join him.

Was it really true that scandal only existed if it was found out? It was what she believed about her sister's situation.

'It's a lesson easier taught if we are sitting next to each other.'

Very well. She sat down with the bag as a buffer between them. How odd it was that a moment ago, Joseph had his hands on her, and it did not feel wrong.

It was only…they were not dancing on the bed.

Heaven help her. For a distraction she opened the bag.

Peeking at what was inside, she laughed. 'Joseph? What on earth?'

He took the bag from her and dumped the contents onto the mattress between them. Four colours of embroidery thread lay on top of a rectangular piece of muslin. Three needles pinned into the fabric glinted in golden lamplight.

'Ladies spend a great deal of time sewing fancy stitches. I can't say whether they enjoy it or not, but it is what they do while they visit and talk.' He picked up a skein of green thread. 'But perhaps you already know how?'

'I know how to mend. And stitch sheets…plain work. I am good with knitting.' She should not be laughing at his frown, even if her mirth was on the inside, as much as she could keep it there. 'Do you intend to teach me to embroider?'

'You think I cannot?'

Oh, that grin was going to destroy her one day. Everything about it made her barmy inside, from the glint in his eyes to the turn of his lips.

'I do have my doubts.'

He held a needle up to the light, pushed the end of the thread toward it and missed the tiny hole.

'Aye, so do I. But I did watch this afternoon when Mama and Hortencia were busy at it.'

'Here, I will thread the needle,' she said. 'Mending and fancy needlework cannot be so different.'

'Does your sister know how? Perhaps she will help us.'

'Our mother knew how, but she never had time to do it or to teach us.'

'Here, then.' He took the threaded needle from her. 'I paid close attention when my mother was sewing a leaf.'

'She must have thought it odd, you watching her sew so intently?'

Joseph pushed the threaded needle into the fabric, down, then back up.

'I doubt she noticed. She and Hortencia were discussing our guests. One of them especially— Curse it!' Joseph tugged at a knot in the thread which would not pull through the fabric. 'Forgive my language, Olive. This is trickier than Mama made it appear.'

'Let me try.' She took the cloth from him. 'There are supposed to be hoops to hold it flat.'

'Hoops are tricky things to make off with.'

'We will manage as best we can.' It was a stubborn knot.

She had to bite it with her teeth in order to get the thread loose. 'You hold the muslin tight while I try a leaf.'

Her attempt failed, her foliage looking more like a thistle.

'Perhaps I will plead a sick headache,' she mumbled.

'Shall we practice that instead? I believe it is a social skill. That and fainting.'

'I refuse to feign a faint. If you see me go down, it will be genuine.'

The closest she had come to fainting was when Eliza had confided that she was with child. If she'd survived that without a swoon, she supposed nothing would fell her.

'Tell me about the guests. Why was one of them being gossiped about?'

'Ah, Vivienne Curtis. She has the misfortune of wishing to become a photographer and not a marchioness.'

He took the needle and thread from her fingers, apparently wishing to make another go at a leaf. Joseph Billings was unique among men. She could not a recall ever seeing a fellow attempt fancy-work…plain work either, for all that.

'Surely she can be both?'

'Her father is a noble, so no, she cannot.'

'I pity your class, Joseph. It seems that no one has a choice at all when it comes to their future. It is a shame, really, that you must one day wed for position, and that the unfortunate Miss Vivienne cannot have her camera as well as a husband.'

'Rebels have little hope of finding fulfilment in society. Worse if the rebel is a woman.'

'I always considered Eliza's plight to be desperate, but at least she has a chance at love.'

'Have you spoken to her? Has she revealed her secret to James?'

'Not unless she has done so since this afternoon, when I met her to pick up cheese.'

'It is rather urgent, I think. What if our ruse fails? She must be safely wed by then.'

'It is what I've told her time and again.' Olive well knew this was one of those easier-said-than-done situations. 'The odds against us being successful in our deception are not good, not now that we must keep at it longer. And I do not know how long Eliza will be able to trick our father into believing I am away on a honeymoon trip. Especially with the increased traffic on the path. He will be curious. It would ruin everything if he came here.'

'I wonder what he thinks of our marriage?' He shot her an owl-like wink and a teasing and oh-so-compelling grin. She would miss seeing it each day once this was over.

'I am sure he is more thrilled than he is confused. But don't you think the bigger question is, what will he think once we end it?'

'The one good thing about having guests is that it gives us more time to discover a way to become unwed,' he said.

'Us? As I recall, you told me you would think of a way.'

'A reckless promise, that. Now that we are mentioning it, I might need your help.'

'I have no idea whatsoever. We could be falsely wed forever, trying to come up with a way out of this mess.'

His laugh rumbled deep, giving her a curious tingle. 'It's not all a mess, Olive. But can't you see us? A pair old dodderers sewing leaves on handkerchiefs?'

'We will be rather good at it by then, I imagine. My question is, will I be a false viscountess, or will you be a false goat farmer? It seems some sort of choice will need to be made.'

Although they made jest of the situation, the problem was a real one.

Joseph bent his head to the task of demonstrating how to embroider a leaf. He poked his finger with the needle, then pressed his thumb to the wound.

'Wicked little weapon,' he muttered.

'It takes practice, I think.' She took the weapon and the wrinkled muslin from him. 'Does your mother knit? Some ladies do, our Queen among them.'

'I cannot recall. Until now, I never paid attention to what sort of stitchery she was creating. Is there such a thing as fancy knitting? It might do.'

'Most knitting is practical, but years ago, my mother taught Eliza and me to knit flowers to decorate our bonnets. They were as elegant as anything you ever saw.' It had been great fun for a while. 'But it has been years since either of us had time for it. Pretty stitches are very nice in their way, but they do not earn much money.'

'Knitting flowers will have to do, because I do not think we will learn this…' He took her needle, punched it into the muslin, then scowled at it. 'It would take a wizard and a magician working together to make a leaf out of thread.'

'I will ask Eliza to bring my needles and yarn when we meet tomorrow morning.'

'Be careful. It would not do for Hortencia to see the two of you together. We know she is watching.'

'We have the advantage, Joseph. She is not aware that we know it.'

'I nearly pity the woman, having to outwit you.'

'Not me, us.'

She took the moment to appreciate the turn of his mouth when he grinned, the laughter shining in his eyes made all the more intriguing because of where they were sitting.

The truth was that they would not be falsely wed forever, would not spend their doddering years stitching in their armchairs side by side while sharing stories about the exploits of their children and grandchildren.

Nor would she do it with anyone else if her sister did not admit her secret to James.

Once Father learned that Olive had not wed a viscount, he would push her at the baker again.

Not that he would succeed. No one could force her to marry Eliza's one true love.

'You are troubled.' Joseph reached for her hand. 'Tell me why.'

'It is what you just said about Hortencia watching Eliza. My sister needs to tell James the truth before it comes out on its own. I wish I could take her to James and stand beside her until she tells him the truth.'

'Shall we kidnap them and spirit them away to Gretna Green?'

'If only.' But the mental image of it did cheer her up.

'What will you teach me next about being a lady, Joseph?' she asked in an attempt to divert their minds away from the worry.

'I haven't decided,' he said softly, then touched her hair, drew a lock back over her ear. 'You are rather perfect as you are.'

The urge to lean across the heap of muslin between them and kiss him was too strong.

Nothing would come of it but heartache. More and more

often, she had to remind herself of who she was…and who he was.

They got on so well together that sometimes she forgot.

'Well, then, perhaps I will teach you something,' she declared, eager to redirect her thoughts to the display. 'How to make goat's cheese. That way, when our lie is revealed and you are disowned, you will have a skill to make a living at.'

'If you want to know the truth, given a choice between attending a season of balls in London and making cheese in Fallen Leaf, I would always choose cheese.'

She smiled at his playful jest, but not from the inside.

Joseph would never be free to make cheese any more than she would be free to dance at a ball.

He still had not let go of her hair, but twirled it around his thumb.

'You have pretty hair. I like it better when it is loose like this.'

She pulled the strand from his fingers, but slowly and with regret.

'I like it better this way, too,' she admitted.

She must not wish for something which was impossible. Once she did, she feared that she would never be able to un-wish it.

What kind of life would she have, longing for things which could never be? For a man who could never be hers?

A bitter life, that's what. In the past she had given little thought to love and its role in her future.

Now there was Joseph…and she did.

Two days later, Olive joined Lady Claymore and Hortencia in the solarium for an hour of stitchery.

Taking her place on a bench across from two ladies experienced in fancy needlework, she knitted her flower. It had taken three hours of practice in her chamber to remember how to make the complex stitches Mama had taught her.

She smiled looking down at it now. It was as pretty in its way as what Hortencia was stitching.

Not that she was not nervous. Although the Queen favoured knitting, it was slower to catch on in society.

Inhaling, she drew on her fictional self, who would be confident in everything she put her hand to.

When she exhaled, she was Lady Olive, her smile smooth and welcoming, as if these women were guests in her home and it was her place to make them feel at ease.

'Isn't this the best time of day?' she asked with the intention of beginning a pleasant conversation.

She removed a skein of yellow yarn from the satin bag, intending to show off her skill by changing colours. Last week the knitting bag had been made of an old shirt of Father's. Eliza had sacrificed a portion of her favourite petticoat and sewn her a new one.

'A lovely time of day, Olive, my dear. It is my favourite,' Lady Claymore commented.

The endearment made her feel wonderful. She also wondered if Joseph's mother meant it, or was she simply trying to mean it?

To find her son married to a woman she had never met, never even heard of, would be utterly shocking.

'It is getting cloudy.' Hortencia's sigh was heavy, dripping with drama. 'Solariums are meant for sunshine, and look how dreary it is becoming.'

Lady Claymore cast Hortencia a barely perceptible

frown. From what Olive was learning, ladies of rank did not frown, but smiled congenially in all situations.

'Olive, what a pretty flower. I envy your skill at knitting.' It gave Olive a glow inside, hearing Lady Claymore's praise even if it was only to be kind to her supposed daughter-in-law. 'I have never been able to hold the needles in the proper way to be skilled at knitting.'

'We are the same, Lady Amelia,' Hortencia put in. 'Knitting needles are far too cumbersome for my smaller fingers. I do not mind, though, since embroidery needles produce finer work. So much more delicate, don't you think?'

'I do not. In fact, I grow weary of doing the same thing over and over again. I have lost count of all the flowers I have embroidered over the years.' Lady Claymore secured her needle in the fabric and set it aside on the small round table beside her chair. 'Perhaps I should have another go at knitting. Would you be so kind as to teach me, my dear?' she asked Olive.

'I would be honoured, Lady Claymore.'

Amelia Billings rose from her spot, then joined Olive on the bench. 'Pah, I am not Lady Claymore to you, my dear. Please call me Mama. I know we have only recently met, but I would like it if you did.'

Resentment pulsed off Hortencia so hot it was a wonder it did not melt her delicate silver needle.

No surprise that she was provoked. To all appearances, Olive was taking the position Hortencia had fully expected to have.

Rather alarmingly, Hortencia had the skill to paste a smile over her anger. If Joseph had not warned Olive who this woman was at heart, she too might have been deceived by winsome blue eyes. By a smile sticky enough to trap the unwary.

'How wonderful,' Hortencia declared sweetly. 'We despaired of our Joseph ever making a marriage commitment. He must love you very much, Olive.'

'Some things cannot be hidden… I suppose it shows. But I love him just as much.'

'May I be honest, my dear?' Lady Claymore asked. 'I was taken aback when I first saw you standing on the steps with my son.'

'It is completely understandable, Mama.' Olive felt wicked and wonderful at the same time, calling her that.

'It is a marvel we did not faint, isn't it, Lady Amelia?'

Olive held her smile even though it was past annoying that Hortencia inserted herself into every turn of a conversation.

'Speak for yourself, Hortencia. I was quite steady.' Lady Claymore returned her attention to Olive. 'It is only that, had my son informed us beforehand, we would have been prepared for—'

'That was not well done of him, was it?' Hortencia disguised the insult with her sticky smile.

Olive wondered if Lady Claymore saw the woman for who she was. Perhaps not, or she wouldn't have been so set on a marriage between her and Joseph, no matter the social coup Hortencia's fine lineage would bring to the family.

'We all make mistakes, Hortencia, dear. Seeing how Joseph looks at you, Olive, it is quite forgivable. Not every couple is blessed with sudden love for one another.'

Hortencia set her sewing aside rather harder than she might have wished to. The action did cause the viscountess to raise her brows.

'I would adore learning to knit, if you will teach me as well,' Hortencia said.

'I would be delighted,' Olive said, but really, it was a pity that she could not answer with an honest no.

Hortencia squeezed in on the bench even though there was not proper room. Skirts and petticoats popped up at odd angles.

'Teaching others to knit must be something you enjoy, Olive.' Steely blue glinted in Hortencia's wide, blinking eyes. Seeing innocence and craftiness all in one glance was a bit unnerving.

The woman was laying some sort of trap for her, but Olive could not imagine how knitting could be a snare. Well, it could be if one was attacked by a large needle, but Hortencia was more subtle than that.

'It is not something I do all that often. But since you are my friend, I am delighted to instruct you,' she lied, because there was no way not to.

'I cannot tell you how thrilled I am to learn from you.'

She could not, because she was not. Still, Olive managed a smile while placing the needles in Hortencia's 'small' fingers in the proper position.

'I am confused about something, Olive. You say you do not teach knitting often? And do you only teach friends?'

'Yes,' Olive answered warily.

'Oh...but didn't I see you with that cottager who sells cheese? You had your knitting bag with you.' Hortencia snapped the needle tips together with a click. 'The two of you did seem particularly friendly. If I did not know better, I would have thought you to have been acquainted with her for a long time. But of course, it could not be, since you only just arrived at Falcon's Steep.'

The trap was sprung, and Olive was neatly snared.

'Hortencia, it sounds as if you are shooting some sort of jab at Olive. Although I cannot imagine for what purpose,' Lady Claymore said disapprovingly.

'There is no jab, I assure you. I only noticed the two of them while I was walking and thought they seemed friendly. But of course, I must have been mistaken, since our Olive would not have such a friend as that.'

'You were not mistaken.' Olive turned her attention to Lady Claymore because her approval was the object of this skirmish. 'I was teaching someone from the cottages to knit. The poor woman had suffered an injury. She is the one we purchase our cheese from, so I do see her upon occasion. I meet her in the meadow because she cannot walk the full distance to the manor to deliver her product, which is excellent, I have to say. Lately the poor woman's pain has grown worse. I was showing her how to make pretty knitted things to sell on market day. It seems easier than selling cheese.'

'It is commendable that you are able to have a friendly association with someone not of our own rank. I do not know if I could,' Hortencia declared.

'If you wish to make a first-class match, Hortencia, my dear, you must learn to do so.' Joseph's mother smiled when she spoke. Was it training which made that possible? Olive doubted she would ever learn that skill. 'A lady of breeding must know how to act congenially towards people of all classes.'

'Of course. I shall strive to be more like our Olive. I fear, though, that I will never learn the knack of making merry with my inferiors.'

'Making merry and being courteous are not quite the

same thing.' Lady Claymore's voice was crisper than Olive was accustomed to hearing.

Perhaps now that she had no hope of Hortencia wedding her son, she was beginning to look at her with more clarity.

Which was exactly what Joseph had hoped would happen.

'Olive, my dear,' Lady Claymore said, laying her hand companionably on Olive's arm. 'Shall we continue with the lesson? I cannot say how anxious I am to learn a new way to use needles.'

There was something in the older woman's gaze which looked different than it had mere days ago. In the beginning she had looked at Olive with reservation…suspicion, even. All for good reason.

Now the look appeared softened, as if she were welcoming Olive to the family. Perhaps even felt a bit of affection for her.

This was a complication Olive had not considered in the beginning but ought to have. At first, everything she had done was justified…necessary to protect Joseph and Eliza.

Nothing was too dear a price to pay for their well-being.

Only now did Olive fully understand that other people would pay the price as well.

She would leave wounded hearts behind when this charade came to its certain end.

Who among the ladies sitting here was the wicked one, she had to ask?

Before she entered the solarium, she would have known it to be Hortencia. But now she wondered.

If Hortencia was deceitful, what was Olive?

Birds of a feather, were they? Kindred spirits, perhaps?

There was one difference between them. Olive felt remorse for what she was doing. Hortencia probably did not.

Quite suddenly, Olive wanted to run from the solarium and weep.

To do a wrong and feel no remorse for it was far less wicked than feeling remorse and doing it anyway.

No wonder lying was a sin. It injured both the victim and the sinner.

'If you will excuse me,' she said, standing. 'Quite out of the blue, I need a breath of air.'

'Perhaps you are falling ill.' Hortencia gave Olive a considering look, one that said she suspected Olive did not need air, nor was she becoming ill.

'Do take care, my dear. We hope to see you at dinner.'

In that moment, Joseph entered the solarium, his smile so handsome it gave her an ache all the way to her soul.

She would fight Hortencia for this man with all she had…and in the end, she would lose him anyway.

However much guilt she felt for deceiving Lord and Lady Claymore, she would carry on.

Ending the ruse would only give Hortencia the victory.

Eliza would suffer. Joseph would suffer.

She would do this so that one day he could marry a woman who loved him.

Not Olive, because even if she did love him, it could not be her.

If she loved him?

Well, glory fire, she could not honestly say she did not feel anything akin to it for him.

Lady Amelia crossed the room and stood beside them.

'Are you well, my dear?' She pressed the backs of her fingers to Olive's cheek.

Tears cramped her throat. Having not had a mother's touch since her own beloved mama had died, she suddenly felt the loss and the longing quite intensely.

If she and Joseph were wed, she would have a mother again.

'Are you ill?' Joseph touched her cheek, frowning.

'I am not ill, I promise I am not. All I said was that I needed some fresh air.'

'We all need a walk in the garden,' Hortencia announced, reaching for Joseph's arm to claim him for the stroll.

'I believe my son came here seeking his wife. We shall give them some time. I will walk with you, Hortencia.'

Skirts brushing, Joseph's mother and Hortencia went out of the solarium doors, which opened to the back garden.

Joseph led Olive through the house, then out to the front gardens.

'You look as if you are about to weep.' His arm snugged tighter about her waist. Tears pressed harder against her eyes.

'I am not far from it.'

'Did Hortencia say something to you before I came in?'

'It was not Hortencia. It was your mother.'

'Mama? Was she pressing Hortencia on you? I hoped she would stop. Shall I have a word with her?'

Olive blinked, and even though she fought it, tears dampened her lashes.

'That is just it, Joseph. You have not chosen me. I am not the woman you love. This is all a great trick we are playing on the people who love you.'

And on her own father, too. He would be vastly disappointed to discover he was no longer the father-in-law of the wealthy neighbour.

Joseph had been looking intently into her eyes but then suddenly his gazed shifted to the rosebush to their right. The afternoon was dim with increasing cloudiness, which made the flowers look brighter against the foliage.

He picked a lavender-hued rosebud, twirled it in his fingertips.

'Maybe I…' His brows lowered in a frown. He tucked the rose into her hair behind her ear. 'Never mind…but in the end we will all survive it.'

'Yes, in the end we shall go back to being the neighbours we were always meant to be.'

Except they would not. For her part, she would always remember what it felt like, the fantasy of playing his wife. Every time she saw him pass by on the road, or spotted him in the village, she would wonder what could have been if he was not a viscount…if she was not a goatherd.

The thought had occupied too much of her mind lately.

She was far too taken with his smile, with his voice when he spoke softly to her…and how combined, they enamored her.

'The last thing I wish is for you to be sad, my dear.' He carefully swiped his thumb under each of her eyes, taking his time.

Had he noticed that he called her 'my dear' even when no one else was nearby to hear it?

Of course, it would be a slip born out of habit, nothing more.

'I am not sad, not really. It is only, your mother was so kind to worry about me. Her concern made me miss my own mother.' Sweet fragrance from the rose filled her senses, bolstered her. 'I hate deceiving her like this.'

His great, broad thumb touched her chin, lifted it while he looked deeply into her eyes.

What did he see?

That she wished for him to draw her in close to his heart?

Loving him was not a part of their agreement.

'This will all come out right,' he murmured, his fingers gentle while tracing the curve of her cheek.

Perhaps she was winning the battle against Hortencia, but she feared she was losing her heart in the process.

Chapter Ten

A scatter of lightning caught Joseph's attention as he strode past a window facing the front garden. He stopped to gaze out.

It had been two days since he'd walked in the garden with Olive, placed a rose in her hair and came so close to kissing her.

The moment left him unsettled, as if he stood on top of the black, roiling storm clouds, trying to keep his balance.

Thunder vibrated the glass, as much a warning as any he had ever received.

Kissing his pretend wife, except for the occasional peck on the cheek or the forehead, was not a scene in their show.

If he did kiss Olive, it would be because he wanted her in the way a man wanted a woman.

Damn it…a man who wanted a woman he could not have. Even if there was a way, he would not take it. To make Olive a lady of society would change her. He would never shackle her with those chains. Would that he could shed them himself.

A moment ago, he had left Olive in the kitchen, discussing the menu for tonight. It was an important meal since the guests arriving from London later today would be dining with them.

Mama had meant to instruct Cook, but Olive had stepped in first to perform her duty.

She was a wonder, his make-believe wife. He was amazed how anyone could look so natural playing a role she had no experience in.

When he'd left the kitchen, Cook was smiling and nodding her head. From all he had seen, she was not an easy woman to please.

Olive pleased everyone. Especially him.

No matter how he resisted wishing all this was not a farce but true life, he was failing.

Perhaps because his feelings for Olive were not what they had been in the beginning. He cared for her…deeply. More than friendship would account for.

He would never look at the lavender rosebush and not see the flower in her hair, not breathe in the enticing scent urging him to act on what he yearned for.

Turning away from the window, he continued down the hallway, lost in thoughts of lively green eyes and lips that were pretty no matter their expression.

The library door was open. He heard a fire crackling, his mother's voice in quiet conversation.

Perhaps Father was with her. A visit with his parents would be just the thing on this dreary day.

'There is something not right about them.'

Joseph came up short. Even if his father was in the library, so was Hortencia.

But what did she mean, something was not right? He stood very still, listening.

'It is just your imagination, my dear,' his mother said. 'Unless you have proof of wrongdoing, I think it is best to keep such nonsense to yourself. There is really no reason whatsoever for Joseph to pretend to be wed to someone he is not.'

'Perhaps he does not wish for you to know he has a mistress, Lady Amelia. If she acts the part of his wife, she can consort with him right under our noses.'

Of all things, his mother laughed.

Suddenly his clothes felt too tight, too hot. Hortencia had a scorpion's tongue…pure poison.

'You, of all people, know my son has never kept a mistress. You have had a close enough watch on him over the years to realize he would not. Do you want to know what I think?'

'Of course I do. We have known each other too long for anything but the truth between us.'

'Yes, well, you will not like it, Hortencia. What I believe is that you are seeing things which are not true because of your disappointment that our plans for you and my son have not worked out.'

'Surely you are also disappointed.'

'At first I was. But what mother can see her child so happily in love and not be glad for him?'

Was he in love? If so, he was not happy. Loving a lady who could not be his would only bring him misery.

In that moment, he did feel rather miserable, so what did that mean? He was in love?

'But you always said that having love in a marriage was not the most important thing. You believed that young love is gone too quickly to grasp. Did you not tell me that the family name is what matters, what lasts?'

'I did say that…but now, seeing my boy so happy, I begin to remember how it was early in my marriage. I wonder if I advised you wrongly.'

'You did not. I, for one, am not so quick to give up on our plans. I tell you, something about this feels off to me.'

'You must give up, Hortencia. We have no more plans. My son has made his choice.'

Joseph had had enough. He spun about.

'We shall see…' he heard Hortencia say.

Oh, aye, they would.

Olive felt snared in her elegant gown, trapped by the rain which forced everyone to remain indoors.

Not that she could go outdoors even if the afternoon was sunny.

The London visitors had arrived, and she was, right then, pouring tea. Hopefully, she remembered all the details of Joseph's instructions. This was a ceremony as much as just getting tea into cups.

What Olive needed to be doing was going to her sister, warning her that Hortencia might come snooping about. It was true what Joseph said about her. She was a bloodhound.

However, she was quite stuck here entertaining guests. Guests who already knew Hortencia from London. Friends who had socialized with her from forever ago and would probably believe every rumour she presented.

Joseph stood across the parlor, near the fireplace, speaking with two gentlemen he had known from university.

Peter was tall, Charles was short, but both of them displayed manners so polished they gleamed.

Joseph must have felt her attention on them, because he looked away from his friends and gave her an adoring smile, one so sweet everyone was sure to believe it sincere.

Nearly everyone. There was always Hortencia to threaten the show.

The taller of the gentlemen noticed the shift in Joseph's attention and nodded to her.

The reason for his friends' presence, Joseph had explained, was not only to celebrate with them. It was to balance the numbers. Two single ladies required the presence of two single gentlemen. His mother had insisted upon it.

Society was an odd bird, Olive thought, and not for the first time.

However, that being the case, the balance was off.

What gentleman was there for Hortencia?

The married one? Oh, but no... Joseph was not married. And yet her first reaction had been that he was.

It was not right for Olive to be possessive. Only Hortencia made her feel that way. When the right woman came along, the one who loved Joseph for the good man he was, Olive was sure she would not feel like that.

Not in the least.

For an instant, she forgot what she was doing. Hot tea from the china spout dripped on her fingers.

'Oh, let me help!' Viscount Helmond's daughter, the one who wished to take photos rather than wed, leapt up and dabbed Olive's hand with her napkin.

Olive blinked, came to herself and what she was doing.

'I know I shall never learn the knack for serving tea,' Vivienne Curtis declared.

'Olive has the knack,' replied Grace Curtis, the viscount's younger daughter. 'It was only when Joseph looked at her that she forgot herself. How perfectly wonderful it must be to be wed.'

'Nothing quite like romance to put one off-kilter,' Joseph's father announced. 'Isn't that right?'

The comment seemed to be made to everyone, but it was Lady Claymore who blushed.

Although she smiled, Hortencia's face flared.

The woman was hiding her animosity less with each day that went by.

It was time and past for Eliza to tell James the truth about Laura.

This marriage ruse would soon come to an end. Olive was determined that it would be on Joseph's terms, not Hortencia's.

Tonight, once everyone was retired for the evening, she would go to the cottage and make Eliza know how urgent it was.

'Please let me serve tea, Lady Olive.' Grace Curtis took the teapot from her, handling it with skill. Quite clearly she was presenting her accomplishments, showing what a beneficial wife she would make.

The young men flanking Joseph seemed to get the message, because they smiled at Grace, both of them clearly besotted.

Vivienne took the moment to slip her arm though Olive's and guide her to a couch. They sat down side by side.

'Please do tell me, Olive, what birds and wildlife inhabit the area. I am ever so anxious to capture them in a photograph.'

After a few polite words about nature, Vivienne said, 'I have always admired your husband. He is different from most society dandies. I cannot say how pleased I am that he married you. I feared that it would be that awful Hortencia, or no one.'

'Surely there were many ladies he could have chosen from, although I am glad he did not.'

'I am not certain if Joseph is aware of it, but Hortencia chased away his admirers with threats of ruin. Oh, she was subtle, but she could have done it with a word. No one dared cross her. But now look. Joseph is wed, and she is in danger of being left on the shelf.'

This fascinating conversation was cut short when Joseph crossed the room to stand behind her chair. In a touch that would appear loving, he caressed her shoulders with his thumbs.

How, she had to wonder, could he touch her this way and feel it a mere performance?

Her response to his touch was sincere. When she reached up to cup his hand, to caress his fingers…it was no act.

More and more often, when she touched him or smiled at him with tenderness, it was not a performance meant to fool others. If she denied how natural showing affection for Joseph had become, the only one she would be fooling was herself.

Head bent against the rain, Olive tugged her coat around her neck and hurried along the path toward the cottage.

The hem of her nightgown was getting caked with mud, but she refused to sacrifice an expensive gown to the downpour. It was not as if any of the dresses in the wardrobe truly belonged to her. Once this marriage ruse ended, she would sell them and donate the money to a charity.

She would not miss the gowns, not terribly. But she would miss the man who had purchased them, quite terribly.

That was a thought for another time. Right now, she

must warn Eliza about the urgency of being honest with James.

Rain and mud made it difficult going. Made it cold going, too.

If she had to drag her sister out of bed and take her to James, it was what she was going to do. Olive had every confidence in James to do the loving thing and take both Eliza and Laura to his heart.

Only a thunderbolt in her path would keep Olive from making her sister do what she must.

But what was that noise?

She stood suddenly still, rain dripping off her nose and sleeking down her hair while she listened.

Not thunder but horse hooves clopping in the mud. She knew the sound too well to be mistaken.

Knew the figure of the rider too well to be mistaken about him, either.

It took only a moment for Joseph to catch up.

She looked up at him, shielding her eyes from the rain with her hand.

'What are you doing here, Joseph?'

'Following you.' He bent low to peer down at her. 'What are you doing here?'

'I am going to tell my sister she must reveal the truth to James.'

For no apparent reason, he grinned.

'In that case, I am here to bring you back home.'

Bring her home? Did he think so?

Home was the cottage at the end of the lane. The manor was no more than Olive's stage.

'You go back. I must take my sister to James.'

'Come.' He reached his hand down for her, but instead

of clasping her fingers, he bent lower, caught her around her waist with his arm. He drew her up, then settled her in front of him.

'Put me down. I need to—'

'Trust me.'

'Do I have a choice?' It did not seem so since his arm held her snugly to him.

'No, you do not. I'll not have you becoming ill for no reason. Look at you, soaked to the skin.'

Judging by the arch of his brow and the glint in his eye, it was not all she looked. One would think a coat to be enough protection against that sort of gaze, but it was a short coat and bunched up about her thighs.

Joseph had not bothered with a coat. All of a sudden, the rain was no longer a nuisance but her friend. Water drenched his white shirt, making it nearly transparent.

Even though it was an indulgence she would pay for when the time came, she snuggled her shoulder against his chest, pressing her cheek to the wet shirt.

Heavens, how could a man feel steely and cosy at the same time? She was not going to waste precious moments wondering. She was simply going to appreciate the essence of Joseph Billings.

She was going to miss her pretend husband. Grieve his loss dearly. Although he lived close by, he might as well be an ocean away. Swimming the social distance between them would be impossible.

Joseph was silent on the ride back to Falcon's Steep, but they arrived at the stable in short time. He settled Dane himself rather than waking the stableman. Then he struck a fire in the stove.

'Sit here.' He pointed to small bench in front of the stove. 'I'll get you a blanket.'

He went into a tack room and came back out carrying a blanket of red and green plaid.

He heated it over the stove for a few moments before sitting beside her and placing it around both of their shoulders.

She was warm because of the blanket, but more because of the man next to her, who was as wet as she was.

He picked up the end of the blanket and dried her face with it.

'I was perfectly safe,' she said, fending off the scolding that was sure to come.

'I'm aware. I was behind you most of the time.'

'If you knew I was safe, why didn't you just let me continue on? Eliza's whole future is at risk.'

'Because she is not at the cottage.'

'If she is not there, where is she? And how do you know she is not in her bed?'

'Oh, well, I suppose she is in her bed…but in Gretna Green, with her new husband in it with her.'

Olive leapt to her feet. She stared at Joseph's grin for several seconds before she exclaimed, 'What! But how?'

'It was easy enough to arrange a few things and send them on their way.'

'Arrange a few things?'

'The trickiest part was getting them together in a private place so they could talk. Once that happened, it was simple enough to arrange the travel and the accommodations for them.'

'I cannot believe it!'

'All they needed was a bit of a shove. They were eager enough to go once they made up their minds.'

She sat down, and gave him a quick, wet hug. 'You, Joseph Billings are my hero.'

'Oh, aye?' He gave an impression of preening. 'A grand fellow, am I?'

'The best false husband a woman could want. Joseph, we are halfway there, then. All we need to do is get through a few more days until everyone goes home.'

And make up a believable story about why they were no longer wed. One that would keep Hortencia from coming back and beginning her pursuit of Joseph again.

He frowned. 'There's another reason I got them off to Gretna Green in a hurry.'

'Not for true love to find a way?'

'Because Hortencia suspects we are not wed and has told my parents that.'

'Oh no.' This was worrisome news. Not terribly unexpected, though. 'You may count on me to do my utmost to convince her that we are.'

Even though it would lead to her eventual broken heart, Joseph deserved everything she could give him, especially after saving Eliza and Laura.

Chapter Eleven

Except for the niggling worry of what Hortencia might do, the next few days passed pleasantly.

The thing for Joseph to keep in mind was that there was nothing Hortencia could do. The woman could not prove he and Olive were not married. They presented a convincing show of being in love. His parents believed it, and as far as he could tell, everyone else did, too.

In spite of it all, Joseph found he was enjoying himself. Entertaining friends at Falcon's Steep was not as stressful as he had expected it would be. It was different from in London, where one dashed from ball, to tea, to the theater, and all for the main purpose of being seen. Here in the country, he had time to leisurely enjoy the company of his friends.

But enjoying leisurely company was not all of it—not most of it, even. Joseph's greatest pleasure came from watching Olive playing mistress of the manor.

He had to remind himself that she was, indeed, only acting. She played her part so well that sometimes he forgot.

For Olive's sake, he was glad it was an act. It would be wrong of him to want her to be who she was not. To try and keep her with him, even though it was not what would make her happy, would make him selfish in the worst way.

Just now, he stood in the shade of the porch, watching while Olive walked near the edge of the woods with Vivienne, pointing out trees and birds.

Despite everything he had just considered, Olive looked like she belonged at Falcon's Steep. Or maybe it was simply what he wished to see, and so he did.

Judging by their gestures and smiles, the ladies were looking for the best spot for Vivienne to take her photographs.

He wished for a photograph of Olive as she was right in this moment, gripping the ribbons of her bonnet while her pale blue skirt ruffled in the breeze.

It was sad that all he would keep of her was a photo. Not even one he could hold, but only the one which existed in his mind.

When he was not with her, all he thought about was when he next would be. To say he ached for her company would not be an overstatement.

The only thing preventing him from telling her so was the circumstances of their births.

Star-crossed, were they?

No, that would imply that they were lovers, which they were not. And yet, he would be a fool not to recognize that whatever was between them was changing. What had begun as an alliance had quickly become friendship, and now…

Now he ached for her company.

Ach, well…it was foolish dwelling upon what could not be.

Olive would not be better off for bearing a title.

When he wed for real, it could not be to a commoner, no matter how uncommon she was.

He was supposed to wed a woman of noble birth in order to help secure the family's social status for generations to come. If he spurned that duty, it would harm the family name…the name his parents had spent their lives keeping above reproach.

While he could largely avoid London by living here, he could not avoid his duty to the title. One day he would be forced to fill his father's shoes.

'A damned curse is what it is,' he mumbled, not that he resented his life or his family…only the demands society placed on a first-born son.

He was startled by the rustle of skirts approaching from behind.

'My dear, unfortunate friend…a curse?' Hortencia gave a great sigh, then stood beside him. 'Have you come to regret your hasty marriage so soon?'

'I only regret that I am forced to share my wife's company with other people.'

'Surely you do not mean me.' Most men would be delighted to be the recipient of her engaging smile. He was not among them. 'I have been your dear friend for a long time. I do recognize when you are troubled. You may confide in me, you know.'

Oh, aye, he was troubled. It was because she was standing so close to him.

'Hortencia, there is something you need to understand. I am well aware that my mother held hopes that we would wed. She has finally put those hopes aside. I need for you to do the same.'

'I would, of course, if I did not have your best interests at heart. But, in all affection, I must tell you of my suspicion.'

'You must?' This was interesting. He would humour her for a moment, discover what she might reveal.

'It grieves me to say so, but I believe you have been duped by your wife.'

'Oh, aye? Tell me why you think so.'

'I believe she has a close friend who is of a lower class.'

'I cannot think what that has to do with me. But since you believe it does, who is it, and why do you think I would even care?'

'It is that woman with the limp who sells cheese. I believe they were acquainted before you met.'

'Would it make a difference if they were?'

'Oh, Joseph, you are too trusting. Can't you see that there is something not above board here? You will not wish to hear it, but I believe that Olive and the cheese maker conspired in some way to catch you.'

'Do you have proof of it? If you do, I would like to hear what it is.'

The trap was neatly set. Come, Hortencia, fall into it and reveal what you are up to.

'It is a feeling only. However, I shall discover what it is, I do promise you I will. On my honour as your closest friend.'

Honour? There was very little of that in Lady Hortencia Clark.

'You are greatly mistaken in thinking so. My closest friend is my wife.'

'So you believe. But tell me, Joseph, why do you only ever kiss each other on the cheek? For a couple in the full embrace of romance, I would expect to see you more enamored of each other.'

'I will not enlighten you on what happens behind our closed chamber doors.'

A respectable woman would blush and drop the conversation; however, this was Hortencia.

'I am not blind, Joseph. Olive does not share your chamber, and you leave hers very early each night.' He wondered if she realized how her smile looked in the moment. Cunning, ugly in spite of its perfection. 'You are being duped.'

'Whatever the state of my marriage, it has nothing to do with you. But back to what you said about the cottager. If my wife was friendly with the woman, it is purely because she is friendly with everyone.'

'I suppose that might be true. Just look how happy she seems with that awkward Curtis girl. It is as well she does not wish to wed, since no man would have her anyway.'

'You cannot be speaking of Vivienne?' It was stunning that his mother had ever wished for him to be bound to this viperous woman. 'She is intelligent and lively. I know many gentlemen who have spoken highly of her.'

In fact, he had not heard them do so, but he ought to have done. She was an engaging woman. Yet it was the lady's sister who seemed to get all the attention.

'You are a guest in my home.' He must try his valiant best to be firm without antagonizing the dragon. 'I would appreciate it if you did not malign the other women. And as for what goes on between my wife and me? It has nothing to do with you. You would be well-advised to turn your attention to other matters.'

'You only say so because you do not see what I see. But I will be patient. When your wife shows her true colours, I will be here. You and I will have the future we were meant to have.'

She went up on her toes as if she intended to kiss his cheek. He stepped back so that her lips only smacked air.

'You cannot put me off forever, Joseph. You have always been meant for me.'

True colours indeed.

So much for his valiant best. He'd stepped on the viper's tail and made her hiss.

Let her then. It remained to be seen who would be the first to strike.

Hortencia struck first.

Until the moment she smiled and buried her fangs into him, it had been a good evening.

Joseph had been at ease during the last dinner of the house party, confident that the visit had been a success and would end well.

With the exception of Hortencia, everyone seemed to approve of his marriage.

In the morning, the guests would be returning to London, so the after dinner gathering in the parlor tonight was especially enjoyable.

Everyone spoke of how they must get together again soon.

Grace sat side by side on the piano bench with Charles. The fellow grinned broadly while she played a lively tune.

Peter caught Hortencia's hand, spinning her about in a playful invitation to dance. Poor man was neatly rebuffed.

Olive twirled in, saving Peter from embarrassment by grasping the hand Hortencia had just slapped away. She filled in the dance step which went wanting.

They were a happy sight, his friend and his wife—

Wife! The endearment that came so naturally had him catching his heart, shoving it back between his ribs.

At any rate, Olive and Peter made everyone smile with their silly, happy dance steps.

After a moment, his father caught the mood. He kissed Mama's hand, then twirled her about the parlor. They laughed together in a way he had never heard them do.

Eleanor and Thomas Curtis joined in, making the parlor dazzle in a whirl of colourful skirts. Laughter added to the music from the piano.

And then it happened. The serpent's tongue flicked. Hortencia clapped her hands in apparent merriment and declared for all to hear, 'Do you know, Joseph, I have never seen you give your bride a proper kiss.'

Grace stopped playing.

The dancers stopped and stared.

Everyone must be wondering if the comment was playful or critical. What they would all know was that it was highly inappropriate. She was getting desperate.

'Hortencia, my friend, you do say the funniest things.' Olive hurried to his side while everyone looked at one another, clearly at a loss to know if they should laugh or not. 'No one can make a jest as well as you can. Now tell me, what sort of kiss is it that you seem to believe my husband is negligent in giving me?'

At that, everyone relaxed, smiled. Everyone except for Vivienne, who looked wide-eyed and offended on their behalf.

Hortencia opened her mouth, closed it…then frowned. 'Well, never mind, perhaps—'

Father cleared his throat. 'Perhaps all of us married men have been negligent in the matter. What do you say? Each of us give our wives a resounding kiss!'

'On the count of three, then,' his mother ordered. 'Married kisses all around.'

Dash it. He was good and trapped. Kissing Olive in the

way which was expected of him was risky. A man could only resist so much temptation. Now here it was and no way out.

Olive whispered so quietly that he could not hear her words, but he read the message well enough.

They would survive this one kiss. She understood what it was and what it was not.

Lord, give him as logical an approach to the matter as Olive seemed to have.

Glancing to the side, he decided to follow the example his parents set.

Hortencia would accept their example as to what made a respectable show of affection.

He and Olive must have both thought the same thing, because they turned as one to look at Lord and Lady Claymore.

Well then…it was not that kiss they could copy.

He had not ever seen his parents kiss that way before. Somehow this visit to the country must have revived the flame in their marriage!

He lifted Olive's chin, deciding the best course was to kiss her a degree cooler than his parents were doing and a degree hotter than the Curtis couple were.

Dipping his head, he felt her breath, hot and quick, on his lips.

'Forgive me,' he whispered against them.

'No,' she breathed, her lips moving on his.

Anyone looking on would imagine they'd exchanged romantic endearments in the instant before kissing.

But 'no'? What did she mean by that? Was it 'no need to', or 'no, I do not'?

Wondering was the only thing which kept him from becoming fully consumed by Olive, caught up in her scent, in her shape as she pressed against him.

'How delightful!' Grace exclaimed. 'I can hardly wait for the day when I may play this game.'

He was aware of conversation and laughter buzzing about the parlor, but dimly.

'No?' he whispered against Olive's ear. 'What does that mean?'

'No more,' she whispered back.

'My, but wasn't this fun? I think we will start a new trend in parlor games.' Joseph heard his mother say. 'Have you seen what you wished to, Hortencia?'

This was not Joseph's first kiss, but it might as well have been. As distracted as he had been during it, a question came to him.

Was this a kiss to build a lifetime on?

'Come with me.' He grabbed Olive's hand, and drew her out of the parlor, down a long hallway, and then into the solarium.

Moonlight shone through the glass. He heard wind huffing around the eaves and Olive's quick breathing.

He needed to know. Now that they were alone, would he still feel the future in her kiss?

If he did, it might be the greatest regret of his life.

A shaft of moonlight etched a path across the solarium floor. Joseph tugged her along, then stopped abruptly beside a small tree.

He jerked her against him, frowning.

She arched her brows in question, because what was this about?

Then he kissed her. Or claimed her. Whichever, she was consumed…possessed.

And then it was over except for the heat. There was not an inch of her which did not sizzle.

Although he took a step back, he did not release her arm. Breathing hard, he looked intently into her eyes. 'No more what?'

She reached up, touched his bicep. It was tense and firm. She felt a tremor race over his skin.

'No more wondering what kissing you would be like without acting being the reason.'

'Now we know.'

'Aye, now we do.' He kissed her again, and she allowed it.

This time the kiss did not have a sense of urgent possession. Rather, it was slow, and she sensed it held a hint of regret.

This intimacy would not happen again. She knew it was true as well as he must.

How sad to put something so wondrous away in the very instant it was acknowledged.

'I cannot be sorry. How can I regret a moment of knowing you?' He made as if to kiss her again, but she shook her head, broke his hold on her arm, then stepped away.

One more taste of the forbidden would make her weep. And she was not sorry for a moment they had shared, either. But grief for what they would be missing might crush her.

'We shall call this…' she waggled her fingers at her heart and then his '…a moment out of time.'

The wonder was, how she had squeezed the words from her throat without weeping.

Society was a beast, keeping people from one another. After his kisses, she knew if things were different, then... Never mind. Things were not different.

'Yes, I suppose that is what it was.' He touched her hair, drew his fingers over the curve of her bottom lip. 'It was a wonderful moment, Olive. I will never forget it.'

Nor would she, and yet remembering was the saddest thing she could imagine.

Olive gave up pacing across her chamber floor and plopped heavily into the chair in the bay of the window.

No matter how hard she tried to, she could not sleep. Not surprisingly, Joseph's first kiss lingered on her lips, as did his last.

She had been too close to confessing she was in love with him. What a grand and heartbreaking mistake that would have been.

She stared out the window. Above the treetops, she saw a pair of smoke columns curling from the cottages below.

Her secret love for Joseph would go with her when she went home. The last thing he needed was to have her confession haunt this house while he tried to make a life with some perfectly lovely and acceptable woman.

For all that she valued truth, sometimes it was better kept to oneself.

Chapter Twelve

Peter Helms and Charles Barlow departed for London after breakfast the next morning.

Joseph regretted seeing them go. Not only because they were men whose company he enjoyed but also because once everyone was gone, Olive would be, too.

Mother, Father, and Hortencia would be here for another week only, which meant his time with Olive was growing short.

Then he would no longer need a wife.

But Olive…would he no longer need her? Her presence seemed as natural as breathing did.

Before all this, he had counted himself lucky to be living at Falcon's Steep by himself.

Look at him now, waving goodbye to Charles and Peter and feeling sad about it…feeling lonely.

If it was this difficult saying goodbye to them, what would it be like when he had to say farewell to Olive?

True, she only lived down the hill. The distance would not be all that great. But there would be a gap between them of another sort. Because of it, she might as well be a hundred miles away. Once she was no longer lady of the manor, she would go back to her old life. He would go back to his.

Provided he had a life to go back to. He feared everything had changed. He still loved the estate and did not wish to live anywhere else, but after Olive, what was he to do with himself?

Perhaps he should wed. The manor needed a mistress.

No, curse it. The manor needed Olive. He needed Olive.

The thought of some lovely stranger taking her place left him feeling odd. It fisted his belly into a knot.

The knot only tightened as the day went on.

A few hours later, Olive stood beside him, giving hugs and wishing the Curtis family a safe trip home.

'Where is Hortencia?' Grace asked. 'One would think she would come and bid us goodbye.'

'Perhaps remorse over her behaviour last night is keeping her indisposed,' Joseph's mother said.

Maybe. Yet her absence made Joseph itchy under the skin.

'Remorse? I rather doubt it,' Vivienne answered while handing up the tripod for her camera to the driver to be stored with the luggage. 'I saw her chatting merrily with a crofter down the hill not an hour ago. They did not give a whit that they frightened away the bird I was trying to photograph. More is the pity. It was quite beautiful.'

Olive went stiff, glanced up at him and whispered, 'Father?'

'It might be anyone,' he answered.

'Let us hope. My father is not known for his discretion.'

He caught her fingers, squeezed them. She squeezed back.

All of a sudden, he wished the week was over. That everyone was back in London with no secrets having been revealed.

As long as he was wishing…

But no. There was no magic lamp that was going to grant his greatest wish.

Throughout dinner, Mama carried the conversation.

Joseph had never been more grateful for her gift of steering talk to pleasant topics. She was a lady born and bred, and it showed even when she presided over a group of five, and four of them family…no, three. Too often lately, he forgot that Olive was not family at all.

Hortencia was stewing, and her mood would have tainted the meal if not for Mama.

The nasty glances she cast at Olive were unusual. Ordinarily, she at least managed a put-on smile.

If Joseph had any doubt that the cottager she had been speaking with was Cedric Augustmore, he no longer did.

Hortencia would have been seeking proof that he and Olive were not wed. She would not have received it from Olive's father. He believed they were. But Cedric couldn't have mentioned his relationship to Olive either, because Hortencia would have crowed about it. They'd been unbelievably lucky—this time.

As soon as dinner was finished, he would whisk Olive away. With any luck, they could avoid Hortencia's accusations for a bit longer.

The second Mama nodded to the footman that dinner was finished, Joseph stood.

'It was a lovely meal,' Olive said, then also stood and grasped his hand.

Clearly she, too, understood the urgency to be away at once.

While they might manage to avoid Hortencia for tonight,

with seven more days before she went back to London, it would be impossible to avoid her altogether.

Only not tonight. It had been a busy and tiring day with all the socializing first and then the goodbyes. When he denied whatever his foe had to say, he would need his wits about him.

Yet there was very little she could do other than accuse. If it came to their word against hers… Olive was the more convincing player.

'Good night, my dears,' Mama said, then slipped her hand into the crook of Father's elbow.

Lady Claymore gave her husband a glance which made him grin. He led her from the dining room at double pace.

Who were these people? Where was the woman who believed that marriage was intended purely for social advancement? That love could not be counted on to endure for a lifetime?

Her attitude about everything seemed so changed, Joseph scarcely knew his own mother. Father knew her, though, and he looked exceptionally pleased.

'Good night, Hortencia,' Olive said. 'My husband and I have had a full day. We shall retire to our chamber.'

'Not just yet.'

Hortencia stood, faced them across the table. She smiled but not in good humour. Once again she looked like a cat with feathers in her sharp little teeth.

It was another ugly image which made the small hairs on the back of his neck leap to attention.

Joseph nodded at the footmen standing beside the door. 'Thank you, Densley… Wilson. You may go.'

Whatever Hortencia had to say, he did not wish for the staff to overhear.

Once they were well out of earshot, Joseph said, 'Speak your mind so that my wife and I might retire to our chamber.'

Hortencia tapped her fingernails on the table.

Click, click, click... Her eyes narrowed, and her smile quirked up at one corner.

'Oh, Joseph, how perfectly wicked.' What was wicked was her giggle. He pressed Olive's shoulder to encourage her…and himself to stand firm.

'When two people are in love, it is what they do. Good night.'

When they were only steps from the doorway, she let her arrow fly. Her point hit square between his shoulder blades.

'I do not doubt that you love the woman, Joseph. But you are not married to her.'

She could not know that for certain. Only Eliza knew the truth, and she would deny it.

'Surely you are not suggesting that Joseph and I are living in sin.' Olive gave a perfectly horrified gasp. 'It is beneath you, Hortencia. A lady would never utter such a lie.'

'Which of us is the true lady, Olive? Show me a wedding gown. Present me with a certificate of marriage. Otherwise, I will assume I am correct.'

Olive closed her eyes, took a breath. He knew what she was doing, had seen her draw deeply into her character on several occasions.

When she opened her eyes, she was so completely mistress of the manor that he nearly believed it to be fact.

'I confess. I am utterly bewildered, Hortencia.' Olive stepped around the table. She clasped her foe's hand. 'Have you feigned our friendship all along?'

The only answer the woman gave was to shrug.

'Oh dear, do not tell me we are not friends? Have I assumed something that is not true?'

Olive dropped Hortencia's hand.

'You are beneath me. Surely you do not think we could ever be friends,' Hortencia spat.

Olive was not beneath anyone! He was about make it clear, but a cool head was called for in that moment, and he did not have one. Olive might not either, but she acted as if she did.

'Dear Hortencia, I believed you to be a lady of quality. I now see that you fall short of the role. I made an incorrect assumption. Just as you have made an incorrect assumption about my marriage to Joseph.'

'Oh, you are good under fire, Olive. Still, I am no fool. I recognize a liar when I see her.'

'Enough, Hortencia!' Anger pulsed under his skin, matching the thud of his heartbeat. 'I am finished with your accusations.'

No matter that they were true, he was finished with Lady Hortencia Clark.

'You have three days to make arrangements to leave my home.'

Of all the reactions he'd expected, it was not to hear her laugh.

'Do I, now?' *Clip, clip* went her shoes on the tile as she walked around the table to him. 'I give you the same three days. You will confess the truth, send this woman back to where she came from and return with me to London. We will be wed at once. I grow weary of waiting for you, Joseph.'

'All you will do is grow wearier, Hortencia. I will never love you.'

'Yes, anyone can see that Olive is the one you love. Not

that I care one way or another. Love whoever you wish to. Marry me.'

'Why, you immoral creature!' Olive had the presence of mind to exclaim this quietly. It would not do to have the household aware of the drama happening in the dining room. 'Leave our home at once! You will not take my husband to London or anywhere else.'

'But I will. In three days. Produce proof of your marriage or I will ruin you, Olive.'

'Come, my love.' He snatched up Olive's hand, kissed her fingers, then tucked her under his arm. 'This is nonsense. She can do nothing to us.'

'How do you think Lord and Lady Claymore will feel about being played the fool?'

Olive went rigid, but she said quite coolly, 'Presumptions will be your downfall.'

Hortencia snorted.

'Come, husband.' Olive's hand trembled. He gripped it tight to keep Hortencia from noticing. 'We shall retire to our chamber.'

The door had not been closed for a full minute when Olive decided what she must do.

Hortencia had run mad if she thought Olive would just hand Joseph over to her.

'Three days, indeed,' she grumbled.

He did not seem to have heard her, or if he did, he did not respond.

Pointing at the bed, he mouthed, 'Bounce.'

When she gave him a blank look, he caught her hand and took her to the bed, where he proceeded to sit and show her, causing the mattress to creak, the bedding to rustle.

She followed his lead but had no idea how this helped with anything. It was amusing, but right now she did not feel that amusement was called for.

Action was. And she had a plan.

'Good,' he whispered. 'Now moan.'

'Why ever would I do that?' she whispered back, her breath coming in huffs from exertion.

'Because Hortencia followed us. She is probably listening at the door. So act as if you are in the throes of passion. We do not wish for her to think we are worried about what she just said.'

'What? Joseph, I have never been in the throes of passion. I have no idea how to sound like it.'

Could she act something she had never experienced? She had read of it, imagined it…so perhaps.

'Very well. I shall try.' Being already breathless was bound to help. So would picturing Joseph without his shirt, his chest glistening because he was emptying a bucket of water slowly over himself… How delightful were those liquid droplets sliding over bare, pebbled muscle?

She made a low sound, added a gasp, and said, 'Oh, Joseph… Joseph…'

With her eyes closed, she bounced and imagined his hair wet, his eyes all smoky desire.

Bit by bit, she became aware that Joseph had stopped bouncing, that in fact, he was no longer sitting on the bed.

When she opened her eyes, she saw him standing, looking down at her. The smoky desire was real and hotter than in her imagination.

Glory fire, but he made her bones go soft. It was difficult to love a man, to see him giving her such a look, and not react by stretching out on the bed and offering herself up to him.

Mentally, she grabbed her heart and gave it a good stiff shake.

She inclined her head toward the chamber door, arching her brows in question. Was Hortencia still snooping outside?

He whispered for her to get beneath the blanket.

While she scrambled under it, he walked toward the door, yanking open his shirt buttons, kicking off his shoes.

He gave her a wink, a grin, and then he bent to curl one sock off his foot.

If Hortencia was on the other side of the door, Olive's show of heaving lust would be convincing…and unfeigned.

Joseph yanked the door open. No eavesdropper had her ear pressed to the keyhole, but footsteps did echo in the hallway, tapping out a quick retreat.

He closed the door, leaned against it, the long toes of one bare foot wriggling.

Scrambling out of the bed, she took a moment to gaze about the grandest bedchamber she had ever seen.

Dark wood gleamed with polish. Velvet drapes of hunter green hung from ceiling to floor, drawn shut over a window which probably took up the better part of one wall.

Olive did not belong here. Not that she had any notion of how she was going to stop being here, especially now.

More than ever, their lie must prevail, and the truth must fail. She had never imagined a more tangled web.

What would Joseph think when she turned it all on its head?

Her idea was easier to come up with than to present. She had no notion of how he would respond.

There was only thing to do if this situation was to come out in their favour.

She loved Joseph, and there was nothing she would not do to protect him from a tragic future.

She respected his parents with all her heart. To have them discover the truth of what they had done was unthinkable.

No amount of explaining would make it acceptable for her and Joseph to have been living together without being married.

There was really no way to say what she needed to gently, so…

'We will wed.'

In the face of his gaping stare, she added, 'You do have experience with arranging marriages in Gretna Green. We will stay in this room tonight and leave at first light. Then we will return home with a licence.'

'It is generous of you to offer to sacrifice yourself for my sake. Only, I cannot accept.'

'You must. Unless you see another way out of this.'

'I do see another way. We shall admit to the truth.'

'And live with the disaster that would follow? I might as well hand you over to Hortencia on a silver platter. No other woman would have you with your reputation so blackened.'

'Aye.' He shook his head, frowning until his brows nearly met. 'Yours would be, too.'

'I would be utterly ruined, an outcast in the place where I was born and raised. Of course, I did expect to be a spinster anyway.'

With his hand working through his hair in clear agitation, Joseph paced to the window and back.

'You would make a terrible spinster.'

'You know I am right about this.'

'I see the wisdom in the idea. But it is not as if we can

seek an annulment afterwards. We have done too good a job of convincing people we are in love.'

Far too good a job. She was utterly, madly in love with him. Not that she was free to admit it.

She owed this man more than she could ever repay. What would have become of Eliza, James, and Laura had it not been for him? Instead of living apart, they were now a family.

Marrying Joseph was small recompense for all he had done.

An easy price to pay.

The difficult part would be carrying on, day by day, without him knowing she was in love with him.

Which she must do so that he could go about his life as he would have done before all this.

He had saved her family from disgrace. Now she would do the same for his.

'Once we have done this thing, we can live separate lives. Me at my cottage and you in your manor house.' She swallowed hard, because this was a wickedly difficult thing to say to the man she loved. 'If you wish.'

If he wished! None of this was what he wished.

To wed the woman he adored and yet live apart from her?

It was madness. Clearly, it was also what she wished.

Cursed awful was what it was going to be…trading one lie for another.

He was not certain he could pretend this was only a convenient marriage. The honest truth was that he was in love with Olive, and he was not certain he could act as if he was not.

'We will not live in separate homes. Separate chambers would do…if you wish,' he said, giving her own words back to her. Not to mock her but only to agree with what she seemed to want.

He could not understand why she would wish such a thing after the way he had kissed her, after the way she had kissed him back.

There was plenty to build a marriage on.

'Olive, I…' He did not understand but he would not pressure her for her reasons. 'May I have my grandmother's ring?'

Blinking, she looked away while she slipped it off her finger and pressed the warm circle of gold into his palm.

Had she misunderstood? Thought he was refusing her?

'Will you look at me, Olive?'

She still did not, so he turned her chin in his fingers. Moisture shimmered in her green eyes. She was hiding herself behind them.

The sight made his gut clench. Here they were, hours from being wed, and she was hiding herself from him. She had never done it before.

All he could think of was that she was sorry for the sacrifice. Even though she was pressing for it, and he did see there was no other way, it was evident she did not wish to wed him.

He couldn't blame her. He had promised this charade would last a week, and now she was to give up a lifetime.

'I will do my best to be a decent husband, Olive. I promise.'

The vow given, he went down on his knee and took her hand.

'Olive Augustmore, will you do me the great honour of becoming my wife?'

He put the ring back on her finger and noticed her hand trembling. So were the corners of her mouth.

It took a moment, but she nodded. 'Yes, Joseph, I will marry you.'

She looked at the ring on her finger, then pressed it to her bosom.

The moisture in her eyes spilled over in a single tear. He wiped it away with the pad of his thumb.

He wished he knew what the tear meant. But then, perhaps it was better he did not.

Chapter Thirteen

The next morning they left for Gretna Green at dawn.

By noon, the minister declared Joseph to be Olive's husband, and Olive to be his wife.

He pledged his love and fidelity to her and wondered if, in spite of the circumstances of their marriage, she had any sense of how deeply he meant that promise.

Standing in this quaint church, his marriage only seconds old, he had the same sense of coming home as he had when he first rode up the drive to Falcon's Steep.

He wished he could tell Olive that he did not regret marrying her, that there was a sense of wonderment to the morning, but he held this tongue.

She would not appreciate knowing…not if she did not feel the same way.

The ceremony ended quickly. It was time to go home.

As they walked down the front steps of the church, a dragonfly buzzed over a silk flower on Olive's hat.

A sign of good days to come? What wouldn't he give to regain the easy way that used to be between them?

Something had happened to change it. Perhaps being the husband she wanted would get it back.

Dash it, though. The husband she seemed to want, which was no proper husband at all, was not the one he wanted to be.

It was a fine line he would walk with Olive Billings, but he would choose no other.

'Olive Billings,' he said, taking his bride's arm and leading her toward their waiting carriage.

'Yes?' She glanced up at him, her expression neutral.

It cut him to see it, because brides were not supposed to be neutral. Typically, they were blushing with joy.

The dragonfly still hovered about. Its wings glistened blue and green in the sunshine. There had not been time for either of them to procure more elegant clothing. The flowers she carried were purchased from a street seller.

The dragonfly, though—to him, it added a little magic to the moment, rescuing it from neutrality.

'I'm just trying out your name, now that it's real.'

'Mrs Billings,' she repeated after him. To his great relief, she smiled and seemed more herself. 'It sounds honest, at least.'

Perhaps now, with the vows spoken and their futures secured, they could once again be the friends they had been.

What he must not do was press her for any more than she was willing to give him. Which was her whole life.

While he could not give her everything he wished to as a husband, he could at least give her his restraint.

The dragonfly alighted on the bodice of Olive's travelling gown. It flexed its wings on a shiny button. Lucky insect.

To his way of seeing it, the insect was a messenger reminding him to be patient, and one day he and Olive would find their way to a true marriage.

She nudged the insect with her finger, but instead of flying off, it crawled on her fingertip. 'Isn't it amazing?'

'Oh, aye. Quite a splendid insect.'

She blew on its wings. It took flight, circled their heads, and then off it went.

'Well, something advantageous has come of the morning,' she said.

'The dragonfly, you mean? A portent of good things to come?'

'A lovely sentiment, of course, but what I mean is that we no longer need to think of a way to end our marriage,' she said.

Ach, no. It was now more about finding a way of carrying on with it.

Home by teatime, Olive sat with Joseph and his parents, eating small sandwiches as if this was a day like any other.

The only difference was that Hortencia was absent. Since Joseph was safely beside her, Olive did not worry over where Hortencia was or what she was doing. It was pleasant not to have to feel anxious about the woman's scheming for an hour.

The rest of the afternoon and evening went much as they always had, each of them doing what they always did. As far as Olive could tell, no one even wondered where they been together this morning.

When it was time to retire, Olive was exhausted. The steps to her chamber seemed a mile high.

Then Joseph looped his arm about her waist, helping her up.

She tried not to lean into his strength. Yes, he was her husband now, but not much had changed except having a piece of paper to say so.

The truth was, she had gone from having a pretend husband to a husband in name only.

It was simply more of the same. To let herself believe otherwise was folly.

Had it not been for the fear of being discovered, she would never have demanded he marry her, and he would not have gone on his knee to propose.

They had spoken the vows required to secure the marriage certificate…no more, no less.

Now they needed to speak of what came next.

This was their wedding night. What would Joseph wish to do with it?

She knew what she wished for, but the last thing she would do was seduce him into her bed. Just because a woman offered her body did not mean she would be loved in return.

Now here they were in front of her chamber. She opened the door to her room, but closed the imaginary one on the pining and sighing from her heart.

Joseph stepped in behind her like he always did in case anyone was watching, and closed the door behind him, like he always had.

The bed was ten feet away, like it always was.

And yet it loomed so much larger tonight, occupying far too much of her attention.

Her tricky imaginary door must still be cracked open an inch, because the bed seemed to pulse with temptation.

She really must grab hold of her emotions…focus on the fact that conjugal bliss was not going to be a part of her marriage.

She knew very well why they had married, and so did he.

'Are you worried that now I'm your husband, I will press you for my rights?'

Glory fire, not that. It was more that she would demand what he was not willing to give!

An honest answer to his question would be that she feared offering her heart only to have it rejected.

Better to keep what was between them as it was… friendly, amicable. Going through life as allies.

'No, Joseph. It is not what we agreed to. I trust you to… to refrain.'

'Good, then, we have that settled. It is late, and I am tired. May I just sit on your bed for a while?'

In the past he had done so without asking…when he was instructing her on how to act like a lady.

'This is your home. You may sit anywhere that suits you.'

With a sigh, he sat on the bed, then flopped onto his back with his knees hanging over the edge.

He waved his fingers for her to join him on the mattress.

When she hesitated, he sat up, then rose from the bed and came to lead her by the hand.

'It is difficult to speak to you when you are standing over there.'

It was not the speaking which concerned her; after all, they had done it many times before. The difference between now and then was that a marriage licence lay between them.

Things that used to be forbidden no longer were…except for the boundaries they set for themselves.

Joseph's boundary was that he would not press his marital rights.

Although he did not know it, her boundary was the same.

He drew her down onto the mattress. Together they lay

back. Like before, his legs dangled over the edge. Hers did, too, only his feet were closer to the floor.

'What do you wish to talk about?' she asked quietly.

'Our friendship. I wish to have it back, like it was before we wed.'

'I do not think it has suffered.'

'Good, then may I hold your hand as we have done in the past?'

'Of course.' He caught her hand, drew it to his chest.

She felt his heart beat hard against her fingers. Odd since they were supposed to be relaxing from their long, weary day.

He turned on his side so that they faced one another. He arched his brows, then grinned.

Instinct warned her that he was about to break their rules. She must be the firm one, then. If she was not, she might admit that she loved him.

Folly, folly, folly! She must not be reckless.

'I've kissed you before, too.' He drew her hand to his mouth, lingered over the kiss he placed on her knuckles.

'Only when people were watching.'

'No…there was the time when they were not.' He moved closer. The mattress squeaked with his weight shifting. 'I think you recall it?'

'We have agreed to a friendly marriage.'

'Kissing is friendly, aye?'

Too friendly and yet… 'Would you want kissing in our marriage? Since we are setting our boundaries, we ought to know what they are.'

'We must try one or two in order to know.'

'Don't we know from before?'

Then, kissing had been nearly more than she could resist. Now that he was her husband, he could take things further if he wished to.

His breath came quick, warm on her cheek. His open palm pressed her closer toward him on the mattress.

'My Olive.' Her name, so softly whispered, branded her heart. The sizzle of the burn went all through her body. It cindered her resolve and blew the ashes of her good sense all over the mattress.

And that was even before he kissed her.

When he did, well…she had no argument. She loved him and would show him with every sigh and moan he drew from her, with every stroke, every touch of every part of her that had been forbidden.

Her brain was fuzzy. Her body was not.

It knew what she wanted and insisted on having its way.

She gave herself over to her husband because surely it was impossible for him to touch her with such loving tenderness unless he did, in fact, love her.

This was right. Joy hummed through her at every kiss. The small sighs and noises his touch drew from her was a love song.

All at once his hands fell away from her. He rolled off her with a muffled curse, then all but leapt from the bed.

'I never meant to…' He backed toward the chamber door, jerking his hand through his hair as he did when he was agitated. 'I got carried away, Olive. Forgive me, it will not happen again.'

Within seconds, she was alone in the room.

There was no mistaking what he'd meant.

Joseph had never meant for her to believe he was in love with her.

Her 'love song' must have shocked him out of the trance

that had led him off course. He'd only wanted their friendship back as it was.

She lay down on the bed again, not a button undone on her gown, not a stocking rolled down, silently weeping.

And alone in her love.

The next afternoon, Olive stood in the centre of the entrance hall of Falcon's Steep. Absently, she plucked a dried frond off a potted fern.

What she ought to do was go home. She could not, of course. This was her new life now. She had chosen it, and there was no going back. It was not as if going home would help with her heartache anyway.

Looking back on events, which was all she was doing, it was fair to admit last night was not completely Joseph's fault. There had been two them sharing embraces on the bed.

She had known better and yet still set good judgement aside. Had she been firm in what she knew to be right, none of it might have happened.

When next she saw him, she would not act as if she resented him.

To resent someone because they did not love you as you loved them would only lead to further heartache. Last night she had shed hours of tears, feeling sorry for herself. She was done with it.

As far as she was concerned, she and Joseph were friends and would continue to be. Only, next time he asked to sit on her bed, she would point him to the chair.

Looking about the grand beauty of her new home, she knew there was only one thing to do, and that was to move on.

The question was, how?

No longer was she acting the part of Lady of Falcon's Steep. She was its true mistress now.

In the past, she had managed by drawing on her fictional self. Acting, though, was quite a different thing from reality.

This sudden turnabout in her life would be challenging. Which was probably what she needed right then. Discovering how to remain who she had been, while becoming who she was required to be, ought to keep her mind busy enough.

No longer was she responsible for a goat herd, whose only requirements were to be fed, milked and sung to. Now she was accountable for a household and the well-being of all those who worked here.

And she was to do all this without pressing Joseph for affections he did not feel for her.

Oh, yes, during their wedding vows, he had promised to love her, but everyone said that. It was a requirement.

In this moment, all she hoped for was to regain the friendship which had blossomed so naturally between them.

Footsteps strode across the tile floor from behind. She recognized whose they were straight away.

She had not seen Joseph since he left her chamber last night and had been nervous about what their first encounter would be like.

Distant? Friendly? Resentful? Forgiving?

He did not speak, but plucked the dried frond from her fingers and placed it back in the pot. He managed to do so without his fingers even grazing hers.

'No need to trim the plants. We have servants to do it.'

As far as she could tell, he was neither distant nor

friendly. Not resentful, nor forgiving, either. The best she could figure was that he was as confused as she was.

'You have staff to do everything. Really, Joseph, no one is going to believe I am a baron's daughter.'

'Olive.' He reached for her hand, but at the last moment drew it back. 'Last night I overstepped. Please do not hate me. I have no excuse except for bad judgement.'

'Mine was as bad. We shall go on as if it did not happen and consider it a lesson learned.'

'Aye,' he said, his expression sombre. 'A lesson learned. I hope you will not hate me for the teaching.'

'I've too much on my mind to cling to misplaced resentment. Going forward we shall respect the boundaries of our marriage.'

'Agreed. Now, tell me what is pressing on your mind?'

'How am I to go from being a goatherd to Lady of Falcon's Steep?'

'You have been doing it already.'

'Acting it.' The same as she was acting as if she was not in love with him.

When she thought about it, she had been acting in one way or another since before she met Joseph. At last she was free to be herself.

The last deception must be settled today, this very hour. It was going to come out at some point if Hortencia kept digging for gossip. Better if it was by confession than discovery.

'We must tell your parents who I am at once.'

'It's true. Even if she found out, Hortencia would have nothing to hold over us then.'

'Let's do it now before we lose our courage.'

He extended his hand to her. 'This is acceptable?'

For her, touching this man in any way was risky. And yet they had done so as friends, and she did wish to have a friendly marriage.

'This will have to be said just right. Once they recover from the surprise, I am sure they will want nothing but our happiness,' Joseph said.

'Will we be happy?' she asked. It was blunt, but she did not regret the asking.

'We were, I think…before.' An endearing frown crossed his brow. 'Olive, I was not the husband I ought to have been last night. From now on I will be.'

Fine, except that the husband he thought she wanted was not the one who'd walked out of her chamber.

It was the other husband, the one who'd kissed away all her good judgement.

There was nothing in Hortencia's attitude to indicate that she had so recently threatened him and Olive. Yet Joseph was not fooled by her pretence of congeniality.

The cheerier the woman seemed, the more it worried him. He had given her three days to make arrangements to leave his home.

This was the morning of that third day. She gave no indication of being ready to travel. But he was still not of a mind to bring out their marriage certificate since the ink was still fresh and the date was proof that she had been correct when she claimed they were not wed.

While she chatted with Mama, he did not get the sense she was saying goodbye.

More than ever, he would need to keep a watchful eye on her, because not only was this her day to leave, but it was the day she had given them to produce proof of their marriage.

He had tried a few times to get his parents alone so that he and Olive could tell them who she really was, but aside from Hortencia clinging to them, they'd spent most of yesterday and this morning visiting friends.

The longer the moments ticked by, the more urgent he felt it was to reveal the truth. Something was not right here, although he could not quite put a finger on it. Except that Hortencia was acting far too congenially.

'There is something different about you, son.' Joseph's father stroked his chin in thought.

Quite a bit more than his father knew. He was not aware that being in love and having to act like he was not, showed!

'Something is different about you, too, Father.'

His father laughed joyously. Mama tapped his arm in clear affection.

He had never seen this loving, playful part of his parents' marriage.

It must be that spending time away from London and society had made them look at one another in a new way… or perhaps an old way.

Whichever it was, it seemed that they had revived their first love. Joseph could not have been happier to see it.

Hortencia stopped conversing with Mama, then went to the window and stared silently out.

Probably she was knocked off centre by Cupid's arrow darting between his parents. With luck she would not notice it going off target where he and Olive were concerned.

All at once, she turned away from the window. She smiled that cat smile she had.

'Lady Amelia, I have invited a guest to join us. I hope you do not mind.'

His mother raised her brows, but Father spoke up. 'Have you met a young man, Hortencia?'

'I have met a man. I didn't realize exactly who he was at first, but now I do. I'm sure he's someone you will be most anxious to meet.'

Hortencia slid a look at Olive, sending her a slow, malicious grin.

Olive's face drained of colour.

Joseph stood.

'What have you done?' he asked with a scowl.

'I have merely invited a charming gentleman for tea.'

Footsteps clicked in the hallway.

'Mr Cedric Augustmore has come to call, sir.' The butler sniffed, bowed at the viscount and then backed out of the parlor.

Olive rose from the couch, she had recovered nicely. She did not appear to be distressed, and he admired her for it. No, he loved her for it.

'Good afternoon, Father.' Olive hurried across the parlor, then gave him a hug.

There was nothing to do but introduce him. This meeting had come before she'd hoped for it to, but now that it was upon her, she must push through.

What a blessing that she did not smell alcohol on her father's breath. The situation might be far worse.

'Lord and Lady Claymore, I would like to introduce you to my father.'

Neither of them spoke. Apparently they were struck dumb, wondering how this man could be the baron they had been told he was. Although Father had worn his best suit for the occasion, it was still patched and out of fashion.

To complete his look of cottage farmer, he held a pair of small bleating goats, one under each arm.

'A gift for you, my lord, my lady.' He extended the kids, adorably speckled, one with brown splotches and one with black. In Father's estimation, this was a grand gift which anyone would appreciate.

Her mother-in-law gave a great blink. What, Olive wondered, was the biggest surprise? The goats or the man she had greeted as her father? He did not resemble a baron in any way.

To her credit, Lady Claymore recovered quickly, hiding her surprise behind a gracious smile.

The viscount took the kids, awkwardly cuddling one in each elbow. 'We haven't owned goats before. Thank you, sir. They are interesting little fellows.'

Interesting and nibbling the shiny buttons on Lord Claymore's sleeve.

'It was kind of you to come all this way to pay us a visit, Mr Augustmore.'

'Oh, but it was not all that far, Lady Amelia,' Hortencia announced. 'Mr Augustmore lives only down the hill… the first cottage you come to on the path. I met him again by happy circumstance when I was out walking earlier today. Once I knew who he was, it only seemed appropriate to invite him to tea.'

Olive uttered a mental curse. She and Joseph had missed their chance to tell his parents who she was and introduce her father to them on their own terms. Now it was Hortencia steering the moment as she wished to.

'I did want to give my best wishes to my daughter and

my new son-in-law. And to make your acquaintances.' Father gave a polite nod to each of them. 'I am pleased to be able to call you family.'

'It is a great pleasure to meet you, Mr Augustmore.' Lady Claymore indicated the tea tray with its assortment of delicate sandwiches. 'We are delighted that you are able to join us.'

Hortencia gasped, probably horrified seeing her scheme turn against her. 'Oh, but I do not think—'

The viscount interrupted her to say, 'Please do stay, Cedric. I hope I may call you that? As you say, we are family now.'

'I thank you kindly, my lord.'

'No more "my lord". We shall be Marshall and Amelia.' Her father-in-law's smile looked so like Joseph's it took her breath for an instant. 'Until we are called Grandfather.'

'And Grandmama!' Lady Claymore exclaimed. 'Hortencia, will you serve tea?'

Knowing she would not be giving these dear people grandchildren made Olive want to weep on the spot.

Hortencia flinched. 'All of a sudden, I do not feel—'

'A word, my dear.' This was not a request but an order given by a viscountess. Hortencia did not dare ignore it.

Lady Claymore walked towards the corner of the room, where she was sure to be out of earshot of the men who chatted easily with one another despite the difference in their social stations.

The conversation was not out of Olive's earshot.

'Hortencia, you have invited a guest. You will now have the courtesy to serve him tea.'

'Of course, Lady Amelia. Forgive me. I do not know what came over me. I feel recovered now.'

Hortencia's words were certainly not genuine, but uttered in order to save face with Viscountess Claymore. It would not do to make an enemy of such a lady of wealth and influence, one whose son she had designs on.

Clearly, she still did not wish to burn the bridge she believed she must cross to get to Joseph.

Once again, the trickster was all gracious smiles, especially to Olive's father.

Olive doubted that her father was aware of what Hortencia was about. Papa would be feeling grand having such a beautiful lady treating him so attentively.

Flirting was what the hussy was doing. To see her father being so used made her sizzle to the tips of her hair.

She was saved from visions of mayhem by Joseph, who finished his conversation with the men and joined her. He led her to the bay of the window, where he could speak and have it appear to be a tender whisper.

'I knew my parents would not change how they felt about you. You may feel more at ease now, aye?'

'Not aye. We are not free of her scheming yet. The wicked besom might still demand to see our certificate of marriage. There is the date to worry about. Your parents are still coming to terms with my low birth. Now to discover we are only recently wed? They would not easily overlook that scandal, I'm sure.'

Joseph nodded, his mouth set and his frown square on Hortencia's back.

'I suppose not.'

Chapter Fourteen

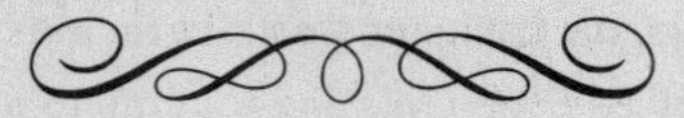

With afternoon tea finished, Olive's father asked her for a word in private, and told her he could not return home without speaking of an important matter.

She took his arm and led him outside. They sat on a bench which gave them a view of the front garden and the driveway.

'Do you mind that I did not marry James?' She might as well get to the heart of it…her defiance of his dictate.

'Ach, no. You did very well for yourself. All is as it should be.'

'You do understand that I would not have wed the baker, no matter how much you insisted. He was Eliza's beau.'

'And now her husband. They have brought Laura home to live with them already.'

'They have? That is wonderful news! Then you are right about all being as it should be. I only pray that no one suspects the truth of who she is.'

'You girls did a good job of keeping the secret.' He caught her hand and held it in both of his. She could not recall the last time he did that. 'I have a confession…and a promise to go with it. Seeing how everything worked out so well for you and your sister made me want to brag about how I succeeded in bringing it all about. Then it was pointed out to me that I had nothing to do with any of it.'

'By Eliza, I suppose.'

'No, by your mother…in a dream. She told me I was high-handed and had nearly ruined everything for her girls.'

'You saw Mama in a dream?' She wished it was true, but he'd probably been drinking.

'As clearly as I see you. She told me to apologize.'

'I accept your apology.' She squeezed his hand, blinked away the moisture gathering in her eyes.

'Ah, I'm glad, then. Now for the other part, the promise. You will recall that your mother was a virtuous woman. Well, she gave me strong words about seeking comfort from a jug. It paid her no honour whatsoever. She made me promise to quit immediately. I have never broken a promise to your mother, and so I sit here beside you, a sober man.'

'This is the best news! But it must have been difficult for you.'

Mama must have come to him, then! He would never have promised to stop drinking otherwise.

'It is odd, but no. The reason I indulged in a wee dram was to ease my sorrow. I missed your mother so. Now that I have seen her, it makes me think she was never gone. Only out of sight, you see?' Olive nodded, because she earnestly wanted to see. 'My good wife gave me a hard scolding. You will recall that she used to, sometimes. She pointed out that I was not the father I ought to have been.'

'Oh, Papa, you were the best you could be. I could burst, I am that proud of you.'

When he smiled, she nearly did burst. Her Papa, the one who had swung her about as a child, told funny stories and tickled her…it was that father's smile she saw now.

'It is good to hear, but lassie, I sorely regret the years I've wasted. I need for you to know it. I promise I will not miss the time with my grandchildren that I did with you and your sister. I suspect that man of yours will do his part to provide plenty of them.'

As true as this was, it was not a thought to indulge in while sitting beside her father.

'I am glad you came to visit. The kids were an adorable gift,' she said in a quick change of subject.

'They were your mother's idea. Your sister said I was daft and should not bring them.'

'If Mama visits you again, you may tell her they were well received.'

'We had a good visit, your mother and I. It was a long dream. She told me she would come to me again as long as I behaved myself.'

The front door opened. A whisper of rustling skirts and the sharp click of shoes on tile announced Hortencia's arrival.

'Ah, there you are, Cedric. I was afraid I had missed giving you a proper goodbye. Please allow me to walk you to the end of the drive.'

Olive wanted to growl. No matter how Hortencia acted the part of a lady, she was not one.

Father stood. Then he bent to kiss Olive's cheek.

'Do not trust her,' Olive whispered.

'Ach, I am fool enough to enjoy her attention but not fool enough to think she means it.'

The day could not end soon enough. Matters might have come out far worse than they had.

They still might.

To add to Joseph's misery, he was once again alone with Olive in her chamber. Echoes of last time came at him from every corner—especially, though, from the bed.

He did not dare even glance that way, let alone think of it.

Olive directed him to sit in the chair beside the window. He settled in and closed his eyes.

Something dropped down onto the mattress. Heaven help him. How would he survive this torture? Had his wife undressed and climbed under the covers?

No, there would not have been time.

'I thought you two would never come upstairs!'

'Eliza?'

Eliza!

Olive gawked at her sister as if she might be a vision and not standing next to the bed, pointing at the valise she had tossed on there. 'What…where did you come from?'

'From behind the curtain, naturally. The pertinent question is, do you know where that awful woman is?'

'Hortencia was in the parlor when we came up,' Joseph answered with a shrug. 'I assume she is still there.'

'It would be a mistake, assuming anything about her.' Eliza opened the latches on the valise. She withdrew the highwayman's costume and tossed it at Olive. 'She is going to the tavern tonight to expose us. You must stop her.'

'She knows?' How could she? Anyone who knew the secret about Laura would take it to the grave. 'Help me with this, Joseph,' Olive said while fumbling with the button of her bodice.

'I suppose it is my fault. I made the mistake of sitting out in the sunshine with Laura on my lap this afternoon when Hortencia walked by with Father after tea. I was kissing her nose and tickling her belly. I may have said something about being her proud Mama, I cannot recall…but as you said. The woman is part hound.'

'How do you know she is on her way to expose us?' Olive asked.

'Hortencia made the mistake of believing I couldn't hear her from the garden. You should have heard her grumbling to herself about what she was going to do tonight. It was fascinating to be privy to what was going on in her mind. And a good thing I did hear it. We must hurry. What sort of vile creature would label a child a bastard in order to gain her own selfish ends? You being her selfish end, Joseph. I heard her say so several times.'

'The woman is daft as well as wicked.' Joseph plucked the red plumed hat off the bed and placed it on Olive's head. 'I will have a horse saddled for you.'

'No time for that,' Eliza said. 'Star is at the edge of the woods already dressed in her costume. I think she is anxious to perform one last time.'

'How do you know she is?' Joseph thought it unlikely.

He was not anxious for this performance. The last thing he wanted was for his wife to go out in the dark and face Hortencia alone.

'Perhaps it is the apple she is anxious for, but she knows that when the gauze goes on, an apple will soon follow,' Olive pointed out while she picked up her sword. She turned it in the lamplight, making the steel glimmer.

'I hope you run her through with it,' Eliza snapped. 'No, never mind. I would not have you commit murder.'

'Joseph and I are now wed,' Olive announced abruptly.

'Well, then. I am happy for it. I am only surprised it took you both so long.'

'You are not stunned?'

Eliza gave a short snort-laugh. 'Any fool can see how much you love one another.'

Olive shot him a stricken look. What did it mean?

There was no time to dwell on it now.

How close was Hortencia to the village? Perhaps she had already arrived.

He would forbid Olive to take this risk if there was any other way. But curse it, his wife was probably the only one who could turn her away from The Shepherd's Keep.

'I will check the stable to see if she has taken a horse. Pray she had not got ahead of us.'

'Joseph,' Olive caught his sleeve and gave it a tug. 'Try and imagine this as an adventure. I find it helps.'

'Adventure, is it? I shall follow behind to make certain it remains one.'

She looked as if she would object, but Eliza cut her off by saying, 'Do not worry. We will stay well-hidden.'

Olive closed her eyes and took a slow, deep breath. He knew the look. She was drawing the highwayman into herself.

'Ho, me lads,' Olive said once she opened her eyes. 'Let us venture out into the storm and slay the wicked plans of our villain. Defend the reputations of the fair Eliza and Laura.'

Her words were playful, but the urgency of the outing could not be overstated.

Luckily, the storm Olive had mentioned did not exist. The villain did.

The three of them went out of the house, as silent as the mouse they frightened on the back stairway.

It could not be denied that there was a splash of adventure to the outing.

More, though, there was risk. Much could go wrong.

Olive waited in her spot under the shadow of the tree. There was no telling when their villain would come along. Joseph had reported that she had not taken a horse, but he had seen her walking towards the stable.

It could only be assumed that she meant to take one, and where else would she be going than where she said she would?

Olive glanced over her shoulder. She did not see Joseph or her sister, but she knew they were there, crouching in dense shrubbery.

Joseph's fears of her, once again, hitting a branch or dashing her head on a rock were unfounded, probably.

Honestly, she did not mind that they were keeping watch.

Ah, just there…a muffled sound. Olive strained to listen. Hooves clopped on the dirt, coming slowly closer.

It was not likely that anyone but Hortencia was riding this particular stretch of the road.

Within seconds, the woman was going to get a fright to last a lifetime.

The ghoul withdrew her sword from its scabbard. The hiss of steel on leather sounded ominous. Flashes of silver in beams of moonlight would give the rider a terrible fright.

Ah, here she came, the hood of her cloak dipping over her face.

The highwayman and her fearful steed stepped out of shadow. Olive gave a shrill, awful wail. Star rose, pawed the air while neighing and showing the whites of her eyes.

How gratifying to know what a wild sight those eyes must be in the darkness.

While Olive had never enjoyed frightening her father, glory fire, she was enjoying this.

Hortencia drew her mount up short, and stared hard as if questioning what had just dissolved out of the darkness to block her way.

Humph…apparently she was not as easily convinced as Father was that she was facing a spectre from the underworld.

A low, creepy moan issued from the shrubbery. Hortencia's mouth went wide at the sound, but no shriek emerged. Her face was as pale as the moon, though.

Clearly her composure was shaken now. She jerked hard on her mount's bridle, probably in an attempt to make him run for home. But Ben was the gentlest horse in the stable and seemed to want nothing more than to stand in place and gaze at Star.

Bless the beast for doing his part.

Star trotted forward, then pranced in in a circle around their 'victim'.

Since Ben understood nothing about highwaymen or phantoms, he offered Star a friendly whicker.

Being well-trained, Star remained in character, snorting and stomping.

The ghoul in Olive grinned. She extended the tip of her sword. Feeling fiendish, the highwayman flicked the hood of Hortencia's cloak with the blade tip.

The hood flipped back on her shoulders. A respectable gash showed in the deep blue velvet.

Ordinarily, Olive would not ruin a perfectly lovely garment, but in this case, it was necessary.

Once the fright was finished, Hortencia must not discount it all as a vision and then decide to go to the village later on.

A high-pitched scream burst from the bushes, then faded to a whimper.

Bless a gust of wind for rusting the leaves overhead just then, and double bless an unseen owl who took that instant to whistle a hoot.

Hortencia jerked, lost her balance, then tumbled off the saddle. She crumpled into a heap on the path and, covering her face with her skirt, she sobbed.

Given how pretty she was, a passerby might think her an angel being accosted by some depraved creature.

Luckily, there were no passersby.

This little stage served as a lesson that one could not always believe what one's eyes saw.

No matter how pretty she looked, this woman was a menace.

But where to go from here?

Olive could not speak a warning for her to turn around. For all that she looked a highwayman, she sounded like Olive… Billings.

There was nothing for it. The sword must do the speaking.

Olive swung it in a circle overhead. It struck a low branch, slicing a shower of leaves down on her.

One of the leaves brushed Hortencia's hand. Her head jerked up.

There was no reason whatsoever Olive should feel regret for the tears tracking Hortencia's cheeks. And yet, she did. Even knowing what the woman intended to do, Olive disliked seeing the terror she'd instilled.

Still, with the sword circling, Olive pointed her other

hand at Ben. Hopefully conveyed the message that she was to mount.

Pointing her sword toward the village, she wagged the weapon, a clear warning not to go that way. Next she nodded, pointed the sharp-looking tip up the hill toward the manor house.

When Hortencia merely blinked up at her, Olive gave the silent signal for Star to roll her eyes.

Ben, sweet horse that he was, nudged his fallen rider.

Without taking her eyes off the phantom highwayman, Hortencia rose shakily from the path. She stood beside Ben for a moment, her gaze sharp on Olive. Then she mounted the saddle.

Swiping tears from her cheek, she turned Ben's head toward home, all the while casting the spectre a speculative frown.

Once she was gone, Joseph and Eliza came out from hiding.

'We must reach home before she does.' Olive slid off the saddle and hurried to undress. She shoved the costume at her sister. 'I did not like the way she looked at me, at the last. I think she suspects.'

'She is a canny thing,' Eliza said. 'You did keep your hat low? No moonlight shone on your face?'

'I was involved in the moment and cannot say for certain where the moon was shining.'

'No hope for it now, if she did recognize you,' Eliza said. 'You and Joseph ride Star to the manor by way of the stream. It is a quicker way back. I will follow, find Star, and bring her home.'

Joseph made a leap onto the saddle, drawing Olive up in front of him. Without a further word, they were off for home.

It took only moments to reach the woods near the stable. Joseph secured the horse out of sight. Then then he grabbed Olive's hand while they ran for the back door of the kitchen.

The door was not quite closed behind them when Olive heard Ben's hooves trotting into the yard.

Joseph looked out the chamber window, watching for Hortencia's arrival.

The excursion had been a success in that Hortencia had not made it to the tavern, but the problem remained. She knew their greatest secret and meant to reveal it.

Olive was stepping into the gown she had discarded at the beginning of this caper, and he was watching that, too.

'Hurry, love. I see her crossing the paddock.'

All at once, Olive ceased fastening buttons and gave him a quizzical look.

Clearly she had not missed his slip of tongue.

Turning from the window, he hurried across the chamber, then finished buttoning up Olive's gown.

And then…then, with his hands on her shoulders, he drew her to him. Kissed her hard, urgently.

Hortencia would be halfway across the meadow by now, so he had no time to explain, even if he knew how. Only this afternoon, he had promised Olive he would be the husband she wished for him to be.

'We must hurry,' was all he said in the face of her astonishment.

They dashed downstairs, rushed through back hallways, passed by the kitchen and at last entered the parlor.

Grimacing, he greeted his parents with a nod. Mama and Father glanced at one another, brows raised.

'Back again?' his father asked. Who could blame him for seeming surprised? They had said their good-nights only an hour ago.

Joseph snatched a book from a shelf on the way to the couch. Pulling Olive down next to him, he opened it.

'*The Migration Patterns of Songbirds*,' Olive read the book title aloud. 'I have always wondered how it works.'

Three paragraphs into discovery, Hortencia burst into the room, breathing hard…but glaring harder.

At Olive.

'My word,' Olive exclaimed. 'You look a fright. Have you encountered some sort of mishap?'

'Indeed, my dear,' Mama said. 'You have ripped the hood of your cloak.'

Hortencia had something curled in her fist. Crossing the room, she let it fall on the open pages of the book.

'I found this in the hallway outside of the kitchen. It is a leaf.'

'I am sure my daughter-in-law will have a word with the housemaids in the morning. Certainly there is no reason to be distraught about a leaf on the floor,' Lady Claymore said.

'This woman is not who you think she is!' Hortencia swirled her cloak off her shoulders, displaying the damage done to the hood even though it had already been noted and commented on. 'She is a deceiver…a trickster! You see what she did with her sword.'

'You are overwrought.' Mama patted the couch, the spot between herself and Father. 'Please do sit down. I will ring for a cup of tea.'

'I was accosted by a phantom…her.' Hortencia pointed her finger at Olive.

'There have been rumours of a highwayman in the area. Although, who would believe it?' Joseph commented, snapping the book closed. The leaf fell on the floor. 'When did this happen?'

'You know very well when. Not twenty minutes ago. That was you howling in the bushes, wasn't it?'

'Really, Hortencia.' Father frowned. 'My heir howling in bushes? I rather doubt it.'

'We shall send for the doctor.' Mama rose. Crossing the room, she looked at Hortencia's face for a moment and then pressed the backs of her fingers to her forehead. Mama used this gesture to ferret out any sort of illness.

'People do take delight in spreading fearful tales,' Mama said.

Joseph wondered if his mother sensed the anger pulsing from her would-be patient.

Even sitting several feel away, he felt it. But it was probably because he knew why she was so angry.

'It is no tale. Olive is the highwayman.'

Mama shrugged, then frowned. 'You are speaking irrationally, although I do not detect a fever.'

Hortencia spun out from under the other woman's touch. She marched jerkily to the hearth, turned her back on them all and hugged her arms around her middle.

A tempest was about to be released in the parlor.

He reached for Olive's hand. Gave it a reassuring squeeze. She gave him one back. There was something very right about touching his wife. He was close to telling her so. Only not now. Later, if he was lucky enough to be allowed in her chamber. After kissing her again, he might not be.

For the moment, Hortencia was silent. The only sound in the room came from her skirt shifting across her hips while she swayed. Damned if it did not bring to mind a cobra in the moment before it strikes. This viper was rising for a final attack.

He prayed that they would all survive her venom.

'No matter how my parents react to this, you remain my wife,' he whispered to Olive. 'We have things to discuss.'

Olive nodded in the second that Hortencia pivoted, her eyes pinpoints of hatred. 'Oh my…isn't that the sweetest thing you have ever seen?'

'Aye, it is. As I have told you before, I love my wife.'

He felt Olive jerk at his words. She might be displeased to hear it was the truth.

'This would all be ever so admirable, so utterly charming…if there was any truth to it.' Hortencia's walked slowly toward his parents.

'What has come over you?' Mama's patience appeared to be at an end. 'Anyone can see how much my son and his wife love one another.'

'Nothing you have to say will change that, Hortencia,' Joseph pointed out, although he did not believe it would deter her from what she was bound to reveal.

It was only that he wished for his wife to know it.

'Dear Lady Amelia.' Hortencia took his mother's hand, her expression suddenly soft and sorrowful. 'I hate to be the one to reveal the truth, but no one else will, and I can no longer see you being taken advantage of.'

'I have no idea what you are going on about. Perhaps we should all retire before I discover what it is.'

'Hortencia does not believe that Olive and I are wed,' Joseph declared, deciding it would be better to lead the charge. Let the accuser be the one to defend herself.

'It is true, Lady Amelia. As I tried to tell you before,

they have been living in sin right under all of our noses. I cannot imagine a worse insult.'

'I see,' Mama said, her voice sounding calmer than it ought to after such a revelation. 'Please tell us why you think he would do so?'

'Our Joseph has been bewitched…clearly ensnared in some sort of enchantment.'

How right she was. At the end of this, Olive was going to know it, too. She might reject him. Regardless, he could no longer lie to her about his feelings.

'You are undone, Hortencia. Olive and I *are* wed. You cannot change it.'

'I would be undone, wouldn't I? Joseph and I are to wed. You, you wicked thing, have trapped him in an immoral liaison.'

'You are wrong,' Joseph stated.

'It must be true. Why else would you dally with a common goatherd when you could marry me?'

'Olive Billings…' he emphasized her new last name, making it clear that she belonged to him and this family '…is the finest lady I know.'

'You see? He is possessed. Surely, Lady Amelia, you will not allow this behaviour to carry on under your own roof. Tell your son to put her away and wed the woman he was intended to wed.'

Hortencia stepped close to Olive, her face a sneer.

In spite of the finger wagging near her nose, Olive appeared unflustered.

No acting the part of a lady, this. Olive was one, no matter her birth.

'I will not allow you to marry my husband.'

'Show me a wife who would?' was Father's comment on

the matter. He sat back on the couch, watching the drama unfold as it would. 'And just to be clear. This is Joseph's roof, not ours. A wedding gift from me and his mother.'

Mama caught Hortencia's finger, drawing it away from Olive's face. 'My dear, kindly act the lady you were brought up to be.'

'I was meant to be the future Lady Claymore.'

'Son, this matter can be cleared up easily enough. Be so good as to fetch your marriage certificate,' Father said, draping one arm across the back of the couch.

'Oh, by all means do that. He would never show it to me!'

'I cannot imagine why he would need to.' Father's casual pose belied his annoyance. Joseph knew the posture well.

'Lord Claymore, you are about to face a ruinous scandal. I will protect you from it by wedding your son, even though his behaviour of late is unforgivable. I will not let your family be brought to shame.'

'If there is shame brought upon us, it will be done by you, not me, Hortencia.' Joseph narrowed a gaze at her, then addressed his father. 'I will bring the certificate.'

Joseph strode the short distance down the hallway to his office and plucked the document out of the desk. He sniffed it. Close up, the ink still smelled fresh. Hopefully no one would notice.

More than that, he hoped his parents did not notice the date in the corner.

If they did, what Hortencia accused them of, living in sin, would appear to have been true for a time.

When he entered the parlor, Father and Mama stood close together.

His mother took the certificate. Father peered over her shoulder.

'This is…' Mama looked up sharply at him. Then she subtly covered the date with her thumb. 'Hortencia, come and have a look. We would appreciate putting this matter behind us.'

Mama gave her three full seconds to study the document before she snatched it away, folded it in quarters and handed it back to Joseph.

'Now that we have that nonsense settled,' Mama declared, 'I am certain you will be anxious to return to London, Hortencia. I have no doubt you miss society. You do seem out of sorts without it.'

'I am not out of sorts. However, you will be. There is something else. I would not normally bring it up as it is so indelicate. However, my hand is forced. I have knowledge of a matter which would ruin this family in society's eyes. You will not be welcomed into a decent home again.'

Mama grew pale. A respectable name was everything to her.

'You know of what I speak, Olive. Give Joseph back to me or I vow, I will tell everyone.'

Chapter Fifteen

When the moment came, it was worse than Olive could have imagined possible.

Seconds ago, she had believed that no matter what, she would never give in to Hortencia.

Joseph was her husband. She would not give him to anyone.

Now here she was, facing a decision. Who was she willing to ruin?

Would it be her sister? Sweet and innocent Laura?

Would it be her husband?

Or would it be the reputation of her new family?

No matter what choice she made, Olive, herself, was ruined, because whichever way she went with this, she could not live with the guilt.

A wave of nausea hit her hard. She pressed her fingers to her middle.

In the moment of stone silence which followed Hortencia's threat, a gust of wind whipped around the eaves, howling and putting her nerves further on edge. Probably everyone else's, too.

Joseph gave her a look which she could not interpret. Fear, perhaps, that she would hand him over to their enemy.

When she'd pledged herself to Joseph in marriage, she'd

meant it. Her life recently had been a series of lies, but those vows had been the truest words she had ever spoken, despite playing a part.

Would she now forsake him? Let no man separate them, the minister had said.

If she did not, Hortencia would rip her sister up without a qualm. In doing so, she would ruin the family only just begun. The damage to Laura would be unspeakable. What kind of twisted soul would label a child a bastard knowing the shame would follow her all her life? Fallen Leaf was a small village. It was not as if they could hide from the scandal. Even Mary and Harlow Strickland would suffer for their part in it.

'You have half a minute more. Then I will reveal the truth.'

'The truth, Hortencia?' Joseph placed a reassuring arm on Olive's shoulder. 'There is nothing you can say which will change the fact that Olive is the woman I chose to marry. Whatever she decides, I will not wed you.'

Strong words, determined ones.

And yet there was more to it. If she truly loved Joseph, and she did, would she allow the Claymore title to be besmirched?

Joseph's parents had accepted Olive, commoner that she was. They took her to their hearts when they might have rejected her. Back in London, her low birth was going to be gossiped about. These good people were willing to risk tainting the family name for her.

The truth that Hortencia threatened to reveal would be another thing all together. To accept a fallen woman as a part of one's family would be unthinkable. Their son's sister-in-law would certainly be a family member.

The truth that Olive had always valued was about to take her around the throat and choke her.

'Joseph,' she gasped, hugging him tight.

He pressed her head to his chest with his wide palm. His fingers curled in her hair, and his heart thumped hard under her ear.

None of this was his doing.

She loved him.

That was the end of it, was it not?

At their beginning, all he'd wanted was to escape this horrid woman who would have ruined his life. No one could fault him for it.

How could she now sacrifice him?

Joseph and his family or Eliza and hers?

No.

She could not.

Either way she went, she could not.

She had the impression Joseph wanted to say something to her but bit it back.

'What do you choose?' Hortencia actually stomped her foot in childish temper. 'I am finished waiting.'

Olive hated what she must do. Lives would be ruined.

She pushed out of Joseph's arms.

How was she to survive this?

'I choose my husband.' Grief for what everyone else would suffer brought tears to her eyes. 'Do what you will, Hortencia.'

'I have heard all I need to,' Lady Amelia declared, then walked to the bell pull and yanked on the cord. Within seconds, a footman entered the parlor. 'Ready the carriage for Lady Hortencia, please. Inform her maid that she will be leaving for London within the hour.'

'Right away, my lady.' The footman spun about and hurried to do as he was bid.

'Oh, but Lady Amelia, you know I only wish the best for this family,' Hortencia said. 'And so I must tell you what I know. It will break my heart, of course. Trust me, though, once you have heard the truth, it is that woman you will put on the coach.'

'Olive, my dear, it is apparent she is going to reveal something that should not be revealed. Would you like to be the one to tell us what it is? I do not trust Hortencia to present this in the most favourable light,' Lady Amelia said gently.

She would not like to, no…,it was the very last thing she wished, but she was grateful to be offered the chance.

'Thank you, I—'

'Her sister is a fallen woman! There is no favourable light.'

Hortencia's face looked harsh and unhinged. With her mask off, her genuine character made her pretty face ugly.

Her mother-in-law flinched.

Joseph's mother had overlooked a great deal when it came to Olive, but this…it would be too much to accept.

'I know it is a blow, Lady Amelia,' Hortencia cooed. 'The trollop is the woman who sells us cheese. I can only imagine she gave up her virtue for a penny and got stuck with the unhappy outcome.'

'She's called Eliza,' Olive put in. 'Her daughter's name is Laura.'

'Unhappy outcome?' Joseph snorted, his disapproval palpable. 'You are greatly mistaken. No mother cherishes her child more than Eliza does…or more than her aunt does.'

'Do you believe children to be a blessing, Hortencia?' Lady Amelia's voice was mild, but it was her viscountess voice, so Olive knew better than to believe mild was what she felt.

'Certain children, of course. This one was kept in the care of a neighbour. Can you believe it? Right next door to her disreputable mother. The apple does not fall far from the tree.'

'I believe that to be true…in some cases,' the viscount said, staring at Hortencia in disgust. 'Don't you agree, Amelia?'

'It does seem to be true, although I am sorry to say I did not recognize it until now. I do beg your forgiveness, Joseph.'

'I do not understand what we are talking about.' He lifted his brows, clearly as confused as Olive was.

'They are grateful I spoke up and saved the family from shame…before it all came to light from someone who did not care. We can be together now, Joseph, just as we were meant to be,' Hortencia implored.

'It would be prudent of you not to take this conversation any further than this room.' Lady Amelia leveled her weighty stare at Hortencia.

'It shall be our secret, Mama.'

'You do not seem to understand. I am *not* your mama, not in any sense of the word.'

'But I soon will be…' Lady Claymore shook her head one time, but once was all it took. 'Surely you are not suggesting that you will choose a commoner over me?' Hortencia exclaimed.

'I believe that *is* what she means,' the viscount said.

'Precisely what I mean. Understand this, Hortencia. Although you are a high-ranking lady of society by birth, you will still need to marry well to maintain your respectability.'

Hortencia lifted her perfect little nose, giving an imperious sniff. 'I have every intention of marrying well, with or without you.'

'I am sure you expect to. But let me ask, do you know how long it is between a child's conception and its birth?'

'A foolish question, and not to any point I can think of...but nine months.'

'Surely you are aware that many pregnancies, even in proper old London, are shorter? Some much shorter than others.'

Hortencia blinked, apparently not understanding.

'Our Joseph was a little early,' the viscount announced. Was that a gleam in his eye? Yes...quite clearly, it was a gleam. 'Eight weeks, wasn't it, my dear?'

'Yes, dear, eight and a half.'

'I was—' Joseph gasped, coughed, so Olive patted him helpfully on the back.

'You were a lusty nine pounds when you were born in spite of it.' Lady Amelia smiled at her son, then gave her attention back to Hortencia. 'You do understand what that means?'

'Well, I suppose...it means... I dare not say.'

'Do you not? I shall say it for you then. It is not all that rare for children to be conceived before the vows are spoken. I need for you to understand this before I continue with what I am going to tell you.'

'Very well.' Hortencia rolled her eyes as if saying none of this had to do with her or their present situation.

'To begin, your mother and I were friends, but not terribly close ones.'

'I know that. Everyone does. I do not know what it has to do with—'

'You were born at six months, Hortencia. Your mother conceived you well before she wed.'

'Ah,' the viscount declared with a grin. 'You and young Laura share a bond…being not quite the blessing other babies are, I mean.'

'What a vile thing to suggest! My birth was…it was… My mother was no fallen woman. She was a noble lady.'

'You are fortunate that she was. Because of it, your arrival in the world, at every bit of seven pounds, was remarked upon, but soon it was politely overlooked.'

The footman stepped into the parlor and nodded at Joseph's mother, indicating that the carriage was waiting.

'Well! I will make my escape. To think I nearly allowed myself to be attached this family.' Hortencia gave a smirking smile to each of them. 'I would say I wish you well, but I do not. There is no hope for any of you.'

'Be that as it may, Hortencia, but if you speak a single word against any member of my family, I will remind people of your…unusual birth. Do not think they will not recall it. No proper gentleman will have you.'

Storming towards the hallway, Hortencia cast a glare over her shoulder. 'You are cursed, the lot of you.'

As one, they gazed at the now empty doorway.

'I for one, feel blessed,' her father-in-law announced.

'Greatly,' his wife agreed. 'That woman would have crushed our boy. Olive, my dear, we are so pleased that it is you and not her.'

'And we are anxious to meet your niece.' The viscount grinned at his wife. 'What relation is she to us? Not granddaughter, but surely she is something special.'

'I do not believe there is a term for it, but she is our son's niece, and so we shall simply call her our special girl.'

Olive sat hard on the couch and began to weep. She and Joseph had survived the ordeal. Eliza and her family had as well. There was such relief and joy inside of her that tears were the only way of letting her emotions out.

A weight settled beside her. Motherly arms wrapped her up.

'No one will learn any of what went on here tonight. We may be a family with secrets, but all families have them. Dry your tears now, daughter. All is well.'

'It could not be better, if you ask me,' her father-in-law declared, patting Olive on top of her head. 'I never did trust Hortencia, even as a girl. Too much like her mother. The apple and the tree, and all that.'

'I am sorry to my soul that I pushed her on you, Joseph.' With that, Lady Amelia kissed Olive's forehead, then rose from the couch. She hugged her son about the ribs. 'Please forgive me.'

'Always, Mama,' he said.

'I am quite done in, Marshall.' She sighed. 'Take me upstairs.'

Arms about each other's waists, Lady and Lord Claymore walked towards the doorway.

Without turning, Joseph's mama said, 'Tomorrow we shall discuss your marriage licence…that bit about the date.'

They disappeared down the hallway.

'Just when I thought our troubles were over,' Olive said.

'A small skirmish, that's all.'

Joseph wondered what would Olive do when they reached her chamber door.

Now that Hortencia was no longer a threat, there was no reason for her to invite him in.

No one else to be fooled…no more lessons to be learned.

She reached for the doorknob, but he caught her hand.

'May I come in? I wish to have a word.'

'It would probably not be wise.' She slipped her fingers out of his, opened the door and stepped into the room.

She pushed it closed, but he caught it with his hand. 'I am done being wise, Olive.'

'I am not sure what you mean but…' She let go of the door and stepped aside to let him in.

Good so far, but it was not her chamber he wished to be in. It was her heart.

How to get there, though? What words were there to open that door?

None.

He cupped her cheeks, lifted her face, then bent his head to kiss her. Actions were better than words. He might stumble over finding the right ones, but it was his heart speaking.

She did not struggle against him, so that was hopeful. But dash it, she did not lean in and give herself over to him, either.

'I have something to say to you, Olive. If it makes you unhappy, I will not stop you from going.'

'Going where?'

'Home.'

'Humph.' She pushed against his chest, freeing herself of his embrace, although she did not step away. 'And where do you suppose home is?'

'At the cottage, with your family?'

'I say this in friendship, but you are a fool, Joseph Billings. We shall discuss it further after you explain why you are toying with me by continuing to kiss me when you have made it perfectly clear that—'

'That I love you.'

'You…' Her cheeks flushed, and her eyes shimmered. 'I do not believe you. Only last night, you ran from—'

'Aye, love, I was a fool.'

'Maybe this is you being a fool again.' She crossed her arms over her chest, narrowed her eyes.

'Put me to the test. See if I flee or I stay.'

'How do you know I will not be the one to flee this time?'

'All I know is that I love you. If you do not love me, too, you may tell me to go at any time, and I will. But if we are together at the end of it, then we will have gained the world.'

'At the end of what?'

'Our conversation.'

He took her by the shoulders and backed her toward the bed.

The mattress made all sorts of creaking sounds when he tumbled down onto it, drawing her on top of him.

He kissed her again. This time she warmed to it but cautiously.

'This is not talking, Joseph.'

'It is, love, only without tricky words to get in the way.'

'I need to hear the tricky words. Last time we spoke without them, I thought certain things, and then…well, I was wrong about them.'

'You were not wrong. I was.' He picked the pins from her hair. It tumbled over his face in a soft tangle. 'I was wrong about how I felt, wrong about how you felt.'

She squirmed on top of him as if shuffling out of her slippers, one then the other.

'I never told you how I felt, Joseph.'

'Oh, aye, love. You've told me many times.'

She lifted up on her hands, shook her head. With her

hair falling all around, it seemed as if they were enclosed in a silky tunnel.

'When?'

Since she was lifted up, he took the opportunity to free the buttons of her bodice.

'There was the time you came to me that windy night and agreed to help me.'

'I did not say I loved you then. I only agreed that we could help one another.'

Ah, things were looking up now, as she began unfastening his shirt buttons.

'Then you will recall the time when you tried to leave me wearing only your shift?'

'I do not know how you can take that as saying I loved you, either.'

'I can, because you stayed.' With her gown open, he discovered a delicate blue bow holding her chemise closed. He tugged it open. 'Then there was the time you knocked me off the log and urged me to ravage you. That was love.'

'No, it was protecting you from a viper.' She undid a button on his trousers. Words were working better than he'd expected.

She rolled off him so that they lay facing one another.

'Truly, love, I knew it when you chose to save me.'

'Oh…' She touched his cheek, drew her fingers across his lips. 'Well then, you were not wrong.'

'I need to hear the tricky words, too.' Joseph looked vulnerable all at once. Her heart rolled all over itself. 'That night, the reason I left your bed was that I thought you did not want me to love you.'

'But I did.' She kissed him softly on his lips, then moved

so it was easier for him to get her arms out of her gown. 'I do now… Joseph, I love you. You hold my heart.'

'Aye, and you hold mine. It will always be in the palm of your capable little hand.' He kissed her fingers. 'Now, we must put our words to the test, aye? If neither of us flees the bed, we have our proof.'

'The suspense will be too much.'

'Not to fear, I will assure you as we go.'

Olive closed her eyes, feeling reassurance in each touch. When she opened her eyes, she saw love reflected back at her.

The last thing she intended to do was flee. She meant to have this spot beside him, and in his heart, for the rest of her life.

The night went on speaking in tender touches. For the longest time, they did not even need words at all.

At last, when the first bird began to sing, Joseph said, 'Here we are then. Neither of us fled.'

'But I wonder, maybe we should give it another hour or so, just to be sure?'

Three hours later, Olive watched her husband busy at the shaving bowl. His back moved with each stroke of the razor.

What a fine, strong back it was. She had reason to know.

She sighed, not bothering to hide the sound. She did not bother to hide anything from Joseph now.

'What?' he asked, turning to look at her with white froth covering half of his jaw.

'I was just thinking how good it is to look at a finely made naked man and know he is yours.'

'Oh, aye? You think me finely made?' He grinned through

the shaving cream. 'I am not naked, though. There's the towel.'

'In my mind you are.'

'Ah.' He loosened the towel and let it drop. 'You do my ego a great deal of good.'

'What do you think, Joseph? Did we start a child last night?'

He grinned, nodded, wiped his face and then strode towards the bed. 'We were rather diligent in our efforts. But just in case, we really ought to give it another go.'

'Are you certain you are not saying that simply to avoid facing your parents this morning?'

'A grandchild would go a good way towards them looking kindly on the date of our marriage.'

Olive sat up, reaching for Joseph's trousers, which were in the exact spot he had dropped them last night. 'Put them on. We must face our comeuppance.'

'I don't regret what we did, love, no matter how it looks to anyone else.'

Nor did she. Life was coming about as nicely as if it were a book which she'd written with her own hand.

Chapter Sixteen

All during breakfast the next morning, Joseph expected to be called to account for the discrepancy of when his parents had believed him and Olive to be wed and the actual date on their marriage licence.

It never did come up, but something else did.

Between his last chew of ham and his first bite of toast, his mother asked, 'Would it be appropriate for us to take a walk to the village and meet your sister-in-law and her family?'

'We are anxious to get acquainted with little Laura,' Father said. 'We have not had a child in the family since our boy was small. Will your sister mind if we come by?'

'She will be over the moon, I am certain. No one in Fallen Leaf has ever had a visit from a viscount and viscountess.'

Which was the point of the visit, Joseph suspected. If there was anyone in the village who questioned Laura's sudden adoption by Eliza and James, or speculated about her birth, a visit from peers of the realm would forever validate her.

To be accepted by Lord and Lady Claymore would place Eliza's family above reproach.

'Isn't this the day James bakes our favourite bread?' Going to the village seemed a fine outing. 'It is worth every step of the walk just to smell it baking.'

Once along the way, he noticed his mother looking at the swathe of pure blue sky visible beyond the treetops.

'It is no wonder you love it here, Joseph. The weather is lovely. I can nearly taste autumn coming.'

'We will miss it here, son.' Father breathed in a deep, dramatic breath of crisp air. 'But we must return home. Lady Green has her autumn ball in two weeks. Everyone in society will be there. Also, it would be wise for us to keep an eye on Hortencia for a while.'

'It would not hurt to find her a husband.' Mama stooped and picked up a leaf whose edges were beginning to turn yellow. She twirled it in her fingers, looking thoughtful.

Thoughtful about last night, Joseph suspected, and wondering why Hortencia had put so much focus on a leaf.

'Ah, I pity the poor fellow, though.' His father shook his head. 'Tell us, son, why is your wedding certificate dated after you claimed to be wed?'

'There is a good reason for it.' Hopefully his parents would think so. He might be a man grown, but still, their approval was important to him. 'I was desperate to avoid Hortencia. I knew she meant to compromise me. It would not have been so difficult to do here with so few people around.'

'And at the same time, there was my father,' Olive said. 'He had it in his mind that as the oldest daughter, I would wed first. He was insisting I marry James, who was Eliza's true love. I could not have done it, naturally.'

'It only made sense for us to pretend we were wed… We meant to go our own ways once everyone went home.'

'A sensible plan,' Father said with a nod. 'But how would you have explained going your own ways?'

'We never did come up with an explanation.' He grinned at Olive. 'It's why we wed.'

'He is making that up. We had to wed because Hortencia suspected we were not.'

'Are you claiming you were forced to wed against your will? If so, I do not believe you,' Mama said archly.

'Forced, yes…but glad for it,' he answered in all truth.

'It is not for me to pry, or to judge, and yet…' He had never seen his mother blush, but she did it now. 'Joseph, you… How do I say this?'

'We did not share a chamber until after we wed.' Olive blushed as deeply as his mother did.

'Only the once,' Joseph amended truthfully, thinking of the night before their wedding.

'Heaven help me,' Mama muttered. 'And you, dear Olive. I believe you will need what help you can get.'

'Nothing untoward happened that night.' His bride cast him a frown. Not a terribly annoyed one, though.

'It is true. But it did make it clear that we wanted something untoward to happen. So when Hortencia forced the issue, we were well and gone, past willing.' He and his father shared a grin.

'Men…incorrigible, the lot of them, no matter their age.'

Olive slipped her hand into the crook of her new mother's arm while they walked, Joseph and his father a step behind.

High up, tree limbs on each side of the road met, making a canopy and giving the path a pretty dappled look. All around, leaves rustled and whispered.

'Joseph makes it sound as if he was a rogue. The truth is, you raised your son well. He was always respectful.'

'I am not one to judge in any case.'

'That is not our job, is it…to judge?' Olive said. 'Ours is to forgive. I hope you forgive us for tricking you.'

'Oh, quite.' Mama patted Olive's fingers. 'I trust there are no more secrets.'

'I do not see how there could be.' Father laughed when he said so.

Joseph took a long step, bringing him alongside Olive. He gave her a wink and a grin. She shrugged…nodded.

Taking his elbow, she drew him back a step. 'From now on, I am going to live a strictly honest life. I do not wish to take part in any more schemes.'

'Agreed.'

His parents turned, probably wondering what the whispering was about.

'There is just one more thing.'

'Will I require a fainting couch, son?'

'I think not, Mama…only… You have heard of the fearful highwayman ghoul?'

Both his parents blinked, silent and clearly puzzled.

'The one with the fire-eyed horse…sprung from the underworld?' he clarified.

Father's brows nearly touched. 'Oh, that one. Indeed we have.'

'Aye, well…it was Olive.'

Two weeks after Joseph's parents returned to London, Eliza invited Olive and Joseph to dinner, along with the sisters' father.

It proved to be a happy time which dissolved the last of her concerns that the lives of a viscount and a cottager would not mesh.

She ought to have known it would be this way between

the families since it had always been so between her and Joseph.

Even in the times when her mind warned her they could never be together, her heart knew the truth. She and Joseph were destined for one another. How else would they have overcome what obstacles society had placed between them?

While they ate, laughed, and talked about everything from making cheese to the proper way to hold a dance partner, it became clear that they, all of them, high born and common, were family.

She'd got a sense of kinship taking root on the day they had walked to the village with Joseph's parents so that they could meet Eliza, James and Laura.

Tonight, before the meal was finished, she no longer recognized a separation of class, only people coming together to celebrate.

It was after sunset when she and Joseph walked her father home. In the west, lightning glittered over the hilltop. Cooling air smelled damp with a coming storm.

Father had no sooner waved them goodbye and closed the cottage door when rain hit hard.

If they ran for home, they would get drenched. If they took shelter in the cottage, they would not be alone.

'The stable.' Joseph snatched her hand. They dashed around to the back of the cottage, then along a short path.

Olive drew open the stable doors, breathing in the mingled scents of goat and fresh straw. She loved living in the manor house, but she also loved it here. One more illustration, she thought, of how the two sides of her life could meld.

She did not need to choose one over the other. Because Joseph was hers, both lives were as well.

'What is behind that pretty smile, love?'

'Well…it's love.'

Gilroy rose from his straw bed, gave a bleat and then nudged Olive's hand to be petted.

'Looks like I am not the only one in love with you.'

Olive stroked the goat between his ears. Gilroy leaned against her, clearly content.

'He misses me, I suppose.' Although she did visit the flock nearly every afternoon. 'I used to sing to them in the morning.'

'Can't blame the poor fellow. I'd miss it if you did not sing to me.'

'When do I sing to you?'

'You don't know?' His eyes warmed, and his mouth quirked up at one corner. He touched her lips with his thumb then drew it down her throat in slow circles.

When he kissed her, she sighed, gave a little moan.

'Aye, just so.'

'That is not singing,' she protested.

'But it is, the sweetest love song a man could hear.' All of a sudden, Joseph jerked and spun about, swiping at the seat of his trousers.

'Gilroy! You little beast! You should be ashamed.' But then she grabbed her middle and laughed.

The sight of the goat placidly chewing a torn piece of Joseph's trousers was too much. The humour could not be ignored.

Not by her, at any rate.

'Curse the beast!' Joseph plucked the shredded threads of the hole Gilroy ate in the wool.

'And to think, that at this very moment we could be attending the Autumn Ball,' she said.

They had been invited to the grand event but had promptly declined the honour.

Not that Olive wasn't curious about that side of her husband's life. One day she would be required to be a part of it.

Not yet, though. For now, they did not wish to share each other's company with anyone.

'I do not mind missing it any more than you do,' he said while brushing a curious kid away from the hem of his trousers.

Joseph took her by one hand, twirling her in a circle. 'We shall enjoy a private ball, right here among our four-legged friends. See how they enjoy our skilful steps.'

He waltzed her over bits of straw on the stone floor. Star whinnied when they whirled by her stall. Olive did enjoy dancing this way, the steps so smooth and elegant. A day was coming when she would wear a fine gown and spin about a crowded ballroom, but it could not be as lovely as this moment.

No orchestra would match the soft bleats of the kids, the whicker and stomping of hooves…the rush of Joseph's breathing.

Joseph changed the pace of the dance. Slower, then slower still, until they were simply standing and swaying…looking at one another in a language which went beyond words.

She touched his chest, tapped her fingers on one button of his shirt. Her message was clear…she wanted him…quite impatiently.

When he pressed his big hands on her waist and drew her tight against his hips, she supposed it was his answer. She would have him…and he would have her.

'That ladder,' he whispered. 'Is it solid, and where does it lead to?'

'Solid.' She lifted her chin, indicating the top of the ladder. 'We keep fresh straw up there…and blankets.' The loft was her favourite place to read.

'Come then, love.' With his fingers pressing her waist, he walked her backward, step by slow, sultry step. 'I wish to hear you sing.'

Epilogue

Claymore House, London,
December, one year later

'Are you nervous?' Joseph murmured.

Olive nodded. 'Does the trembling show?'

Members of proper society were beginning to enter the grand parlor. She and Joseph stood beside his parents, her father, then Eliza and James next to them.

Lady Amelia had promised this would be a comfortable evening at home with some of their dearest friends stopping by to meet the newest members of the family.

She was certain introducing one's country kin to society was not usual, but having country kin was not usual either.

She admired her new parents for being so comfortable in their social position that they did not fear doing so. To Olive's way of thinking, they set the trends which others would imitate. Hopefully, they would. If they did not, she would follow Lord and Lady Claymore's example and not be troubled by it.

As it turned out, a few of Viscount and Viscountess Claymore's dearest friends made up a large crowd. In fact, they would add up to more than the population of Fallen Leaf.

Olive could only wonder what her father thought about

being stuffed into black formal wear and glossy shoes. He did look wonderful.

While he was so fine and dapper, his own goats would run from him, not recognizing who he was.

Olive scarcely recognized him either. The change in her father made her soul sing in gratitude. He had kept his promise to Mama and gone all this time without drinking. She had every hope he would continue that way. These days when he went to The Shepherd's Keep, it was to visit friends and puff out his chest over who his new relatives were.

More voices came from outside. She must have shivered or gasped or done something to alert Joseph she was nervous.

'Draw on a character, the way you used to do,' Joseph suggested softly. 'It will settle you.'

'No, I cannot. I am standing here as myself. People will accept me or not. I will not present a false character.'

'Good then. I like you fine as you are. Everyone else will, too.'

'They will pretend to, anyway, for your parents' sake.'

'It's true. All my life I have had to puzzle over who is a friend and who only pretends to be.' He squeezed her hand. As always, his strong presence calmed her. 'We will be home soon, and it will not matter. Let us muddle on.'

'You do not need to muddle, Joseph. You were born knowing what to do.'

His gaze grew suddenly warm with the expression she knew quite intimately. 'I know what I want to do.'

She did, too, and longed to run away upstairs with him.

'Later.' She jumped when he discreetly tickled her ribs. 'But look who has just made their entrance, the Curtis family. Your mother says that Grace is betrothed.'

Olive watched the sisters walking side by side. One Curtis girl had the fair good looks and proper attitude which society adored. The other Curtis girl was taller than most ladies, and slim, with eyes a deep shade of warm brown.

To Olive's way of thinking, Vivienne was lovely, even if she was not society's prescribed beauty.

'I do like Vivienne,' she remarked. 'I hope she gets what she wants from life, even if it is not a husband.'

'It is different for daughters of a lord. They wed for advantage. Same as first-born sons do.' He gave her a wink and a grin. 'I wed for great advantage.'

'Our daughters will wed as they wish. They will have the futures they want to have. We shall see to it.'

'So we shall. But if we have a son, he will be born to obligation.'

'Such nonsense you speak, Joseph. You have the life you chose.'

'By some miraculous good fortune, I do. I wonder if good fortune can be passed from father to son. I will say it can and believe our boy will be as happy as I am. But so far, we do not have a son or a daughter.'

'I hear an orchestra beginning to play. Dance with me.'

Waltzing with Joseph was rather like floating on a delightful cloud. For those few moments with her feet not touching the earth, everything was perfect.

'I've had news,' Joseph said, grinning in the mischievous way he had.

'Good news, I hope.'

'Depends upon who you are. For us, it is.'

'Then who is it not good for?'

'Hortencia.' He gave her a quick spin. 'It seems that she has fallen into her own trap. She set her cap for a marquis's son. Meant to trap him in the dark where she would compromise him.'

'As she enjoys doing.'

'It did not end well for her, though. Seems the wrong fellow came by and fell into it, a second cousin to the fellow she wanted. A good man, but not of the highest ranking. Well, she pounced upon him. Then, when her chaperone discovered them, as they had arranged for her to do, Hortencia was in the embrace of the wrong man. They are to wed next week.'

'Poor fellow.'

Olive was kept from laughing aloud when her sister walked past.

'Will her babe wait until the party is over to be born, do you think?' Joseph asked, his eyes going wide at his sister-in-law's large, cumbersome form.

'She has a bit of time yet, she thinks.'

'She also says her children need cousins.' He waggled a brow at her. 'All children need cousins. Makes life happier.'

A cold December breeze blew in through an open garden door, fluttering her skirts and ruffling Joseph's coat sleeves. The air was refreshing, and she took a deep breath to savour it.

'Come to the garden with me,' she said, leading him out of the door and ignoring his warning that it was too chilly outside.

With all the talk of cousins, time alone was called for. The house so full of people that she would need the privacy of the garden.

Joseph sat on a bench, drawing her down beside him. With a sigh, she snuggled close, as content as she had ever been in her life.

How could she have ever doubted that life would be easy between them, despite their birth?

Only a few people strolled in the garden. Some of them nodded, and others stopped only long enough to offer their congratulations.

London was not as bad as she had imagined it would be. The people of high society seemed polite and gracious for the most part.

Still, she would be glad to go home. There was much to get ready before spring came.

Olive snuggled deeper into Joseph's side. How delightfully big and warm he was. 'I am so happy I could burst.'

She said this as a clue for him to follow…a crumb to a puzzle's end.

'I'm so cold I could shiver.'

He lifted her chin with one knuckle, then kissed her.

'Hmm, you are cold; that was certainly an icy kiss.'

'I reckon you will need to warm me up. You know how.' What a wonderfully suggestive grin it was, given in the most inappropriate location.

Still, she could not resist kissing him over and over again. He was correct about it being cold outside. However, she needed a bit more time out here.

Eventually, light in the garden grew dim. Distant voices grew fainter. The guests must be going inside.

'We should join them before we turn to ice statues.'

'Soon. Just… I am so happy I really could burst,' she repeated.

'I'd just as well have you whole, if it is all the same to you.'

'Very, very whole, then,' she said, but he was still not catching on. 'Immensely whole.'

'Can you be immensely whole indoors, please?'

He tugged her up from the bench, curled his big body around her and rocked back and forth for a minute.

His breath felt wonderfully warm on her hair.

'It is more that I will be immensely whole, late next spring.'

He cocked his head. 'You are speaking in riddles, love. Tell me directly what is on your mind so we can go back in. Your lips are turning blue, and I think I just saw a snowflake.'

She could do that, but this was so much more fun. In spite of the weather, she wanted to drag out her fun for as long as she could.

Not his fun, she thought, since he was beginning to frown. He would cheer up when she got to the end of it.

'Do you recall a few moments ago when you said that Eliza's children ought to have a cousin?'

A light flashed in Joseph's eyes. Comprehension, she hoped.

'And you are about to burst in the late spring…with the cousin?'

'With your son or daughter.'

'Ah, my sweet Olive. You make me a grateful man, a thousand times over. You will be the loveliest bursting woman come spring. I cannot wait to see it.'

Snow began to fall in earnest now. It seemed to wrap them in a blanket of white, silent velvet.

'It is as if we are alone in London,' she murmured.

'Not so alone, aye?' He pressed his hand to her only slightly rounded stomach.

'I think I felt it move.'

'Not yet. That must have been me shivering…or you.'

'Must be me since now I'm shivering with joy. But let's go inside before our wee baby freezes.'

They were steps from the door when Joseph stopped short.

'Did you see it?'

'See what?'

'Just there, a flash in the shrubbery near the door.'

Oh, dear, she ought to have let him come inside sooner. Now he was imagining things. She peered into the bush, though, just to humour him.

But then...she squinted her eyes at something, its blue and green wings fluttering gently.

'It's a dragonfly! But I can scarce believe it. It is long past their season.'

'Like the one from our wedding day. It was on your finger. I took it then as a hopeful omen.'

The insect flew away and disappeared among the snowflakes.

They blinked at one another.

Olive was the first to recover her voice. 'Did we really see what we thought we did?'

'Maybe...or maybe not. Except it was both of us seeing it.'

Olive took his hand, leading him inside, where a rush of warmth wrapped them up.

'Do you think that was the point? To remind us of that day...that it's the two of us, always.'

'Maybe so. I like the romance of it.' Then he kissed her for a long time. 'The thing of it is, I do not need an insect to remind me. You do it every day.'

'When do I do that? I do not recall saying so.'

'But you do. When you smile at me...when we laugh together, and when you snuggle up to me during the night... especially then.'

He kissed her yet again, a long, slow, forever sort of kiss.

'And when you make those sweet little sighs and moans like you did just now. Oh, aye, love. There is good fortune and forever in it.'

Something mysterious bubbled deep inside her belly, a sweet private tickle.

Good fortune, wonderful blessings.

* * * * *

Keep reading for an excerpt of a new title
from the Special Edition series,
TAMING A HEARTBREAKER by Brenda Jackson

Prologue

Sloan and Leslie Outlaw's wedding...

"Sloan definitely likes kissing you, girlfriend."

Leslie Outlaw couldn't help but smile at her best friend's whispered words. "And I love kissing him."

She'd married the man she loved, and she'd had her best friend Carmen Golan at her side. Leslie followed her friend's gaze now and saw just where it had landed—right on Redford St. James, who was being corralled by the photographer as Sloan took pictures with his best man and groomsmen.

Unease stirred Leslie's insides at her friend's obvious interest.

Leslie had known Redford for as long as she'd known Sloan, since she'd met both guys the same day on the university's campus over ten years ago. Redford had been known then as a heartbreaker. According to Sloan, Redford hadn't changed. If anything, he'd gotten worse.

"Carmen, I need to warn you about Redford," Leslie said, hoping it wasn't too late. She'd noted last night at the rehearsal how taken her best friend had been with Redford. She'd hoped she was mistaken.

"I know all about him, Leslie, so you don't need to warn me. However, you might want to put a bug in Sloan's ear to warn Redford about me."

Leslie lifted a brow. "Why?"

A wide smile covered Carmen's face. "Because Redford

St. James is the man I intend to marry. Your hubby is on his way over here. I will see you at the reception."

Leslie watched Carmen walk toward Redford. Marry? Redford? She had a feeling her best friend was biting off more than she could chew. Redford was not the marrying kind. He'd made that clear when he'd said no woman would ever tame him.

Chapter One

Two years later...

Redford St. James froze, with his wineglass midway to his lips, when he saw the woman walk into the wedding reception for Jaxon and Nadia Ravnell. Frowning, he immediately turned to the man by his side, Sloan Outlaw. During their college days at the University of Alaska at Anchorage, Sloan, Redford, and another close friend, Tyler Underwood, had been thick as thieves, and still were.

Redford had been known as the "king of quickies." He would make out with women any place or any time. Storage rooms, empty classrooms or closets, beneath the stairs, dressing rooms …he'd used them all. He had the uncanny ability to scope out a room and figure out just where a couple could spend time for pleasure. He still had that skill and used it every chance he got.

Although he, Sloan and Tyler now lived in different cities in Alaska, they still found the time to get together a couple of times a year. Doing so wasn't as easy as it used to be since both Tyler and Sloan were married with a child each. Tyler had a son and Sloan a daughter.

"Why didn't you tell me Carmen Golan was invited to this wedding?"

Sloan glanced over at Redford and rolled his eyes. "Just

like you didn't tell me Leslie had been invited to Tyler and Keosha's wedding three years ago?"

Redford frowned. "Don't play with me, Sloan. You should have known Leslie would be invited, since she and Keosha were friends in college. In this case, I wasn't aware Carmen knew Jaxon or Nadia."

Sloan took a sip of his wine before saying, "The Outlaws and Westmorelands consider themselves one big happy family, and that includes outside cousins, in-laws and close friends. Since Carmen is Leslie's best friend, of course she would know them." Sloan then studied his friend closely. "Why does Carmen being here bother you, Redford? If I recall, when I put that bug in your ear after my wedding, that she'd said she intended to one day become your wife, you laughed it off. Has that changed?"

"Of course, that hasn't changed."

"You're sure?" Sloan asked. "It seems to me that over the past two years, whenever the two of you cross paths, you try like hell to avoid her. Most recently, at Cassidy's christening a few months ago." Cassidy was Sloan and Leslie's daughter. Redford was one of her godfathers, and Carmen was her godmother.

"No woman can change my ways. I don't ever intend to marry. Who does she think she is, anyway? She doesn't even know me like that. If she did, then she would know my only interest in her at your wedding was getting her to the nearest empty coat closet. The nerve of her, thinking she can change me."

"And since you know she can't change you, why worry about it?"

"I'm not worrying."

"If you say so," Sloan countered.

Redford's frown deepened. "I do say so. You of all people should know that I'll never fall in love again."

Before Sloan could respond, his sister Charm walked up and said the photographer wanted to take a photo of Jaxon with his Outlaw cousins.

When Sloan walked off, leaving Redford alone, he took a sip of his wine as he looked across the room at Carmen again. Sloan's words had hit a nerve. He *wasn't* worried. Then why had he been avoiding her for the past two years? Doing so hadn't been easy since he was one of Sloan's best friends and she was Leslie's, and both were godparents to Cassidy. Whenever they were in the same space, he made it a point to not be in her presence for long.

He could clearly recall the day he'd first seen Carmen at Sloan and Leslie's wedding rehearsal two years ago. He would admit that he'd been intensely attracted to her from the first. It was a deep-in-the-gut awareness. Something he had never experienced before. He hadn't wasted any time adding her to his "must do" list. He'd even flirted shamelessly after they'd been introduced, with every intention of making out with her before the weekend ended.

Then he'd gotten wind of her bold claim that he was the man she intended to marry. Like hell! That had wiped out all his plans. He was unapologetically a womanizer, and no woman alive would change that.

Carmen wasn't the first woman to try, nor would she be the first to fail. Granted she was beautiful. Hell, he'd even say she was "knock-you-in-the-balls" gorgeous, but he'd dated beautiful women before. If he'd seen one, he'd seen them all, and in the bedroom they were all the same.

Then why was he letting Carmen Golan get to him? Why would heat flood his insides whenever he saw her, making him aware of every single thing about her? Why was there this strong kinetic pull between them? It was sexual chemistry so powerful that, at times, it took his breath away.

Over the years, he'd tried convincing himself his lust for

her would fade. So far it hadn't. And rather recently, whenever he saw her, it had gotten so bad he had to fight like hell to retain his common sense.

Although Sloan had given him that warning two years ago, Carmen hadn't acted on anything. Was she waiting for what she thought would be the right time to catch him at a weak moment? If that was her strategy then he had news for her. It wouldn't happen. If anything, he would catch *her* unawares first, just to prove he was way out of her league…thanks to Candy Porter.

Contrary to her first name, he'd discovered there hadn't been anything sweet about Candy. At seventeen, she had taught him a hard lesson. Mainly, to never give your heart to a woman. Candy and her parents had moved to Skagway the summer before their last year of high school. By the end of the summer, she had been his steady girlfriend, the one he planned to marry after he finished college. Those plans ended the night of their high school senior prom.

Less than an hour after they'd arrived, she told him she needed to go to the ladies' room. When she hadn't returned in a timely manner, he had gotten worried since she hadn't been feeling well. He had gone looking for her, and when a couple of girls said she wasn't in the ladies' room, he and the two concerned girls had walked outside and around the building to find her, hoping she was alright.

Not only had they found her, they'd found her with the town's bad boy, Sherman Sharpe. Both of them in the backseat of Sherman's car making out like horny rabbits. The pair hadn't even had the decency to roll up the car's window so their moans, grunts and screams couldn't be heard.

Needless to say, news of Candy and Sherman's backseat romp quickly got around. By the following morning, every household in Skagway, Alaska, had heard about it. She had tried to explain, offer an excuse, but as far as he'd been concerned, there was nothing a woman could say when caught with another man between her legs.

Heartbroken and hurt, Redford hadn't wasted any time leaving Skagway for Anchorage to begin college that summer, instead of waiting for fall. That's when he vowed to never give his heart to another woman ever again.

That had been nearly nineteen years ago, and he'd kept the promise he'd made to himself. At thirty-six, he guarded his heart like it was made of solid gold and refused to let any woman get close. He kept all his hookups impersonal. One-and-done was the name of his game. No woman slept in his bed, and he never spent the entire night in theirs. He refused to wake up with any woman in his arms.

Redford knew Carmen was his total opposite. He'd heard she was one of those people who saw the bright side of everything, always positive and agreeable. On top of that, she was a hopeless romantic. A woman who truly believed in love, marriage and all that bull crap. According to Sloan, she'd honestly gotten it in her head that she and Redford were actual soulmates. Well, he had news for her, he was no woman's soulmate.

When his wineglass was empty, he snagged another from the tray of a passing waiter. When he glanced back over at Carmen, he saw she was staring at him, and dammit to hell, like a deer caught in headlights, he stared back. Why was he feeling this degree of lust that she stirred within him so effortlessly?

There wasn't a time when she didn't look stunning. Today was no exception. There was just something alluring about her. Something that made his breath wobble whenever he stared at her for too long.

He blamed it on the beauty of her cocoa-colored skin, her almond-shaped light brown eyes, the gracefulness of her high cheekbones, her tempting pair of lips, and the mass of dark brown hair that fell past her shoulders.

Every muscle in his body tightened as he continued to look

at her, checking her out in full detail. His gaze scanned over her curvaceous and statuesque body. The shimmering blue dress she wore hugged her curves and complemented a gorgeous pair of legs. The bodice pushed up her breasts in a way that made his mouth water.

"Now you were saying," Sloan said, returning and immediately snagging Redford's attention.

"I was saying that maybe I should accommodate Carmen."

That sounded like a pretty damn good idea, considering the current fix his body was in.

"Meaning what?" Sloan asked.

A smile widened across Redford's lips. "Meaning, I think I will add her back to my 'must do' list. Maybe it's time she discovers I am a man who can't be tamed."

Sloan frowned. "Do I need to warn you that Carmen is Leslie's best friend?"

"No, but I would assume, given my reputation, that Leslie has warned Carmen about me. It's not my fault if she didn't take the warning. Now, if you will excuse me, I think I'll head over to the buffet table."

He then walked off. At least for now, he would take care of one appetite, and he intended to take care of the other before the night was over.

"I wish you and Redford would stop trying to out-stare each other, Carmen," Leslie Outlaw leaned over to whisper to her best friend.

Carmen Golan broke eye contact with Redford to glance at Leslie and couldn't help the smile that spread across her lips. "Hey, what can I say? He looks so darn good in a suit."

Leslie rolled her eyes. "Need I remind you that you've seen him in a suit before. Numerous times."

"Redford wore a tux at your wedding, Leslie, and he looked

good then, too. Better than good. He looked scrumptious." Carmen watched him again. He definitely looked delicious now.

She knew he was in his late thirties. He often projected a keen sense of professionalism, as well as a high degree of intelligence far beyond his years. But then there were other times when it seemed the main thing on his agenda was a conquest. Namely, seducing a woman.

Carmen knew all about his reputation as a heartbreaker of the worst kind. She'd witnessed how he would check out women at various events, seeking out his next victim. He had checked her out the same way, the first time they'd met.

She'd also seen the way women checked him out, too and definitely understood why they fell for him when he was so darn handsome. His dark eyes, coffee-colored skin, chiseled and bearded chin, hawkish nose, and close-to-the-scalp haircut, were certainly a draw.

Then there was his height. Carmen was convinced he was at least six foot three with a masculine build of broad shoulders, muscular arms and a rock-hard chest. Whenever he walked, feminine eyes followed. According to Leslie, although he made Anchorage his home, his family lived in Skagway and were part of the Tlingits, the largest Native Alaskan tribe.

Since their initial meeting two years ago, he'd kept his distance and she knew the reason why. She'd deliberately let it be known that she planned to marry him one day, making sure he heard about her plans well in advance. And upon hearing them, he'd begun avoiding her.

"Granted, it's obvious there's strong sexual chemistry between you and Redford," Leslie said, interrupting Carmen's thoughts. "Sexual chemistry isn't everything. At least you've given up the notion of trying to tame him. I'm glad about that. You had me worried there for a while."

Carmen broke eye contact with Redford and looked at Leslie. "Nothing has changed, Leslie. I'm convinced that for me it was love at first sight. Redford is still the man I intend to marry."

Leslie looked surprised. "But you haven't mentioned him in months. And at Cassidy's christening you didn't appear to pay him any attention."

Carmen grinned. "I've taken the position with Redford that I refuse to be like those other women who are always fawning over him. Women he sees as nothing more than sex mates. Redford St. James has to earn his right to my bed. When he does, it will be because he's ready to accept what I have to give."

"Which is?"

"Love in its truest form."

Leslie rolled her eyes. "I've known Redford a lot longer than you have, and I know how he operates. I love him like a brother, but get real, Carmen. He has plenty of experience when it comes to seducing women. You, on the other hand, have no experience when it comes to taming a man. Zilch."

"I believe in love, Leslie, and I have more than enough to give," Carmen said softly.

"I believe you, but the person you're trying to give it to has to want it in return. I don't know Redford's story, but there is one. And it's one neither Redford, Sloan nor Tyler ever talks about. I believe it has to do with a woman who hurt him in the past, and it's a pain he hasn't gotten over."

"Then I can help him get over it," Carmen replied.

Leslie released a deep sigh. "Not sure that you can, Carmen. Redford may not ever be ready to accept love from you or any woman. You have a good heart and see the good in everyone. You give everyone the benefit of the doubt, even those who don't deserve it. I think you're making a mistake in thinking Redford will change for you."

Carmen heard what Leslie was saying and could see the worried look in her eyes. It was the same look she'd given her two years ago when Carmen had declared that one day she would marry Redford. She understood Leslie's concern, but for some reason, Carmen believed that even with Redford's reputation as a heartbreaker, he would one day see her as more than a sex mate. He would realize she was his soulmate.

"I'm thirty-two and can take care of myself, Leslie."

"When it comes to a man like Redford, I'm not sure you can, Carmen."

Carmen shrugged. "I've dated men like Redford before. Men who only want one thing from a woman. I intend to be the exception and not the norm." Determined to change the subject, she said, "I love June weddings, don't you?"

The look in Leslie's eyes let Carmen know she knew what she'd deliberately done and would go along with her. "Yes, and Denver's weather was perfect today," Leslie said.

"Nadia looked beautiful. This is the first wedding I've ever attended where the bride wore a black wedding dress."

"Same for me, and she looked simply gorgeous. It was Jaxon's mom's wedding dress, and she offered it to Nadia for her special day."

Nadia not only looked beautiful but radiant walking down that aisle on her brother-in-law Dillon Westmoreland's arm. Both the wedding and reception had been held at Westmoreland House, the massive multipurpose family center that Dillon, the oldest of the Denver Westmorelands, had built on his three-hundred-acre property. The building could hold up to five hundred people easily and was used for special occasions, family events and get-togethers.

Carmen glanced around the huge, beautifully decorated room and noticed the man she had been introduced to earlier that day, Matthew Caulder. He'd discovered just last year that he was related to the Westmoreland triplets, Casey, Cole and Clint. It seemed the biological father Matthew hadn't known was the triplets' uncle, the legendary rodeo star and horse trainer, Sid Roberts.

It seemed that she and Redford weren't the only ones exchanging intense glances today. "You've been so busy watching me and Redford stare each other down, have you missed how Matthew Caulder keeps staring at Iris Michaels?" Carmen leaned in to whisper to Leslie.

Leslie followed her gaze to where Matthew stood talking to a bunch of the Westmoreland men. Iris was Pam Westmoreland's best friend. Pam was Nadia's sister and was married to Dillon. "No, I hadn't noticed, but I do now. Matthew is divorced, and Iris, who owns a PR firm in Los Angeles, is a widow. I understand her husband was a stuntman in Hollywood and was killed while working on a major film a number of years ago. I hope she reciprocates Matthew's interest. She deserves happiness."

Carmen frowned. "What about me? Don't I deserve happiness, too?"

"Yes, but like I told you, I'm not sure you'll find it with Redford, Carmen, and I don't want to see you get hurt."

"And like I told you, I can take care of myself."

At that moment, the party planner announced the father-daughter dance, and Dillon stood in again for Nadia's deceased father. While all eyes were on them, Carmen glanced back over at Redford. As if he'd felt her gaze, he tilted his head to look at her, his eyes unwavering and deeply penetrating.

Like she'd told Leslie, she didn't intend to be just another notch on Redford's bedpost. Their sexual chemistry had been there from the first. It was there now, simmering between them. He couldn't avoid her forever, and no matter what he thought, she truly believed they were meant to be together. She had time, patience and a belief in what was meant to be.

She would not pursue him. When the time was right, he would pursue her. She totally understood Leslie's concern but Carmen believed people could change. Even Redford. His two best friends were married with families. She had to believe that eventually he would want the same thing for himself.

Was he starting to want it now? Was that why he'd been staring tonight after two years of ignoring her? Her heart beat wildly at the thought.

When everyone began clapping, she broke eye contact with Redford and saw that the dance between Nadia and Dillon had ended. Now the first dance between Jaxon and Nadia would start. As tempted as she was, she refused to look back at Redford, although she felt his eyes on her. The heat from his gaze stirred all parts of her.

When the dance ended, Jaxon leaned into Nadia for a kiss, which elicited claps, cheers, and whistles. As the wedding planner invited others to the dance floor and the live band began to perform, Jaxon and Nadia were still kissing.

Carmen smiled, feeling the love between the couple. She wanted the same thing for herself. A man who would love her, respect her, be by her side and share his life with her. He would have no problem kissing her in front of everyone, proclaiming she was his and his only. He would be someone who would never break her heart or trample her pride.

How could she think Redford St. James capable of giving her all those things when he was unable to keep his pants zipped? Was she wrong in thinking he could change? She wanted to believe that the same love and happiness her sister Chandra shared with her husband Rutledge, the same love Leslie shared with Sloan, and Nadia shared with Jaxon, could be hers. Even her parents, retired college professors now living in Cape Town, were still in love.

People teased her about wearing rose-colored glasses, but when you were surrounded by so much love, affection and togetherness, you couldn't help but believe in happily ever after. She was convinced that everyone had a soulmate. That special person meant for them.

Unable to fight temptation any longer, she glanced back at Redford. His eyes were still on her and that stirring returned. He smiled and her heart missed a beat.

Then her breath caught in her throat as he began walking toward her.